C

of the
Currawong

by
Alwyn Lewis

About The Author

Alwyn Lewis was born in New Zealand and
lived three years in Canada but has spent
the major part of her life in Australia. She
has written eight plays, including the award-
winning *Gert and Daisy*, two books of poetry
and a book of short stories.

For the past twenty years, she has been the
Australian co-correspondent for the New York
music magazine *Cadence*. Her current play, *Four*

Photo: Gustavo Reyes

Different Women, is about to be staged in Melbourne, where she now
resides with her husband Laurie.

Other Titles by the Author

Join 'em on the Riff
Australia on the Riff
Sometimes the Pavement Sings

Published in Australia by Sid Harta Publishers Pty Ltd,
ACN: 007 030 051
23 Stirling Crescent, Glen Waverley, Victoria 3150, Australia
Telephone: 61 9560 9920, Facsimile: 61 9545 1742
E-mail: author@sidharta.com.au

First published in Australia 2008
This edition published November 2008
Copyright © Alwyn Lewis 2008
Cover design, typesetting: Chameleon Print Design

The right of Alwyn Lewis to be identified as the Author of
the Work has been asserted in accordance with the Copyright,
Designs and Patents Act 1988.

Lewis, Alwyn
Call of the Currawong
EAN13: 978-1-921362-14-9
ISBN: 1-921362-14-6
pp328

For Laurie, Jeff and Marty

Acknowledgements

This book is entirely a work of fiction; however, I am deeply indebted to Rhoda, Victor and Laurie Perry, all members of the Wonnarua Tribe in New South Wales, and to their mother and grandmother, Tribal Elder the late Jean Miller, a woman of incredible dignity and grace who shared her reminiscences and opened not only our eyes but also our hearts.

My heartfelt thanks also to the late Dr Philip Groves, for helping me understand that the impossible exists only in our own irrational fear, to Clare Allan for her support, editor Annette Hansen for her eagle eye and unflagging encouragement and last, but not least, to Laurie, for everything.

Painting on Front Cover: Reg Livermore AO

Contents

Beginnings

She loved the morning, the way the soft-grey mist disengaged itself from the earth's embrace, hiding away from the sunlight to return like an eager lover under the safety of darkness. She loved walking away from the camp to collect food for the group, an activity some of the other younger women considered a chore. She loved the feeling of endless space, the quiet that seemed to contain all sound within its silence, the solitude, the beautiful peace that enveloped her, and the marvellous sense of a place of belonging that the open country away from the camp gave her. Everywhere she looked, the untouched splendour of the land delighted her, its vastness and grandeur simultaneously, clearly reaffirming her insignificance and her importance.

She pushed her long, brown, bare feet deeply into the warm, red earth, drawing its energy upwards through her gradually warming soles, feeling the sympathetic, given-for-the-asking strength pass from her ankles through the muscle fibres and fibula, the warmth spreading, encircling her own creative parts, moving upwards through her abdomen, under her rib cage, around her heart to then run down each arm, through and around her neck, warming her face from the inside while a generous, all-knowing sun warmed the outside. She didn't speak; there was no one to speak to and nothing to say. She had always felt that the solitary moments like this were the real moments of clarity, the moments given for pondering and understanding, a time when spoken words could appear to contain a crudeness which might intrude and interrupt the sacredness. Words were things of man, the symbols needed for mere humans to interact, and understand each other; feelings were innate, given by powers other than mortal.

She stood very still so as not to disturb the tingling energy rising gently through her being, letting her eyes rest softly on the smoothness of the moss-covered, sacred rock outcrops behind which she knew existed caves housing paintings from ancestors who so long ago walked this way, leaving their spread-eagled hand prints on walls and their teachings suspended in the air to be caught generations later by ears sensitive enough to hear the message and pass it on down through the line.

Slowly the willowy woman in the faded print dress turned, stretching out her slender brown arms as if to embrace affectionately all she saw before her. No scarring roads or man-made buildings to defile the landscape here. As far as the eye could see, the monumental rock outcrops arranged somewhere long ago in the Dreamtime kept their silent vigil of truth. Scribbly gum and paperbark, pink flowering tea-tree; blonde, feathery pampas grasses with their long manes flying in the wind like mythical galloping horses; gentle, white flannel flower and spiny spinifex sprang energised from the same earth that warmed her slim, brown feet.

She let her eyes feast on the rainbow of colours before her, the varying shades of bush green framed by the pale blue of the cloudless sky behind them which also served to starkly outline the darker blue of the surrounding hills, the particles that constituted their being almost visibly dancing before her in the sun's light.

A gentle flutter of blue-black familiarity almost brushed her face. 'You here again?' she asked the currawong. 'You come to tell me something?'

Girlie knew she had been given the currawong as her totem, also knowing that for the rest of her life, she must respect the bird that had power to help her in countless ways. Ways she might only dream about.

She watched until it was no more than a tiny black dot, almost out of her vision. The bird turned and swooped sharply then disappeared over the far-flung rocks. Time stands still here if you are quiet enough, she thought, knowing that time simply measured the space given on earth for learning and experiencing. Reluctantly she shook the red soil from her feet while her mind silently thanked the earth, her mother and teacher, for the lesson.

With the woven grass dilly bag of bush tomatoes over her shoulder, the tall woman they called 'Girlie' walked slowly back over the hill to the group of huts built out of bits of corrugated iron, cast-off timber, whitewashed wheat bags, or whatever the twin gods of providence and determination had provided; one hut which she shared with her husband and two year old daughter Pearl. Life was changing for her people since the white man had come to claim this vast land as his own. Traditional hunting grounds were now owned by white farmers who thought nothing of putting a bullet into any trespassing Aboriginal hunter who 'strayed' onto land they now considered theirs. She shuddered at the recent memory of a black corpse hanging with a corncob stuffed in its mouth. No amount of reasoning would ever convince the white farmer who perpetrated that act that the boy, whose family were near starving, had only taken the corn from an area where, in years past, he had freely gathered food. So, now the menfolk exercised caution by hunting further afield, leaving only some women with children, and the old people behind in the camp.

But now she smiled as the small brown youngster, calling out in her wordless chatter, interrupted her thoughts by running towards her, arms outstretched, the girl eager for their familiar placement around her mother's neck. In one motion, she picked the child up and danced in a circle, her head back, large brown eyes momentarily closed, lost in the ecstasy of motherhood. She held the child tightly, savouring the smell and feel of her, not wanting to put her down, only doing so grudgingly when something caught by the sunlight blinked back an unseeing eye, momentarily drawing her attention away from the child in her arms.

The paralysing fear that travelled like a cloud ahead of its henchmen swept through the settlement like thick molasses as Girlie noticed the old people gathering quietly behind her while the horses bearing the dark-suited white men wearing the unseeing eyes on their chests rode up alongside to surround the encampment. Spiralling red dust stirred into life by horses' hooves made Girlie put the child down and rub at her own watering eyes momentarily blinding her to the two-horse dray in the centre of the group of horsemen.

Something on the duckboard seat of the dray made the child at Girlie's knee whimper and hide her face in the soft cotton of her mother's skirts. The mother held tightly to her daughter's hands, uneasy as two figures stepped down from the back of the dray. The strange looking man, white as chalk, wearing a stiff black suit and an even stiffer looking back-to-front collar with his reddening neck overflowing around its rim, led his sallow-faced female partner over to stand in front of Girlie. The woman ignored Girlie and stood dabbing with a white handkerchief at the perspiration forming around her upper lip, her wispy brown hair scraped into a thin little bundle at the back of her head. Her white, claw-like hands were reaching forward, reaching out for something. Girlie heard the old people around her crying as she slowly realised in horror just what the eager fingers were reaching for. The child at her knee buried her face even deeper in her mother's skirts as Girlie struggled to keep the clawed hands away.

One of the horsemen with the blind button eyes grabbed and held Girlie's arms as the terrified child was dragged away from her. Shocked into immobility, she watched helplessly as Pearl was placed in the back of the dray between the black-coated white-face and his companion. Echoing around her Girlie felt, rather than heard, a high-pitched sound unlike anything she had ever heard before, as if the Earth herself objected to what was taking place on her surface, but then she realised that what she was hearing was a wailing. A keening in heart-rending unison from the old people standing behind her. Quite suddenly, roaring blood pounded at Girlie's temples as, with her insides screaming, she drew deeply from her morning's earlier gift of energy. She kicked out with her feet and bit, drawing blood from the hand holding her.

'Bitch bit me,' her captor muttered as Girlie fought with all the inner strength she could muster, kicking her feet, struggling with her arms until it took two of the horsemen to hold her arms with a third to grip her feet.

Long after the dray had disappeared, showing the last glimpse of her daughter's terrified, tear-stained face, her mind's eye held a scene it would repeat to her with agonising clarity for the rest of her life. Long after all her energy had been spent, long after her arms had been released, long after the horses had disappeared, long into that night and the countless nights to follow, she cried desperately for her stolen daughter. Only when the torment inside her slid mercifully into a kind of dulled resignation did the well of tears inside her dry enough to allow her to think back, back to the beginning, to the day of her daughter's birth. The day a girl child had been born differently from other children.

This child had not cried when she entered the world; she had lain in the crook of her mother's arm as if she had enjoyed the experience, almost smiling. It was then that Girlie knew that her child had been born to help others have their children, that she was to have the gift.

From now on, every night, just before she fell asleep, Girlie recalled her two year old daughter and tearfully sang the name of her gift into the darkness. Somewhere, she hoped, the song might find her daughter and help her to know her life's direction. Somehow, if a mother tried hard enough, her daughter might be allowed to know. Somehow, somewhere, if the winds and the fates were kind, the message would be delivered. Delivered and understood.

As the seasons passed and the new settlers expanded their holdings, game became more and more scarce for Girlie and her clan. Kangaroo, a staple diet, moved further afield and became more difficult to locate as farmers eradicated anything that interfered with their English-style farming. Girlie moved away reluctantly at first, fearing to be too far from the place where she had last seen her daughter. But as time progressed, necessity dictated her whereabouts, and although it did nothing to ease the ache that never left her alone, neither did it completely destroy her hope.

Hope had led her today to where she now stood, breathless, her heart pounding from the exertion of the climb so far and with still half of it ahead of her, she gradually pulled herself over the enormous grey boulders, patchworked with lichen. Every few yards she stopped, her eye caught by the simple beauty of a white flannel flower or her ears filling with the trilling of a nearby bird. Beyond one rock, a frill-necked lizard expanded his neck ferociously, his tough grey skin shining in the sunlight like some ancient coat of armour. But Girlie was used to such posturings and simply smiled as she passed; her mind was set on one thing and one thing only. Hadn't her dream told her to visit this place?

Three nights in a row, the same dream had seeped into her consciousness and through her system, its insistence barraging her with the information as to where her feet were to lead her. She stopped for a moment and looked behind her, down across the bush-covered valley dense with blue-green foliage under a cloudless mantle of blue. Around her, nature pulsated as the breeze, nonexistent one moment, refreshing and cooling the next, made her recall the throbbing of the didgeridoo, the way the sound of the instrument had always reached deep inside her to touch and reveal thoughts and feelings, sometimes with a soothing effect, other times to disturb but always as if realigning her own feelings with those of the universe surrounding her.

Lean, brown fingers wiped beads of perspiration across her forehead as she turned to continue the climb. She emptied her mind, trying to allow powers other than her own to direct her to her destination, and in a short time she knew without question that she had arrived.

She found herself at the entrance to a cavernous opening, formed naturally in the side of a rock face. Beside this cave extended a wide, flat plateau with indented areas in the rock face worn smooth by centuries of forgotten, grain-grinding hands. A sacred, ancient place to which her dreams had directed her.

Quickly, she gathered a small pile of twigs and branches, setting them together just outside the cave entrance. Patiently she fired the twigs, blew gently on the flame and stood downwind, so that the smoke enveloped her in its cleansing smell of eucalypt, breathing steadily, letting the smoke filter through her being. Then she carefully extinguished the fire and stepped into the cave.

It was then that she heard it. Clearly reaching down through the centuries, a baby cry, a universal newborn sound reaching down from some other level to touch and comfort, bringing with it the knowledge that she had been directed here to find an age-old birthing cave. Girlie fell to her knees, arms crossed over her torso as the tears of gratitude poured down her face. For she had been brought here for a reason, of that she had no doubt. Her night-time singing had not fallen on deaf ears; the Powers had heard and wanted her to know. Somehow, somewhere; Pearl, her daughter, had received the gift.

The Decision

Long, flickering flames from the ironbark logs in the huge stone fireplace momentarily caught their own reflections dancing in the dangling lustres of the kerosene lamps to give the parlour of the Mitchell homestead a slightly forlorn appearance. Hugh Mitchell, still wearing his mud-spattered riding boots together with an air of total irritation, sat thoughtfully probing the fire's embers with the poker. His mood was one of melancholy, staring into the flames, his other hand cupped around a half-filled brandy balloon, alternately warming and sipping its contents. The fierce Australian sun had weathered, even enhanced his good looks over the years, bleaching his greying fair hair as it tanned his skin a rich golden colour. But dammit he was tired. Tired of fighting a losing battle in this insane country where one year, the land cracked open with its surface baked so dry with sun and drought that even your piss was steam before it hit the ground, and the next you lost stock, buildings, crops – and the occasional station hand – in gales and floods. There was an intense ferocity here that he just could not handle any longer.

He put down the poker, stood to place the brandy balloon on the mantelpiece and, with a sigh, leaned down to pull off his riding boots. 'Twenty-five years of heat, flies, droughts, floods and snakes,' he mumbled. Lately he had found his thoughts returning to England more and more. To Kew and lilacs, to the joy of four changing seasons and the sight of the first budding yellow crocus. Even the London fog laden with consumptive promise seemed attractive from this distance. Only two damned seasons here, he thought. *Hot and dry and then wet and cold*. It had rained solidly for the past month, and he had yet again lost stock, crops, sleep, and of course income. He was, putting it simply, getting too old for it. The thrill had long ago worn off, leaving him with stiffened joints and worsening arthritis as his only companions now.

In anger, Hugh reached out and forcefully rang the bell to summon the young kitchen girl Pearl to pour him another brandy. Oh, she's obliging enough, he thought, watching her replace the decanter on the sideboard with slender, long-fingered black hands, and humble enough for a fourteen year old, but that was another thing. Servants at home were well-mannered and knew their place. And a man could visit his club and see men of like kind, not the boorish men of the land and the lumpy, plain-as-pastry women he had encountered during his twenty-five years in Australia. Thick ankles and waists, no tits. Dammit, he'd had enough. After Emily left, leaving him with young James, he'd only stayed on to give the lad something for the future. Well, he could have it, the whole 400 000 acres of it. The boy surely would be marrying eventually, sooner rather than later; the timing was right. They could stay on here and have what was, after all, partly their inheritance anyway, and he could go back. Back home to England, to a cultivated and genteel way of life. He'd been wise enough to keep property and an income source there all this time. He would go home and stay there. He was damned if he was going to die in this God forsaken wilderness at the arse end of the world amongst a lot of ratbag, get-rich-quick colonials, most of them straight-out-of-the-bog Irish stock transported here, of course, at Her Majesty's pleasure.

Hugh let his eyes roam around the familiar room as the welcome amber liquid warmed and comforted. He had had this homestead built from the ground up. Sawn his own timber from the surrounding ironbarks to build a large wooden structure surrounded on all sides by a wide verandah. French doors opened from all five bedrooms onto the verandahs, allowing for cooling breezes to circulate through the mosquito nets in summer, but they also each boasted a fireplace for the long, cold winter nights. That's of course if you could get the staff to remember to set and light the fires and keep them banked for you.

Most of the furniture in the parlour in which he now sat had been brought from the old country when he had convinced Emily that their futures lay together in the brave new land. Funny, he hadn't thought of it before, but she hadn't wanted to take anything back with her. It seemed she just wanted to forget the whole Australian experience and that included her husband and young son. Hugh sighed, taking in the unadorned but comfortable sofas and armchairs, the glass-fronted bookcases with the float glass panels that rose each side of the fireplace, filled with Shakespeare and Dickens. Try though she would, Emily could not interest their son in literature. He wanted to know about stock and station right from the very beginning and the boy was certainly good at it. Good enough to leave alone to manage it all. Hugh knew there was no way he could coerce James into returning with him to England. The thought of inheriting his father's 400 000 acres and the success of his stock and station investments were all that James needed.

Hugh stood, stretching his stiffening joints, mulling the brandy in his hand as he took in the house. Apart from the parlour, the building contained a formal dining room furnished with a massive oval mahogany table and Regency striped chairs for twelve, a study for himself, a sewing room for the staff, and a huge kitchen and adjoining wine cellar. There were numerous outbuildings, some housing the station's staff; there was a smokehouse, barns, sheds, stables for the horses and a huge well, thanks to the talents of that woman Nettie from the neighbouring McManaway farm. Never seen a water witch like her, he thought. *Mind you, she'd kissed the Blarney stone – damned Irish, they're all the same.* Oh, she didn't see fairies and little people like Mrs McManaway, but she did seem to know instinctively about the future. Hadn't she asked him when he was leaving? And he hadn't even decided himself. Damned unnerving, if you thought about it.

Hugh drained his glass and walked through to the monstrous roll-top desk in his study. He would write the shipping company and book a berth for right after the wedding. That way, the two youngsters could come back home and continue their lives without his interference.

He sat drumming the base of his pen against a front tooth, thinking of another time, another place and another son, one who had never been spoken of in this house. The boy would be thirty-something now, probably still living somewhere in the old country. Funny how life came and hit you in the face every now and then.

He had married Emily without even a thought for his illegitimate son's deserted mother. Well, she came from common stock, something his parents just would not tolerate. In fact, he had come to Australia to get away from it all. Then, once here, his wife turned the tables on him, leaving him with a second son who considered himself totally Australian, walked on the land like he was part of it. Why, the boy rode almost before he could walk and he had a shrewd head for stock, built up his own herd from age twelve. He was just a natural when it came to living on the land. Well, he could have it, and all that went with it.

Hugh stood and stretched one foot out in front of him. *Blasted arthritis.* He didn't like defeat – financial or any other variety; that probably accounts for my mood of the moment, he thought. And he felt this irresistible draw to his beginnings, the old estate near London with its carefully tended gardens, the lake that never ran dry, not like his dams on the property here which were always a headache. And, dammit, he had to face the fact that he missed the culture, the theatre, the proximity England had to Europe, the sophistication and the art. Yes, being recognised as a gentleman did have advantages over life in the raw in the Antipodes and, God alive, he had given it his best shot, hadn't he? Twenty-five of the best years of his life. He deserved to enjoy the rest of his life in more harmonious surroundings.

He reached for the bellpull with one hand, draining the last dregs of brandy at the same time. He would leave everything in order, as was his way. No loose ends, not in this country anyway. All he had acquired in this country would go to his son. His Australian son, the only son he recognised.

Love in bloom

In 1904, prime land was selling well in the wealthy Parramatta area and people were accumulating holdings in other parts of the country. But ever since Charles Carson spoke at home with admiration about the meteoric success of young New South Wales landowner James Mitchell, he noticed something subtle change in his daughter Hilda. He noticed it even more so after James Mitchell had been invited to dinner at the Carson home to discuss stock and station matters. Something inside his pretty, blonde and skittish daughter grew and blossomed in front of his very eyes. It irritated him unreasonably, but with his irritation arose something new: an unnerving sense of fear.

Early in her life, his daughter had always been able to delight him, so at first, it didn't worry him that she constantly achieved her own way in everything. He even found it amusing to watch as she worked a situation to her own advantage so cleverly that anyone else involved in the circumstance was left feeling they still owed her something, that she had been somehow, slightly short-changed. First he had hoped she was simply exercising a high level of intelligence, but now her interest in his house guest showed all the familiar signs. And James Mitchell was a typical male and did what typical males do; he reacted to, and was flattered by the attention paid him by this pretty city girl.

Such was Charles's concern that after his guest's departure, he cornered his daughter Sunday morning after church and walked her slowly in the pale spring sunshine through the well-kept grounds of their Parramatta home, ostensibly to admire the camellias and rhododendrons, but in reality to try and ascertain just what was in her mind. He placed a guiding hand on her elbow as the sunlight caught dancing red flashes in her fair hair, making her look more childlike than ever to him. He had always put her on a pedestal – he knew that. She was to always be his little girl, his baby. But this little girl had a mind of her own; he had found that out. He closed his eyes briefly to escape looking at the black and white wild cat that shot across their path and into the surrounding bushes, but then opened them sharply, not liking the scene that flashed into his mind. God he knew, of course he knew, that his old pet cat had not fallen from the attic window. Perhaps he had paid the damned cat too much attention, but he had been fond of it. He knew that had annoyed his daughter beyond measure, his pampered daughter who wanted his complete attention, but he also knew that cats are sure-footed, too sure-footed to stumble. Still, he could not comprehend the thought that she, the only one in the house at the time, might have thrown the cat out the window. No, no, he just had too much on his plate at the moment, how could he think such a thing?

Hilda stopped, little-girl like, petulant, cupping her hand tenderly around the base of a pale pink camellia, secure in her own ability to tie her father quite securely around her little finger. 'Is James Mitchell coming here again soon?' she asked provocatively.

Inwardly Charles cursed. Already it was too late. He had never ever said no to her before in her life; she was not about to take no for an answer now. Well, he hoped James Mitchell was as strong as he appeared because he was going to need all his inner resources to tame this child.

Then and there, before the idea of a marriage proposal had had time to bypass the more voluptuous thoughts running through James Mitchell's mind, Carson decided that if there was going to be a wedding forthcoming for his daughter, it was going to be the biggest and best arrangement the district had seen. James Mitchell was going places. After all, he was a businessman; there was no disputing that.

He certainly came from good English stock even if he was a bit rough around the edges for the Parramatta crowd, but success gathered more admirers than failure. He could always be honed down a little and mellowed – less of the land, more of the parlour, that kind of thing. With a little luck, he would polish up all right.

★ ★ ★

Round and round, round and round. The ball of wool grew ever larger as the bony hands, devoid of rings and sprinkled liberally with dark age spots, wound the wool from the almost identical pair of hands holding the decreasing skein. Her new husband Wilf had just poured her an elderberry nip and Leila felt the warmth from it slowly slide down her throat as she sat back in the armchair, watching her twin maiden aunts. The afternoon's trip to the Carson household to take tea with Hilda's new beau, tomorrow to be husband, had left them agog. She held the slender crystal glass with both hands and sat back in her chair, thinking she might have been invisible for the amount of attention her aunts paid her.

Strange how the moving hands and the increasing ball of wool taken from the decreasing skein mesmerised. That wool was not unlike her aunts' lives, come to think of it. Start at one end and finish at the other. Nothing too exciting in the middle either. Both spinsters because 'the right man never came along'. Both living off their ever-dwindling family inheritance until Wilf came along and married her. Then they'd breathed a sigh of relief that the hoped for security had entered their lives.

The two elderly ladies dressed in the fashion of the day, endeavouring in so doing to hide what they considered their 'weak points'. Both wore high-necked chiffon blouses in shades of mauve – lined, of course, for modesty's sake – and both with long, floating panels of fabric tied at the neck, held in place with large cameo brooches. Not for one moment did their manner of dress conceal, as they imagined, the bulge at their throats which announced their enlarged goitres to the world.

Salt, Leila thought, looking at their neckline. Eat plenty of iodised salt with your food, she mimicked inwardly. She had lost count of how many times her aunts had encouraged her to take salt at the table. 'It's the iodine', they would say to her. 'You don't want ugly lumps at your throat like us, do you?'

They meant well, of that she had no doubt. They were just of another age, another time. Since her parents' death, they had been more cloying than ever, or was it just the fact that she wanted to be independent and felt more trapped than she liked.

'Well, she certainly did well for herself,' said Ethel, the elder of the two.

Her younger sister Dorothy nodded. 'Rather attractive in a boorish sort of way, is he not?'

The two women exchanged looks meant to imply a certain knowing, an understanding, even minus the attendant experience required.

'Well, my dear, I hear he practically owns Wellsford, wherever that is. They say he has hundreds and thousands of acres, and a huge mansion of a home,' said Ethel.

Dorothy wrapped the final end of the ball of wool and placed it on the table alongside her. 'Oh yes, but there's more to marriage than possessions,' she said, glancing meaningfully at her niece.

Leila stared out the window, not wanting to get into this exchange. There certainly was more to marriage than possessions. She sat back in the chair and closed her eyes. In some marriages, that is. She tried to imagine what it might be like to live at Wellsford in the Mitchell mansion (wherever it was). James Mitchell filled her thoughts. He was so different from her lily-white husband, a husband more or less foisted onto her by a family decision brought about by shortage of funds. Wilf was, after all, a bank manager and had access to equitable stock. Very reassuring for her aunts, and it did provide security for herself, she had to admit that. But he was no match at all for her daydreams of James. She couldn't imagine James rolling onto her in the middle of the night still wearing his socks and suspenders. Oh no, that would be a much more lascivious coupling. Something that would enable her to realise something of her own emotional depth, untapped and dormant in her present marriage.

'I wonder if anyone has explained her wifely duties to her,' Dorothy said meaningfully, pouring herself a generous glassful from the decanter on the sideboard. 'I doubt that her new husband will be a man to wait.'

The two women exchanged knowing looks and nodded their heads. A pair of bobbing Orpingtons, Leila thought. She loved her aunts, even though they got on her nerves. Wonder what you two would have been like if a James Mitchell had ridden into your lives, she thought. *Would you have untapped passions that you now subjugate with elderberry wine and lewd thoughts?* Gratification by surmise, she thought to herself. *This family has existed on that for years.*

She clicked her glass with a fingernail and held it to Wilf to refill, wondering momentarily if there might be something mentally amiss with her family but knowing, in her aunts' case, their potentials were simply untapped from lack of opportunity; no suitors had ever presented themselves. That was one of the reasons they had been so desperate to couple her with Wilf. Oh, he was kind enough, tried to do the right thing, bit of a lost soul himself really. But she dreamed of passion while at the same time wondering if such an emotion really existed. Or she had wondered that, until she'd met her best friend's intended. Now *that* was a passionate man. Passionate about the land and its possibilities, probably passionate about everything else that interested him. God, everyone could see he just couldn't keep his hands off the girl he called his 'little pink princess', obviously looking forward to starting a dynasty.

Leila found herself wondering how Hilda would be feeling about that. In all the years they'd been friends, the subject of the opposite sex had always been sidestepped or quashed on the few times it had arisen. Hilda didn't seem to like men, just the attention and flattery, a legacy from her life with her father. Leila could see the usual signs again, quite the opposite from what she saw in James Mitchell who was straining at the leash to get started. God, how wonderful, she thought.

She watched her aunts chatter together, realising she should feel sorry for them; no prince in shining armour was going to ride into their lives now. And as for her, well at least she had Wilf and he was attentive. All the same, she found herself looking ahead to a time when she would visit her friend and her new husband at their home in Wellsford. Looking ahead with a definite feeling of anticipation.

Within three months of James's first visit, the grand Carson home at Parramatta had found itself repainted and refurbished, filled day and night with tradesmen, dressmakers and caterers. The service door onto the street danced to a jig played out by its own rusty hinges as the wedding day dawned. Tables covered with fine, starched damask were set out under the green marquee and laid with the best silver. Bibbed, tuckered and white-gloved waiters were given their final instructions, organdie-aproned waitresses made last-minute checks on the huge, flowing floral arrangements as the childlike bride and her wealthy country husband took their places at the official table.

It was only after the event that Charles Carson really felt uneasy about the match, after the speeches and the one too many glasses of punch when Hilda and her new husband waved through the oval back window of their retreating coach; her small, pink face flushed from laughing at the array of boots tied to the back. She certainly was still a child, his daughter. She had always been a child. A child in a woman's body, but a child nevertheless. Would James indulge her the way he always had? Even he had been recently forced into more monetary chance-taking to accommodate her indulgences. So what?

he thought; a little gamble here and there only adds to the spice of life, and the child was certainly worth the wager.

But after the four hour drive from Parramatta, Hilda Mitchell sat morosely beside her new husband. Heat, dust, endless pitted and jarring roads all conspired to tarnish the sheen on the bride's new marital tie. She waved an irritated hand in front of her face as flies, searching persistently for any spot of moisture, pestered the corners of her eyes. When she leaned forward in her seat, Hilda felt perspiration trickle slowly down the middle of her back like a melodramatic tear. 'How much further is it?' She made no attempt to hide her impatience.

Her new husband squeezed her knee with a too hot, moist hand, mistaking the tedium in her voice for a mirror of his own impatience. To his new bride, the drive seemed endlessly boring, dusty and uncomfortable, past scattered farmhouses with their cluster of lean-to outbuildings; Raggedy Andy, grimy-faced children swinging aimlessly on the gates, eager to catch a glimpse of anything passing that might offer a break to the tedium of rainless heat. The majesty of the countryside towering with ironbark trees, grey-green lichen covered rocks and rolling plains escaped her. The dirt roads had covered her pink going-away dress with a thin layer of red dust which puffed into eye-watering clouds as she patted her skirt. She made no sound when the driver of their coach indicated that they had arrived for a change of horses, and refreshments at the Cobb and Co roadhouse.

James escorted his new bride into the main area of the roadhouse, ignoring the knowing looks of the few old-timers embroidering their memories with generous jugs of ale. 'Aye, he'll be wanting to get her home now, then,' one snaggle-toothed old woman confided to her mate with a slap on the knee and a raucous laugh. Hilda ignored them all; they were, to her mind, extremely low class and not worthy of her attention. All she wanted was a cold lemonade, a pitcher of water to refresh her face and to have the new horses harnessed so they could soon end this tiresome journey.

After yet another three tedious hours, they arrived at the main street of the tiny township of Wellsford, travelling along the Wellsford River, clattering over the old wooden bridge and past Devil's Rock then finally to the three miles of poplar-lined dirt road which took them past the burned-out remains of the old gold-digger's shack, over Hugh's Ford to bump along the dusty track leading to the Wellsford homestead. Rays of sunlight danced between the poplars, playing a now-you-see-me, now-you-don't game, but Hilda was completely oblivious to it. Along the road's edge, herds of Herefords grazed contentedly; their large, brown eyes not registering the horses and carriage in their midst until directly in their line of vision, causing them to skitter in every which direction.

'Cows are up.' James was relaxing completely, now on his own territory, feeling in control, with a growing pressure of anticipation in his lower abdomen not helped at all by the jiggling movements of the coach. A black and white dog rushed at the side of the coach, snapping a canine welcome, then raced off ahead as if to herald the master's arrival. On the side of the road, a black snake felt the vibration of the hooves and turned on itself, disappearing into the long grass.

'Did you see that?' asked Hilda, her reverie totally broken.

'Yup,' said James, again squeezing her knee purposefully.

'Snakes,' said Hilda, panic in her voice. 'I can't stand snakes.'

'Get a lot of them at the homestead,' James said. 'You learn to live with it.'

That did it; she had already had enough. Hilda wanted to go home. She wanted to go home to her father, to her orderly pink and white bedroom and to servants who knew exactly how and when to fluff up the warm blanket of her past security.

It was at precisely that moment as the coach rounded the last bend of the journey that she first saw the homestead; an impressive, long, low, white timber house with a green iron roof, surrounded on all sides by a wide, screened verandah. To one side of the verandah steps, arms folded over white aprons, expressionless, stood Pearl and Mary, the house girls. Several farmhands stood alongside them, some chewing a piece of straw but all eyes slanted sideways, carefully watching the coach swing down the roadway in front of the house. Apprehension shuffled feet and made fidgeting hands uneasy as anxiously the staff waited for a glimpse of the new mistress, the boss's missus, all fearful of the unknown quantity of someone from the city. And that someone took one look at the line-up of servants attached to her country estate, straightened her dust-laden skirt and her gaze, mopped her perspiring face and immediately assumed her role as mistress of the Mitchell household. She confidently removed her husband's hand from her knee and with it firmly brushed away all thought of snakes.

★ ★ ★

It had been an eventful few days for the household staff members at Wellsford. They'd known for a while that the young master, James, was going into the city for his wedding, and that his father Mr Hugh would of course be going along, but it had come as a shock to learn that Mr Hugh was not coming back, that he was handing it all over to his son and going back to England.

Only one member, that closest to Hugh Mitchell, Charlie Saddleup, felt sure that this was bound to happen sooner or later as Mr Hugh's loneliness and frustration at being unable to completely accept Wellsford, or in fact Australia, as his home had been becoming increasingly obvious recently. Mr Hugh had been a good boss and quite a close friend. In fact, he had been responsible for giving Charlie his name. When it was discovered at a very early age that Charlie was an absolute natural with animals, and a wonder on horseback, he and Mr Hugh had become like man and shadow. Mr Hugh would bang the door behind him and shout, 'Charlie, saddle up!' as he headed for the stables, and the name stuck. But he'd never loved the land in the way that his son James did.

James, being an only child, had grown up spending most of his time with the Aboriginal kids, and they were all together around the farm and the animals all the time. Although Charlie was a few years younger than James, his aptitude with horses developed earlier, and it suited James to have Charlie by his father's side so much, enabling him to get the feel of running an enormous spread like Wellsford in his own way and his own time.

For as long as his memory stretched back, James had adored his surroundings, the constantly changing colour of the hills; dark navy blue when it promised rain, pink as they caught the last of a sunset. He loved the varying shades of green on the hills and surrounds that changed with each season, never failing to amaze and delight. Even the crazily perverse weather pattern suited him – he liked the unpredictability. Wellsford was his life, and he began training himself early to run it all, as he was confident he certainly would.

That day had come upon them all quite suddenly. Hugh had recognised his son's ability, both with the farm and the business side of things, and encouraged the takeover without mentioning his intentions, just as James had become besotted with Hilda Carson whom he'd met on business trips to Parramatta.

In the excitement of it all, the parting of James and his father Hugh had become little more than a short, formal moment. The moment that James's pulsing brain was looking forward to was when he returned home and took his bride to the nuptial couch. And now that time was almost at hand as James looked smilingly out at the waiting staff, spruced up for their arrival, and they looked back questioningly at him. Once stopped, he opened the door and jumped down, now preoccupied with helping Hilda down and introducing her to her new life.

Charlie looked quickly along the short line-up, in particular at the two teenagers Pearl and Mary who hadn't long ago arrived at Wellsford. My Gawd, he grinned to himself, they scrubbed up all right, especially that Pearl who, unaware of his thoughts, concentrated her attention on the coach.

James was now holding a pink-gloved hand and a moment later, the new mistress emerged. The staff were thoroughly taken aback with their first sight of the new Mrs Mitchell. They'd never seen anything quite like it; a cloud of pink – pink hat, pink cheeks, pink clothing, pink shoes and gloves. 'In the pink,' muttered Mary, 'right in the pink.'

Gawd, thought Charlie, looks like she's made of that stuff they sell at the annual fair in town – fairy floss! How the hell's she going to fit in here?

Mary hid her astonishment and through lowered lids watched as James, completely out of character, from their experience, fussed over his wife as they approached the line-up. What had happened to him? And why did she feel a twinge of envy, even jealousy? Instinctively Mary knew that she could never share anything or have anything in common with this snobbish, pink person, so why did she feel jealous?

Pearl recovered quickly from the shock of this unexpected vision and quietly and correctly assessed the new mistress. She knew it had been a long trip at the end of a big day and had expected her to be tired but not to immediately display an unsmiling superiority and apparent total disdain for the group of them. And not only them; it seemed to also extend to their boss James, Hilda's new husband. A wave of disappointment enveloped her, but there was no disappointment on James's face.

'This is Charlie, Pearl, Mary ...' The names came one after another, but they doubted that even one of them registered as the new mistress walked purposefully and distastefully past them towards the verandah and the front door.

Yep, thought Pearl, we're in for a time with this lot. How can the boss not see that?

After the walk-past, Charlie's face was a study. Fit in? he thought. *She hasn't got a hope in hell. She thinks that everything has to fit in with her! Well, Charlie-boy, you'll be keeping a good safe distance from that. The young boss can have her, Gawd help him.*

The group, embarrassed, stood for a minute; then, realising that that was it, it was all over, went their separate ways.

As she took in her new surroundings, Hilda's confidence grew in her ability to control James as easily as she had always controlled her father. There had been little physical contact with anyone throughout her life although Daddy had always jumped to comply with her every request, so why should this be different? From their first meeting, she had been taken with James's rough landowner approach, his good looks and his ability to let nothing stand between him and what he wanted, not unlike her memories of her father's business dealings. And hadn't he kissed the back of her hand and called her his 'little brooding hen'? – whatever that meant. She felt sure that in no time, she would have James Mitchell eating out of her hand.

But this confidence ended abruptly during the first night at the homestead, a night culminating in a brutal few minutes of totally unromantic realisation that left her dazed, anxious and exhausted while her new husband rolled onto his side and slept soundly.

Utterly mortified by this ravaging, this brutish invasion; Hilda, shuddering, tried in vain to relax. Finally the long day's events forced her into a fitful sleep; however, it seemed to her that she'd hardly closed her eyes when her new partner stirred beside her and, to her horror, began anew as her bruised lips and body were subjected to another outburst. No one had told her about this. Surely, she thought, this couldn't be all there was to it.

At last it was over, but this time sleep was out of the question for Hilda. How could she have been so blind? Why had nobody warned her? Was this what marriage was all about? What had happened to her space, the space between her pedestal and the fawning admirers? How could anyone tolerate, let alone enjoy this? It seemed that her very nerve ends were reacting in disgust. How would she ensure that this never recurred? *Daddy, where are you?* Disgust and a festering loathing for this beast of a man rose like bile to her throat. She lay staring at the ceiling, tossing from side to side until at last, completely spent, she slipped into a troubled sleep.

Awakening early the following morning, she tried to consider her situation, fighting back tears of anger and frustration, and angrily promised herself that regardless of the consequences, there was never, ever going to be a repeat of the previous evening's revolting activities. If it meant unpleasantness, so be it. And it did.

'Gawd alive,' said Pearl, 'did you hear 'em screechin' at each other last night, Her Ladyship and His Nibs?'

Two months had elapsed since James had brought his new wife home to Wellsford. Mary rolled her eyes and bent to add more firewood to that already flaming underneath the boiling load of washing in the outside copper. She smiled. 'This washing isn't the only thing boiling up around here,' she said, 'the two of them yelling hammer and tongs at each other half the night long, like a couple of rowing bush tomcats. Talk about happy newlyweds! Maybe they think we're deaf.'

Pearl picked up the heavy copper stick and began lifting the boiling sheets over the side of the copper and into the adjoining tub of cold water, the exertion creating beads of crystal perspiration on her forehead. She blew at an irritating piece of hair sticking to her face. 'I don't think they think of us at all,' she said. 'Long as we keep our mouths shut and the place runs like clockwork.'

Mary pulled a length of sheet out of the cold water only to drop it quickly as her hand uncovered a pocket of still nearly boiling water. She pushed the sheet down to cool it then wedged a corner of it in the mangle and started turning the handle, drawing the squeezed-out sheet through to the next tub of blue rinsing water. She loved the smell of the boiling clothes almost as much now as later when she brought them in dry off the long station clothes line to be folded and sprinkled prior to the heavy pressing irons transforming the dampness into sweet-smelling steam. 'I dunno,' she said thoughtfully. 'We could be in worse places, much worse places.'

The transition from the stately Parramatta mansion with its tasteful drawing room filled daily with fresh cut flowers and furnished in the period which favoured rosewood and soft pink velvet, where musical evenings were held with like-minded groups of associates and their sometimes rather more vacuous partners, to the sparseness of the Wellsford homestead was something to which Hilda Mitchell could never really adjust. The apple of her father's eye, adored and pampered, given to accentuated airs and graces, the pretty blonde with the silly laugh felt totally lost. That laugh had initially attracted James Mitchell, making him think of the soft pink furnishing of his father-in-law's Parramatta drawing room, a pink he affectionately saw reflected in the desirable cheeks of his wife-to-be. Later in his life, the silly laugh – the soft pink laugh – would send James's blood temperature to boiling and his hands flying to cover his ears. He would learn to loathe the colour pink, learn to change it in his mind to match his mounting rage, from pink to red, to violent blackish-purple.

From the first few days on, Hilda played at hiding her disgust somewhere deep behind her face and threw herself into her idea of planning the running of the homestead. First of all, she would throw out all the heavy old furniture and refurnish. That would give her an interest, even if she now knew she couldn't persuade James to let her renovate his study. Horrid, dark little room, full of age-old English and year old Sydney newspapers. Then she'd reorganise the kitchen staff so that they cooked food that fattened and filled a little less, something perhaps a touch French, introduce a little culture to her new household. She'd set about getting these things done, but by the third month, she felt so nauseous in the mornings she couldn't stand the taste of food or even the smell of it, much less discuss its preparation.

Into the bargain, she was having a frightful time trying to make her new husband do her bidding. Quite often the discussions degenerated into tasteless, high-pitched arguments. The man simply would not understand that she intended to be treated as she always had, as a lady should.

It was during one of those mornings after yet another loud disagreement, as she was sitting in the cane rocking chair on the front verandah, taking in a little of the sun's warmth, feeling piqued, her body aching, that she noticed the dust rising in the distance. A cloud of dust way down the southern end of the dirt road. A cloud of dust that grew larger and moved closer until at last she saw the cause: a lone horseman galloping towards the homestead.

She took the 'special delivery' letter he handed her and, mystified, sat back on the verandah to read it. She sat for a very long time. When Pearl came to announce that lunch was served, her voice fell on deaf ears. Hilda stared at the paper in her hand, the paper from her family's solicitor, the paper that told her that the staff at the Parramatta home had been unable to awaken her father. It couldn't be true, the words would just not sink in and seemed to swim, enlarging and contracting in front of her eyes. She read and reread the letter. Her escape and security no longer existed. Her father, the one constant in her life, the one person in the world who treated her as she wanted to be treated, was no longer able to indulge her whims; he was gone. Daddy was dead.

Hilda sat stunned, unable to move. Pearl again came out onto the verandah, realising that her mistress had literally not moved since she'd announced lunch earlier. Something was obviously wrong, and it had to do with that letter. She'd better get the boss, and quickly.

When James arrived at the homestead a short time later, he had a quick word with Pearl then walked out to the front verandah. He moved to his wife, but she didn't react at all, didn't even seem to notice he was there. He took the letter from her hand and even her hand stayed where it was.

James read the letter quickly then closed his eyes for a moment, kneeling down on the verandah and reaching for his wife's hand. At his touch, Hilda exploded.

'You unutterable boor, don't you dare touch me!' she shrieked.

'Hilda, I'm only trying to —'

'Don't try to ingratiate yourself into my favour, you animal! I've just received the worst piece of information I could possibly imagine and you try to take advantage of the situation by pawing me! You're revolting!'

Throwing herself from the chair, she burst into tears and ran down the verandah to her bedroom. James stood and watched the retreating figure, with the blood pumping at his temples. Furious, he thought, *she*'s had bad news! *She* has!'

As the wind moved the long branches of the pepper tree across the iron roof of the homestead, James stood wondering what joke fate had next in store for him; then, realising there was nothing he or anyone could do, he sighed, stood up and went to clean up for lunch.

★ ★ ★

Hilda could not come to terms with the events that had unfolded over the past few days. She and her husband had made an almost silent coach trip right back to Parramatta and even the thought of seeing her old friends had not been able to cheer her up. Then, when she was among them, not only had they not seemed overjoyed to see her, they'd been surprisingly offhand towards her. Some of them hadn't even attended the funeral, which seemed unforgivable.

It was not until the awful business of the visit to the solicitor's office for the reading of the will that the enormity of her situation had struck her. Charles Carson, the man who had adored and pampered her all her life, had also, it seemed, been a silent but uncontrollable gambler. Not only had he died penniless, but his house and everything in it – Hilda's home – was in the process of being repossessed and sold by the bank. She was to receive nothing; in fact, she could be in debt. Now she'd understood why her acquaintances had been so cool to her – they must have known! The only person who'd seemed unchanged was Leila although even she seemed to pay more attention to James than to her bereaved friend.

After the meeting, Hilda had avoided seeing anyone, quickly arranging the repacking for the trip back, but on the morning of departure, she was pleased to receive a visit from her old friend Leila who called in to offer condolences. After two or three sherries, Leila moved to put an arm around Hilda's shoulders. 'My dear,' she said, 'I know this has been a wretched time for you, and I'm more than a little worried for your wellbeing. I know that your wonderful husband is quite capable of looking after you, but you're not quite looking yourself, dear.'

'Oh, it's nothing at all,' Hilda lied. 'It's all been a trying time and I'm quite tired. Into the bargain, I've been out of sorts in the mornings lately so possibly don't appear at my best.'

A quick light of understanding had shot to Leila's eyes and she'd flicked a glance at Hilda's midriff.

'Well, dear, we'll keep in touch, and when things settle down, perhaps Wilf and I could come and visit?'

This time, when they'd left Parramatta, Hilda knew that that part of her life was over, destroyed. But what was to replace it?

Through the long trip, she'd thought long and hard about her situation, discarding ideas almost as soon as they arose. Obviously, it would all have to revolve around Wellsford, and the baby she felt sure she was carrying although she'd said nothing so she was sure nobody knew, not even James. Certainly not James. Heavens, she could no longer bear to have him touch her.

She would take over the household completely and bring up her child in the image of her beloved father. She would learn to tolerate

James and keep him at arm's length at all times. There was plenty of space at the homestead; she had already arranged separate bedrooms. Yes, it was going to be all right. She only needed to be left alone. She'd handle it all. She'd mind her business, and everyone else could mind theirs.

Something sinister started to unravel deep inside Hilda Mitchell almost from the day they returned. By the time her son John, born later that year, was five years old, the door in her face had slammed completely closed. Closed, locked, bolted. Secured tightly so as to never reveal what lay behind it. Not to her husband, not to her son, not even, if she could manage it, to herself. If occasionally she suffered from little, rat-like niggles of something nibbling at her consciousness, she pushed them back, forced them down and dismissed them. When they re-emerged to pile up like magnetised dust creeping into the deepest recesses of her mind, she pulled the drawstring corners of her awareness even closer together, giving them no room, no space, no way of survival, hemming them in before drowning them with her shrill, pink laugh.

The kitchen girls had their own ideas of the reasons for Hilda's erratic behaviour.

'Maybe she doesn't like doin' it,' Pearl said, giggling from behind her hand. 'It might be that the boss is great riding a horse but ratshit in the bedroom.'

'More likely I reckon that she is,' Mary offered.

The girls laughed to themselves as they simply could not imagine their mistress enjoying any kind of physical activity at all, let alone sex. 'He'd have lost interest by the time she got them stays off,' Pearl chuckled. Mary nodded but said nothing, rubbing the silver polish onto the fork prongs, lost in her own daydreams.

Forbidden fruit

James Mitchell sharpened the pearl-handled carvers brought to this country as part of his long-departed mother's trousseau and started slicing the leg of roast lamb Pearl had placed in front of him on the huge mahogany table. These nights happened rarely, but God, how he hated them, having to sit around the table with some visiting piss-elegant friends of Hilda's. His wife had always had a slight plum in her mouth, but listen to her tonight. *Sounds like she swallowed the whole damned orchard. God alive, shut up, woman.*

On these occasions, Hilda changed from the morose and moody woman who sulked around the house to a brittle, skittish, vacuous socialite. And now, Leila and Wilf were making noises about inviting them back to stay at their Parramatta property. God forbid. The man didn't even know how to pour a decent drink. Last time they'd been together for a meal, he'd been given about enough brandy to wash out a hollow tooth, and that given grudgingly. Probably worried that his country bumpkin guest might not know how to handle his liquor. Well, at least I don't sit down to pee, James thought, enjoying the secret insult.

'Can't tell you how much I admire you taking on the building and supervision of a schoolhouse,' said Leila Branxton, pink-faced from the before dinner sherries, her unsteady elbow narrowly missing the edge of the table and ending up somewhere in her lap. Her eyes, conversely, had no problem focussing just a moment too long on her host's crotch. God, I'd love to take that on, she thought.

'Oh, it's nothing,' Hilda lied through her teeth. 'James insists you know that the children are to be well educated. And of course,

John's still almost a baby, so it will be years before we need a bigger school.'

'But those other children, will they be attending?' Leila stressed the word 'other', pulling her lips as if its very pronunciation tasted of something unpleasant. After all, she thought, it does seem like a total waste of time. It isn't as if those ragamuffins have a normal learning capacity. They can be trained to work at menial things, but everyone knows they are ... well, not the same as us.

'Yes, yes, they will,' Hilda confirmed, flicking her eyes at James. 'Sitting to the rear of the class, of course, not up at the front with our children.'

James was no longer capable of hiding his boredom. He yawned without covering his mouth, took out the gold fob watch that once attended this table adorning the chest of his late father Hugh, and checked the time, drumming his fingers on the lace tablecloth. How on earth, he thought, had he allowed his life to come to this? Sometime back there, he must have been suffering a touch of the sun. Maybe his brains transferred themselves to the head of his dick or something. Well, even that turned out to be a complete fizzer. God alive, the woman hardly twitched let alone responded. In fact, she obviously hated it! So, he did what any normal, red-blooded man would have done; he just stopped trying. Nothing in it at all. She simply didn't like 'his thing', as she called it – or any other part of him whatsoever – near her, so she damned well wasn't going to get it near her. There were, after all, other women in the world; other warm, loving, giving women. Women who kindled a flame and then softly nurtured it, slowly, slowly till your blood was on fire. Christ Almighty, what the hell was he doing wasting time sitting here with silly damned Hilda, her prune-faced friend Leila and her dotty, tight-fisted husband?

By the time coffee was served, James's already shredded thread of tolerance had worn dangerously thin. He filled the brandy goblets from the crystal decanter and served the guests, wished everyone a very good night, bowed slightly then turned and abruptly, without so much as a by your leave, left the room and the homestead.

Hilda, adjusting her pearls and tottering slightly, poured herself and her guests another brandy. She was pleased James had left. He was a boor anyway, didn't know how to behave with sophisticated people. She wound up the gramophone, put on a recording and struggled for a moment to drop the needle in the groove. In the middle of New South Wales on a fine April night, three rather inebriated voices joined in song. The hostess turned away from her guests, just for a moment, to wipe a solitary tear of self-pity from the corner of her eye. This song was about her, could almost have been written for her. She thought of her father and her nights at Parramatta then joined her thin soprano voice in to sing along. '*Oh, if I had the wings of an angel, over these prison walls I would fly …*'

In the kitchen, Pearl washed the last of the cleared away dinner dishes. She heard the scratchy record and the even scratchier voices and shook her head. *They'll be wanting bacon and eggs at midnight, trying to sober up, I reckon.* She knew already that it was going to be a late night for her.

Pearl sat on the edge of a kitchen chair with the tea towel draped over her arm and found herself once again thinking over the events of the last eighteen months and how she and Mary used to joke with each other during the long nights when the homestead was host to visitors. But underneath, she knew she should have noticed Mary's pensive moods and in retrospect now wondered why she had allowed them to slip past her without comment.

It was only when she realised that her friend was with child to that roughneck shearing hand who Pearl had never particularly liked, and who verified her feelings when he disappeared like the proverbial Arab into the night once the shearing ended and before Faith was born, that things fell into place. But even that didn't seem to worry Mary. Oh, she had known all along that Mary slipped out at night and certainly wasn't spending her time looking at the stars. Her blood flowed too hot in her veins for that. And when she'd helped her in the barn to deliver Faith, the dearest little girl, wasn't her delight boundless?

It was after that when things just didn't seem to add up. Why would Mary go swimming near Devil's Rock alone when she knew full well how dangerous it was? She had asked herself that question countless times and never found an answer. Pearl shuddered at the too recent memory of Charlie finding Mary's body. Dear, sweet Mary who'd left behind a tiny little daughter she had loved above all else. Dear God, Pearl wondered, would the hurt never leave her alone?

Pearl sighed, picked up the towel and dried the rest of the dishes. 'Not for me to question,' she said, but her heart ached for her lost friend and her mind wandered back to the institution where they had met.

Mary was always filled with the joy of life, eager to experience it to the full. Pearl smiled, recalling one Saturday morning when hastily pulled roller blinds followed by sharply pushed-up casement windows had indicated to the sleepy girls that Matron was once again that morning not in the best of moods. Red-faced, mouth set like a piece of pulled string, she'd strode purposefully down between the dormitory cots, pulling back covers, slapping her hands, if not together, alongside any head or limb that came within flailing distance.

'C'mon, c'mon, you girls, it's Saturday morning, you have your chores to do.'

Pearl and Mary raced to the washroom, eager to be as far away as possible from whatever had caused the rise in Matron's bile. They washed quickly as it was obvious that this was not a day for throwing water bombs or wet washcloths at each other. To avoid a hiding, it was much better to just get on with the day's chores. All of them had experienced these mornings too frequently not to know that keeping moving was the only way to avoid the whack of a tortoiseshell hairbrush across a cheek or side of the head.

Once breakfast was over, the dishes stacked on the enamel bench and the younger girls dispersed to do their morning tasks. Pearl collected the potato and vegetable peelings left by Cook in the staff kitchen and mixed them together with the bran and warm water, ready to take and feed the chickens. She mixed the mush carefully, savouring the grainy smell of the bran before tipping the slush into half a kerosene tin and motioning to Mary. 'C'mon, we'd better feed the chooks and collect the eggs, or we'll be in the poo.'

The two girls giggled, hands over their mouths, sharing the thought of the absurdity of their ill-tempered mistress. Carefully they walked, one on either side of the kerosene tin, struggling with the weight, the wire of its handle cutting into their hands and leaving dark welts. Every few moments they would stop, spit on their reddened hands and rub them together before changing sides to rest the tired hand and continue down the hill past the barn to the chicken coops. Once inside the wire enclosure, the hens and roosters clucked and gathered around them, knowing full well the usual feeding routine. A large black rooster pecked at Mary's hand.

'Cor, he's a greedy one, that,' she mumbled to Pearl, rubbing the back of her hand.

Pearl said nothing, tipping the chicken feed into the long wooden trough and scraping the last of it out of the tin with a wooden paddle, shooing the chickens away and brushing one off her shoulder. While the chickens scrapped and pecked over the food, the two girls ran around inside the coop, picking up the day's eggs and putting them carefully in the now empty tin. Mary straightened her back and shielded her eyes with a hand holding two fresh eggs.

'Them blackberries look just about ready,' she said, pointing to a clump of brambles outside the boundary fence.

Pearl nodded. 'Out of bounds, though,' she said.

The two girls stopped for a moment and looked at each other, then without saying a word, they left the coop, placed the tin of eggs carefully outside in the shade and moved quickly together to the boundary fence. Mary held up the top line of barbed wire as Pearl climbed through, but then, climbing through herself, she snagged her dress, pulling a small hole in the skirt. She pushed the ragged edges of the small hole together, hoping it would not catch the notice of Matron later.

'There'll be hell to pay if Matron sees that,' Mary mumbled, but then, taken by the freedom of being outside the fence promptly forgot all about it. Behind the bramble clump, shielded by its density from the institution buildings, the girls gave themselves to the freedom of the moment. Even the native shrubs, tea-tree and pink and white boronia seemed to look and smell differently outside their usual daily confines.

'This boronia smells sweet,' said Mary, lying flat on her back and holding a sprig of the gentle pink blossom to her nose. Pearl sat alongside her, holding her face back to the feel of the sun's rays, her strong hands flat on the warm earth. Mary rolled onto her side, holding the boronia for her friend to admire. 'Race you to the blackberries,' she said.

Long fingers carefully plucked the luscious berries and the two girls ate their fill, wiping their hands on their skirts and their mouths on the backs of their hands. Then slowly, reluctantly, they made their way back through the fence, picking up the can of eggs before hurrying to the institution kitchen to be told by Cook that Matron awaited in her office and would see them both – at once.

The two girls stood sheepishly as the red-faced Matron read the riot act about their going out of bounds, destroying government clothing, generally being disrespectful, unthankful, ungracious and behaving in a manner not acceptable to the institution. Matron's voice rose in a dramatic crescendo of warning to then fall to hushed tones, promising dire consequences that evidently couldn't be spoken of as one thing became crystal clear. The Devil, this fearsome entity they were unquestionably connected with, who must be avoided at all costs, was not exactly a horse of a different colour but was definitely, obviously, totally different in skin colour from Matron herself. That meant he was probably black. Could this be the reason the girls had been gathered together to be scrubbed, moulded and changed here at the institution? Was there some devilish meaning in the language he spoke that was also akin to theirs so that it had to be silenced and not even thought about as their language had been? Could this apparition hide bits of himself in their hair, their ears, under their nails even, to climb unseen into body openings from underneath nails that were not scrubbed clean of his every vestige? If that were so, what havoc would he play once he got inside their bodies, inside their thought processes?

That the Devil's powers were awesome was not something they doubted at all. One look at Matron's reddening face was convincing enough without the spreading patches of dampness under her arms and the nervous twitching that seemed to have taken up residence in her left eyelid. He was fearsome all right, and what's more, he was probably one of them.

'When will you remember what you have been taught here?!' Matron ranted, hitting the desk in front of her with the flat of her hand. She took a deep breath and reached into her top drawer to bring out the thick leather belt she used on such occasions. For a moment she stood, little raised spots of red deepening on her cheeks, her blue eyes becoming just a little too bright as she fondled the leather of the strap.

Matron moved around to the front of the desk and whacked Pearl roundly on each leg, making her hop up and down, endeavouring to avoid the next inevitable stroke of the leather. Then Matron told her to wait outside. It wasn't Pearl she was after; she wasn't the troublemaker. Oh no, she knew very well who that little madam was. It was that Mary all right. Well, she'd show her a thing or too, beat it out of her if she had to.

Folding the strap in half, the older woman walked to the front of her desk. 'Bend over,' she told the child in front of her.

But Mary stood straight.

'Bend over, girl, and bare your backside.'

Mary refused to move.

Matron was furious now. She lashed at the child with the strap, letting it hit where it fell, but she had underestimated the smaller girl whose hand grabbed the end of the strap and held on.

'Let go, let go, you little devil!' called the older woman, but to no avail. With a mighty wrench, Mary pulled the strap from the older woman and stood defiantly in front of her, holding it.

'Have your damned strap,' she said as she threw it at the feet of the older woman and strode out the door.

Ten days later, Pearl and Mary were both told to pack their few belongings together. They were to leave the institution, the only home they had ever known. It seemed a gentleman from a place called Wellsford, a Mr Mitchell, needed staff for his country station and would be sending for them.

'There'll be no shenanigans there,' Matron told them knowingly. 'Either of you play up there, you'll know all about it.'

Pearl sighed at the remembrance. Yes, Mary's sense of adventure had led them into dire trouble, all right. They knew exactly why it had happened. They had brought it on themselves, all right, by slipping through the fence and grabbing the taste of freedom firmly in their mouths. If Pearl pushed her tongue up against the roof of her mouth, she could still savour the first time she knew freedom's blackberry-tinged flavour.

But the very next morning, Sunday, all the girls were ushered into the dining room, surprised to see that the tables had been removed, the chairs lined up like the neat rows of carrots in the institution garden. In walked Matron clutching a heavy, leather bound book, her sparse hair pulled back from her face and thin, scarecrow-like body corsetted. Pearl had covered the lower half of her face with her hand as if to prevent as much as she could of what stood in front of her from entering Matron's vision.

'God has no time for sinners,' Matron informed them, hot spots of colour on her cheeks, walking between the rows of girls, hands reaching out and whacking at any angle any head that appeared to be unimpressed. Pearl thought she would never again see anything like it in her life. For a start, the old girl was ranting and raving like a loony about some kind of lamb which didn't seem to be connected at all to the rabbit stew that was having all the flavour boiled out of it in the adjoining kitchen, leaving even its aroma weak and unpalatable.

Pearl felt her forehead; it was hot and sweaty. Maybe Matron had some catching sickness and had thrown it at her along with the disgusted looks that she shot her way. She glanced across at Mary who rolled her eyes and received a Bible across the forehead for her trouble. Pearl tried hard to swallow, but her throat was parched and sore. She loosened the neck of her blouse and grabbed greedily for air. Must've been those damned chickens, she thought as, oblivious to all around her, she slid, in the grip of fever, onto the floor and out of range of the sanctimonious voice.

'You've got chickenpox,' Mary told her later, 'all over you. You look a real mess.'

Pearl laughed. 'I knew them chickens would do me in,' she said, feeling better now the spots had walked their way through her system to emerge triumphantly all over her.

'You got to drink lots of water and have calamine lotion on you,' Mary giggled behind her hands. 'You just did this on purpose, didn't you,' she laughed. 'Just trying to miss all that stuff she was telling us about the Devil having hold of our souls.'

But underneath, the two girls were concerned. Of late, it seemed to them that Matron was losing the thread more and more. Not only that, but she'd agreed to allow some of the local landowners to convince her of their Christian beliefs and now they were coming in quite regularly to take a young girl of their choice out for the day for a treat. These days must have been exhausting as when the girls returned, they all wanted to go straight to their beds and not speak about the day's events. Pearl noticed that some of them walked funny for a day or two after the outing and most of them waited until they thought the dormitory was asleep before shyly holding on to their pillows, the closest thing they knew to a mother, and spilling their tears.

Often, during hot summer nights at the institution when the breeze unabashedly displayed its moodiness, swinging this way and that, soft as a downy feather one moment, irritable and blustery the next, Pearl occasionally felt a sense of some kind of belonging. Perhaps it was not so much the capricious breeze as the fact that on summer nights, the girls' cots were placed outside on the wide wooden verandah, head-on to the peeling tongue-and-groove timber of the outside wall, feet-on to the iron lace balustrade but away from the dormitory's swelter, enabling the girls to lie on top of their beds and gaze up at the sky, wondering tearfully if in some other place, but under the same sky, someone thought about them. But try as she would, Pearl could not get her thinking to step back into her past further than the trip on the great steam train. At least I know I belonged to someone once, she thought, feeling her sympathies rise for girls like Mary who had been brought to the institution as babies, knowing nothing of belonging to anyone other than Matron and old White-face.

Day after day, the girls were taught to 'learn to be of service'. The ultimate fate awaiting them.

Pearl closed the eye closest to her pillow and squinted the other, taking in the fullness of the moon; the great, never-ending expanse of sky with its creamy, sparkling splash of the Milky Way.

For a moment, she let herself imagine buds of little wings sprouting from her shoulders. She concentrated her energy and her thoughts until a tiny part of her stepped out of the bed, over the iron lace railing to soar meteor-like through the vastness.

She sighed with the hopelessness of her situation. If I was up there, she thought, I could look down and see them, see where I came from. I could look down and know. Know for sure that they want me with them.

She pulled the tissue-thin sheet up over herself as the wind displayed yet another change in temperament and she cast one last sleepy glance at the Milky Way. One day I'll know, she promised herself, one day when I'm old.

Eight days later, with Pearl still shaky but back on her feet, the two girls were summoned to Matron's office to be given the news about their imminent departure. That night, the two girls pledged their friendship. Whatever was ahead, they would share and support each other. They would be to each other the family neither knew. They would not, under any circumstances, desert one another or their heritage, even though they were unsure just what that heritage was. They would trust in something unseen yet felt, and they would do it together.

Yes, it hurt her to the quick all right that Mary had tragically died so young, a hurt that started somewhere deep inside her and rose up as if to choke her breath with the pain of it. She could feel Mary's life force everywhere she looked; in the swaying of a eucalypt in the west wind, in the soft rain that turned new leaves green; in the mad, uninhibited sundown chase that the station dogs periodically indulged in around the house and, worst of all, in the upturned face of Mary's young, motherless daughter.

Faith was almost like a daughter of her own. After all, hadn't she helped her into the world and heard her first cry? But her friend's death seemed such a meaningless tragedy for such a joyous child of the earth, her cup of passions overflowing every which way regardless of the danger such spillage might invite. There had been a bond of sisterhood between them that was more than mortal, even though they were so different from each other.

Pearl smiled, recalling a time behind the barn when she herself had given in to a little enticing, but not really wholeheartedly, more in the hope that she might discover a little of whatever it was that put such a spring in Mary's step. But it hadn't been anything at all, really, just a bit of fumbling and then Charlie's weight on top of her. Made her laugh later, thinking it was all a bit 'this will be good, wasn't it?' Oh, she could have taught him a thing or two if she'd had the inclination, from intuition rather than from experience, but as far as she had been concerned, Mary was welcome to as much of it as she could handle. It certainly didn't compare to the thrill of holding a newborn little-un by the feet and hearing its first cry.

Perhaps it might be different if she had happened to meet someone who had been 'sent' for her. She would recognise that immediately. If it were to last one night or a whole lifetime, she would know when it was right. Oh, she'd heard what they said about people who never married – 'old maids' or 'maiden aunts' who never shared their lives and therefore never looked at things from the wider perspective of two viewpoints. The missus and her visitors were always talking about those things over too many tipples in the big dining room.

Better look in the big oval mirror in the master bedroom next time I clean it, Pearl thought. *Check if I'm walking lopsided, if that's the way those of us who don't share their lives with a partner are, like their balance isn't quite right.* She dismissed the idea before giving it too much life. Not that I'm alone here, she thought, putting down the tea towel and straightening her skirt as the bell from the dining room impatiently summoned her presence. *Hardly a minute to meself.*

★ ★ ★

'They mate for life, you know.' Hilda shooed the geese away from the path she and Leila were taking, then laughed. 'Wouldn't it be dreadful to be a female goose stuck for an entire lifetime with an ill-tempered gander. Now, that's really being a goose.'

Brittle words skirting the borders of a growing fragility gave her friend just the opening she was seeking.

'My God, Hilda, doesn't it irritate you, the way James just rushes off like that in the middle of a meal without so much as a by-your-leave or beg your pardon?'

Hilda knew Leila was prying, but the seedy state of her head after the previous evening's carousing prevented her indulging herself in a sense of annoyance. The two women were taking a head-clearing stroll along the river bank where crystal clear, bubbling waters of the Wellsford River sang joyously over the river stones after the recent rain. Native king parrots sat eating berries in the white cedars; oblivious, in their growing intoxication, to the human intrusion. Small floral parasols protected the female faces from the already hot morning sun as the two women ambled, constantly brushing bush flies away from their faces with their free hands.

'No,' answered Hilda rather too firmly. 'The man's a bore. He's always been a bore, I suppose. I can't imagine for the life of me why I found him amusing in the beginning. I must have been quite blind. I mean, I even found his misuse of words attractive. I recall one time at Daddy's when I offered hors d'oeuvres and he made some crude remark like 'Oh, God alive, girl. Horse's ovaries, no thanks'. I thought it so funny then. About the closest he ever got to understanding the subtleties of the French language.'

Hilda stopped, bending to pick a long-stemmed flannel flower. She turned the flower around slowly by the stem and then, losing interest, dropped it to lie forgotten in the grass. 'The man is an oaf,' she continued, 'crude and lecherous. I stay here,' she looked at Leila as if answering an unasked question, 'because I am mistress of the house and I have my child. My own little John, and soon the school children.'

Hilda smiled at her friend. 'Really, Leila, James has no ardour, no real emotional intensity. He thinks a crime passionelle is some kind of sticky, morning tea bun.' She hesitated, leaning forward to rest her hand on her friend's arm. 'Of course, my life would have been different if Daddy ...' The voice trailed off as if a ghostly finger reached from another level to cover her lips. 'Anyway,' she continued, shaking her head as if to remove the melancholy, 'James isn't setting up the schoolhouse to perpetuate any kind of cultural endeavour; he simply wants his pennies and pounds taken care of.'

The two women continued their walk in silence, but Leila's mind was racing with curiosity. She knew that Hilda's father had died penniless, frittered his life's savings away gambling. She knew Hilda had nowhere else to go and was dependent on James, but she seemed to be developing a veneer around herself as fragile as an eggshell. If given one tap, the whole exterior might crack wide open, and who knew just what that might reveal. Leila shuddered.

'But where does he go when he runs out like that?' The slight whine in Leila's voice belied her contrived look of open-eyed innocence and revealed that she had her own suspicions.

Hilda sighed and slid her eyes under their lids to take a quick sideways look at her friend. 'Out carousing with the servants, I suppose,' she replied flippantly, adding quickly as if enjoying the opportunity to shock, 'Certainly I have made it quite plain that I have absolutely no interest in his monstrous grunting and groaning his way to a one-sided ecstasy.'

Precisely what Leila wanted to hear. Her look of concern camouflaged a smile of delight, unveiling only on the inside of her face. She had thought as much but nevertheless feigned shock at her friend's attitude. A blatant lie would have been more acceptable; it was unthinkable to freely admit to the man's infidelities. God alone knew there were times when she was, well, less than interested with Wilf, but she always managed a few little encouraging whimpers. Better to keep him home than to have him out and about with heaven only knew who. Besides, she thought, even though Hilda considered James an oaf and a boor, there was something devilishly attractive about the man. Something too good to just send out into the night. Something about his vulgarity that was definitely seductive.

'But don't you ever want to … you know … with him anymore?' Leila stood in front of her friend, toying with the web of the topic in the hope that she might motivate the spider into revelation.

Hilda turned, pulling over her face a low-hanging branch of the pepper tree she was standing under. Obscured for a moment behind the lacy shadow of its leaves, her eyes lingered to partner the dancing prisms of light on the Wellsford River. 'No,' she answered.

There was an edge in her voice that made Leila think of the time she'd dropped a pan of toffee, shattering the contents into an abundance of pointed, glassy shards.

'No,' she repeated, letting go of the pepper tree's branch. 'I don't ever want to again. Not ever. Not with him, not with anyone.'

The two women made their leisurely way back to the house. Leila wanted to pack right now; she was impatient and anxious to be on the move. She had juicy, gossipy bits to share at Parramatta and she just couldn't wait. She'd suspected that Hilda might be a little on the cold side, but just wait till this hot stuff hit the old crowd. Her ears would be burning then, and no doubt about that.

Leila had a warmth of her own building up. The revelations had her head spinning. She thought about little else as they packed up, put their ports in the carriage, went through the farewells and left Wellsford.

The servants, she thought. *And Hilda knows! How could she talk about it so casually? Wasting a man like James on the servants. Dear God, I wish I lived closer. If Hilda doesn't want it, I'd have it.*

The fantasy coupled with the bumping and vibrations of the coach were working Leila into quite a state of excitement which steadily built with the passing miles. Unconscious of the hours on the road, she was almost jumping out of her skin by the time they arrived at their home.

Hardly inside the door, Leila suddenly embraced her husband and said, 'Wilf, take me to bed.'

Flabbergasted, he answered, 'But we've just got … What, now?'

'Yes, *now*.'

Great heavens! thought Wilf. *Where did I go right? Usually she needs at least some coaxing*, but instead he said, 'What a grand suggestion.'

Leila's smile seemed to come from far away as she started loosening her clothes and dropping them on the floor on the way to the bedroom.

Providence

Nettie felt the heaviness of the weight inside her, a heaviness that never left her for a moment. When she lay down at night, she was reminded of what caused that heaviness. She had had it from the day her daughter had died in childbirth. She rubbed the left side of her ribs, underneath her heart, to ease the burden. Albert was all she had now since her husband Jack had gone without trace. Gone out to mend fences three months ago and not returned, not even been heard of. But he was gone, Nettie was sure of that, and she felt pretty bad herself with this constant pain in the chest.

The McManaways were all right. They kept their distance while Nettie did her chores, but she worried about what might happen to Albert if she wasn't there to look after him, and he was far too young to work yet. Anyway, James Mitchell was coming over today. He wanted to sink another bore and needed her water-divining skills again.

She liked those trips out onto the land. Mr Mitchell was always at ease with his helpers and very appreciative of any special abilities. He knew how good his offsider Charlie was with animals and how Nettie always found the precious water. Come to think of it, that Pearl; she'd be a good one to see to Albert if it could be arranged.

Her thoughts were interrupted by the sound of horses' hooves outside, and some minutes later; Nettie, silently gritting her teeth against the jolting, was riding out with her two neighbours.

By the time Nettie reached the area for where the new bore was intended, she knew that she was not at all well. She'd ridden horses most of her life and this wasn't a heavy trip, but she was exhausted.

Now, added to her worries about Albert, a new problem nagged at her: what if her weakness made her lose her divining powers?

She slid down off the horse then leant back against the animal for a moment. Closing her eyes, she whispered, 'Don't let me down now, please,' then reached into the saddlebag for her twisted piece of fencing wire.

'What do you think, Nettie?!' James called to her.

She looked around the landscape and from deep down, the stirrings began again, and she started to relax. 'Thank you,' she whispered, then called, 'Not right here, but close!'

'You're the boss, Nettie, go for it!'

That always made her smile inwardly. 'I'm the boss? That'll be the day,' but secretly she liked hearing Mr Mitchell say that, something he had always said all the years they'd been taking these search trips. And Charlie beamed at her as he liked to hear that easy familiarity from Mr Mitchell too. Also, he loved to watch Nettie moving around with her wire in front of her between her hands, but today, for some reason, it took some time and a lot of moving about before Nettie said, 'Okay, this area's better.'

Charlie watched as she moved off in a definite direction, her bare feet sliding as though attached to the earth, a part of it. A few gliding steps further, the wire between her hands moved slightly and she slowed her movements a little. As she moved forward, the wire began to revolve gently, then after two or three paces more, it took life and started to spin in Nettie's hands. Another pace and the spinning was too strong for her to hold without it burning her hands, and as she dropped the wire; James, with a confident smile, reached for one of the stakes he'd brought and walked over to mark the spot.

This business of finding water often made Nettie feel tired and a little dizzy, but this time it was definitely different. She didn't feel at all well, almost as if she might faint.

She moved over to one of the horses and held its bridle for support until, much to her relief, the feeling passed. Charlie and Mr Mitchell were busy driving in the stake and fixing markers, so luckily, she thought, they didn't notice.

'Done it again, Nettie,' James said. 'You're one reliable water witch. Damned if you ever miss. After all these years, think what I owe you.' He smiled fondly at the small woman. 'Wish there was some way I could repay you, something special I could do.'

Nettie couldn't believe her ears. Immediately, she blurted out, 'There is, Mr Mitchell, there is!'

Slightly taken aback at the urgency in Nettie's unexpected reply, James looked into her eyes and his smile faded. The open face in front of him had worry written all over it, something he had never seen in all the years he had known her.

'What is it, Nettie? Is there something you want?'

'It's not for me, Mr Mitchell, I got all I want. But if something happens to me, what'll happen to Albert? He's too young to work and I don't want him taken away. The McManaways are nice people, but ...' Her voice trailed away.

James's voice was almost gentle. 'I'm not sure what you're on about, Nettie, but you can rest assured there'll always be a home for Albert at Wellsford. Don't you worry about that.'

The ride back to the McManaway property left James worried; something was getting at Nettie. He waited until she was tethering her horse and asked, 'Nettie, are you sure you're all right?'

He was relieved to see that the worried expression she'd shown earlier had gone, to be replaced by a wide, open smile.

'Oh yes, Mr Mitchell, I'm all right now, just fine.'

Nettie felt the worry in her mind dissolve as the weight in her chest increased. Mixed with the pain of memories past, she now felt the stirrings of hope. The two steps up to her place felt difficult today. Bed was what she needed – bed and a rest.

She lay back on her mattress and closed her eyes. That was where Albert found her later when he came running in to show her the speckled bird's egg he had found.

The next day, James Mitchell rode from Wellsford to take Albert home.

★ ★ ★

Hilda considered the gap between herself and her staff to be so vast as to never allow for any real personal contact. Every morning, she stood in the huge kitchen and designated the day's jobs only to Pearl, without ever meeting her eyes. She ate the food she prepared, wore the clothes she sewed and mended with minute, institution-trained stitches then faithfully washed and ironed, slept in the beds she made, all in the same manner that she addressed her; with no sign whatsoever that she even acknowledged her existence.

Pearl's existence was, however, noticed and enjoyed by Hilda's young son John. In the growing child's uncluttered mind, the household was all one. The fact that some members lived in the outhouses and tended to the needs of others who never went near those buildings meant not a thing to the boy. He accepted the affection of the household staff naturally and they returned his in the same manner. As far as he was concerned, they all lived together – a mother who fussed constantly, a father who was out on the land all day, and a Pearl who took care of necessities.

'Bet I know why you're hangin' around.' The boy looked up at her from the kitchen doorstep. Her white apron was pulling over her full bust as she stood in front of him, one arm holding an oven cloth, the other resting on the back of a pine kitchen chair, that ever-truant piece of hair again pulled out of its tie and falling down the front of her face. She blew from the corner of her mouth to move it away then smiled and repeated her statement.

'No reason,' John replied, looking down. 'Just thought I'd sit here with my toys.'

'Nothin' to do with the fact that half the week's bread is in the oven and the kitchen smells like the closest thing to heaven?'

John blushed. He could never resist bake days, when the smell of bread cooking filled the entire house and half the surrounding outbuildings as well. Besides, he knew the routine. If he sat quietly, Pearl always cut off a hot, crusty delight for him, straight from the oven.

Pearl rubbed her hands on her white apron and opened the oven door, releasing a mouth-watering wave of heat. 'Oh, lovely,' she said, removing the trays of bread and placing them on the long wooden bench. She turned the containers upside down, tapping the bottom lightly, allowing the crusty hot loaves to fall onto waiting wire trays to cool.

'Don't suppose I could tempt you with a slice?' she asked.

John stood alongside her, watching her cut the steaming crust from the loaf, then sat cross-legged on the floor, picking at the feather-soft dough, savouring every mouthful. 'Dad says you're the best, Pearl,' he said through his chewing.

'Don't speak with your mouth half full,' Pearl chided. 'Fill it right up.'

Pearl ruffled his hair. It was easy to love this lad. He had inherited his father's affection for the land and regardless of Hilda's constant efforts had seemingly missed out on any of his mother's idiosyncrasies. And he came straight to the point though people would probably not like that about him later in his life, especially the ones who preferred to colour the truth.

'What did your mother and father look like?' asked the boy innocently.

Pearl started to speak, then stopped herself. She took a long breath, sat on the chair and leaned her forearms over her knees. 'I don't remember,' she said slowly. 'I try and try, but I just don't remember.'

John put down his crust and walked over to Pearl's chair. He reached up and touched her cheek with the back of his hand. 'I love you, Pearl,' he said. 'I think you're the best in the whole world.'

She stood up and flicked her oven cloth at him. 'Get outside, you young time waster, or I'll call your father in,' she threatened. But she bit her lip as she watched his retreating back and blew her nose just a little too loudly. Then she ran her hands down the sides of her white apron. 'Well,' she said to herself, 'that's one for the books. First time a man ever told me he loved me.' She laughed inwardly. 'Don't matter if he's only a whippersnapper, feels good all the same.'

She turned to the bread loaves on the bench and cut herself a generous slice. She felt good. Why not treat herself? She turned to the pantry. Might as well spread the slice with some farm butter and homemade jam. After all, not every day a young man declares his love.

John sat on the bottom step of the back porch, still picking at the bread crust and taking in the landscape before him where the paddocks rolled up to and past the river, fading into a mass of differing greens before merging with the darker blue hills on the horizon. He couldn't imagine ever leaving Wellsford. He rolled the remaining piece of bread into a cigar shape and bit through it. He would never leave Wellsford. That's where he was born, where his father was born. He would always live here, always. But his heart felt uneasy and he shuddered in spite of the sun's heat, a cold shiver brought on by just the thought of being taken away from everything familiar that surrounded him. Away from everything he loved. Then, catching sight of Faith and Albert, he shook the feeling off and ran to join them in the yard.

Kicking up the minuscule fragments of sawdust carried on the west wind, Hilda walked around the verandah surrounding the Wellsford house, watching the station hands raising the timber frame of the building that was, whether she liked it or not, to become her schoolhouse.

Ring-a, ring-a Rosie,
Pocket full of posy,
A-tishoo, A-tishoo,
They all fall down.

She looked at the group of children holding hands in a circle and singing the song. Her eyes lingered affectionately on her son still munching the last of some rolled up bread and then moved on to the ragamuffin child next to him. She shook her head in disgust. Mary's brat Faith holding John's hand. There was something about that brat she didn't like, hadn't liked since Pearl helped Mary bring her into the world in the old barn. Bastard kid, the daughter of that shiftless station hand who'd worked here a while back.

The smell of fresh sawn timber grew long fingers and tantalised her nose. All around the valley echoed the sounds of men hammering and nailing. The building was coming along – her schoolhouse. Her schoolhouse, but not her idea – his idea. One room, with a fireplace, a blackboard and five or six desks. One for her son John, two for the neighbouring McManaway children and one she supposed for that brat Faith. She saw this as an unnecessary intrusion, an area in which she had no interest and fought against fiercely, but to no avail.

James, for some reason she could not understand, insisted on having all of the station children taught in the schoolhouse and that was that. There was simply to be no argument (God knows there had been enough of those), in the same way that, as mistress of the station, she had no option other than to be their teacher. That was the way on the land; she just had to accept it. The fact that she had no idea how to teach children, much less what to teach them, made no difference at all to her unyielding husband. He wanted his child and the children of his staff to be able to read, write and calculate. Once that was done, his wife could indulge herself, read them all the Dickens she wanted, fill their heads with it if she liked, so long as they were prepared in the basics for the business life he had planned for them, the business in which he was now spending all his time. The Mitchells of Wellsford, and their staff, were not to be trifled with – oh, no. The Mitchells just about owned the whole district of Wellsford and that was just how James Mitchell liked it. Even in these tight economic times, he would not change his mind about the next generation's education. 'They might be in a mess and gearing up for war in Europe,' he said to her, 'but we're hanging on here. We'll ride this through.' His answer to everything.

Eyes slanted and watched from Hilda's closed-door face as Pearl called the children together. She brushed sawdust from John's clothes and wordlessly brought him over to his mother and then walked away, taking the brat Faith, bits of sawdust all through her hair, with her. That child was like Pearl's own since Mary had died, found dead one morning down by the river at Devil's Rock stark bollocky naked. Thinking about it, Hilda sucked in her cheek. The woman was stupid. Everyone knew that no one ever swam down at Devil's Rock. The water had always been dangerous and there she was in the middle of the night in the raw, going for a swim. It was no wonder at all that she drowned.

Hilda lovingly took John by the hand and started to walk him inside to tidy up before Pearl came to bathe him and give him his tea. She paused, casting a brief glance at Pearl walking the small girl in the other direction. For a moment, her green eyes almost revealed something deep behind her face. Only for a moment. Then it was gone.

* * *

James could not hide his disgust; Hilda had invited Leila and Wilf to visit again, and they were to be arriving the next day. By car, in fact.

'Not only do they have a daughter who I've never seen,' Hilda had sniffed at him, 'but they have a car.'

'Only because the bank provided it,' James snorted.

'Never mind how, do I have a car?' The voice was sharp, vitriolic.

Red-faced, James could only glare at her. Goddamn, he thought, the nose has gone up and the plum's back in her voice already, and they're not here yet.

'No, you don't,' he growled.

'Exactly,' she said flippantly, then turned and left the room.

James knew this visit was really going to be a trial. He was positive that Hilda would have told her precious friend nothing about the past few years' developments, the separate bedrooms, the constant fighting, the never-ending coddling of her son which had driven the boy to his father and the staff. Not to mention the increasing consumption of alcohol, which she thought nobody noticed. Nobody noticed! Great God. Well, they'd find it all out tomorrow. They might be as dull as ditchwater, but neither of them was blind. He'd have to keep as far as possible from them during the next couple of days and try to conceal his feelings when they were together.

Excitement rose around the station with the dust caused by the car's wheels as visitors arriving from the city was only an occasional occurrence in Wellsford. Of the few cars to visit the area, most were driven by travelling salesmen from big city companies, so almost everybody on the station gathered for the occasion and Leila's behaviour became even more brittle and skittish, loving being the centre of attention.

But it was not long after Wilf and one of the men had unloaded their luggage that Leila started to see things as they were; quite different from the contents of Hilda's letters. Although Hilda was genuinely pleased to see them and skipped to meet her, Leila was inwardly shocked at how she had physically deteriorated and as they embraced was staggered by a wave of gin fumes. And James was not even there.

'Oh, how lovely,' Hilda said, 'and this is Celia.' She bent forward with outstretched arms, almost losing her balance. The child did not move; just made a distasteful face then ran to hide behind her mother.

'Celia, say hello to your Aunt Hilda,' Leila said, but the girl hid her face in her mother's dress.

'Ah well,' said Hilda, straightening up, 'perhaps a little later on. Do come inside.'

Over what was ostensibly a cup of tea, although Hilda's was generously laced with gin, the two friends caught up on all the gossip from the city while Celia sat or moved about the room with a sulking expression on her face.

'This isn't much fun for you, dear,' Hilda said to her gaily. 'Would you like to go out and play with the children?'

'No thanks,' the girl replied sullenly.

'Oh dear, I think the trip has tired her,' said Leila.

Leila tried to intervene, embarrassed. 'Perhaps you'd like to have a lie down, dear?'

'No, I wouldn't. I didn't even want to come here. Just leave me alone, please,' and she sat sulkily on a pouf with her back to them both.

Leila rolled her eyes at Hilda. 'Awkward age,' said Hilda, inwardly seething.

The day got steadily worse. James did not put in an appearance; Wilf sat with a fixed smile for as long as he could manage then excused himself to walk outside to, as he put it, 'stretch his legs after the journey.'

Leila thought it strange that not only did the head of the house not appear, but neither did his son and heir.

Late in the day, the woman Pearl came into the room, bringing John Mitchell with her. He'd clearly been spruced up, so Leila correctly deduced that the servant looked after him, not his mother.

'Ah, here he is,' said Hilda, beaming as the boy walked to Wilf and shook his hand, then to Leila who kissed his cheek. 'Come and meet Celia, John, dear,' said Hilda. 'She's almost your cousin, you know.'

John looked around anxiously for Pearl, but she'd gone. He wasn't sure what to do next, so he walked towards the girl with his hand out.

'Don't talk to me,' said Celia petulantly. 'I saw you playing with the servants and my mother says that's disgusting.'

Silence hung heavily in the room on air that could have been cut with a knife.

'Celia! I never said any such thing,' blurted Leila.

'I told you that would have repercussions one day, Leila. The girl is too young to understand,' said Wilf, pleased to have the advantage for once.

'Heavens, is she really only three years old?' said Hilda, shaken not so much by the statement as the rebuff to her son. 'How discerning.'

John casually shrugged his shoulders, dropped his hand, turned and walked out of the room.

'Surely it's time for a drink,' said Hilda, heading for the safety of the sideboard.

They were on their third when James returned to the house, kicked his boots off, washed his hands and, to Hilda's mortification, walked into the lounge to confront, rather than greet his wife's friends.

'Hello there,' he said and having quickly assessed the situation walked to the liquor cabinet, poured himself a stiff Scotch, downed it and poured another.

'James,' said Hilda, the alcohol-induced acid level already high in her voice, 'could you not have dressed a little more appropriately for the occasion?'

'What occasion? Oh, you mean meeting these two?' He smiled disarmingly. 'Well, I wouldn't want them to think I'm anything but a farmer, you know. How are you both?'

Wilf said, 'We're fine, thank you, James,' but didn't move, while Leila sat stunned. For years, she had had erotic dreams of this man, but the memories of them were crashing around her. She managed to bleat, 'Yes, we're well, thank you.'

'Motherhood seems to be agreeing with you, Leila,' James said. 'You've put on a bit of weight.'

Hilda gasped and Leila cringed, then bristled.

'And you, Wilf,' he continued, 'doing well at the bank? I saw the car on the way in. Must be nice to have your company buy you one of those?'

He threw the second Scotch down his throat and headed for a refill. He'd been gearing himself for this and wanted it over with as soon as possible.

'And where is the third member? Ah, there she is. Hello, Celia, what a pretty dress. Did Mummy make it?'

'No, she didn't,' the girl pouted, and walked behind her mother.

'Oh. Well, I just thought I'd ask. Now, if you'll all excuse me, I'll clean up for dinner.' And he left.

Hilda left her sherry beside her chair and poured herself a large gin with a splash of tonic water, took a gulp and had a coughing spasm. When it finally settled, she dabbed her eyes with a lace handkerchief and inquired, 'Can I offer you two something perhaps a little stronger?'

The strained atmosphere at the dinner table resulted in a veil of ominous silence. Wilf, now completely withdrawn, looked so uncomfortable that one would think his plush chair was a bed of nails. Celia sulked, and toyed with the cutlery in front of her.

'Don't fiddle, dear,' said her mother, taking her embarrassment out on the girl.

'I'm not fiddling,' said Celia, 'I'm hungry. I hope these people know how to cook.'

Young John, again tidied by Pearl, gaped at her in amazement.

God, thought Leila, can it get worse?

It could.

'Oh, I don't think you need worry, young lady,' their host said, smiling. 'If you don't like the witchetty grubs, just push them aside. There are plenty of other things to eat.'

The girl made as if to get down, but Leila held her arm. 'Just sit there, Celia. Mr Mitchell is having a joke with you.'

Unimpressed, the child sat back and stared into her lap as Pearl came into the room with the trolley and began to serve the soup.

'Ah, lovely,' said James, 'kangaroo tail.'

'James, stop it!' snapped Hilda, her cheeks taking a deeper shade of pink.

'Oh, sorry, m'dear,' now with an affected accent, 'just a little bit of fun, what?'

Leila was now shaking. Wilf had frozen. John couldn't understand what was going on so didn't try. Instead he enjoyed his soup. Hilda closed her eyes to try to regain her composure, then picked up her soup spoon, carefully pointing her little finger across the table. James had already all but emptied his plate.

When Pearl came back a few minutes later to collect the dishes, not another word had been spoken. She moved from place to place, finally arriving beside Celia whose soup was untouched. As Pearl picked up the dish of soup, Celia said, 'I'd like a glass of milk.'

'Please,' said her mother, but the child ignored her.

Pearl took the trolley from the room and soon returned with the milk, placing it before the girl.

'You can go now,' said Celia, without looking up.

You can go now, thought James. *Jesus Christ Almighty, the bloody brat is not yet four years old – you can go now!*

'Dad,' said John, 'why is Celia so rude to Pearl?'

Still making the monumental effort to control his temper, James said, 'Well, son, she can't really help being ignorant. As your mother has said so often, it's all in the breeding, you know.'

Pearl beat a hasty retreat from the room.

Leila choked, her face flaming while Wilf huffed and said, 'Oh really, James.'

Hilda stood up suddenly, sending her chair flying backwards. 'You pig!' she spat, and strode to the gin bottle.

'Dad, can I go and eat in the kitchen, please?'

'Certainly, John, go ahead. As a matter of fact, I've lost my appetite too.' Sliding his chair back as he stood, he looked around the table. 'You can all go to buggery,' he said, and walked out of the room.

Hilda dropped into an armchair, crumpled and crying.

Leila slowly opened her eyes, signalled to Wilf, collected Celia and left the dining room to repack for their departure as early as possible the next morning.

The picnic

Although James had little truck with social occasions in his home, he was well aware of certain outside celebrations that had become part of the language of the land. Like the picnics on New Year's Day, the one day landowners traditionally put aside to treat their workers. It was simple bush psychology: if you attended to your staff, they attended to you.

In spite of herself, Hilda usually enjoyed these functions, even though it meant the barrier she had placed between herself and her staff was, for the day at least, somewhat relaxed.

All summer, Albert had been feeding a magpie he had found as a nestling, a raggedy, brown, black and white bird which followed him everywhere and spent its nights teetering in a half-sleep on the door of his 'room' in the barn. 'It can talk, you know,' Albert confided in Pearl. 'It copies me.'

She didn't disbelieve him. She had watched the boy with the bird and it wasn't inconceivable that it had picked up a few phrases. She laughed to herself as she remembered an old white cockatoo who used to shout 'Get stuffed!' whenever anyone came within cooee, a phrase taught it by a shearer with the DTs, now long dead.

'And he can do tricks,' Albert disclosed. 'I'm teaching him one for the picnic.'

If anything ever gave Pearl a sense of almost remembered family, it was the New Year's Day picnics. The pleasure generated by the gathering, momentarily at least, wiped from her mind the obvious gaps that existed between the station owner's wife and her staff, and something about the sharing of food and spontaneous laughter took her back almost to the outer shadows of her beginnings.

Picnic day brought trestle tables covered with white tablecloths to house a feast otherwise unknown to farmhands used to 364 days of damper and roast or stewed mutton. From the kitchen, Pearl and the neighbouring wives lugged huge jugs of lemonade, their surfaces floating invitingly with mint and slices of lemons cut from the station trees. Roasted pork, a leg of ham, garden vegetables and salads, along with every kind of sponge cake, cream puff, fruitcake and nose-taunting dampers covered the tables to capacity as the station people gathered around.

One by one, each of the stockmen arrived at Wellsford when required, unheralded, as if led by some intuitive notion, usually carrying all his belongings wrapped in a roll on his back, on horseback or walking, their closest friend a cattle dog always yapping at their heels. They were shy at first, unused to silver tableware and stunned by the array of available food. Some of the itinerant hands might only share this occasion once.

Pearl looked affectionately at the assemblage, her eyes lingering sadly on the small figure in dungarees sitting alone, away from the crowd. Although she only saw her occasionally, she had a strong affection for Millie, the cattlehand, poor Millie who'd had the words stolen out of her mouth, never to return.

Pearl sucked in her cheek. There was so much that didn't seem right, it made her wonder sometimes what right was. Or was the world so lopsided with wrong that right just slid off into some nameless void?

Four roughnecks – shearers, they were – had stolen the words from Millie's mouth. Rode into her camp one night drunk and found her alone, tied a rope around her neck as if she were some kind of animal. Tied her up to a tree and beat her and raped her till she had no words to tell about it and the only thing that spoke was her eyes. Nobody ever found out who they were; they just moved through. Now she wore men's clothing in the hope that she would pass unnoticed, as a man. Cut her hair and looked out through her haunted eyes and never again found her lost words.

'C'mon, Pearl, me girl, how about a dance?'

Charlie, the chief hand, grabbed Pearl around the waist and tried to waltz her out to near where Jimmy Flaherty's violin invited all to dance a jig. Pearl gave him a push. 'Gawd,' she said, 'you might have shaved, Charlie, but you still smell like horses. And I believe you may have had a drop or two.'

'Aw, Pearl, c'mon,' said the crestfallen Charlie.

'Buzz off,' she replied. 'Can't you see I'm busy?'

Calling the children together into a line, Pearl handed them a silver dessertspoon and a hard-boiled egg.

'Winner takes a bag of marbles!' Hilda Mitchell called, momentarily forgetting herself but sure nonetheless that her son would win the egg-and-spoon race. Her triumph was as short-lived as her smile, however, as it was not John who won the race. Hilda turned away from the winner to slyly empty half the marbles into her skirt pocket before presenting the winner with the remainder. No point wasting the prize on someone like that, she thought to herself.

Then she resumed her place in a deckchair to one side of the group, near her favourite jacaranda, which shielded her face from the sun as she seemingly enjoyed the relaxed atmosphere and the gentle breeze.

James and the men congregated to one side of the table, safe in the mateship of male company, most of them embarrassed and tongue-tied in front of the women who sat in another group, exchanging gossip, heads bobbing.

'It's nearly ready,' Albert confided to Pearl. 'You watch and see what happens.'

Albert had taken his magpie and placed it on an overhanging

branch of the jacaranda, then walked to the far end of the picnic group. He put his fingers to his lips and whistled, a piercing whistle which brought Bluey the favourite cattle dog hurtling into view to skid to a dusty stop in front of him, tail wagging expectantly. Albert raised his hand in signal to the magpie sitting on the tree's branch. The bird whistled, a piercing whistle indistinguishable from Albert's. Reacting to ingrained discipline, Bluey raced frantically over to the tree, turning every which way, looking for the originator of the command. With this the magpie flew to the other end of the picnic group where it sat on a branch on another tree and at a sign from Albert gave another piercing whistle. Once again, Bluey rose to the command. Muffled laughter followed, almost a snicker at first, but then as the bird continued to give the command, changing his position after every signal, and the obliging dog obeyed, the laughter increased. Pretty soon, hands were reaching into pockets for handkerchiefs to wipe away the laughter-induced tears.

'You king for a day, boy.' Pearl patted Albert on the shoulder, wiping her eyes and laughing. 'Yep,' she added, 'you certainly got that bird doing what you want and that poor dog confused.'

Albert didn't answer, his attention taken by something he had just noticed floating on Wellsford River. He pointed at the same time as James leapt across the bench in front of him, half running, half hopping, removing his boots as he ran. In a moment he was in the water, striking out to reach for the something that had caught Albert's vision. Then he was back at the bank, handing up a bundle; a small, wet bundle which suddenly emitted a wail.

Careful hands placed the now crying child on the bank where she coughed and spluttered and struggled for breath. Pearl raced to her side, having been so engrossed in the antics of Albert's game, she hadn't even noticed Faith wander off.

Albert knelt alongside also, his heart pounding. He watched anxiously, willing to promise all Gods everywhere anything just so long as the little girl was all right, cursing himself for taking everyone's attention with his silly joke.

Under the jacaranda tree, something behind the panicked look on the face of her husband James infuriated Hilda, so much so that she made her mind up then and there that there would be no more New Year picnics for the staff at Wellsford. From now on, all of them would learn and learn well to keep within their boundaries. There was nothing to be discussed with anyone; she had made up her mind. Look at all this stupid fuss, and all about that little bastard brat Faith! The station picnics, as of this day, were finished.

* * *

Like many other small country townships around New South Wales, Wellsford had, since its formation, been considered an appropriate place to rest and change horses for the Cobb and Co coaches moving between the main cities. Through years of pounding hooves and coach wheels, the track had become a dusty road and the original coach-house had grown from one big room with an attached stable to a tavern of sorts with a bunkhouse, kitchen and dining room and separate bathroom.

As the traffic slowly became heavier, with more passengers and their supplies aboard, a blacksmith's shop and a general store were both added, and because of the natural beauty of the area, several expressions of interest were shown in the possibility of the establishment of a real township. Due to a strange formation of rock across and just below the surface of the river, there was quite a safe place for the coaches to cross and this, added to the name of one of the district's early explorers, Edward Wells, led to the crossing becoming known as Wells's Ford, which very soon became Wellsford.

The area was sheltered on three sides by a small range of low hills topped with ironbark trees, and as the land for miles around was very sparsely treed and flat except for an occasional hillock, with the river winding through it all, it had soon been reported back to the cities by surveyors and acquired by graziers.

One of the first of these had been Hugh Mitchell whose original holding increased as neighbours falling on hard times became disenchanted, so that by the turn of the century, his station was huge, along both sides of the river, east of the Cobb and Co stopover.

Little in the way of town expansion occurred before the years of the First World War, with news and all contact with the world outside arriving by coach. It was a hard and lonely existence, one with which many settlers, including Hugh's own wife Emily, could not cope and, coupled with the fickle weather pattern veering without notice from one extreme to the other year by year, it eventually beat Hugh himself. But the new generation, born to the country and knowing nothing else, developed a great love for it all and, disregarding the hardships to which they'd become accustomed, began very successful businesses which soon attracted other people to the area.

James Mitchell had sensed this interest early and had called meetings with outlying neighbours to discuss the formation of a town council for what he fully expected would be a minor boom period not many years ahead. Some of these neighbours had shown interest in James's schoolhouse and its success which was due more to the pupils' eagerness for knowledge than the capability of its teacher, definitely filling a need. If this council could attract more settlers to the township, a state school was a must, along with other service establishments.

Meanwhile, Hilda's reasoning that it was not surprising she had been forced to become a secret drinker was not only becoming less reasonable of late; it was also becoming less of a secret. The station school had been in operation for years now, during which time she had taught the children the rudiments of the three Rs, but 'dear God,' she asked herself, 'at what cost to my health and sanity?' And what if she *had* started to tipple? After all, it was just a little nip to get her through the morning class, until that little nip failed to blunt the raw ache around the edges and needed to be topped up during morning recess.

Not that she really minded teaching the children. At least it passed the time, and of course John was a perfect student. Luke and Jane, the McManaway children, were manageable and Albert was harmless enough, sitting at the back of the class.

Albert's facility with figures never failed to surprise her although Hilda was sure he was helping the brat Faith whose hand shot in the air every time a question was posed. Not only did she shoot her hand into the air, but the damned child stood and called out, 'Please, missus! Please, missus!' Horrid little wheedling, conniving brat. And she was developing already and had a pretty enough face, she supposed, so God only knew what she would be getting up to with the station boys. Probably end up the same way as her mother – stark naked on the river bank one summer night. Better to get her tied up with someone as soon as possible. Albert maybe. Albert never took his eyes off her and was never far away from her either.

Hilda rubbed the chalk figures from her blackboard, beat the soft side of the duster gently against her palm, raising a cloudy white puff of chalk particles, then walked to her table to ring the small brass bell, indicating the end of school for the day.

'Faith!' she called to the young girl sitting cross-legged at the rear of the class. 'Stay behind, please, and sweep the room, then dust the desks and empty the inkwells. And the water in the bowl of flowers on my desk needs freshening.' She paused, brushing a film of chalk from her dark skirt. 'You'll be working in the big house full-time next year, so you'd better get good and used to it. I like my girls to be thorough. After you have cleaned the room and before you go over to help Pearl, make sure you wash your hands.' Hilda gave an involuntary shudder. 'Pearl might want you to help with shelling peas or something.'

Faith hung her head and shot a sideways glance at Albert. She knew he would stay and help her after the old girl had gone, even though he had to chop wood and fetch and carry for whoever needed it after school finished. Dear Albert; she couldn't even think of a life without him. The times when she felt down about her lot – about being motherless, about having no future other than working for the Mitchell family – didn't seem so bad when she thought about Albert being there with her. These thoughts made her feel selfish when she realised that Albert never even knew his mother; the only kin he knew were his grandparents, who died a long way back, and his cousin Freddie who worked on a station miles away. Freddie showed up occasionally when, as he put it, he had 'had enough of their shit' and would sleep in the outbuilding with Albert until someone came and took him back to work again.

When Hilda rang the bell, Albert left the school room with the others but hid for a few moments behind the barn until he was sure Hilda had gone. Then he scampered back to put his head impishly around the door, flashing a wide smile at Faith.

'All right, Miss Smartypants,' he said, imitating their teacher, 'tell me what six times eight is.'

'Forty-eight,' answered Faith, smiling widely.

Albert raced around the schoolroom, putting his hands over his ears. 'I've suddenly gone deaf and how dare you be such a smart little so-and-so, because I only want to hear the answer from my darling little boysie woysie John,' Albert mimicked. He picked up the cane and pointed to a blank spot on the blackboard. 'Oh dear, I feel so shocked,' he mocked, 'that such a nobody could know the answer, I'll have to go immediately and have a drink.'

Faith put her hands to her face, giggling behind them. She picked up the chalk duster and threw it at Albert. 'You be careful. She'll catch you one of these days and there'll be hell to pay,' she laughed.

Albert ducked from the path of the flying duster, picked it up when it hit the wall of the room then walked over and put it back near the blackboard. His brown eyes shone as he looked tenderly at Faith. 'You going to be my woman, Faith. One day soon, no doubt about it. You never going to be for anyone else.'

He turned and walked out of the schoolhouse as Faith picked up the broom and started sweeping, singing softly and smiling to herself.

Loose ends

The whirring of the egg-beater took a firm grip on Albert's ear, leading him in its determination to the outside door of the farm kitchen. Brown eyes peered through the screen door as he pulled his cheeks inward in an effort to control the juices accumulating in his mouth and waited for Pearl to turn and hand him the cream-laden beater to lick.

'Nuthin' wrong with your ears, young Albert,' Pearl said as she smilingly handed him the beater. 'Minute you hear that beater, your ears tell your legs to bring you to my doorstep real fast.'

Albert sat on the white, sandsoap-scrubbed step, leisurely running his tongue down the curves of the beater, licking every vestige of cream from the cool metal. 'They got visitors coming?' he asked, nodding his head towards the array of delicacies on the kitchen table, glimpsed through the throw-over of fine embroidered muslin. He also noted the silver tray with the gleaming, ornate tea service polished at the ready.

'Her Ladyship has,' Pearl replied. 'Got the priest coming over for afternoon tea again, probably to get his palm greased.'

She spread the thick whipped cream on the base of a sponge cake, dropping another sponge cake over the cream, dusting its top with icing sugar. She stood back, the way an artist would, to survey her handiwork.

'She's spent the entire morning dolling herself up like a sore toe, and she smells like she rolled in the lavender patch,' said Pearl. 'Mind you, they'll be getting into the sherries after the tea, though, then Her Ladyship will play the piano and the prune-faced ponce will sing his hymns, same old stuff.'

Same old stuff was right. She'd seen Father O'Malley's sanctimonious hand linger just too long on the shoulder of her mistress. The routine with the holy father's visits seldom changed and almost always ended with James and Hilda red-faced and yelling at each other, out of control.

She clearly remembered the last time she'd been in the room collecting the tea tray and glasses. James had strode in to find his less than steady-on-her-feet wife handing over a substantial cheque for the church fund. The red-faced theosophist had taken one look at his benefactor's spouse, picked up his belongings quick smart and without another word had hastily made his exit.

Pearl had dearly wished she could also have got out, but her only access to the door was blocked by the two partners, by that time both in such a blind fury that her presence was not even noticed. She had frozen.

'That useless, bloody, pansy member of the non-practising celibates!' James had roared. 'Are you quite mad, woman? Do you damned well think we're made of money? That idiot spends at least half of that cheque restocking his not insubstantial wine cellar. You don't honestly think that red face comes from sitting with the parish ladies, sticking his little finger out, taking tea, do you?'

Hilda had poured herself another generous sherry and stood unsteadily, looking at her husband, dislike emanating from every pore, carried to him on body heat laden heavily with lavender. Two bright-pink spots stood out on her cheeks as she'd slowly and purposefully drained the contents of her glass. She'd replaced the glass on the sideboard alongside the crystal decanter and then turned, facing her husband, her back arched, feral, ready to pounce.

'You hideous, ignorant boor.'

She had spat the words rather than spoken them, then picked up the decanter and slowly refilled her glass. Faltering footsteps of fury had moved her towards her husband where she had thrown the contents of the glass in his face.

James didn't move for a moment; then, as a muscle at the corner of his right eye had started to twitch, he very slowly raised his arm to wipe the back of his shirt sleeve across his face. He had closed his eyes momentarily, then quickly opened them, taking in the flushed cheeks of his wife, wanting with all his might to smash his fists into them. Then suddenly he had turned and stormed from the room. Hilda had hurled the empty glass against the wall near the doorway, burst into tears and run out of the room.

Pearl, terrified, hadn't dared to move until it was all quiet, then had quickly made her way to the safety of her kitchen, thankfully sinking into a chair and promising herself that she'd never get caught like that again.

And now this afternoon, another visit was arranged. Well, thought Pearl, if nothing else, the Reverend Father got guts.

She took the beater from Albert and held it up to the light. 'You missed a bit,' she teased, noting the licked-clean silver gleaming.

Albert stood for a moment, allowing himself to enjoy the look of the older woman in front of him. When he closed his eyes and tried to remember his grandmother now, it seemed she looked like Pearl. It was hard for him to remember. He shuffled his feet shyly.

'Better get out there and collect them eggs,' Pearl instructed, handing him a cane basket and making a shooing motion with her hands. 'And,' she continued, noting the dreamy look in her young friend's eyes, 'don't spend all day talking to each and every chook. You got jobs to do, remember.'

Albert took the basket and ran to the henhouse. It was all right here at Wellsford Station most days. So long as Pearl was around, it was quite all right. Pearl didn't cuff you over the ear or tan your backside like the mistress did for something that occurred only inside her head. Sometimes it seemed even the sight of Albert's face – or worse still,

Faith's – acted like a trigger on Hilda Mitchell's hand, making it lash out like it had a mind of its own, and that mind set on beating the devil out of the two kids.

Albert ran his tongue over the roof of his mouth, remembering a recent lashing received at the hands of Hilda Mitchell. The smell of fresh jam tarts had caused that ruckus. He had crept to the kitchen knowing that Pearl had just made a batch of jam tarts; golden, luscious tarts filled in the middle with the rich, red tomato jam she had made a few weeks back.

When Pearl had left the kitchen momentarily, leaving the cooling tarts on the window ledge, Albert had quickly reached through the window and nicked one of the treats. He had turned to find Hilda Mitchell striding towards him from the kitchen garden with a face dark as a thundercloud and he had hurriedly pushed the still hot tart into his mouth. What he hadn't allowed for was the heat-retaining properties of the jam, and he had screamed in agony as the searing hot mixture stuck to the roof of his mouth.

Not that Hilda had any sympathy for his pain. Like someone possessed, she had picked up a stick and whacked his legs until blue-black welts appeared, lashing until it seemed that even her energy left her in disgust, and then Pearl, dear Pearl, had gently bathed his wounds with vinegar and sung to him.

In spite of the warm sun, Albert shuddered at the thought of how things might be if he lived at Wellsford Station without Pearl and Faith. Not much, he thought, not much at all.

While the First World War raged, planning went ahead, as the few children in the area were too young to enlist and the graziers were unavailable for military service so that by war's end, a whole blueprint had been drawn up ready for development should Mitchell's dependence on his intuition be proved right.

And it was.

After the shocking and bitter experience of a war, trying to settle to life in the busy cities was not an attractive option for many ex-service-men, and the quieter lifestyle of a country town somewhere seemed much more acceptable. Several discovered the open-arms policy of this little place called Wellsford, and before long the town began to look very different. Soon there would be a school large enough to service secondary education; a bank, a newsagent/post office, a town hall attached to council chambers and the police station; a small building housing a doctor's rooms, a butcher's shop, a bakery and a fledgling newspaper, *The Wellsford Herald*. The old coach-house had enlarged into a hotel and the smithy had branched out into general metalwork, a saddlery and all manner of leatherwork while the general store was a thriving establishment with an inventory including an enormous variety of household necessities and a clientele which spent much of the day in chairs or on the floorboards of its verandah, having a smoke and a yarn.

Growing pains

lthough John Mitchell was only a nine-almost-ten year old,
he seemed quite a bit older than his years. Growing up in
the secure knowledge that his family's station would provide for him
as it had for the past two generations, he nevertheless felt himself to
be in a rather strange situation. He'd never known grandparents on
either side of the family, and his parents lived separate lives. In fact
his father, who he idolised, was spending more and more time away
from the homestead, attending personally to the supervising of the
now-regular meetings with town planning associates.

John's situation with his mother was uncomfortable at the best
of times as she, for years now, had seemed intent on treating him as
still a baby. Oh, she knew he was growing, but she showed little to no
involvement in his interests, all of which were developing outside the
home. Schooling was a chore and becoming an embarrassing one as
Hilda constantly favoured him above the other pupils. In fact, lately it
seemed that the others did not even seem to exist, in her mind. Luckily,
because all the pupils had grown up together, they understood the
situation, tolerated Hilda's favouritism and were good friends with
him, but now there was another problem. John felt quite sure that the
teaching was reaching a stalemate; that his mother's inadequacies in
that department were increasingly apparent, and before long, it might
all grind to a halt.

Because of the strained relations between his parents, John didn't
feel like bringing this subject up with his father as it would inevitably
lead to another screaming match with James taking off and Mother
hitting the bottle.

Outside of school hours, Hilda was content to leave the boy to his own devices which was when John gained so much knowledge from the farm staff, to whom he gravitated as he grew. With endless but discreet encouragement from Charlie, he became quite adept at handling the horses and took to working with the animals quickly, so much so that he surprised James one afternoon with his unexpected ability.

'Hey, Charlie!' James called, 'you got yourself a talented student, it seems.'

'Yes sir, Mr James, he gonna be all right. He catches on fast.'

James beamed at his son, who turned away to hide his embarrassment. It seemed that he was seldom in a position to do something to gain his Dad's admiration, and he liked the feel of it.

Later, as father and son were walking back to the washhouse to clean up, James said, 'You're doing very well with the stock, John. Very well. Charlie's obviously leading you in the right direction. Learning about live animals is a lot different from the three Rs, right?'

Inside, John glowed but could only say, 'Yup, it is.' This was the first time he could remember receiving a real compliment from his father.

'I'm sorry I haven't been much help lately,' James continued, 'but that Charlie is a wonder. You stick at it, son.'

Inside, John smiled. Sticking at it was precisely what he had in mind.

'Well, there's something else coming up soon that will interest you too,' James continued. 'The council has put in for a grant to help build a secondary school in town because you and the others will need secondary levels pretty soon. We're confident, or at least I am,' he added, smiling, 'that when this war's over, the town's going to grow, so we're getting ready early.'

A nice feeling of relief flowed through the boy's body as the niggling worries about the home-schooling dissipated in a moment.

'How about Albert and Faith? Will they be able to go to college?' John asked. 'Albert's much better than me at arithmetic.'

James stopped walking and turned. 'Well, son,' he said thoughtfully, 'not everybody feels the same about their staff as you and I do, so we'll have to meet that when it comes. I just hope it all works out,' he grinned. 'In much the same way that I hope the town's development works out; otherwise all my talking's going to look a bit silly if it doesn't.'

But the situation with John and his mother was deteriorating quickly. The school lessons were getting more and more haphazard, almost useless. For some time, Hilda had resorted to reading to the pupils most afternoons, but as the lunchbreak alcohol intake steadily increased, the students found themselves hearing the same passages time after time. Not even John would dare to point this out to her as it would certainly lead to a verbal tirade and probably tears, so they suffered in silence until the clock mercifully released them in midafternoon.

Then one afternoon, Hilda did not return to class after the lunch recess and when her son went to the house to check through a window, he saw her sitting in the lounge room, holding in her left hand a letter, which must have been delivered that morning, and in her right hand a tumbler, the contents of which had come from the half-empty bottle on the table. She was crying, so John backed quietly away, deciding it was best not to interfere. Already the young boy had learnt to read the signs and knew what to avoid. He went back to the classroom and a few minutes later, by popular consent, school was dismissed for the day.

An hour or so later, John sat outside the stables in the sun, practising tying and untying rope knots the way Charlie had shown him earlier, when Albert came up to him quietly.

'John,' he said, 'you'd better come and give me a hand.'

'Sure,' replied John, getting to his feet. 'What is it?'

'It's not too nice. You'll see in a minute. I hope the two of us can fix it up.'

Puzzled, John followed his friend down past the kitchen to the area where the big garbage drums were kept. Near one of them, lying on her back on the ground, was Hilda, his mother, and near her right hand was the empty bottle. She had vomited over herself before passing out, and the area reeked of gin. John recoiled at the sight, not sure whether it was the smell of vomit or the ever-present smell of gin which was turning his stomach.

'We'll have to move her into the house if we can,' said Albert. 'You take her feet.' Then he tried to lift his mistress from under her arms, but to no avail. 'She's a dead weight, out cold. We'll have to call Pearl.'

When Pearl arrived, she paused, closed her eyes briefly then took over. The boys took a leg each and the three of them half carried, half dragged Hilda back into the homestead. Pearl then shooed them out, telling Albert to send Faith in from the kitchen with a basin of warm water.

John resumed his knotting practice but found he couldn't concentrate. Thoughts raced around inside his head. Why did she drink so much? Why was it she hated the place so much? What could it be that she so disliked about it all? Everybody else seemed to like it, why couldn't she? Even in the late mornings when she seemed at her best, she hardly ever smiled – hadn't for ages, it seemed to him. She never spoke a civil word to his father any more and at any sign of disagreement headed for the bottle. And always gin. That sickly-sweet smell of gin pervaded everything around her now. Why?

No answers would or could come.

With a sigh, John looped his rope over a protruding nail beside him and went to see if he could find Charlie.

* * *

'Wake up, sleepyhead.' His father's voice. 'Come on, jump to it! It's your birthday, no day to sleep in.'

John grinned up at him. It had been a whole lot better the last few weeks. His dad had spent much more time with him, and while John had always loved him, they had recently developed a different sort of closeness, a wonderful feeling of family. Although he hated the thought of it, he knew that he could never have this feeling with his mother. Both he and his father had tried but were locked out. And now he was ten – one oh, into double figures!

He jumped out of bed to wash and dress for breakfast. For a fleeting moment, he hoped that his mother might be at the table, but no. Dad was there, at his usual place, and Pearl, beaming at him, stood behind his usual chair.

'Happy birthday, young John,' she said, waving him towards his seat as Faith peeked around the door at the goings-on.

'Yes, happy birthday,' said his smiling father. 'I forgot to say that earlier.'

As the boy moved to his seat, he saw that resting on it was a big parcel. 'Oh wow,' he said, 'can I open it now, please?'

'Go ahead,' said James. 'We all hope you like it.'

Pearl produced scissors from behind her back and John put the parcel on the floor and cut the strings. As the wrapping fell away, his eyes grew like saucers.

'A Meccano set, a great big Meccano set!' he cried, then ran around the table to hug his dad. 'Gee, thanks,' the boy said, then ran round the other side of the table and hugged a giggling Pearl.

'That's enough of that, young man,' she said. 'Now, aren't you going to open it up?'

John carefully removed the top of the box and just looked at the huge assortment of parts in their separate compartments.

'Wow,' he said, 'wait till Albert sees this!'

'All right,' said James, 'put it away for now. You'll have plenty of time after breakfast.'

The morning flew by. John carried his gift out to the big side verandah and, after showing it off to Albert and Faith, settled down to experiment, and in no time at all, Pearl was calling him for lunch.

His mind was so engrossed with perforated strips of green-painted metal, tiny nuts and bolts, and patterns that he was halfway through his midday meal before he realised his mother had not yet put in an appearance. Oh well, she'd probably forgotten the date. But as his father had had to go out to work and another meeting, it would have been nice to have had some company for his birthday lunch, he thought. Then he realised why Pearl was fussing about the room with a duster and a huge smile; she knew what he was feeling. He smiled back at her and finished his lunch, eager to get back to the Meccano.

Just as he was sitting down on the verandah, Albert came over to him, looking a bit sheepish.

'I'm sorry I couldn't buy you a present, John,' he said, 'but I've been saving up something to show you till today.' The beginnings of a smile were pulling persistently at the corners of Albert's mouth. 'Come and look at this.'

John stood and followed the older boy across the yard and down towards the backwater pond near the river. Motioning to him to keep quiet, Albert moved stealthily forward towards the bullrushes at the pond's edge. After a few minutes of gently moving leaves and debris about, he paused then shot his hand quickly into the water. 'Gotcha!' he said, holding up a large bullfrog for John to see. 'Now, watch this. Charlie showed me.'

With his free hand, he snapped off a long stalk of grass then from it broke another section about six inches long. He scratched then peeled at one end and, using his teeth, removed the centre of the grass, leaving a hollow stem.

'Come closer,' he said, motioning to John, then inverting the frog, he inserted one end of the pipe into its anus, took a deep breath then gently blew into the other end. The struggling frog inflated like a small balloon. Although half of him thought it cruel, John couldn't resist laughing at the sight.

'Now watch,' said Albert, removing the straw and releasing the bloated frog into the water. The two boys screamed laughing as the hapless frog, releasing a stream of bubbles from its backside, tried frantically but unsuccessfully to dive under the water.

'Hey,' laughed Albert, 'I hope it's not *his* birthday,' and they collapsed again.

'Doesn't it hurt him?' asked John when they started to settle down.

'Charlie says no,' answered Albert, grinning. 'He says a real good fart never hurt anybody.'

Again they rocked with laughter and were still giggling when they got back to the verandah.

'Thank you, Albert,' John said, wiping his still watering eyes on his sleeve.

'Glad you liked it,' said Albert. 'But now I better go and see if Pearl needs a hand with anything.'

Alone again, John concentrated on his Meccano until the unmistakeable smell of roasting lamb caught his nose, then a few minutes later, another wondrous smell – chocolate cake. Knowing very well what that all meant, he decided to transfer operations to a spot closer to the kitchen and, carefully collecting all the pieces, took it all back into the dining room, spreading it all out again on the big Persian rug. Now another delightful smell came through. Mint. Freshly-picked mint for the sauce.

John closed his eyes and inhaled deeply. The smells had caught him by the nose. He stood up and crept to the kitchen door, peeping around it. Faith was at the sink, washing the mint, and Pearl had her back to him and was spreading icing from a bowl onto his cake. She turned to put the bowl beside her and noticed the small figure beside the doorway. Laughing, she said, 'Now you'll just have to wait till I'm finished, young John. You can lick the bowl then. It's your cake, after all, so I'll call you in a few minutes.'

John smiled and headed back to his Meccano.

Suddenly, from in front of him, a heavy crashing sound, and the door from the hall flew open. All smells and smiles were forgotten as his mother lurched into the room, calling, 'Johnnie wannie, where's my Johnnie wannie?!'

Seeing him by the rug, she tottered towards him, arms outstretched. Instinctively, he started to back away. He'd seen her in this condition so many times lately. She was out of control again.

'Ah, my little darling, do you know it's your birthday?'

Before he could say anything, she was near him, reaching out her hands and breathing that smell all over him again. Leaning over as if playing some awful game, she came closer to the boy who was as unobtrusively as possible backing away into the kitchen doorway. Now it seemed everything happened in slow motion. The boy's head was starting to spin and he bumped backwards into Pearl, now sitting by the table. He was aware of a rhythmic banging sound from outside, probably Albert chopping firewood. Faith stopped what she was doing and stared fixedly into the sink. Pearl put down the knife she'd been using and held the icing-filled bowl, still not looking at Hilda. John's hands moved behind him to grip Pearl's dress. And towards it all, the drunken apparition that was his mother, now out of focus to the boy, coming ever closer, her voice wheedling, cajoling.

'Who do you love best in the world today, Johnnie?' The unsteady hands reaching, the twisted smile, the reek of gin. 'Come on, Johnnie. It's your birthday. Who do you love best?'

No more slow motion; now it all happened suddenly. John swung around, leapt up onto Pearl's lap and threw his arms around her neck.

'Pearlie, it's Pearlie, I love Pearlie best. I love Pearlie best in the whole world. I wish Pearlie was my mum.'

His mother stood back, straight and still, her face flaming. Faith still motionless, one hand on the bench. Pearl sat, almost not breathing, staring straight ahead at a spot on the kitchen wall.

'You piece of shit. You rotten, ungrateful little shit.' His mother spat the words at him. 'You are your father's son, all right. Blood's thicker than water. You'll grow up with just the same habits as well.'

Hilda banged her fist on the table, leaning across to raise that fist in Pearl's face, her eyes wild, but then, as if thinking better of it, she turned and ran crying down the hall.

Only later that night did the smell of gin dissipate, along with the dull hurt throbbing inside John's head; after the lonely birthday dinner without his mother. Much later that night when Pearl and Faith had gently washed their mistress, undressed her and put her into bed between crisp white sheets. His senseless, comatose, drunk-as-a-skunk mother.

Changes

The evening's business at the council meeting was now almost over, and James Mitchell, as usual, had presided over several interesting matters pertaining to the development of their town, with unanimous acceptance and encouragement from the council members; however, as had happened at several recent meetings, James sensed as proceedings drew to a close that there was a hesitancy in the air, that something was bothering some of the men, something that nobody felt qualified to mention.

Tonight that feeling was even stronger, so as soon as the secretary had finished scribbling his notes for the meeting's minutes, James slowly eyed the men around the table. 'Right,' he said. 'Now, something is preying on the minds of some of you gentlemen, and I'd like to know what it is. For some weeks, we've reached this point in the meetings and I've had a definite feeling that something unspoken pertaining to me is upsetting you. Now if you feel that I'm waving the big stick too much, acting like a boss rather than a member of this council, I would appreciate knowing this as it is certainly not intentional, and I'd be happy to stand aside for someone else, if that's the problem.'

Silence. Averted eyes and shuffling feet. 'Come on,' James continued, 'we've all been neighbours and friends with common interests till the present, and I know something's wrong. Now, please, what is it? The meeting's over, so let's get this out in the air.'

Still nothing. Looking right at his closest neighbour, Fred McManaway, James said, 'Mac, we've known each other for years. What's this all about? The fact that nobody will speak proves to me that there is a problem, so let's hear it.'

'Well,' James McManaway said, looking past him, 'it's nothing to do with any big stick. In fact, all of us are pleased to have you in charge of operations. It's good that you've chosen to put me on the spot as we've been friends and, as you say, neighbours for a long time, so I can speak out.'

James felt irritated at the pussyfooting. 'Please do, Mac,' he said abruptly. 'Let's get rid of this. Come to the point.'

'All right. It doesn't concern you personally at all, James. It's about Mrs Mitchell, your wife.'

'Hilda?' James was surprised by the statement. 'How can this involve her?'

'Well, it's really about the schooling over at Wellsford, you see. All of the youngsters are growing up, and they're losing interest in the school because they feel they're not learning anything anymore.'

James looked around the room at the other men. 'Heavens above,' he said, 'surely I'm not such an ogre that none of you could have told me this earlier? Anyway, thank you Mac for speaking out. I blame myself for this, of course. I've been so engrossed in other things I obviously haven't been paying attention to matters closer to home. Actually you've all done me quite a favour as my own son John has been showing disinterested signs himself, and it's now obvious to me why.

'All right, we'll make a determined effort from the next meeting on to find premises in the town for a schoolroom until we can build a full school later. Then all the district's children can learn, not just those near our place. And we'll obtain the services of a trained teacher, too. I know Hilda will be delighted to have the burden removed. How does that sound to you all?'

Relieved expressions and 'hear, hear' came from the assembled men.

'Now, anyone for a drink before we break things up?'

Glasses and a bottle of Scotch were produced, and as they all milled around, James grinned to himself. Fancy having some good news for Hilda! She might even be civil to him for a change. That would be one for the books!

Preparations for the establishment of a new temporary school went ahead quickly. The large meeting room in the back of the town hall could easily be adapted for the purpose as it was seldom used in the daytime. And to the council's delight, reaction to the inquiry letters and advertisements for staff was much better than expected. Several older teachers were foreseeing employment problems with the return of other younger people currently on active service and liked the idea of a country lifestyle after the war, so the council members were faced with the odious task of the selection of applicants.

Even that was simplified by the enthusiasm shown in one application from a husband and wife who were both teachers of long experience, and in short order, Cec and Jean Watt were welcomed to Wellsford. They were to share the position offered, with Jean to teach primary levels and Cec secondary.

One afternoon, not long after things had settled down into set routines, James ran into Cec Watt in the town and asked how the schooling was coming along.

'Just fine, James, just fine,' the teacher replied. 'Jean and I feel confident that once the town has a proper school, it will all go from strength to strength. Are the townspeople happy with developments?'

'They certainly are,' said James. 'You can rest assured about that, Cec. And it will be great to have your input about planning the new building. As it's still a top priority project, there'll be no shelving that.'

The two men walked along without speaking until, after loudly clearing his throat, the teacher asked, 'James, may I bring up a rather personal subject?'

'By all means, by all means. You and your wife wouldn't be here if

I hadn't brought up a personal subject at council some months ago,' said James, smiling at the thought.

'Well, it's about your son John. He's a very bright boy with a wide range of interests, James, and Jean and I feel that you should consider enrolling him soon in a city boarding school, to let him broaden his education. I'm sure you understand that there's a limit to what we can achieve here, particularly in the current circumstances, and it could be advantageous to the boy – very much so, in fact.'

The teacher had touched right on something that had occupied a lot of James's thinking of late. In a rapidly changing world, he felt a much greater need for his son to have a sound education. Thinking about it later, James came to appreciate Cec Watt's suggestion more and more, realising that the two teachers' city experience was just what the growing town needed, particularly as each of the Watts had a very open mind on most subjects and their advice would surely be of great value in the future.

James's father, Hugh, had had an education in England before coming to the colony and James himself had come through at a time when life in the country was much simpler, with the accent on practical rather than theoretical matters. A basic education had got him through, and his father's background coupled with the passed-on skills of the various staff members had been enough for him to cope with most situations, but he knew that more learning and certainly wider social contact would have made some aspects of his life to date a whole lot easier. Particularly with my selection of a partner, James thought, now something he accepted as the worst mistake of his life so far.

Without a mother, and with all feminine contact in his early life either hearty country stock or staff; the effect, as a late teenager, of being suddenly thrust into the city's social whirl during their business visits – thanks to his father's money – had sent his mind spinning. All the perfumes, soft clothes and fluttering eyelashes had completely overwhelmed him, and life on the station between visits had become a torment of fantasy and erotic dreams, all titillating but totally unrealistic, as it turned out.

With James's introduction to Charles Carson, one of Parramatta's leading lights, and when his daughter Hilda obviously encouraged James's attention, the young man's control reached bursting point. By the time they'd entered that particular return journey to Wellsford, the image of Hilda Carson in James's mind was changing constantly from a pretty face above a ball gown to a smiling face above female undergarments to a longing face above a naked body. Nights were a perspiring torment of discomfort, controlled by his overpowering sexual awakening. Never at any stage had it occurred to him that he didn't even know the woman. They'd only met under strictly chaperoned, formal conditions, had hardly shared a proper conversation, let alone an improper one. They'd married before any of this got through to James's brain, and then the enormity of what he'd done hit him.

At first he'd been furious with his new wife, but as realisation sank in, he'd turned his fury on himself. It had all been his fault. The signs had been there when he thought about it; he'd just refused to see them. All the sexual connotations that he'd read into their meetings were complete fantasy. The object of his mental passion had only been looking to better her social and financial status and had no interest whatsoever in marital activity. The woman was frigid and now, goddamn it, they were married.

One had to be grateful though, he thought, that John had grown through the terrible rows and Hilda's endless pampering basically unscathed. 'A very bright boy,' Cec Watt had said, and James had felt real pride in hearing the words. Boarding school and a wider education should be just the thing for John. He'd pick his time to break the news to Hilda.

★ ★ ★

The timing for John's changeover to the Sydney boarding school could hardly have been better. The war had just ended and there was a strong sense of celebration everywhere in the city because it was over at last, and the young people would soon all be back home.

The city in general and certainly the school itself were both overwhelming at first to the boy from Wellsford, but as the staff were slowly restructuring, the whole environment was constantly changing, so he very soon adapted to it all. He made friends easily and because of his country-bred abilities was avoided by troublemakers. One or two encounters established that factor very early in the piece.

John very much enjoyed participating in team sports – something he had never really known – and being surrounded by boys of his own age group, quickly developing skills in a variety of sports, making him much in demand by the end of his first year. The main difference in his new lifestyle that he took the longest to adapt to was the almost totally male environment, both in terms of students and staff.

Before too long, he learnt about and understood the strict discipline the school regimen worked under, realising that in a crowd of hundreds of developing young males living together twenty-four hours a day, there had to be rules, and those rules had to be adhered to. Regardless of whether one agreed with them all to the letter or not, they were there and they were to be obeyed.

The only females he saw, let alone had contact with, were the office and kitchen/laundry staff and occasional visiting parents, but John soon came to accept this situation. In fact, it made him really appreciate the term holidays and the resultant trips home.

During his second year, however, John did begin to feel a little disoriented as though he was living in two completely different worlds simultaneously. His school persona in the city was all discipline and compromise while the holiday persona at home was totally different; to John's mind, far preferable. Within minutes of arrival on each trip to Wellsford, he relaxed and fell back into the comfortable ways of his earlier years, delighted to shuck off the uniform and all its accompanying strictures, pull on old clothes and get back among the animals and his 'family' again – the smiling, ever-present faces of Pearl and Faith around the house, the heavy farm work with his father and Charlie, and also now, Albert.

He did, however, feel differently towards his mother. On each of his term-end visits, he could see her regular deterioration and felt genuinely sorry for her while feeling no closer emotionally. Being separated for months at a time had given him plenty of opportunity to think about the home situation and while in no way blaming his father, he could understand the impossible predicament his parents had found themselves in after their marriage. Totally unsuited to each other, it must have been hell for them both, and while John could never condone his mother's constant reliance on alcohol, he was starting to understand the frustration that caused it. But strangely, he felt that he was watching it happen to somebody else's mother, not his. As far as he was concerned, Pearl had brought him up. For as long as he could remember, his mother had treated him as some kind of plaything to show off. His birth, and the endless reminders of it, had somehow caused her to believe he had never grown up, and now that she was completely losing touch with reality, they were like strangers, a little more estranged with each visit.

His mother was by now alone in some world of her own making, completely dependent on Pearl. If she saw anyone clearly, it was Faith, but on more than one occasion, John had seen a look of loathing, of a seething hate in his mother's eyes as she looked at the girl, now developed into quite a beautiful young woman. This look puzzled John. Why did she so dislike Faith? It had occurred to him several times lately that this was nothing new; she'd always hated the girl and never attempted to hide the fact.

From Faith's angle, there was no show of animosity whatsoever, no wondering why, just acceptance of the fact that the situation existed and didn't bear any examination. She made sure she kept out of harm's way and, like everybody else, felt sorry for Hilda Mitchell, quite content to help Pearl clean up after the mistress's deranged misadventures. Faith was happy in the knowledge that all the things Albert had said to her down the years were true, that she was soon going to be his woman.

John had seen this partnership solidifying too, more strongly with each return. Watching its development term by term, he began to wonder about his own future. Faith and Albert had been together as long as he could remember and knew and trusted each other utterly, completely the opposite of his own parents who'd come together absolutely ignorant of each other's personalities. How would he, John, meet someone and develop that sort of trust? Almost certainly not in the city; it held no real appeal at all. He was not really interested in continuing on to university, far more drawn back to the land, but what about a partner? Ah well, plenty of time for that later. At least he had the slow growth of Albert and Faith's relationship and the collapse of that of his parents' as role models to think on.

Steadily the town of Wellsford grew and developed its own personality, giving James Mitchell a strong sense of pride. Some of the newer arrivals among the businessmen were building a good deal of commitment to the wellbeing of the area as well as to their own establishments, and James was finding the council meetings very lively affairs which of course were also increasingly time-consuming as the very welcome suggestions for betterment had to be followed through. The ultimate responsibility for this fell to him.

There was now quite a lot of debate at the meetings, to James a very healthy sign. Geoff Powers, a returned serviceman who had taken over the newsagency, had developed a much more reliable post office as part of his premises and had also begun producing a town newspaper, *The Wellsford Herald*, bringing the surrounding populations into closer contact with each other. The bank manager, Alec McBeath, was an affable man who soon had the confidence of the town, confounding people with his astonishing memory for names. In what seemed no time, he not only knew all his clients by both Christian and surnames, he also remembered their spouses and most of the town's children. The regulars at the hotel swore that McBeath even knew all the names of the town's dogs.

Another popular couple in the town were the Craigs, who now operated the general store and had extended the range of available stock to try to meet every country contingency. This fact was greatly appreciated by the women of the town as not only was it a real novelty to actually do some shopping rather than use what had been a shaky postal system for mail order from city catalogues, but Mrs Craig had turned an alcove in the large shop into a tearoom, so a weekly gossip over tea and scones was now a natural and much-enjoyed occasion.

And a big, likeable Yorkshireman had become the entire staff at the police station; his uniform, walrus moustache and black labrador now a familiar and much-respected sight in the town. Known to adults and children alike as Robbo, only the council members and a couple of close friends knew that he'd been born Ted Robinson.

Now the town boasted a local telephone system, mostly party lines, operating through the exchange, another small office in the town hall building. The operator's name was Louise, a lady blessed with a delightful voice leading one afternoon to a situation which quickly became an item of local folklore. As there was no dialling facility, all outgoing calls had to be made through the operator, and farm people – particularly the men – were charmed by the lilting voice on their telephones. One man, a fortyish bachelor from well away from town, developed a real crush on this velvety voice and decided to take some direct action about it. Unlike most of his neighbours, he took great pride in maintaining a lovely flower garden and, collecting a large armful of his best blooms, he wrapped them in some cellophane he'd kept from the previous Christmas, put on his Sunday best, including a tie, and headed for town.

He reined in outside the town hall and by an unfortunate mistake of timing, unloaded his huge bouquet just as Robbo, and Geoff Powers, the new journalist, came along the main road. Embarrassed, he mumbled a greeting to the two men then hurried past them into the building.

Walking down the short passage to the pebbled-glass door marked 'Telephone Exchange', he took a deep breath and after gently knocking, walked through the door, having to turn a complete circle to do so while navigating the huge bundle of flowers before closing the door after himself.

Against the wall ahead of him was the switchboard, an item which stunned him with its banks of plugs, wires and, on a table opposite, the machine – a typewriter. Apart from this, the room was empty, something else he had not foreseen. He stood, pulling at the inside of the unaccustomed shirt collar with one hand, balancing the flowers with the other when the door behind him opened and a neat little, middle-aged woman with rimless glasses, her greying hair pulled back in a faultless bun, entered. She stopped, startled a little at the sight of the unexpected visitor.

'Good afternoon, ma'am,' he said. 'I'm looking for Louise, the girl who operates the phones.'

'Well, I'm no girl, but I am Louise,' said the immediately recognised, lilting voice. 'What can I do for you, sir?'

The bachelor, now dragging at his collar, gaped at her. 'You're not ... I mean, are you ... I'm ... look, I'm ...' he bumbled; then, thrusting the big bouquet at the amazed telephonist, he said, 'These are for you.'

Staggering under her hefty gift, Louise said, 'How lovely, thank you very much. But what for?'

'Oh. Ah, no particular reason, ma'am, just for being so nice on the phone. My name's Bourke, Larry Bourke, and I was, ah … just passing …'

'Mr Bourke: 1017D, I believe?'

'Yair, that's me.'

'Well, thank you again,' the soft voice said. 'My husband will be delighted as we haven't been here long enough to get a garden going.'

'Oh. Oh, well, that's good, then. Um, well, I'll say good day, ma'am.'

As he strode to the door, he dragged the tie and top shirt button undone and before Louise, who was smelling the blooms, could say goodbye, he was gone.

Stumbling through the front doorway into the blinding sunlight, Larry was met by Robbo and Powers, now joined by McBeath standing beside his gig.

'That what she'd ordered, was it, Larry?' asked Powers. 'You got it right?'

'Ah, shuddup,' said Bourke, climbing sheepishly into his saddle, and while his three friends slapped their thighs, howling with laughter, he clucked the horse and quickly left the township.

The story, already with a little added embroidery, appeared in the next issue of *The Wellsford Herald*.

A day or two later, as the regular coach from the city was unloading outside the hotel; a small, serious-looking man in his mid to late twenties, accompanied by his even smaller, bright-eyed wife, stepped down onto the roadside and went to the coach's rear to claim their meagre luggage. Carrying the two small cases, the two entered the hotel, and when the man had seated his wife at a table in the ladies lounge, he put the bags down and walked to the bar.

'May I speak to the proprietor, please?' he asked the big man behind the bar.

'You're speaking to him, friend. What can I do for you? After I've given you and your good lady a drink, that is. I assume you could both use one after the trip?'

'That's very kind of you, thank you,' the little man said. 'My wife will take a lemonade and I'd love a glass of ale.'

'Consider it done,' the barman-proprietor said as he went about fixing the drinks, 'and there'll be no payment. These are on the house.'

'There's no need for that, sir, we can pay for your service.'

'You probably can, and I know there's no need for it, but when two tired travellers come into my bar carrying suitcases, I always have a strong suspicion they're looking for accommodation and I don't like starting a friendship with a bill.' The barman's huge hand reached across the bar and the handshake paid for the drinks.

'Of course, you are right,' the man said quietly. 'Do you have a room?'

'Yes, we do indeed. Nothing flash, but you're welcome. Sit down and enjoy your drinks and I'll look after these other gents, then take you through.'

A half hour or so passed and the little man emerged from the back part of the hotel and walked to the bar, still wearing his jacket and tie.

'Ah there, everything all right back there?!' called the big barman.

'Thank you, yes, just fine. But I would like another glass of ale, please.'

'Coming up!'

'I must apologise for a lapse in manners, sir. Not quite myself after the trip. Not only did I not ask your name, I didn't offer mine either. I'm Ian Sanders, and my wife, who is presently taking a rest, is Jessie.'

'Glad to meetcha,' said the smiling proprietor, handing Sanders the glass. 'I'm Barry Collins, but everybody calls me Bazza. You'll meet Liz, my wife, when she gets back from the tearoom down at Craigs.

She and some of her mates are providing Geoff Powers with gossip for the local paper. You know how women are!'

'Hey, Bazza,' a loud voice from down the bar interrupted them, 'you want a man to die of thirst?'

Winking at Sanders, the barman moved to attend to the voice's owner then a minute or two later returned. 'You two resting before going on?' he inquired.

'Well no, sir ... Bazza. We may be staying here a while.'

'Oh. Is that right? What brings you to this neck of the woods?'

The visitor slowly sipped his ale before replying. 'Well, I worked at a trade before the war. Just out of my time, then joined up. The last few years haven't been very pleasant, you might say, and Jessie and I want to forget it all as quickly as possible, so we decided to leave the crowds in the city.'

'Good thinking, Ian, good thinking. So, what trade are you in?'

'I work with boots and shoes, making and repairing them. I seem to have been around the smell of leather all my life.'

The barman stood by a full tray of glasses, polishing each and stacking them on the shelf behind the bar. 'That's great!' he exclaimed. 'One of the things this town needs badly is a boot repairer. You should have a word with Ted Hunn the smithy. He and his son try to look after the town's leatherwork, but it's more like a sideline really.'

'Did you say Hunn?' Sanders gaped. 'Edward Hunn?'

'Edward? Well, I suppose so, but he's Ted to us all hereabouts. You seem surprised?'

'Well, I am, Baz, I am. There's a wonderful leather tradesman in Sydney who taught me almost everything I know, and he is one of the few city people who understood why we wanted to get out of it. He said an old friend of his had headed for the state's north-west years ago and had never regretted the move. He was a blacksmith and his name was Edward Hunn.'

'Dammit, man, you've hit the jackpot,' Bazza laughed. 'That's such an uncommon name, it must be Ted. I reckon you're in luck.'

The small man slapped his thigh with an open hand. 'Surely it must be him. Where can I find him?'

'Well, you can't miss the smithy, it's just down the road. But Ted's away at the moment, shoeing some horses away out of town. The boy's with him, but they'll probably be back tomorrow.'

'That's great. We'll just rest up for a while and see what happens then. In the meantime, Bazza, I'd like another ale.'

'Done!' the barman replied, grinning.

Sanders returned to their room, quietly removed his jacket and tie and his beautifully crafted boots and lain on the bed, gently so as not to disturb his wife who he assumed was sleeping. To his surprise, she reached out and took his hand. 'I like it here, Ian,' she said. 'I've hardly been outside, but it feels good, welcoming. For the first time since you got back from overseas, I'm feeling warm inside again.'

He squeezed her hand gently as a loud knock at their door stopped the conversation. Sanders walked over to open the door to a smiling, round-faced woman.

'Ah, you must be Mr Sanders. I'm Liz Collins, the boss of this establishment although Bazza harbours the fond illusion that he wears that hat. I'm sorry I wasn't here to meet you and your wife earlier, but we'd just like you to make yourselves at home. We don't have a real dining room but hope you'll join us for dinner in the kitchen a bit later. I'll belt the gong when it's on, all right?'

'That would be lovely,' Sanders said, a little overcome by their hearty hostess. 'Thank you very much, Mrs Collins.'

'Liz, the name is, Liz. Mrs Collins is Bazza's mother. See the two of you later.' She turned and strode off down the passageway.

The little man closed the door, suddenly realising that he was in shirt sleeves and socks. Turning to his wife, he said, smiling, 'See what I meant, Jessie? They all seem the same – open and friendly. It's wonderful. And so far not one person has mentioned the damned war.'

Jessie looked thoughtful; she didn't like tempting providence. 'Let's not get too excited yet, Ian. We've only just left city life, and there might be a bit of adjustment yet. But I did say before, it feels good to me, and I think we're just at the start of something. You can leave all that horrible war behind you once and for all.'

'Great God, I hope so. You'll have to bear with me a while longer, Jessie, but every day it gets easier, and this one has been a real beaut.'

'Lie down and rest, love. I feel quite sure we'll hear the dinner gong,' and they both laughed, the first time in a long while they had laughed so freely together.

★ ★ ★

Towards the end of John's third year in Sydney, several of his teachers were putting pressure on the boy to continue his education into university as he had by now shown real ability in several different fields. His examination marks placed him near the top in most subjects and he was a definite asset in both summer and winter sports. To the academics, it was nothing short of a crime that he should even consider going back to the bush. But to John, very little had changed. He enjoyed the sport and his studies, but it never occurred to him to stay in the city at term's end. He loved his country home, especially as the town was now changing so often, and couldn't wait to get back into the swing of things each holiday break.

John was a little worried on each visit that his father seemed to be ageing quite quickly, and he guessed that the continuing additions to his workload were the cause of this. All the more reason, then, to get through the schooling and be able to lighten his father's load. Of course, this would have to be decided by James, not him; he had no thought of becoming the conquering hero from the city taking over the farm – far from it. He just wanted to be there alongside his dad and Charlie, and if he had acquired any new skills that might be useful, so much the better. The better for Wellsford, both the station and the town.

So, when he stepped down from the train for the Christmas break, knowing that he had only one more year of college to complete, he was already gearing his thinking ahead past that year. He was looking forward to some solid conversation with his father over this break, to assess what lay ahead.

★ ★ ★

Although James maintained his fierce affection for the land, especially that around his home at Wellsford Station, he was now developing a new attraction to the political life opening up to him through the council. Up until the present, he had maintained a share and share alike attitude, even if always with a keen eye to stock and station, but during the past few months he had found himself liking the leading role and the feeling of command. He convinced himself that his decisions to brook no nonsense were good for the town and if he noticed the questioning looks passing between the other council members as he overrode their opinions, he ignored them.

The news broken to him tentatively by his son John on his last Christmas trip home from school fitted perfectly to suit them both. By the end of that following year, John had completed his matriculation examination, returned permanently to Wellsford and taken over the responsibility of running the farm with Charlie and Albert which gave James the time he wanted to devote to his new interest brought about by the growing township: the acquisition of wealth.

James found a way to support the town's growth by becoming the major shareholder in several of the emerging businesses, which of course enabled him to control the finances. After a while, nothing was passed through council unless it was to his advantage, and the townsfolk soon learned that the only way to make progress was to have James Mitchell on side. Not only did he own the station called Wellsford, he also had what amounted to the controlling interest in the town.

One person who quickly noticed the subtle change in James and rightly assessed its cause was Pearl. The man now seemed determined to distance himself from his household staff. He became more demanding in his requests, constantly widening the gap between them.

Charlie also felt the brunt of the change. No longer the friendly repartee between them; in fact, not much conversation at all. Even the conversations between James and his son John were all to do with business, not that John seemed to mind one bit; he loved the farm. And so while Charlie was concerned with James's changed attitude, he was quite happy to be all day with the lad he had always felt to be a natural. But to everyone else, James seemed simply to be becoming. Becoming politically viable, becoming domineering and demanding and, sadly, becoming a heavy drinker.

The liquor had been occasionally broken out on celebratory occasions at council meetings, but as the months went by and James steadily developed his obsession with power and control, celebrations became an excuse. Soon the Scotch bottle was within easy reach and needed regular replacement.

At the conclusion of each meeting, James took it upon himself to usher everybody out, then sat at the big table with the books and applications, carefully assessing how every suggestion could be manipulated to his gain by changing a word here, a phrase there, then preparing a plan to ensure a majority, and therefore assent, at the next meeting. And the bottle and glass were ever-present. Even Hilda's example did nothing to dissuade him. Heavens! After all, she was weak, and a woman! If he had the power to control a whole township and demand its respect, he could certainly handle a drink or two! And if Bazza felt inclined to keep close to the action by slipping him the odd bottle or two, so much the better. No council book entries, nice and tidy.

James sat at the boardroom table sipping from his ever-present whisky glass. God, he was tired. Another drink would help, but the bottle was empty. Ah well, I'll go without, he thought, draining the glass's contents.

Some time later, he reached for the glass again, reacting angrily when he remembered that it was empty. Blast, I just felt like one more, he thought, but knew that at this time of night, he couldn't call on Bazza, particularly as Liz was unaware of the two men's understanding. Damn, damn, damn, he thought, then smiled to himself. Hadn't that new fellow in town made an application recently for alterations to the old place down by the river? Yes! And hadn't James heard a whisper that the man might be involved in sly grogging, among other things? Yes, again. And didn't he have his phone line? Right, let's find his application file.

'Hello, am I speaking to Mr Raymond Corcoran? Oh, Ray, you say. All right, Ray. I'm sorry to call you at this time of night, particularly as we've never met ... Yes, I realise you've not long arrived in town. My name is Mitchell, James Mitchell and I'm ... Oh, you know of me, then? Good, good. Look, the reason for this call is that I'm caught in a slightly delicate situation. I have a late business meeting tonight and have just realised to my horror that I forgot to replenish my Scotch supply this afternoon. Now, I'm led to believe by some colleagues that you might be able to help me out of this predicament? Official? Heavens, no, it's just that ... You have? Wonderful. Then I'll just drive down ... Yes, I know where you live. A gesture, you say? Well, that's very generous of you, Ray. Right, then. I'll be there shortly.'

James checked a few details in the Corcoran file to refresh his memory, then left the office.

The following day, James had a call from McBeath, the bank manager, asking him to call by the office the following afternoon. As soon as his guest was seated in his office, James said, 'All right, Alec, you sounded very formal on the phone, so something's up. What is it?'

'Well, James, I want you to be the first to know that I've been offered a big promotion in Sydney and have accepted, as I'd be a fool to turn it down. So as soon as the bank can arrange a suitable replacement, I'll be leaving Wellsford.'

James scratched his cheek and checked his fob watch. Damn, he thought, talk about bad timing. *Another bank manager to win over*, but he offered his congratulations.

Alec stood, looking out the window, his hands joined behind his back. 'Thank you, James. It's bound to be some weeks before the changeover, but I wanted to tell you straight away. Now, can I talk to you frankly on another matter? This time as a friendly financial adviser.'

'Go ahead, Alec. You know I value your advice.' God, here it comes, he thought, the friendly pep talk.

The banker turned, both palms of his hands now facing inwards towards each other, fingertips touching. 'James, as your banker and a member of the council, I can see clearly how solidly you are establishing yourself in this community, and I applaud it, but it worries me a little that you might just be getting in too deep. You have interests in so much small business in Wellsford that if there should be any substance in the rumours of disquiet on the world financial market, you could be in hot water, my friend. I know you're a prudent man, but I hope that you're looking carefully at all these investments.'

James smiled. 'Thanks, Alec, but have no fears. I'm very confident in every move I make and am always looking ahead; however, I had no idea this change was coming and will be genuinely sorry to see you go. Can I interest you in a glass to toast the occasion?'

'Thank you, no. I've an awful lot to attend to before the date's set, you understand, surely?'

James stood, extending his handshake. 'Of course, of course, thanks for calling in.'

The late evening meeting with Ray Corcoran had led to quite a friendship as the man, while obviously a rough diamond, was quite different from James's other acquaintances. A big, burly character with an attractive, outgoing personality, a ready smile and an endless supply of coarse jokes (which, however, he never aired in the presence of a woman), he brought a breath of fresh air to the town and a source of laughter to balance some of the formal reticence. James appreciated the light relief Corcoran provided, but he soon, like others in the town, started to wonder about the new resident. He always had well-lined pockets but no apparent source of income, and if any query or mention of his past was raised, the subject was invariably sidestepped with a loud joke.

Soon it was noticeable that men were coming and going from Corcoran's house at all hours of the day and night, and although nothing obvious was going on that might attract Robbo's interest, a shady element seemed to have infiltrated the town. What the man considered a service in after-hours liquor was discreetly taken care of, and though it seemed strange to the bar regulars, Bazza didn't appear worried about this illegal competition. That is, not until one Saturday evening when an unknown small, flat-back truck with a tarpaulin-covered load and sagging springs drove into Wellsford and parked behind Corcoran's, leaving much later in the dead of night with a folded tarpaulin and the rear wheels well clear of the tray.

Quite quickly, Bazza's demeanour changed, although he said nothing. He also noticed that several of his regulars left the bar at measured intervals on Saturdays, returning either smiling widely or grunting with morose displeasure, some buying drinks for the house while others skulked moodily in corners. It was fairly obvious to Bazza that Corcoran had also set up a bookmaking operation.

Next it was noticed that torn-up lottery tickets were appearing on the ground around the town, little pieces of paper pounced on by the local children and collected like darkening autumn leaves, but naturally their source was not positively known as those buying them were not at all keen on an interview with Robbo.

The man was certainly clever as while still being accepted in town as an affable character, everybody's friend, he was getting himself set up by placing many of the town's citizens in his debt in a way that could not be reported.

This situation came to a temporary halt one afternoon with the arrival of the city coach. A small, neatly-dressed woman among the passengers stepped purposefully down from the coach and made her way to the bar in the hotel.

'I'm led to believe a man named Ray Corcoran has recently settled in this town,' she said to Bazza over a gin and tonic. 'Do you happen to know where I can find him?'

At the mention of the name, several of the bar's customers turned with interest towards the woman.

'As a matter of fact, I do, ma'am,' answered Bazza, taking in the woman's well-worn coat and precisely folded gloves. 'At this very moment, he's on these premises, assisting me with a stock count.'

'Ah, that's wonderful, Mr ...?'

'Collins, ma'am, but everybody calls me Bazza.'

'Thank you, Mr Collins. Would you be so good as to fetch him, please?'

Bazza turned and disappeared through the door to the stockroom, a moment later reappearing, laughing, saying to his visitor, 'He'll be here in a sec, ma'am. Reckons it must be his lucky day.'

The woman drummed her fingers on her glass. 'Perhaps, perhaps not,' she said, unsmiling.

As Corcoran emerged, the wide smile on his face evaporated and he gasped. 'Phyllis! What the hell ... Why didn't you let me know you were coming?'

The woman put down her glass and gloves and worried her left forearm with probing fingers. 'Well! That's a nice greeting for your wife!'

A ripple of shock went around the bar. There'd never been any mention of a wife.

'Ah, struth, woman, you might have warned me ...'

'What, and give you the chance to take off before I arrived again?'

Corcoran ignored the inquiring looks from other men in the bar. 'Ah, come on now. Where's your bag? Lemme give you a hand over to the house and we'll have a good old yarn, straighten a few things out. Damn, you look good, Phyl, real good.'

'Words are cheap enough,' she snapped. 'If you don't mind, I'll finish my drink.'

'Eh? Oh yeah, of course.' He looked around the grinning faces in the bar. 'I'll wait for you outside.'

This juicy bit of gossip emptied the bar much earlier than usual and shot around the town like wildfire with James, Robbo and particularly Geoff Powers pricking up their ears.

After a short walk to the little town's outskirts, Corcoran stopped and pointed. 'There,' he said, 'didn't I tell you I'd find somewhere nice and quiet for us?'

Phyllis looked at the house with its little fence and large outhouse, with big trees along the river bank beyond and had to admit to herself it was very nice, almost lovely. But she'd been a city person all her life, and so had Ray, so she was more than a little suspicious of this apparent sudden change.

'Ray, what's this all about? You take off and I don't hear a word for ages ...'

'Not out here, Phyl. Let's get inside and sort things out, all right?'

For the next couple of weeks, Corcoran became a model citizen, walking the main street, introducing his wife to all and sundry and truly acting the gentleman, but several in the town felt that all was not as it seemed and for just that reason, nobody was really surprised when late one morning, Phyllis Corcoran stomped into the hotel's bar with a red face, carrying her suitcase.

'Give me a gin and tonic, please, Mr Collins,' she said, 'and tell me when the next train is due to come through.'

'About twenty minutes if it's on time, Mrs C,' said Bazza, fixing her drink, 'and they're not usually late.'

'Well, I hope to God they're on time today. I can't wait to get shot of this place. Shouldn't have ever come in the first place.'

Handing her the glass, Bazza said, 'There you are. Now just relax and take it easy, Mrs C. It's a long trip.'

'I'm so bloody annoyed I'll probably hardly notice the trip,' she blurted.

Bazza stood polishing a glass, pleased that by lucky coincidence, nobody else was in the bar at the time. 'Something wrong, then?' he asked gently, 'not that it's any of my business.'

'You're right, it's not,' she snorted tearfully, then, 'Ah, what the hell. You'll know soon enough anyway. That rotten bastard, talk about a leopard changing its spots. Do you know what he's doing?'

Bazza wiped the bar down without comment.

'That big shed out the back of the place – used to be stables. You know where I mean?'

Bazza nodded.

'Well, he's getting it nicely set up. There's enough grog out there to send an army on its ear, he's got a phone line to every damned racetrack in the state and he's got another to Tatts in Melbourne. No wonder he didn't want me to see the place! If the wallopers cop onto him, he'll be gone again. Dammit, I've had enough. I'm off – not a minute too soon, if you ask me.'

As if on cue, Bazza heard the steam train coming in at the top end of town and said, 'Well, it looks like you won't have to wait, Mrs C. The train's early. It won't take too long to reload. Be away on time, I reckon.'

She drained her glass in a couple of gulps.

'That's on the house, Mrs C. Sorry things didn't work out.'

'Thanks, Bazza,' she said. 'You're all right, you know that?'

'Always ready to help, particularly a maiden in distress,' he said.

'Ha! Some maiden,' she scoffed. 'A few years passed under the bridge since I fitted that term.' She smiled at Bazza, picked up her bag and headed for the door.

Bazza was very thankful the bar was still empty. He'd known of course about the old stables but wasn't sure how many others knew. He'd have to watch his p's and q's, that's for sure. He didn't trust Corcoran any more than his wife did. He would have to be extremely careful.

Going social

Isobel Craig was neatly fitting Robbo's grocery purchases into a large paper bag, finally adding the small, brown paper bag of eggs to the top.

'Now, watch those eggs, Robbo. Don't go tripping over Blackie or you'll have your eggs scrambled before you reach home.'

Smiling, the big policeman said, 'Thanks, Isobel. I'll get it all home intact. Now, do you have a few minutes for a chat?'

'Of course,' she answered brightly. As a matter of fact, I'd just put the kettle on when you came in, so sit down and we'll have a cuppa.'

Robbo sat in the tearoom area and was soon joined by the shopkeeper with a tea tray.

'It's very seldom that one of the town's men wants to chat with someone of the opposite sex, Robbo, so this must be serious,' she said, smiling broadly.

'I'll come straight to the point,' Robbo said, stirring three spoonfuls of sugar into his tea. 'As we all know, the town is making steady progress, and this little area of ours is bringing people in from far and wide, and a whole lot of them (particularly the new arrivals) have growing children. Now, apart from during school hours, they've nothing much to do, and it's not going to be long before some of them will be up to mischief. Kids will be kids.'

Isobel nodded. 'Precisely what some of the ladies and I have been talking about lately.'

'Of course,' Robbo continued, 'especially this last couple of weeks when the school's on holiday. All right. Now, how would you feel about starting a dancing class? To get the kids together, like.'

Isobel put the teapot back on the tray and looked across the table, wide-eyed. 'Me? A dancing class? Why me?'

Robbo slurped tea from the side of his cup. 'Isobel, it's part of my job to know a bit about everybody's background, and I know you were quite a dancer – won a medal or two a while back.'

'Quite a while back,' she laughed, flushing pink. 'That was before I took up with Fred and found that he has two left feet, so dancing became a thing of the past.'

'So much the better. I'll bet you'd still like to dance, wouldn't you?'

'I have to admit that there have been times when I've missed it.'

'Right, there you go, then. Why not pass on your abilities to the youngsters? You'd probably have girls only at first, if I know this town's boys.'

Both of them laughed.

'I think you'd be right there, Robbo,' she said.

'All right,' said the big policeman, 'so when do we start? I'll help any way I can. I'll track down a gramophone and some records, then all we need's a bit of space.'

'Now, wait a minute, wait a minute,' Isobel protested. 'I haven't agreed yet, and it's not quite that easy. I'll have to talk to Fred about it at least.'

'Well, if he's as good a dancer as you say he is, he'll probably be pleased to look after the counter and keep out of the way,' said the policeman, and again they both laughed.

But the seed had been planted. After Robbie left, Isobel found herself practising a few steps behind the counter, already busy in her mind setting up a way to begin classes.

During the school holidays, the change of management at the bank had taken place. While the town's populace were indeed sorry to lose the knowledgeable Alec McBeath; his replacement, Brian Wills, made the transition easily and smoothly. In a matter of days, he had made himself known personally to all except the members of the community living in outlying areas. Even so, he'd made a point of introducing himself to most of those by letter.

Wills and Belle had two children: Elizabeth, fourteen and Timothy, twelve, who were both to be enrolled when the new school term began. Wills had begun his banking career in a country town and had progressed to a responsible position in Parramatta, but he and his wife Belle had never really settled to city living, and when the Wellsford position was announced, he applied and was accepted. While in name the job was a promotion, the bank's attitude was that a rural managership was somewhat of a step down, but as Wills was so keen on the position, it was his.

Wills was a man of medium build with unruly, curly black hair above an open face with piercing brown eyes. He looked and moved like someone who always felt uncomfortable in a suit, so he adapted to the basic informality of Wellsford from their time of arrival. But his appearance had no bearing whatsoever on his ability with figures, and as he sat in his office poring over the books and ledgers, he very quickly assessed what was what in the town. Alec McBeath had made this task much less daunting by leaving him a copious letter outlining the personalities of many of the town's citizens and, typically of the man, the books and documents were absolutely correct, clear and up to date.

On the afternoon of his first day at the bank, while Belle and the children were still unpacking in the living quarters upstairs, a man came confidently through the main door and moved towards the new manager. Thanks to McBeath's descriptive outlines, Wills was not surprised to hear him say, 'You must be Brian Wills. My name is James Mitchell. There's just a chance that Alec may have mentioned my name to you?'

'Glad to meet you, Mr Mitchell,' said Wills, shaking the proffered hand. 'Yes indeed, I do of course know of you.'

'Just popped in to say hello and welcome you to our town. You and your family quite comfortable?'

'Very much so, thank you. Still unpacking, of course, but already we have a nice feeling of having come home. I feel sure we'll all be fine here.'

'That's good, then. Please call me James. Almost everybody else does.'

'Righto, I will, and I'm Brian. As little as possible of this "Mr" stuff. We've had enough of that over the past few years. Respect and formality don't necessarily go hand in hand, do they?'

James had the feeling that the piercing eyes were assessing him carefully as he said, 'Couldn't agree more, Brian, you're quite right.'

'I'm pleased you've come in, James, as I was intending to seek you out today. Acquaintances of ours in Parramatta suggested we should contact you on our arrival – Leila and Wilf Branxton.'

'Ah, the Branxtons.'

Wills was quick to notice the reaction, the change in voice tone.

'Haven't seen them for years. Leila was … is quite a close friend of Hilda, my wife. How are they and their daughter … er …'

'Celia,' offered Wills.

'Celia, of course. It's been some time since we've been in touch. Well, Hilda may have heard but not passed the matter on. My wife is not at all well and unfortunately, she and I do not communicate quite as we should, or could.'

'Oh, I'm sorry to hear that. Perhaps I should contact Mrs Mitchell direct.'

'No, I don't think that would be the best thing to do at present, Brian. I'll pass the information on and suggest that Hilda contact you when she's ready. I presume the Branxtons are fit and well?'

James was again drawn to the searching eyes as Wills said, 'Oh yes, fine, although ours is not a close friendship. They, or in particular Mrs Branxton, would prefer to be a little more comfortable in these trying times, but as ever, they're making plans for themselves and their girl.'

'I'm sure they are. Well, I'd best be off. I'm very glad to know you, Brian, and if there's anything I can help with, please don't hesitate to call me. There's not a lot in Wellsford that I don't know about!'

Wills smiled. 'I'm sure that's the truth,' he said as he shook Mitchell's hand.

In fact, he knew that it was the truth as the books and accounts under the Mitchell name spelt things out clearly. While the family's holdings had for many years had a balance large enough to provide a strong annual return, in recent times the figures had jumped about regularly with balances always increasing. It was obvious that the man he'd just met was a very clever, even cunning operator who would use family money to help establish any new business as long as it was lucrative in the long run and the percentage split favourable; however, all was above board legally, so as long as things remained that way, James was going to be a valued client at the bank. After all, his business partners also had to effect their transactions through the bank, and if they'd agreed to Mitchell's terms, it was no business of Wills's or anyone else; the bank collected on both sides. The situation, however, did whet Brian Wills's appetite as he ran his practised eye over the rows and rows of figures.

★ ★ ★

On his regular rounds, which were more often to give Blackie some exercise than in the execution of his police duties, Robbo was keeping an eye and an ear open for any hint of a building he might have overlooked that may have clear floor space suitable for Isobel Craig's dancing school, but he was not having much luck. There were several buildings behind those in the main street that were falling into disuse now that the motor car was starting to replace the horse as the preferred means of transport, but as their tenants had previously been animals, the floorboards were badly damaged, if in fact floors existed at all. There was one small house with a large barn attached to its back wall in a handy central position that Robbo decided to investigate, but he was advised at the town hall, much to his surprise, that the property was under negotiation for sale.

'For sale!' he exclaimed to the clerk. 'It's been empty for ages! Is someone in the area after it, then?'

'No, Robbo,' answered the clerk, 'it's another new chum looking to move here.'

'What, someone from England?'

'No, not England,' the clerk replied. 'In fact I don't think he'd be very pleased to hear that remark. He's Scottish, and you can hardly understand a darned word he's saying, or I couldn't. Had a helluva time filling out forms and things.'

'Scottish? Well, he'll be among friends here, eh? The place seems to be filling up with Scotties.'

'Well, they're not all like this one, thank God. You talk about a broad accent – God alive! Anyway, we got there.'

'I can't believe I hadn't heard. Pride meself on knowing everyone. Where's he staying?'

'He's not, Robbo, that's just it. He came into town yesterday morning alone, looked around the town without talking much to anyone, came in here to inquire about the old place, eventually signed some holding documents and left on the afternoon train.'

Robbo looked thoughtful. 'Sounds darned funny. Everything all right, you think?'

'Good as gold, it seems. Just very shy. Said he'd be back in a few days with his wife to have another look with her. Name of Clarke, Stanley Clarke.'

'Well I'll be blowed,' said Robbo. 'Thanks anyway. I'll just have to keep looking.'

'Oh, Robbo!' called the clerk as the policeman walked to the door. 'I just remembered something. Go and have a word with the stationmaster. He was talking about an out-of-use shed or something in the bar last night.'

Robbo walked up to the door marked 'Office' at the railway station, knocked and walked in.

'Hello, Robbo,' the stationmaster Jack Steele said brightly. 'You expecting a remission man on the next train or something?'

'No, Jack,' the big policeman replied, smiling. 'In fact, this visit has nothing to do with trains or dodgy types at all. I'm told you've been talking about some kind of obsolete shed you know of, and I'm interested in having a look if I can.'

'No doubt about it, is there?' Steele replied. 'You say anything unusual in a country pub and the bush telegraph goes to work. In no time at all, everyone knows and funny thing, no one remembers who said it.'

Robbo laughed. 'Well, I've just been talking to the young feller over at the town clerk's office and he told me.'

'And he's right,' the stationmaster replied. 'One of the railway buildings here is full of junk, and I was talking about cleaning it out. I was hoping to round up a few volunteers to help, but no such luck,' he grinned. 'What's your interest, Robbo?'

The policeman gave him a quick run-down on his idea and Steele said, 'Tell you what. This might be just the thing, but there's a bit of work involved, Robbo; it's a mess. And it's quite big.'

The moment Robbo saw the place, he started to expand on his original plan. It was an ideal size for a utility hall and although on railway property, was quite near the main road. Robbo hadn't really noticed it before because there was a large jacaranda behind one corner which partly obscured it from the road, and apart from heaps of outdated equipment, signs etc. piled up against the building, the whole lot was almost covered by an out-of-control tangle of weeds and vines.

'A bit of work, the man says,' Robbo said, laughing. 'It seems the fellers at the hotel knew what you were talking about!'

'Reckon you're right, but a couple of days ago, I cleared a bit away around the other side and got to a door, and the inside's pretty darned good, I think. Come and have a gander.'

The two men moved around the heaps of junk, and Robbo could see where Jack had pulled a lot of old signs, a wide seat and a few wooden cases away from a doorway. The hinges squeaked loudly as they opened the door and as soon as they'd stepped inside, Robbo sucked in his breath in amazement. 'What on earth is the story of this place?' he asked the stationmaster. 'It looks as solid as a church.'

'Not bad, is it? That's why I got interested, so I made a few inquiries and it seems that some years ago, there were plans to make a freight transfer station here at Wellsford, so this place was built as a big stock room to store goods to be changed from train to train. The whole plan was shelved before ever going into use, but the shell of this building was already up. Then the war intervened, so it's just been let go.'

'But dammit, man, look at the floor!'

'All right, isn't it?' said Jack. 'I checked that too and found that ships returning from across the Tasman used to carry New Zealand timber in their holds as ballast, and the railways used it in some of their buildings. This is obviously one of them. Those floorboards are kauri pine, a beautiful timber.'

'And it's in such good shape! Hardly been used, I suppose.'

'No, I shouldn't think so. This rubbish and junk piled up on it might even be original. It's the outside that's the worst.'

Robbo almost ran back to his office where two fingers attacked his faithful typewriter straight away, outlining to the Sydney main office his plans and hopes, with an application for funds. With all due respect, he didn't want James Mitchell taking this over; this was going to be his baby. He wanted official funding and approval to launch the Wellsford School of Arts.

Rein change

Since resettling on the station, John Mitchell had thrown himself completely into farm life and was surprised to find after a couple of months that there was almost nothing of college and the city that he missed at all. The part he did take time to adjust to was the unaccustomed feeling of being boss. While being among the top levels in his class work, and very successful on the sports fields, John had never really aspired to be in a position of authority, having the responsibility of making decisions. He'd never really thought seriously about the inevitability of eventually running Wellsford Station. The fact that he'd not had any desire to enter university was not due to any kind of inertia; it was just that he'd never entertained an idea of a future outside Wellsford. He clearly remembered the look of relief on his father's face when the subject of extended education had been brought up just before the final college year and he'd said that he'd no intention of continuing, rather that he was looking forward to getting back to the land.

John was not, however, quite as ready to be thrust into the driving seat, so the transition over the past few years was not as simple as he'd expected. To add to the awkward situation, James himself seemed to be undergoing personal change which was surprising, not perhaps so much in that it was happening as that John had not noticed it until he was back to stay. His father obviously still loved the station, but his attitude to the staff had hardened and he now seemed much more involved in the running of the town than of his own property. Almost as soon as John had unpacked, the subject of his taking control of the station was raised, and in such a way that James saw it as a foregone conclusion that he was ready to do just that, as if all discussion on the subject was closed.

The one aspect of the change in his father that John found most disturbing was that his attitude to wealth and power now controlled his thinking. As a growing boy, he'd known instinctively that the station was successful enough to provide a high level of comfort, but now that was not enough for his father. Nowhere near enough. The one situation that John had never craved, that of being in charge, was becoming an obsession with his father. He was obviously delighted to hand the reins to his son and was now spending more and more time in the town, displaying his new motor car and other evidence of a bulging bank balance. Often he returned to the homestead at unreasonable hours, well under the influence and expecting, in fact often demanding a meal from Pearl and Faith – with all the trimmings.

The old equilibrium in that area had also become much more threatened; to John, another puzzling aspect. All his life had been relaxed and easy, but now an animosity was developing, not really helped by his own sudden ascendancy into the hot seat, but this change in James's attitude really stung him. It had always been so comfortable and natural, so why had it altered? Answers were simply not forthcoming although John felt he saw similar questions in Pearl's face from time to time. She never complained about the changed circumstances but obviously was very conscious of them. The same open, ready smile was there for John, but the newly estranged relationship with his father clearly showed.

Not so with Faith. If she was upset by, or even noticed the changes, all was swept aside by her absorption in Albert. She clearly adored him and now wore a constant smile regardless of what chore, pleasant or unpleasant, she was busy with. Her future with Albert was assured and she wanted nothing else. They exuded such warmth when together that at times John found himself experiencing a twinge of envy. He'd always felt a closeness to Faith, in fact both of them, and was delighted to see them so happy in each other's company, but on more and more occasions, the thought of his own life ahead surged up. At present, though, he had enough on his plate.

Whether John liked it or not, he was now in charge and was forced to overlook the domestic problems to handle the bigger problems on the huge station. To add to the pressure, while he was still coming to grips with his new situation, his father started making suggestions about alterations which might make the station more productive, more profitable, and gradually the suggestions became commands. Not unnaturally, the boy took exception to this as his new authority was being undermined before it could be established, and it all seemed so unnecessary; the station was already the biggest and most successful in the whole area. Sooner or later, it seemed inevitable that for the first time in his life, he was going to be forced into a confrontation with his father, and from living through many of those between his parents, he didn't exactly relish the prospect.

On serious reflection, John decided to maintain the status quo to the best of his ever-increasing ability, hoping that continued success on the station might avoid any unpleasantness, at least until he felt more solidly established.

★ ★ ★

Robbo looked at the letter in his hands and felt as if he had won a lottery. It had been months since he'd applied for funding for his project and had all but given up. And, wonder of wonders, Jack Steele had said nothing to anyone and had even left the building untouched so as not to attract any unwanted attention. Jack wasn't silly; he knew of course that if he left it alone, the cleaning up would be done by someone else, especially if Robbo's application came through, so it suited them both for him to look the other way.

The policeman couldn't get the grin off his face. Now that he had the letter of authority to proceed, the worry of funding was virtually gone. The more he'd thought about the school of arts, the keener he'd become, and he'd started to think about alternative funding. There were three options: a loan through Ray Corcoran, but that obviously had a fair element of risk involved; a loan through James Mitchell which would basically mean handing him the whole project on a plate; or a loan through the bank. He'd almost brought the subject up a few days before while talking with Brian Wills and his wife but decided at the last moment against it, and now he didn't need to think about it, just get his plans together and quietly go ahead.

He brushed his jacket and reached for his peaked cap, tweaking the peak with two fingers as he placed it on his head more jauntily than usual. He had never been one for seeking status, but the Wellsford School of Arts had a ring to it and he liked the sound. But for now, he had some errands to take care of.

His first port of call was at the home and business address of the newly-arrived Scot, Stanley Clarke, who with his wife Maggie was busily renovating the little place on the main street, changing the old house and barn complex into a shop front with home and workshop at the rear.

The Clarkes had impressed the townsfolk with the speed with which they'd applied themselves to the task. Stanley had arrived back in the town with his wife only a few days after his first brief visit, then they had carefully checked the old property, gone to the town clerk's office to settle the details and moved straight in. Stanley had noticed on his first visit that there were some very basic pieces of furniture left in the house – a rustic table and two chairs, a large wardrobe with its doors removed and leaning against a wall, a double bed with a sagging wire mattress and several other bits and pieces. The luggage which had arrived with them consisted of a suitcase and a trunk containing mainly clothes, bedding and some linen, and

Stanley's toolbox, but the day after their arrival, Stanley was making inquiries about timber availability and the sawing and hammering began almost immediately.

Maggie's accent was as broad as her husband's, so she had a little trouble on her first shopping expedition, but she patiently made herself known in the town as she went from place to place collecting basic provisions for her kitchen and household. Within days, the joinery facing the street had been altered, the twin side-by-side window frames now having been replaced by one large frame divided into twelve smaller windows, and the big front door had been removed, restyled with two glazed panels and replaced. From the doorway to the front gate, Stanley had constructed a pathway paved with flat rocks he'd dragged from the side of the river near the rapids down from the ford. He'd then attacked the ground across the front of their home inside the front fence with a mattock, loosening the soil in preparation for Maggie's later establishing a garden, edging the area with large river rocks. He'd already checked the shingle roof and cleared the guttering for their water supply before starting on the inside. From then on, passers-by could only stare and conjecture about what was going on, but it was obviously plenty.

So, when Robbo, in answer to his knock, was invited in, his jaw dropped in amazement.

'Sorry aboot the mess,' the Scotsman burred. 'We're goin' like mad to get dun wi' it quickly.'

Robbo gasped. 'Great heavens, man, you've rebuilt the place.'

The Scotsman beamed. 'It's comin' along fine, we think. It'll be no too bad when it's done.'

'No too bad, you say! Mr Clarke, it's wonderful already!'

Maggie had come in a side door and now stood beaming beside her man.

'You must be proud of him, Mrs Clarke.'

'Aye, 'e's a clever lad, is Stanley. You must be Robbo.'

'Aye – I mean yes,' said Robbo, thoroughly confused. He loved the way she'd rolled the 'R' in his name and was still coming to grips with the changes to the place. 'I'm sorry,' he said. 'You've taken my breath away, and I forgot my manners. Yes, I'm Robbo, and you are obviously Mr and Mrs Clarke.'

'That's wha' it says on the wee bi' o' paper the Minister gae us, but we're Maggie and Stanley,' the Scot said, quietly giving his wife a hug. 'I'd ask you to make y'self at home, bu' it's no really a home yet.'

'You're wrong, Stanley, it already feels like a home,' the policeman said. Robbo was fascinated. The front section of the building, the original house, had been stripped bare and the doorway to the back widened. What had been a high-roofed barn was now divided into two levels with an access stairway running up one wall. The plumbing had been reversed through the old house's wall, feeding a large pair of tubs on the lower level and a bathroom and kitchen above. Beside the tubs was the copper, moved in from outside and placed on a stone floor area that hadn't been there before, and there was an open hearth between the copper and the wall.

'That's where we'll be havin' a stove an' wood pile, ye ken,' Stanley said, 'and it's flue will go up and oot near the roof. That's tae warm the whole place, ye ken. The workshop will be doon here, wi' the livin' oopstairs. Come 'n' look.'

Silently Robbo followed his host up the new staircase. Although unfinished, the framing was in place, outlining three rooms and a large open area in the centre by the staircase.

'It's no too safe yet, but I'll build posts an' banisters soon. There's no bairns to watch for yet, but that's what the extra rooms are for.'

Now Robbo was flabbergasted. Even in its incomplete state, it looked wonderful to him. In fact, he couldn't believe how different it now was from the only other time he'd seen it, when craning his neck to look in through grimy windows from the outside.

'Tea's on!' came Maggie's voice from below as the two men went downstairs again. 'We're no yet organised,' she continued as they reached the lower floor, 'so the kettle's still doon here. I hope you like oatcakes, Robbo. Them an' porridge is aboot wha' we're livin' on so far!'

Robbo wasn't sure what oatcakes were but found he could manage several with the hot tea.

'Well noo,' Stanley said, smiling, 'you've nae mentioned why you're here. I hope it's nae official business?'

'Not at all, far from it,' the policeman laughed. 'As a matter of fact, having now seen what you've done here, I'm embarrassed to bring the subject up. But I'm hoping for some advice and help, if it's not asking too much.'

Robbo went on to outline his project at the railway yard and when he mentioned the kauri pine flooring, Stanley's eyes shone with interest. 'Aye, me friend, I'd be only too glad to come tae a look. Who knows? I might have a few ideas as well. What you describe as junk just maybe good to reuse, ye ken? Let's go 'n' see.'

'What, now?'

'Aye, mon. There's nae time like the present.'

★ ★ ★

James walked into the walled-off area of the blacksmith's shop which served as premises for the shoe and bootmaker and rang the little brass bell on the counter. Jessie hurried through from the rear of the shop.

'Ah, James,' she said, 'is everything all right with your boots?'

'Jessie, they're quite wonderful. I just dropped in to have a word with Ian about that, as a matter of fact. Is he not in at present?'

'Yes, he's here, just taking a break out in the sunshine. I'll let him know you're here. Excuse me.'

The quiet little cobbler came to the counter. 'Hello, James,' he said. 'You wanted to see me?'

'That's right, Ian. Is there somewhere we can talk for a few minutes?'

'Certainly, out the back. It's beautiful in the sun, come on through.'

'Sorry to appear secretive,' James said as they sat down, 'but it might be awkward for you two if Ted and his offsider heard what I have to say.'

Ian looked at Mitchell quizzically. He knew the man's reputation and was instinctively on his guard. 'Let's hear from you, then,' he said.

'Ian, those boots you made for me are the most comfortable I ever remember owning. They're quite amazing, man.'

'Well, thank you, James. I had a good teacher and take quite a pride in what I do.'

'Not like the army boots you must have had to wear, then?'

'Definitely not like them,' Sanders laughed. 'In fact, I admit I hated those monstrosities, but you're a bit short on choice in the army.'

'Well, I feel sure that once your ability with leather gets more widely known, you're going to be a very busy man,' continued James.

'Lord, we hope so,' Ian replied, wondering just where this conversation was leading. 'Things are a little quiet as yet.'

A feeling of apprehension had lodged itself in Sanders' gut and that feeling was moving, taking over his system.

James leaned forward, rolling his Akubra around between his hands by the brim. 'Right. That's what I'm here for. Would you be interested in setting up on your own in larger premises?'

'I'd be a liar if I said no, James, but we can't think of anything like that just yet.'

'Not even if you had some financial help?' James queried.

'That's just it,' Sanders replied. 'The bank would need some kind of collateral, which we don't have, and nobody knows us yet.'

James put his hat on the chair alongside him and leaned forward to touch Sanders on one shoulder. 'I know you, Ian, and I recognise your skill. I'd like you to think about letting me back you. Naturally I don't expect you to decide straight away, just talk it over with Jessie. I remember your talking about a new style of boot you'd dreamed up, and I liked the idea at the time. After giving it some thought, I like it even more now, and perhaps you should think about producing some to try on the locals. I know Geoff Powers at the paper would give you publicity, and who knows where it could lead? A good strong boot without laces is a wonderful idea.'

Sanders stood up. 'I suppose there'd be very little lost in making a pair or two to try the idea out,' he said as James also rose from his seat.

'Good thinking, Ian,' he said. 'You have a word with your good lady and I'll drop in again in a few days.' He pulled at his trouser leg to display his left boot. 'They really are the goods, you know,' and letting the hem drop, he turned and walked back through the shop to the road.

Sanders stood for a moment, watching the man's retreating back, sucked in his cheek and turned swiftly to walk through to where his wife sat in the room behind the shop.

Feeling a drink coming on, James decided to call on Ray Corcoran down by the river. He walked in just as Corcoran replaced the phone in its cradle, his face ashen, eyes staring straight ahead.

'Sorry, Ray. I've obviously picked the wrong moment to drop in. Bad news?' asked James.

Corcoran jerked back to the present, thoroughly shaken. 'Eh? Oh ... sorry, James, just had a bit of a shock on the phone. Nothing serious.' He forced a sickly smile. *Nothing serious, holy shit!* You're a father, Phyllis had said, and we're coming back to Wellsford next week. Don't be a smart alec and try to leave, or Dad's cronies will get you.

Ray knew who 'Dad's cronies' were. It was only through Phyllis that 'Dad's cronies' hadn't done him permanent damage years ago when he was first trying to muscle in on the wrong side of the law. Phyllis then had no idea about her successful father's business sidelines but had been attracted to Corcoran when he came onto the team. His youthful exuberance had caused him to get a little out of line on a special assignment early in the piece and, completely oblivious to the situation, it was Phyllis whose intervention had stayed her father's hand. So, marrying the infatuated and not unattractive girl was an act of self-preservation more than anything else.

During the first few days of Phyllis's recent visit to Wellsford, things were outwardly fine. They acted almost like a couple of lovebirds, but there was no substance to their arrangement and besides, she expected him to go straight. Now she had had his kid – a daughter. Nothing serious?! Damnation, he was trapped!

'Actually,' he blurted, 'you've come at a very opportune moment, James. I need a drink and I guess you'll join me?'

'You sure? I don't want to intrude ...'

'Never surer,' said Corcoran, pouring two pile-driving Scotches. 'I could use a few laughs.' A few laughs – Jesus! he thought, what a day! *Isn't it bloody ridiculous how often you come up with an idea and just as it's set up and looking good, something comes along to bugger it all up.*

For quite a while now, Ray'd been getting bored with the lack of real activity in the town. His kind of activity. Plenty of money coming in, and all of it black and untraceable, but no excitement. Then out of the blue that morning, he'd had two phone calls. Picked up the phone and a voice he recognised immediately said in his ear, 'Hello, darling. Remember me?' The Pom, of course. Vera, Vera bloody Hogan! His memory had leapt back years. God, she was great in the cot. Just the sound of her voice made the hairs on the back of his neck stand up, and that wasn't all.

They'd been a real item just when he'd been moving into the heavier leagues, but she'd suddenly pissed him off for some high-flying number from overseas. She'd really known how to turn the heat on, not like silly, girly Phyllis gasping and panting and always fishing for compliments every time she came. Lucky he'd always been a smooth liar. But now 'The Pom' was back! Just a few words to clear the air, then she'd said she wanted to get back in tow, wanted to go into business with him! Could she come up and talk about it? Could she? Jesus! From the second he'd hung up the phone, he'd been walking on air, plans absolutely pouring into his head. Then the phone had rung again ...

Ray looked at the empty glass in his hand, suddenly realising that if Mitchell had been talking, he hadn't the faintest idea what about; however, the rich bastard was smiling, so somehow he'd kept some kind of conversation going. Might as well refill and try to come back down to earth. 'Another, James?' he asked.

About an hour later, a red-faced Mitchell, slightly unsteady on his feet, left, allowing Corcoran time to settle his scrambled mind somewhat. The Scotch and the superficial conversation had helped. He thought back about the two phone calls and after weighing up the possibilities decided maybe he could still go ahead with some of the ideas he'd hatched, if he was careful. Just needed some close planning, that's all.

Phyllis had said she was coming up but didn't say when. Now that her old man was really laid low, it mightn't be straight away, so there didn't seem any reason not to look further into whatever business proposition The Pom had in mind. And if The Pom had other more personal things in mind, as he did himself ... well, so much the better.

He reached for the piece of paper where he'd scribbled the phone number, and smiled as he realised what he'd written beside the number: V.H. – Very Hot. Still smiling, he dialled her number.

When word of the school of arts project became known, Robbo was unexpectedly besieged with telephone calls. Before even basic work had begun, he'd had inquiries from townsfolk interested in utilising the hall for meetings of a Red Cross Society, a Country Women's Association, a sewing and knitting circle, the Women's Christian Temperance Union, and for the beginnings of a town band, quite apart from the dancing class and the Police Boys' Club, which were Robbo's original priorities. He'd had a visit from Geoff Powers wanting to know all about it and also telling Robbo that he had a friend involved with the famous touring White Rose Orchestra and maybe they should be engaged for a big event, say an opening ball. The policeman's mind was beginning to boggle at it all. Then one afternoon, young John Mitchell walked into his office and suggested that the feasibility of showing films might also be looked into.

Robbo couldn't stop grinning. The new edifice was going to become the hub of a whole new social life for his community and so far, James Mitchell hadn't been able to grab any of the credit at all.

His reverie was broken by the door opening as Stanley Clarke walked in. 'I've been havin' a wee think aboot it all,' he said. 'If you've got a few minutes to go doon the road, I'll tell y' what I've in mind.'

Liz Collins breezed back into the hotel, still smiling from something Isobel had told her as she was leaving the store, and called to her husband, 'Any excitement while I was gone?!'

'Not really,' he said, rather too casually, she thought, 'but we've another guest. Arrived on the afternoon train.'

Liz dropped her handbag on the bar and walked over to look at the register. 'Is he from Sydney?' she asked.

'It's not a he, it's a she, but yes she is from Sydney.'

Liz noticed that Bazza was avoiding looking at her.

'A looker then, is she?'

Now *he* looked around. 'Why do you ask?'

'C'mon, Bazza. You think I don't know you?' She looked at the register. 'Vera Hogan, a Miss. She's travelling alone, then?'

'Yes. She'll be here for a while. Apparently looking at the possibility of setting up some sort of agency for business friends in the city. She knows Ray Corcoran.'

'Uh-oh,' said Liz, rolling her eyes. 'What sort of agency?'

'How the hell would I know? I hardly spoke to the woman,' Bazza said, almost dropping the glass he was polishing.

Liz looked forward to meeting this 'Vera Hogan' and she didn't have to wait long. She'd hardly replaced her handbag at the back of the counter when the door beside it opened and the new guest came into the bar.

'Ah, you must be Liz,' she said on a wave of perfume, her hand outstretched.

Despite herself, Liz was impressed. A dark complexion, maybe Spanish descent although the accent was pure London; heavy make-up, but not too heavy; dark brown eyes; a full, smiling mouth below a strong, straight nose; a quite lovely, long neck and an hourglass figure with big, firm breasts, a narrow waist and curvy hips. No wonder Bazza had had a shock. Someone like this rarely passed through Wellsford. Well dressed, too.

Liz automatically patted her hair into place before shaking the woman's hand. 'Yes, I'm Liz, and I see from the book that you're Vera Hogan.'

'That's me, dear. I don't know how long I'll be here yet. I'm doing a little scouting for some colleagues in the big smoke. I used to know Ray Corcoran a while back, so as I've never been in the bush before, I decided to start looking around from here. You know Ray, of course?'

'Yes, of course.' Liz smiled, outwardly and inwardly. *Looks great, but if she's a friend of Ray's, we'd better keep our distance.* Bright company though, she thought. *The men'll love this one.* 'Everybody in town knows Ray.'

'That's him all right, everybody's friend. I didn't let him know when

I was due in, so I'd better look him up. Do you know where he might be?'

Following Liz's simple directions, Vera picked her way carefully along the street's rough footpath. It was adequate for boots or sensible shoes but not her fine heels. She'd gone to a bit of trouble to look and smell her best for this reunion. Didn't want to stuff things up again. She knew from the phone calls that he'd got over her earlier dalliance with the Italian, which had been a flop anyway. Just one of those all too familiar situations when a man's financial standing makes him appear more attractive in the short term, so as soon as she'd bled him dry, she'd skipped back to Australia, hoping to patch things up again with Corcoran.

She smiled at his name, as she had lots of times. He was well hung, was Ray, had a bit of a 'Corker-un' and she'd really taught him how to use it. So, if she played her cards right …

She walked into his place without knocking. Ray took one look, sent his chair flying as he stood up and said, 'Holy Christ! You look marvellous!'

Vera relaxed. Got 'im, she thought.

'Decided to just arrive without calling,' she said. 'Too formal in the street. How've you been, Ray?'

He rushed to shut and, she noticed, lock the door behind her, then turned. 'Lemme look at ya … Jesus, I think I could eat ya,' he said, running his eyes over the full body.

'That doesn't sound bad for starters. Aren't you going to give me a kiss?'

'More'n 'at, girl, more'n 'at. We got a whole lot to catch up on.'

He crossed his arms around her from the back, closing a hand over each breast. She kicked off her shoes and stood on his feet.

'Just like old times,' she giggled as he walked her through the doorway from the office.

★ ★ ★

Aha, thought Liz Collins as her observant eye ran over Vera just return-ing to the hotel. *Just a shade dishevelled, it seems*, and she smiled.

'Thanks for your directions, Liz,' said the guest. 'Ray and I have caught up with things now, and my original plans have changed a bit. If it suits you, I'll still stay here, but I'll be in and out quite a bit.'

Suppressing a smirk, Liz said, 'Of course, whatever you like.'

Hell's bells, thought Corcoran, I'm not sure how I'm going to handle this. He'd just hung up the phone after promising to meet the train two days later when Phyllis would be arriving with their daughter Amy. It was going to be a bit of a tightrope act with both women and the little girl all in town at once, but so far, let's face it, things hadn't gone too badly. By altering a few facts slightly, Vera's sudden disappearance had neatly become the reason for his later marriage, so everything might have been fine with Vera, ready to make a new start, but the child made it awkward. He'd never thought of children much, let alone his being a parent, but now it was a fact. And Phyllis had made it quite clear that he was purely a convenience; she disliked him but had nowhere else to turn.

Well, he thought, I'll just have to put on a real good act again until we can sort things out. *At least The Pom's right here and has made several friends already. She'll probably even charm Phyllis! God, I hope I don't hate the kid on sight.*

* * *

Ray fixed a big smile on his face as the train came to a stop, steeling himself for the meeting. The door opened and Phyllis climbed down then turned with outstretched arms to take her child from another passenger. Ray walked forward and pecked Phyllis on the cheek. She didn't react at all, only said coldly, 'This is Amy, your daughter.'

He looked at the tiny girl for the first time. Steeled himself was right. Nothing could have prepared him for this. His whole insides went to jelly. The child had Ray Corcoran stamped all over her face, her eyes, her cheekbones, the cleft chin, the hair colour. He just melted. The girl, his daughter, was gorgeous. His head reeled. Now what the hell was he going to do? It had never once occurred to him that he might feel like this, that he might immediately adore the kid. He'd thought of her as some kind of possible lever in the future if things got rough, but not now.

'Pleased with yourself, aren't you?' Phyllis's voice cut through his euphoria. 'No use trying to tell me she's somebody else's, is it?'

How could I ever have found anything vaguely attractive in this bitch, he thought, and how could she have produced this little beauty? Forcing his smile back into place in case any of the locals were looking, he grated, 'No, it's not.'

'All right, get the bags and let's get out of here,' Phyllis said, and turning, walked away with Amy in her arms.

Carrying the bags, Ray trudged after them, watching the top of the little head as it moved in and out of sight with Phyllis's movements. As he came abreast of Stanley's shop, he had a brainwave. 'Go ahead, I'll catch you up in a minute!' he called.

As he picked up the bags again and hurried towards his home, he couldn't believe what he'd just done. A cot, goddamn it, he'd asked the Scotsman to build him a cot! What the dickens was happening to him?

Vera noticed the difference too, at their next 'business' meeting at her hotel room. The sex was wonderful, but afterwards, Ray was obviously preoccupied. Here's one for the books, she thought. I've had competition before, but never from a toddler! However, when it came to planning the future, she and Ray were meticulous with the arrangements, so she didn't worry too much.

The following afternoon, Ray and Vera were sitting in the general store's tearoom with tea and scones, much to Isobel's amazement, when James Mitchell walked past the window. He saw the couple inside then looked again through the open door as he passed it before walking into the newsagent next door. Corcoran bumped his partner's knee under the table and winked slyly at her. A moment later, Mitchell walked in with a paper under his arm and approached their table.

'Ah, James, how nice to see you,' Ray said cordially.

'Nice to see you too, Ray, particularly in such ravishing company. Perhaps you could introduce us?'

That's right – bite, bite, bite, you bastard, thought Ray. *Bite and I'll reel you in.* 'My apologies, of course,' he said graciously. 'You've not yet met each other. James, this is a long-time friend of mine, Miss Vera Hogan. Vera, this is James Mitchell, one of the town's leading lights.'

Vera beamed and offered her hand, palm downwards. Slightly taken aback, James gently took the hand and leaning forward, kissed it. The perfume made him momentarily giddy, but he managed to say, 'Extremely pleased to meet you, Miss Hogan.'

Vera let her hand linger in Mitchell's for a second or two, gently lowered her eyelashes and breathed, 'Charmed, I'm sure, Mr Mitchell.'

Isobel witnessed this performance from the counter, feeling sure that she saw Corcoran's knee again touch his partner's.

'Do you have time to join us, James? Pull up a chair, my friend.' Raising his voice, Ray called, 'Could we have another pot of tea for James, Isobel?!'

Some time later, as they parted in the street, it had been arranged that James should attend their next business meeting to offer possible advice. At the conclusion of that meeting, James had shown extreme interest not only in the female partner in their project but in possibly becoming a silent partner if their Sydney colleagues agreed. Although the project itself had not been specifically discussed, James could hardly wait for the next meeting by which time, they would have had word from Sydney.

In answer to James's knock a week later, the hotel room's door was opened by Vera who, all smiles, invited him in. He was surprised, on looking around, how delightfully feminine the room was, with just a few touches here and there transforming the atmosphere.

'Ray not here yet?' he asked.

'Unfortunately, James, I hope you don't mind, but Ray's little girl is not well, so he's asked to be excused.'

'Well, everything is very much in its early stages as yet, isn't it? I presume you've heard from Sydney, anyway. Have you?'

'Yes, we have. Sit down and make yourself comfortable, James,' Vera urged, patting the sofa invitingly, 'and I'll bring you a cup of tea. I just had Liz bring in a fresh pot.'

As he sat on the lounge behind an occasional table, Vera picked up a tray from a sideboard and came towards him. As she placed the tray on the table, the neckline of her loose-fitting blouse gaped forward and James let his eyes linger as she poured the tea. Looking up at him from under her eyebrows, without changing her position she cooed, 'Sugar?'

If Vera had at that moment asked him to crawl over broken glass to pick her a flower, he'd have done it – and gladly.

'Er, yes, please, two,' he blurted.

She leaned ever so slightly further forward to add his sugar, then picked up the other cup and stood up. 'I like mine straight,' she said with a wide smile.

James noticed she also had wonderful teeth. *God, what a woman!*

He tried to settle back on the lounge. She kicked off her shoes and folded her legs under herself on the big chair.

'Well, I hope you'll be pleased to know, James, that the people in Sydney can't see any problems, other than maybe a small shortfall in finance, so the next move is for me to return to Sydney to get help in tying up the finer details.'

'Is the help you need financial, Vera? You know I've already offered.'

'That's sweet of you, James, and we do appreciate it, but I also have some other commitments to attend to in the city which I want to clear up and quit. They shouldn't take long.'

James leaned forward slightly. 'Is there any reason why I can't visit you in Sydney?' he asked earnestly. 'I could use a few days away from this place.'

'How lovely, James,' she replied. 'You could stay at my flat, and we can really get to know each other. Let me give you the phone number.'

She unfolded her legs and moved to the sideboard and, taking a fountain pen and a card from her bag, quickly wrote the number. James stood up, looked down to check that his tumescence wasn't obvious and moved over towards her.

She replaced the pen and pad in her bag, picked up the card and, looking at it, swung around to continue the conversation. Walking heavily into James standing behind her, she appeared to lose her balance.

Just as I'd expected, she thought, smiling inwardly. *Hard as a ramrod. This is going to be easy.*

He'd grabbed her shoulders to steady her. 'Thank you, James. You really are very thoughtful,' she said demurely.

Moving away from him, she leant down again to retrieve her shoes, allowing another tantalising glimpse of her cleavage, then went to the door, holding the card out between her first and second fingers. As James took the card, she took his hand gently and, looking right into his eyes, purred, 'Call me as soon as you can.'

'I certainly will, Vera,' he almost croaked, then as she still held onto his hand, he leant down and lightly kissed her.

A moment later, he was out in the passageway, trying to get himself together. He'd hardly touched her lips but could still feel the tip of her tongue as it slipped into his mouth, slid along his inner lip then retracted. He hoped breathing deeply might help, but it didn't. The drumming in his chest and the aching in the lower part of his body refused to subside. God, he thought, I hope there's nobody I know in the bar.

He was lucky, and with a cheery wave to Liz at the far end of the room, he left.

The next few weeks were a continuing torment for James. Vera had returned to the city and progress reports were coming in through Ray Corcoran at infrequent intervals, each one adding to the pressure on James's patience. It was lucky for him that young John had adapted so quickly to managing the station, but he was having trouble with council meetings and business dealings as his concentration was badly scrambled. The one thing that was clear in his mind was that as soon as the call came, he was off to Sydney.

Late one afternoon, James was at the homestead having a cup of tea with John when Pearl came to the table on the verandah to collect the cups. She stepped back a pace and stood, not wanting to interrupt the conversation. After a moment, John looked at her and said, 'Is there something you want, Pearl?'

'Yes, there is,' she replied. 'I'd like to ask a favour of Mr James, if that's all right.'

The senior Mitchell swung around to look at her but said nothing.

'Mr James,' Pearl said, 'before you go back to town, could you spare a minute or two to talk to Albert, please?'

'Albert?' James looked at her, surprised. 'Well, we're about finished here, so yes, of course. What's Albert want of me?'

'That's a favour, too, Mr James, but I'd better let him ask you.'

James stood up. 'Righto,' he said. 'Let's see what this is all about.'

As James walked past, Pearl slid a smile and a sly wink at John, still sitting at the table.

An hour later, James was talking to Robbo back in Wellsford.

'Well, the question came as such a surprise that I thought I'd better check with you. Is it still legal for a station owner to perform a marriage ceremony?'

'For two of your station hands, it is, James. Never been rescinded, to my knowledge.'

'Seems ridiculous. I've known the two of them all their lives but never thought I'd be asked to marry them. Still, since that ponce of a priest was recalled, there's nobody else to do the job, is there?'

'Not without sending for someone, and you know what they're like. Probably won't have too much interest in a long trip for a pair of farmhands.'

'Albert and Faith are a lot more than that, Robbo,' James said, bristling slightly.

'You know it and I know it, James, but outside this town, and to a small extent even inside it, that's pretty much the thinking.'

'Yes,' said James thoughtfully, 'I suppose you're right. Ah well, I'd better drive on and pass on the glad news. See you later, Robbo.' He paused by the door. 'Albert and Faith,' he said, shaking his head. 'I'll be damned.'

Sydneyside

'Vera, it's James. I left the car with John and came by train. Are you far from the station? I'm dying to see you.'

The woman at the other end of the phone ran the long fingers of her free hand through the amber beads she was wearing, twisting the beads around her wrist.

'How wonderful! It's so good to hear your voice, James. I'm in East Sydney, so it's not far from the station. I'll give you the address and you can take a taxi. Please don't be put off by the exterior of the place; this isn't the most salubrious part of the city,' she laughed, 'but it's lovely inside. You'll have to identify yourself with the doorman as my flat is above the business premises, but I'll fix all that and he'll show you the way up. Just give me a few minutes to tidy up?'

In the taxi, James undid the top button of his shirt collar, his excitement steadily mounting, but it was fortunate that Vera had given him some warning as his first impression of the Palmer Street address was one of shock. The exterior was grey on grey, dirty and not vaguely inviting. In fact, James double-checked the street number with what he'd scrawled on the back of his train ticket.

He paid the cabbie, crossed the pavement and used the shabby knocker to tap the door. To his surprise, a small panel below the high doorknocker slid back and a man's eyes appeared. 'Name?' a hoarse voice demanded.

'Mitchell. I'm expected by Miss Hogan.'

The panel slid closed, and after the sound of bolts being released, the door opened. The bullet-headed, bulky owner of the shifty eyes waved him inside then relocked the door behind him. 'Sorry, sir,' he rasped, 'but we have to be a bit careful early in the day. Never know who's knockin'. This way, please.'

James looked quickly around. Vera was right; it was totally different inside. He seemed to be in a nicely appointed vestibule – heavy curtains, potted plants, thick-piled carpet, a plush desk, one or two large armchairs and an open fireplace with a marble hearth and mantelpiece.

His guide, unsmiling, unlocked another door near the entrance and stood back for James to pass through. As the door clicked to behind him, he found himself in a short, carpeted passageway leading to a staircase, again very ornately presented with a carved balustrade and another potted plant and a lustre lamp at the head of the stairs where it led to another short passageway, ending at a closed door.

Taking a deep breath, James knocked. As the door opened, all the weeks of waiting were immediately forgotten. Smiling sweetly, Vera said, 'James, dear, do come in,' but he could hardly move.

'Let me have a moment to look at you,' he said, almost gasping. 'You look absolutely stunning.'

'Why, thank you,' she said, dropping her eyelashes slightly. Her dark skin was offset beautifully with a pale cream, silk-belted house gown with matching feather trim in one continuous line around its edging from neck to floor and back. The material clung to her full figure and with the wonderfully decorated room's low lights behind her, the effect was electric. James smelt the exotic perfume and as she moved slightly, he noticed she also wore slippers to match the gown.

She didn't look up until he finally moved into the room and put his bag on the floor. Vera closed the door gently then came to him, sliding her arms up and around his neck. 'It's been too, too long to wait,' she breathed, and James's world exploded as she kissed him, gently at first, then as if her life depended upon it. Little did James know that perhaps it did.

James couldn't believe that this kind of happiness was obtainable.

As he hugged her, the feel of her body warmth sent surges of energies through him. Into his ear, she purred, 'I hope you're not too tired from the trip.'

'If I felt any better, I couldn't stand it,' he said.

Vera giggled lusciously, and as they parted, she said, 'That's good, because although the old adage reads "business before pleasure", on this occasion I know we'll feel lots better if we reverse that.'

She tugged at the loosely knotted belt, wriggled her shoulders and stood looking right into James's eyes. She was wearing the slippers. Nothing else. There was no doubt about it; Vera knew how to make a man feel good. Any man. She had certainly perfected the art and as she slid across the large double bed, she felt well pleased with herself. Her plan was working beautifully. Just a little more of this masquerade and she and Ray would have the money.

James reached over and touched her hand. He knew he had fallen for the woman. It was a long time since he had been with someone who understood him so well, someone who shared not only his sexual appetite but also his ideas for success.

'I suppose we'd better have a look at this business plan of yours?' he said, gently slapping her on the bottom.

She took his hand and held it to her face. 'Only if you really feel like it,' she said.

He got up and walked over to the table. 'What sort of business is it going to be?' he asked.

She sat up, pulling the satin sheets around herself. 'Well,' she said quietly, 'you probably know that I have a couple of girls working for me here – high-class girls.'

'What, pros?' he asked. 'You run some pros?' The thought hadn't occurred to him.

'James, darling,' she cooed, 'a girl has to survive. It's not easy in a city without some kind of support. I do what I have to do, even though I hate it,' she pouted.

'But surely you couldn't have set up all this opulence?' He waved an arm around the room.

'That's just it. I'm sick to death of doing all this for someone else.'

He nodded, walking back to sit beside her. 'Well, what do you have in mind for Wellsford. Not pros, surely?'

Vera laughed. 'Good God, no. Well, not exactly. What I feel Wellsford needs is some kind of gentlemen's club. A place where men can go and play bridge or cards, have a drink or meet up with talented people. Something really high-class. Ray and I have been looking at a big old house on Henry Street which could be perfect. We'd need to completely refurbish the inside, of course. Similar to this place.'

In spite of his inner rumblings, he was interested. He knew the house well. Wellsford was coming alive; why not give it a touch of class, something with a bit more sophistication than Robbo's school of arts?

Vera traced one long middle finger down his cheek. 'Well, what do you think?' she asked.

James knew that a brothel was illegal, but a club certainly wasn't. He also knew that the town was indeed growing and men were men; he'd seen them lining up at Corcoran's. If Vera's plan was handled discreetly, it would certainly make money.

'Do you know how much you'd need?' he asked.

She swung her legs out the side of the bed and sat with her back to him. 'Quite a lot,' she said quietly. 'We can start pretty soon with just one or two girls in part of the barn that we'll renovate, but then we'll need a lot of money to fix up the other property to eventually house the club. And then we'll have to be able to make the alterations and set up quickly without cutting my colleagues here into the project. This introduces some risk as they won't like my going, but I've found a way to handle that.'

James trailed one finger down her spine. 'All right,' he said, 'count me in, but not by name. I can draw on my Sydney account, so nobody in Wellsford need know I'm involved. Tell me how much you need and let's get started. I just want you in Wellsford, and as soon as possible.'

Vera hid her excitement behind a face that filled with false affection as she turned to him. 'You're a darling. Now, just sit there and I'll bring warm water and a cloth and give you a wash-up.'

James lay back on the bed. God, here was a woman to make a man feel a man, he thought, the idea of the coming wash raising his excitement. And she's a businesswoman as well. So what if the project were a little to the left of legal? Profit would pour into his coffers once she had it set up.

He lay back and let the deft fingers and the warm washcloth smooth away any misgivings.

'Perhaps we could go somewhere quiet for a meal and I'll show you the figures I've been working on,' she said. 'Then we can come back here and cement the relationship.'

'Sounds wonderful,' he groaned.

Vera poured two whiskies, handing one to James as he sat up.

'To the Wellsford Gentlemen's Club,' she said, linking her glass-holding arm through his, making sure she held his gaze as they drank, smiling triumphantly as the glasses clinked.

★ ★ ★

'Ar there, Ray, everything going all right?'

Corcoran had seen Robbo coming down the footpath, and put on a broad smile. I'll just have to brazen it out, he thought. *He may be a country copper, but he's not stupid.*

'Yes, Robbo, very nicely,' he said, slowing to a stop.

'See you've got some alterations going on down there. Must be getting pretty posh, eh?'

'Yeah, well, I really like Wellsford, but from time to time I miss the city, so I thought if I dressed things up a bit, like the old stamping grounds, I'd feel even more at home. Bit tough on the pocket, though,' he said, laughing.

'I'll have to come round and have a look, Ray. It sounds interesting.'

'Sure, why not? The place is full of tradesmen at present. We're right in the middle of things, so give us a couple of weeks then come on round.'

'Thanks, Ray. That sounds good. See you then if not before,' said the policeman, and walked on. Got to hand it to him, he thought, he's got a steady nerve. *Probably thinks because I haven't come down on him so far, I'm either stupid or blind. Wrong, Ray, me boy. Quite wrong!*

The reason Robbo was so far keeping his distance was that he didn't want to put his friends in the town into compromising situations. He knew very well what was happening and to whom, but until things went too far, he kept watch and waited. But it was obviously now coming to a head. Some out-of-town tradesmen were working on the back barn and Robbo smelt trouble ahead. Corcoran might have been using the profit he'd collected recently to finance all this, but now it was getting much more costly, so somebody else must be involved. Unlikely to be city money. Not enough profit in it.

Robbo walked into the hotel. 'Ar there, Bazza, you got a minute for a chat?'

'Sure, Robbo, come on through. Back in a tick, Liz.'

The policeman waved to Liz as he followed her husband.

Sitting at the kitchen table, Bazza said, 'Now, what's on?'

'Well, you're probably wondering why I haven't done anything about our mate down the road although it's obvious things aren't exactly straight. I won't mention how he trapped you into silence, though I know.'

Bazza closed his eyes for a moment then reopened them. The policeman continued talking.

'What's on my mind is that the clever beggar's doing the same thing to others in town, and I don't want anyone badly burned, know what I mean?'

Bazza nodded and made a face. 'Why are you telling me this?' he asked.

'Because I need a little help, that's why. Something's on and I haven't been able to nail it down yet, but there's a lot of money going into that place and it's coming from somewhere. I'm just thinking it may be on loan from some of our citizens, so can I ask you to keep an ear open for me, Bazza? If you get a whisper about investments in the bar, will you let me know?'

'Frankly, Robbo, I'd be pleased to. He's a cunning mongrel, and he's cut into our turnover, of course. Liz doesn't need to know about this, does she?'

'Course not. That's your business.' Standing, he shook Bazza's hand and headed for the street.

Some days later, Robbo was sitting at his desk, trying to put his finger on the missing link to this puzzle. Since his recent conversation with Corcoran, the tradesmen had packed and left, which was all right. What was not so good was that one evening while walking Blackie, Robbo had, from quite a distance, seen a car arrive at the establishment, dropping off two young women. The driver had taken their luggage inside then left.

Alarm bells had rung in his head immediately. Damn, he'd thought, now it's gone too far. But no information to speak of had come from the pub, so either Corcoran had cleverly conned several of his customers into investing, or else … James? Surely not. James had certainly worked some nice business deals for himself in Wellsford, but not in anything shady. Yet there was nobody else, so how could he have got James involved?

The woman, he thought, that's it. *Vera Hogan, Ray's 'friend'. Bet she's got Mitchell by the short and curlies. Maybe I'd just better take a run out to the station tomorrow.*

★ ★ ★

Robbo's car came to a stop near one of the big mustering yards up near the road as he saw Charlie and John with some other men working some cattle. John waved to him and a moment later rode over to the car as Robbo stepped out.

'Hello there, Robbo. What brings you out here?'

''Ar there, John. I hoped I might catch your father at home, for a chat.'

'Sorry, mate, you're out of luck. Dad went to Sydney on business just this morning. Went by train.'

'Don't suppose you happen to know where he's staying, do you?'

'No, Robbo, he didn't say. He'll be back in a couple of days though.'

'Righto, John. It can wait. See you later.'

★ ★ ★

Totally exhausted, James lay back in Vera's bed. Great God, the woman's insatiable, he thought languidly. *We'll be able to do this forever!*

This time, she had met him at the station, and from the moment they'd entered the flat, it was on. Right through the night until now, late morning, they had almost continuously been making love.

He closed his eyes for a second and when he opened them again, Vera was standing beside the bed with a tray. 'Breakfast, sleepyhead,' she beamed at him as he struggled to sit up. 'Got to keep your strength up, you know. Today is the start of a whole new world.'

While he sipped his tea, she said, 'I've been speaking to Ray and he told me that thanks to you, the place looks great and business is booming.' She moved the tray, then knelt on the bed across James's lap. 'Aren't you excited, James? Isn't it wonderful?'

It certainly is, he thought, and with you kneeling like that, I certainly am. *But not about the business.* 'Yes,' he answered lamely, 'of course.'

'He's been able to borrow some extra money from a few regulars, so nobody has the faintest idea that you've been in any way involved. And everything is set to begin working at the club, so as soon as you're ready, darling, we're really in business.'

'Let's do it today, then.' James grinned at her. She took his cup and put it on the side table.

'Wonderful,' she beamed, falling forward onto him.

Later that afternoon, after a visit to the bank, James reluctantly caught the country train.

'I'll be up next week, darling,' Vera cooed. 'Can't wait.'

Once back in her flat, she reached for the telephone and dialled. 'We leave here Tuesday,' she said. She felt Corcoran's hesitation. 'What the hell is it?' she asked.

'Can't get down on Tuesday; it's Amy's birthday,' he said. 'Make it Wednesday.'

The deal was set.

★ ★ ★

Isobel Craig tied the string firmly around the brown paper parcel and handed it across the counter. 'How old is she today?' she asked Corcoran.

'She's two,' he said, 'two years old,' shaking his head.

Isobel had noticed how animated Ray became when talking about his young daughter, the beautiful child with the serious face. 'She'll be thrilled to have this doll, then,' she said. 'It's a beautiful doll. The celluloid face makes it look so real, and the blonde curls ...'

Ray smiled, not listening. His mind was racing. He picked up the parcel and left the shop. God, he wasn't looking forward to the rest of today. He knew Phyllis was going to hit the roof when he told her. And he couldn't tell her till the last minute; he didn't want anyone else in the town knowing until long after he had left. Well, he had tried, hadn't he? Tried to keep up appearances and make a go of it for the kid's sake, but it didn't work, couldn't work. And he knew that once he dropped the bombshell, access to his daughter was finished. Phyllis would do everything in her power to prevent him ever seeing the one person who meant the world to him. Until Vera had come back into his life, that is.

He turned the corner and walked along the street towards the house, hesitated for a moment outside the gate, then purposefully strode up the path and walked in the front door.

There was at least one person who considered that day to be touched by magic – Amy. Unaffected by the goings-on around her, Amy sat on a stool by the wood stove, completely absorbed in her new doll. Her parents' ranting and raving went unnoticed; she'd heard it often before. She shut the noise out with the joy she'd unwrapped with her birthday gift. Only when her mother picked up a blue Wedgwood plate and hurled it at the wall did the child's loving concentration falter. She glanced quickly away from the doll, long enough to see her father's back moving down the hall and out the front door.

★ ★ ★

A forlorn James sat across the desk from Robbo in the police station, unable to believe his ears. 'When did they go?' he asked quietly.

'Yesterday,' Robbo replied gently. 'They must have been setting it up for months. The day before, Tuesday, his daughter's birthday, he took her a present then told his wife and cleared out. Left quite a few debts around the town as well. Hope he didn't owe you any money?'

James felt the perspiration standing out on his forehead. The enormity of the situation had hit him. 'A little,' he answered, 'nothing too drastic. A few quid, that's all.'

The policeman stood up. 'Just thought I'd let you know in case you'd got lumbered,' he said.

'No, no,' replied James, 'only a few quid, a bottle or two here or there.'

Robbo nodded, noticing the perspiration on his friend's forehead. 'What happens now?' he asked the policeman.

Robbo stood up and walked around the room, hands clasped behind his back.

'Well, as I see it,' he began, clearing his throat, 'nothing criminal has actually taken place.' He stopped walking and turned to face his visitor. 'Well, when you look at it, the house of ill repute never actually got up and running, did it? He only had a couple of girls there for a very short time, didn't he?'

James nodded, running his hand over the emerging stubble on his chin. 'Will anyone be charged?'

Robbo sucked in his cheek. 'Well, like I said, nothing really got going, and I have no evidence of anyone staking Corcoran and Vera to establish any kind of shady business ...'

James closed his eyes and breathed in deeply. He had been totally taken in by Vera Hogan. Christ, he was hopeless when it came to women. Couldn't pick 'em at all. He looked at Robbo. 'No fool like an old fool, eh?'

Robbo sighed. 'Bit of a hard lesson, I reckon,' he said. 'If anyone did stake them, I'd say they've kissed their cash goodbye.'

James nodded. He'd always felt there was something fishy about Corcoran, but once his wife and kid arrived back in town, he'd thought maybe he would settle down, enjoy the town. *He and Vera Hogan must have had this all set up, right from the beginning. Smooth-talking bastards.* He stood and extended his hand to Robbo. 'What happens now?'

'Nothing. It's best that nothing happens. You say nothing, do nothing and if anyone asks, stay mum. Anyone who put money into this has lost. They don't have to wear a hair shirt as well.'

James nodded and walked to the door. He turned and looked at the policeman. 'Thanks, Robbo,' he said sheepishly. 'Thanks.'

Stumbling out, James made his way back to Wellsford Station. He ran from the car over the front verandah and into his bedroom where he changed into riding trousers and boots.

'Charlie!' he shouted from the front verandah in a voice to waken the dead. 'Charlie, for Christ's sake! Charlie, saddle up!'

In the kitchen, Pearl bit her lip. She had watched her master storm back into the house and now heard him bellowing for his horse. It brought back memories she would rather not think about. She had only seen this kind of behaviour once before. Years ago. The morning they found Mary's body down by the creek.

Dance partners

'**T**urn to your left a bit,' Belle Wills instructed through a mouthful of pins. 'I'm about halfway now.'

Standing in the unfinished dress on the kitchen table in the residence atop the bank, Elizabeth dutifully obliged. Her mother had spent days making the aqua dress and now patiently measured and pinned the hem.

'That's it,' Belle said brightly. 'You can get down now.'

The girl hurried to her bedroom to look in the mirror and check her mother's handiwork. She turned and glanced over her shoulder to look at the back of the dress and patted the layers of tulle on the skirt. 'It's really lovely,' she said to Belle, now standing in the doorway.

'Give it here, then,' her mother laughed. 'You can't wear it with an unfinished hem.'

Elizabeth slipped out of the dress, handed it to her mother and pulled on her cord skirt and twin-set. She felt a warm glow inside, a glow she thought must be clearly visible to the entire township, and all because of what John Mitchell had said to her this last week.

She leaned forward and studied her face in the bedroom's mirror, then stood back and surveyed her reflection. Not much to look at, she thought. She had always considered herself to be a plain Jane without any particular talents. If she could have viewed herself through eyes other than her own, she might have seen something quite different. A pale face that smiled quickly, surrounded by fine blonde hair that misbehaved irritatingly for its owner but captivatingly for others. Ever since her family had moved to Wellsford and the country, Elizabeth had felt inadequate except, that is, in her own herb garden.

'I grow things to try and make medicines,' she had told John Mitchell one afternoon after the dance class at the Wellsford School of Arts. The two of them had met at the classes three months earlier when they'd both attended, feeling they had tree trunks for legs. After being pushed by Isobel Craig into partnering the shy Elizabeth, John found dancing to be one of life's great pleasures and gradually built a friendship with the girl.

'Makes sense to use natural medicines,' he'd said to her. 'Pearl does that. She's the main housekeeper out at the station. She always cures sniffles and sneezes with some mixture or other she's either grown or picked from the bush. I remember once when I had a sore throat that felt like I'd swallowed razorblades, she put me to bed with this mushed up compress of green cabbage tied to my throat with a bit of old cloth.'

Elizabeth had been fascinated. She had never, ever heard of cabbage curing anything. 'Just simple green cabbage?' she'd questioned.

'Yup. Well, I think so,' John had replied. 'And the next day, she took that cabbage and the rag it was wrapped in and burned them, and my sore throat had gone.'

Elizabeth resolved to try the remedy on anyone who might mention the merest suggestion of a sore throat.

'Burned every bit of it,' John had continued. 'She said the cabbage had taken on my sore throat and it had to be destroyed. Quite often she used to cure Albert and Faith too. Albert told me once that she healed welts on his leg just by singing.'

Elizabeth had stopped walking, her face serious. 'How did he get welts on his legs?' she asked.

John had been embarrassed. He'd cleared his throat and pulled one side of his cheek. 'Beats me,' he'd said softly, knowing full well that the welts were raised by his mother in one of her drunken raves. 'Singing and vinegar,' he'd said, not wanting to discuss the matter in too fine a detail. 'That's what Pearl says.'

'Just like Jack and Jill?' Elizabeth had questioned, laughing. 'Wasn't it Jack who fell down and broke his crown and they fixed him up with vinegar and brown paper?'

John had looked at her for a moment and that's when he'd said it.

'I feel really good when I'm with you,' he'd said, and he had covered her hand with his.

The words still rang in her ears. She had found herself saying them over and over. 'I feel really good when I'm with you.' It was more than she could have dreamed of. And now he was keen to teach her to ride a horse, even though the mere thought filled her with panic. But learn to ride she would. Anything he wanted her to do, she would try to do. After all, he was the son of James Mitchell, the man her father said had an iron will and a snap-shut business mind. His mother was away with the fairies – everyone knew that. But he felt really good with her.

She hugged herself as she thought of the upcoming Wellsford Ball, the new aqua dress she would wear and the young man who felt really good with her who would partner her. Now she herself felt really good. Really good indeed.

The night was a huge success. People came from everywhere, some from well outside the district. Everybody in town had pitched in and decorated the hall's interior with balloons and homemade streamers. Thanks to Stanley's skill, the floor was like a shining sea of honey, there were lights and flowers everywhere and the famous White Rose Orchestra was on stage. Several of the menfolk present smiled knowingly at each other, nodding towards the centrepiece of the hall, the suspended ball of mirrors turning slowly to flash lights around the ballroom, something they'd last seen in the foyer of Corcoran's barn.

Festivities were interrupted at about ten o'clock for a few speeches and announcements, followed by a copious supper provided by the Ladies' Auxiliary.

James Mitchell was in his element, surrounded by crowds of people, almost all of whom he knew personally. His fury had at last subsided and for the first time in weeks, he was able to enjoy himself. After the speeches, he sought out and quickly found Robbo.

'The man of the moment!' he exclaimed, clapping the policeman on the shoulder. 'What a great evening! You must be very proud of yourself. You certainly should be!'

'Thanks, James,' Robbo answered. 'I have to admit I'm a bit overwhelmed by it all leading to this although, of course, a whole lot of people were involved, not just me, by a long shot. Anyway, you should also be very proud, James.'

'Oh?' said Mitchell, surprised. 'Why is that?'

'Lord, man, you've got to have noticed! Every female tongue in the hall has been wagging. They're the best couple in the place by far!'

'Who are? What are you on about, Robbo?!'

'God, man, you've got to give the turps away; you're going blind! Young Elizabeth Wills and John, that's who! They dance like they were made for each other. None of the others come close. Take a look, man!'

James swung around just in time to see his son waltz by, the boy's eyes glued to the beaming face of his young partner. What had happened to the mousy, shy girl he'd seen in the bank? It had to be the same person, but in that frock and with the look of sheer delight radiating from her, she looked totally different. The policeman was right; they did look great together.

'Damn, Robbo, I must be getting old,' he laughed. 'Come and have another drink.'

At the temporary bar, Isobel was dispensing drinks.

'What's this, then? Where's your licence?' said Robbo, smiling widely.

'Oh, I've just taken over to let Liz and Bazza have a dance together,' she giggled. 'It's probably been years!'

Nearby, a small group of people stood around Stanley Clarke

and his wife, apparently urging him on. Looking at Maggie, the carpenter said, 'Ye didn'ae need to tell them that, woman,' but Maggie, her cheeks rosier than usual after a glass or two of fruit punch, just pulled at his arm, saying, 'Please, Stanley, please. They'd love it, and so would I.'

'Oh, all right,' Stanley said, smiling. 'Just bide a wee, I'll be back,' and he left the hall while the music and conversation steadily gained in volume.

Soon the Scotsman was back, carrying a beautifully-tooled wooden case with a single handle on its lid. Placing the case gently on the floor, he unsnapped the two clasps and opened the lid. Maggie's eyes shone. The crowd of bystanders gasped and a few whooped with delight as Stanley lifted out his beloved bagpipes. He'd not touched them since playing a pibroch on the boat's deck as he and Maggie had said goodbye to Scotland receding in the distance. Quickly and as neatly as always, he dismantled the pipes to lick the reeds on the drones, then reassembled them and stood up.

'Ye'll hae t' bear wi' me a wee,' he said. 'It's been a wee while, ye ken.' Then, as the White Rose members took a well-earned rest, he placed the stem in his mouth, puffed a couple of times to inflate the tartan bag, slipped it under his left arm and pressed in with his elbow. An unmistakeable skirl sounded around the hall, changing from one sound to a series as Stanley flicked his fingers at each open end of the pipes to activate the reeds.

By now the atmosphere in the hall was electric, and when the carpenter shifted his fingers to the chanter, and as the melody of *Scotland the Brave* began, the cheering was deafening.

Stanley began to beat his right foot with the music and in moments, everybody was either clapping or stamping their feet in time. Maggie was ecstatic, the tears streaming down her smiling face. Suddenly, up went her hands above her head and up on her left toe, she began twirling, her right foot alternately touching her calf then flicking outwards with the now-pounding beats. The guests spread out to give her room and the Clarkes took over.

The pandemonium finally settled down, and after several more brackets of songs from the White Rose repertoire, and finally *God Save the King*, the memorable evening drew to a close.

As he stood enjoying a last drink with his friends, James grinned to himself. Imagine, he thought, a hugely successful night like this and I've been upstaged not once but three times. First by a policeman fixing the venue and setting it all up, then by a Scottish carpenter reducing half the hall to tears with his bagpipes and finally by my own son who, with his partner, held everyone's eyes on the dance floor. Well, it has certainly put a few things back on an even keel.

He drained his glass, bade everybody goodnight and headed for his car, still grinning.

★ ★ ★

'Thanks for coming in, James.' Brian Wills came around his desk to shake Mitchell's hand.

'It's always a pleasure, Brian, but from your tone of voice on the phone, I feel there's a pep talk coming up. Either that or you want to stop the wedding?' James was irritated but hoped his tone of voice belied his feelings.

'Nothing could be further from the truth than that, James. Just looking at John and Elizabeth makes you feel young again, doesn't it? But as for the other part, I don't think you'd appreciate any pep talk from me; it's more just a chat. There are some nasty-sounding developments overseas that I want you to know about.'

Wills waved James to a chair and resumed his place behind the desk.

'Now it's part of my job as banker,' he began, flexing his fingers till they cracked, 'to keep abreast of the current situation regarding the accounts of our larger clients – you know that.'

'Of course.'

'You also know that yours is obviously our largest account. Now, naturally I've watched the changes you've been making recently, James, and I'm all for them; however, I am worried about the scale of investments you have been undertaking in the cities. Perhaps, though, it's better than pushing Wellsford to bursting point.'

The two men nodded knowingly towards each other, neither revealing their inner thoughts.

'This town is getting on a nice even keel, developing a real country personality, but there are rumblings in the city news on the investment front that are a real worry. If this developing crisis overseas comes to a head – and it could, James, it could – it's entirely possible that the business world could actually collapse. And that's the world, not just America or Europe. If it goes, we'll feel it here in Australia too.'

James scuffed at a spot on the Axminster carpet. 'Good grief, Brian, do you seriously think that could happen?'

'Naturally, like everybody else in this business, I sincerely hope not, but things are definitely teetering, so I felt obliged to pass you on a gentle warning.'

'Thank you, my friend,' said James genially, rising to his feet. 'I'll certainly give things some serious thought.'

As he moved down the street away from the bank, James grimaced to himself. Why is it, he thought, that so many men connected with banking are such doom-and-gloom merchants? *Sure, I pulled my local horns in a bit after that shambles with Corcoran, but for a country banker to know more than my Sydney investment brokers? I think not, Brian, but thanks anyway.*

He headed for the hotel, to pay a social call on Liz and Bazza.

* * *

In the late afternoon sun, John levered off his boots on the edge of the verandah and flopped into a chair. Thank God that's done; bitch of a job, he thought, taking off his hat and dropping it beside him.

The screen door beside him opened squeakily and Elizabeth came through, carrying a tray with a bottle and two champagne glasses on it.

'Hello, hello?' John said, his eyebrows arched. 'What's this? Have we won Tatts or something?'

She put the tray down, then dropped to her knees beside him, grasping his hands. 'It's definite, John, I got the results back today. We're going to have a baby.' Looking a picture of health and happiness, she radiated delight.

'Quick, open the bottle. We've got to celebrate!'

John jumped to his feet, lifted his wife into his arms, hugged and kissed her. 'Wonderful,' was all he could think of to say. 'Wonderful! Who else knows?'

'No one, John. I've been so excited, I wanted to tell everyone, but I kept quiet because I wanted you to be the first to know. Oh, except Pearl. I didn't even have to say anything to her!'

John laughed with her. 'That'd be right, for sure,' he said, reaching for the bottle. 'Let me look at you,' he said, standing back a little. 'No, don't put the glass down; I just want to remember this moment. Dash it, girl, your eyes are sparkling more than the champagne!' And they both laughed.

'Are you really pleased?' she inquired.

'If I were any more pleased, I might explode,' he answered. 'Just a minute ago, I dropped into that chair exhausted. Now I feel I could run a four-minute mile!'

They clinked the glasses and sipped the bubbling liquid, looking deep into each other's eyes.

'Dammit, Elizabeth, we've only been married just on three months!

It's lucky you made me behave myself until the big day. Seems we're pretty well suited.'

'Yes it does, doesn't it?' she giggled as John put down his drink and hugged her again.

'Are the folks home?' he asked.

'Your mother's lying in her room, and your father hasn't come in yet.'

'Good. Let's just keep this to ourselves for at least a few minutes. Somehow it won't sink in.'

'You think you've got troubles. I'm alternately delighted then terrified. But imagine having our own child!'

John suddenly let go of her and, running across the wide verandah, lashed out and kicked his hat flying, then spun around twice with his arms held wide while his radiant wife beamed at him.

Pearl went about her morning chores, her face displaying a wide smile which would not go away. It really appealed to her sense of humour that just as Faith started suffering from morning sickness, so did Miss Elizabeth, almost to the day. So, we got a race on our hands, she thought, and then a double celebration. She rattled the breakfast dishes in the sink and hummed to herself, unable to care at all about the double load she was carrying for a while. The thought of the dopey looks on both men's faces was enough to set her off in another fit of giggling, and she leant against the benchtop.

Faith came into the kitchen, looking decidedly wan, and took a tea towel from the rack, but before she'd walked to the sink bench; Pearl, all smiles, gently took it from her and said, 'Listen, girl. I said I was all right by myself and I am. Now, for Gawd's sakes, go and rest till you feel better.'

Faith stood still for a moment, then without changing her expression gave Pearl a kiss on the cheek and slowly moved out of the room.

Still smiling, Pearl watched her go. You think this is rough, she thought, wait till the other end of this cycle! Never mind, girl, I'll be there to help. In fact, I can hardly wait! The grin got wider.

Birth song

There was something about the way she walked that made her appear taller than she was, almost as if her slender, straight legs moved from her shoulders through her slim hips and continued in an unbroken fluidity down to the ankles. Her thick, prematurely white hair, tied back with a piece of twine, revealed an open face that had lined early, a face that metamorphosed when she smiled, lit from inside, revealing a glow from an ancient source otherwise hidden deep within. There was a swing to her gait, a kind of timelessness about her as if one hip moved in tandem with a sound only she heard, some forgotten music perhaps, its essence carried on the wind.

She stopped for a moment, looking down at the Wellsford River, one hand shielding her eyes, the other on her waist. She particularly liked the river, especially at this time of the year when the banks were lined with flowering gums.

'The bush honey'll be good this year.' She thought nothing strange about directing the remark to a bee which, undeterred, continued moving from flower to flower collecting the season's gold.

Crazy damn shoes, Pearl thought to herself. *Crazy damn laces and besides that, they're a full size too big.* Ugly Wellsford Station hand-me-downs, shabby now, but put in a rag-bag and given to Pearl who was thankful enough for most of it, most of the time. It was just that poor Mrs Mitchell didn't even know that she was doing these things any more. Pearl knew perfectly well that it wasn't generosity; there was an ulterior motive which she'd soon discovered. The woman never spoke to the help, so why did these parcels of junk start being handed over? Pearl would smile gratefully in case there was something useful among it. God knows they never got anything any other way. But usually most of it went in the dustbins.

She stopped and put down the cane basket she was carrying. Its handle had become so old and worn that Albert had found a piece of string and whipped it for her, making it nearly good as new. She slipped off the left shoe and looked at her heel. 'Got a blister the size of a shilling,' she mumbled. She took off the other shoe and put the pair on the basket on top of the old sheets her mistress had given her.

'Been turned once,' she had been told. 'Not too much in them now. Take them if you want.' She knew they had been turned, all right; she and Faith had turned them. 'Fold the sides in to the middle, sew them together so there is more thickness to take the weight of the person in the bed, then cut them down the worn section and hem the sides.' She knew all about turning. First thing she and the girls had learned with those damned sewing machines at the institution. 'Does your mother have a sewing machine? Well, this is the way she works it ...'

She remembered the game the girls had played, kneeing each other in the rear end, mocking the sewing machine's treadle. One of the first things she had done after they'd arrived at the station was fix shirt collars, worn out on one side and then turned until they were worn through on the other. Thin, real thin, shoot peas through 'em and only when they reached that stage were they considered right for roustabout necks.

Very early on, Pearl had recognised the sign of something mean in Hilda Mitchell's face. A shadow of it showed itself sometimes. Pearl couldn't quite put her finger on just what it was. Oh, she would load them up with things she didn't want or had finished with, but there was something hidden in her. Like part of her face had a closed door that no one would ever open or find what lay behind. Pearl had been working in the big house for well over twenty years now, and in all those years, Hilda Mitchell had never revealed what lay behind her closed-door face. Her only child, John, could have the same look occasionally, but she'd had the feeling with the boy from the start that life would turn him around, and it had. He would never be the hopeless case his mother had turned into; there was a kindness underneath with him. Pearl turned up her foot and studied the water-filled blister on her heel.

'Miserable buggers, the older ones,' she said to herself. 'All the money in the world, a great big house, all that land, and they still want more.' She wondered about the new Mitchell grandchild due any time. 'Probably come out acting like his grandad with a ten shilling note held so tight in his hand the King'll have his tongue poking out.' Pearl giggled to herself, pleased with her own joke.

There was something else in the basket underneath the sheets given to her by Mrs Mitchell, underneath the heel of corned beef wrapped in newspaper and the end pieces of bread (both of which Pearl and Faith had of course cooked and sliced). Another empty bottle. They were becoming more and more regular. 'Might come in handy for you for storage,' Hilda Mitchell had said. She honestly thinks I don't know, Pearl thought. *A person would have to be blind to not know that the empty gin bottles had to be gotten out of the house undetected somehow.* 'Wouldn't want to light a match near her.' Pearl smiled to herself. 'The old girl'd explode into flames. Besides,' she conjectured, screwing up her face in distaste, 'you can get a whiff of it downwind from fifty yards. Even a yeller mongrel dog'd skulk away in disgust if it got too close to that lot. Shame, really, all that grog has scrambled her marbles completely and now she's behaving like a real nut case. You have to wonder just who the dickens she thinks she really is.'

Pearl sighed. recalling how Hilda had walked into the kitchen that morning without acknowledging anyone and had moved to the sideboard, picked up the tea-cosy and placed it on her head like it was her best hat. Pearl shook her head. 'Sad, though,' she said softly. 'So sad.'

Pearl could smell rain coming long before it started and quickened her pace along the river bank, pulling her threadbare cardigan around her. She wanted to call in on Faith, just in case. Funny how often she had these feelings and the next minute somewhere around the farm, her particular skills were needed, most times without anyone even getting a message to her.

The first drops of rain pitter-pattered gently on the old rusty tin roof, its rhythm soothing and hypnotic; but then, as if to gather strength joined forces with the wind and in so doing revealed the darker side of their united nature, unremitting and inflexible. Brighter than daylight flashes of lightning which preceded the deafening thunder stripped the one-roomed shack bare of all but the dignity of its occupants. From the roof, several constantly streaming leaks of water filled a blackened saucepan and the bottom halves of two kerosene tins, their overflow making a dark, moving stain on a wooden floor swept clean and smoothed by constant care. The containers could wait; there were more important things going on.

'You gunna have to push harder, girl. This one is a knower, I reckon. Trying to hang on. Sometimes first ones are like that.'

Gripping the sides of the grey and white mattress ticking, with no sheet but covered with several pages of *The Wellsford Herald*, the knuckles of the strong hands turned pale from their straining. Perspiration stood like beads of crystal on Faith's forehead and made rivulets in the satin of her neck as she groaned in agony while the contraction seized her swollen belly.

'Pretty powerful child you birthing,' Pearl said. 'Lucky I just dropped by, I reckon. Sounds to me like the powers want this one to be noticed.'

The older woman walked to the side of the room and lifted a boiling kettle from a wood stove. She held a corner of a threadbare sheet in her strong white teeth and pulled her hands sideways, tearing the piece in two then, kneeling down on the mattress rubbed the back of the groaning woman, singing gently to herself.

'Pretty soon I gunna get you on your knees,' Pearl told her. 'Just as soon as this little-un lets us see the first hair on its head.'

The wind howled and whistled, thrusting itself belligerently under the corrugated iron of the old wooden shack, threatening to lift the roof. Loud though the drumming rain was, it was nothing compared to the resonant, cracking thunder, itself insufficient to smother the sounds of pain of the woman on the floor who groaned, and clutched her belly.

Pearl half hauled, half lifted the younger woman to her knees. 'Come on,' she said, panting from the effort. 'Just lean on me now. Put your weight on your hands and lean your body against mine.'

The pain was constant now, each searing finger of it seemingly matched by lightning flashes and erupting thunder.

'Come on, girl, come on now. Lean on me, come on now.'

Heaving, groaning, crying, pushing.

'Come on, girl, come on now. One more push, come on now.'

'I can't.' Desperation. 'Pearl, I just can't.'

'Course you can, come on now. Every damned person in this world came in this way, come on now. Push hard, girl, come on now.'

'Pearl, no I can't, I can't do it, I can't.'

Raisin splotches of perspiration dripped on the black and white print of the newspaper, both women on their knees now, the older woman behind the younger, rubbing her back, encouraging, concentrating on passing her energy through her hands to ease the pain of the younger.

'Come on, girl, come on now. One more time, come on, girl.'

A clap of thunder reverberated around the room, a clap so deafening it drowned out the scream.

Pearl knelt up, smiling, holding by the feet the small, glistening baby, its dangling cord still attached to its mother. 'You done well, girl. You done well. A boy child, a beautiful boy child.'

Long, anxious arms reached lovingly for the child.

'That's quite a surprise you got for Albert when he gets home tonight,' the older woman said affectionately as she folded the torn sheet to wrap around the baby. 'Got himself a fine son for his firstborn. Gonna give him a real good reason to clean up their mess and build their fences now, I reckon.' She winked at the woman on the floor.

Neither woman noticed that the storm was quietening now, the rain tapering off to a gentle pattering on the tin roof, the sound of the receding thunder replaced by the gentle cries of the new infant.

'First time I ever helped one come into the world like that,' said Pearl, 'and I helped plenty.'

'Like what?' questioned the mother, holding the baby in her arms.

'Like it's so special, it seems the wind and rain only came to make sure we notice this one.'

Pearl bent to mop up the mess on the wood floor, then sat back, wide-legged, on the wooden bench Albert had built against the north side of the room. She wiped her face and hands on a piece of the torn sheeting, but nothing would wipe the smile from her face as she watched the young woman holding her child.

'Say one thing for me,' she ventured. 'Might not be able to read or write much, might never had no young-un of me own, but I know something about birthing. Just puts me heart into it and something guides me. Never lost one yet. Never lost one yet.'

She rested her head against the rough-hewn ironbark wall of the shack and closed her eyes. Never lost one yet was right, but she had never had this feeling of unease before either. Something to do with the night; the sinister, howling wind and driving rain. And the thunder. The thunder was a warning, a warning to the birthing woman about a child born this night. A warning to be mindful, to pay attention. This child entered the world for a definite purpose. There was no earthly reason for a child to be born tonight, no reason at all. Not unless it was a child of thunder.

Across town, behind the double-brick exterior of the Florence Nightingale Hospital, privilege was treating one of her own to a quite different entry into the world. Elizabeth, the pretty blonde wife of John Mitchell, heir apparent to all the Mitchell land making up the accumulated farms and station of his late grandfather, lay comatose between starched white sheets. With a face resembling that of a rather bored basset hound, Nurse Hatfield, dressed in clothing as starched as the bedsheets and her moral sense, walked across the room as she replaced the stopper in the bottle of blue ether. Her uniform crackled like scrunched up cellophane, sensible shoes squeaking on the polished floor. She removed the pad of gauze from Elizabeth's face and turned to survey the newly delivered son.

'Better let the new father off the hook, I suppose,' Dr Sinclair remarked, pulling off his surgical gloves and gown. 'He's done what they all do – almost worn the pattern off the linoleum in the waiting room.'

'Well, he's had the pleasure,' said Nurse Hatfield sniffily.

An extended hand, offered in congratulation. 'A bonny lad,' he said to the new father. 'You've got a bonny lad.'

John smiled at the doctor, relief showing all over his face. 'Good to have a boy first. How's Elizabeth?'

'Pretty groggy at the moment, I'm afraid,' the Doctor remarked, 'but come on through now and see your son.'

John Mitchell looked at the tiny being in the crib, wondering when he would feel some kind of rush of recognition. He looked at the bruises on the infant's head. 'What are those marks on either side of his head?'

'Forceps delivery,' the Doctor explained. 'Unfortunately he's had a rough trip out, but he's fine. They'll be gone tomorrow and his mother will feel much better as well. Do you want to look in on her?'

'Yes, please, if it's all right.'

'Of course it's all right, John, but she's in and out of consciousness right now. She'll know you're there, though,' he grinned.

John looked down at his wife, so wan and tired against the pillow, and fought back tears in a rush of emotion. She looked so helpless, so exhausted, and after all those hours of labour, their new son was born with marks on his head, although Sinclair said that was common, nothing to worry about. But why was the husband not able to help more? They'd made it clear that he was to keep away. Why? Why did the woman have to do all this alone? Even now, Elizabeth's hands were tucked in; he could hardly touch her.

John bent down and gently kissed her forehead, then her nose, and her eyelids fluttered gently for a moment.

The door opened and Sinclair's voice said softly, 'Best let her rest, John. In the morning, they'll both be more prepared for visitors. You probably need a bit of rest yourself.'

'Not much hope of that for a while, I'm afraid. Dad has some of his mates around, waiting for me to wet the baby's head.'

Dr Sinclair walked with him to the front door. He hoped his dislike of John's father wasn't written all over his face.

'I suppose James couldn't help it he was born with a silver spoon in his mouth,' the Doctor told Nurse Hatfield later, enjoying the way her lips pursed at the mention of unlimited wealth. 'The man's so used to everyone doing everything for him, of course he would just expect someone to arrange delivery of his first grandchild. John and Elizabeth seem somehow incidental.'

The nurse leaned over the crib, looking at the new baby. 'Dear little thing,' she said. 'Wonder if he's going to grow up in the Mitchell mould and be like his grandfather. God help him if he turns out to have his grandmother's qualities, her not being wrapped too tightly and all.'

She turned to push the crib to the nursery. One thing was crystal clear in her mind, the same thing that happened every time she attended a birth. There was no way in the world she was ever going through that, ever. Not for any man.

* * *

Albert Franklin ran to open the door of the big Ford and held the umbrella over John Mitchell's head until he had walked up the steps to the house's dry verandah.

'Evenin', John. Nasty night.'

'You're not wrong there, Albert, and I've just come from seeing my brand new son. Helluva night to be born, Albert, helluva night to be born. No wonder the poor little bloke wasn't keen to make his exit.'

Albert sighed and sat on the upturned apple crate outside the kitchen. Pearl and Faith had finished for the day. They would be back at 6 am tomorrow. In the meantime, he had to wait to tidy up after the meeting.

Wish them buggers would finish so I could clean up their mess and go home, he thought. Home might not be much, but it was better by far than something built out of wheat bags and white clay. He hoped Faith was all right. Her time was due and John Mitchell had unnerved him. He was right, there was no doubting it. It was a helluva night for young Mitchell to be born.

Laughter coarse and masculine, loosened by alcohol, made its boisterous exit from the station parlour. Albert sighed to himself, imagining the cigarette butts tossed thoughtlessly towards the ashtray, ashed wherever they fell as the whisky flowed even more freely. Gettin' on the piss, he thought. *Better watch myself. Don't want to be the butt of their jokes.*

Eventually the door opened and six men emerged, red-faced, laughing coarsely. 'At least you got one with a spout.' More raucous laughter and slapping of John Mitchell's shoulder.

Albert watched as the men left the building then he moved in to clean up as he listened to the retreating sound of their car engines. At least the storm had passed, so he could cycle the couple of miles home without getting soaked.

He swept up the mess from the mahogany table and the floor and put the unused glasses and liquor away. The overhead fan whirred gently as he replaced the chairs, straightened the antimacassars and took the dirty glasses and ashtrays through to the kitchen. Finally he checked around and under the table and stood in the doorway looking briefly back into the room before switching off the light.

Albert wheeled the bike from behind the outbuildings, reached into his pocket for two pieces of twine and tied the bottoms of his trouser legs, looking questioningly at the sky. He was pleased the rain had stopped; he hadn't been looking forward to riding through the mud and slush and getting soaked through as well.

As he pedalled the old station bicycle through and beyond Wellsford, Albert looked at the swollen river and thought about fishing. Early tomorrow when the river was down again, he would dig up some worms for bait and take his line and go fishing. He chuckled to himself, remembering Pearl telling him how James Mitchell went fishing.

'Brings 'em home all stuffed into his knapsack,' she said. 'Puts them in the icebox because we can't possibly cook them all and then a week later, when they don't keep, he throws half of them away. They do the same thing with the potato peelings,' she said. 'Throw the best part away.'

Albert pedalled his bike and shook his head, remembering how they had all laughed. There was such an enormous gulf between folk, he wondered if it would ever close up. They might think him ignorant and poorly educated, but he knew without question that the river was full of fish. You caught what you needed for your dinner that night and tomorrow if you needed more, you caught more. Only a fool would catch so much he had to put them in a chest with a squeaking door, half filled with ice. What was it all about? Did James Mitchell think he owned the river too and that all the fish in it were subject to his whim?

Long ago, Albert's grandfather had taught him about sin; not the kind the old, red-faced Father O'Malley had seemed to be obsessed with but real sin. 'Real sin is waste,' his grandfather had said. 'Waste and the inability to share, Albert. Those are the things that make a man a sinner.'

'Funny how you think about things,' Albert said to himself. He thought a lot about his grandfather, who was wise in the ways of the bush. He remembered how he could never tell whether the moon was waxing or waning and how his grandfather had laughed and told him that when the moon looked to the right, it was increasing. When it looked to the left, it was decreasing. Still can't work it out, Albert thought. *Must be really thick.*

He wondered if knowledge weakened as each generation moved away from the beginning source. Take his grandmother's ability to divine for water, for instance. He had tried that. Walked all over the land with a piece of wire, waiting for it to turn this way and that, but no knowledge seeped through his body from the earth to move the wire in his hands. It was as if that knowledge stopped with her. Albert immediately found himself swallowing hard.

From behind the window of his cabinet-maker's store, Stanley Clarke squinted his eyes from the light, caught sight of Albert pedalling his bike and waved goodnight to the shadowy shape.

Albert was pleased he didn't have to stop and talk with the furniture maker. He had had to pick up a chair for Elizabeth Mitchell the week earlier and couldn't understand a single word the cabinet-maker had said. 'He's Scottish, Albert,' young Mrs Mitchell had said, 'and broad. You could cut it with a knife.'

Although he couldn't understand what Stanley Clarke said, Albert liked him. He wished sometimes that he could be invisible and just watch the Scotsman's hands planing and sanding the furniture he made. 'He respects that timber,' he had said to Faith. 'Treats it with respect and somehow it shines back at him.'

The cabinet-maker's wife had invited Albert to sit in her kitchen and brought him a glass of lemonade although frankly, he couldn't understand her either. She had the same kind of voice as her husband and the same smiling eyes. Albert wanted to sit on the back step where he felt at home, but Mrs Clarke would not be dissuaded and had sat him down right inside the house in the kitchen, chattering all the while in her funny-sounding voice, not even noticing how ill at ease he felt or how unused he was to sitting in other people's kitchens.

He couldn't imagine Stanley Clarke filling his ice chest with stiff, dead fish. More likely he'd share what he caught with his neighbours. After he'd delivered the chair, Mrs Clarke had given Albert a paper bag filled with cookies she had just made and a jar of blackberry jam to take home. People – you couldn't pick 'em. Some of them were ignorant and some were just fine. It wasn't as his cousin Freddie had said, that they were all arseholes. He had laughed at that one and told Freddie, 'That's not right. Arseholes are useful. You'd be in a sorry mess without one.'

The rain had so muddied the track leading to the shack that Albert got off the bike and wheeled it along the grassy verge. He put the bike under a sheet of corrugated iron for protection, undid the pieces of twine around his trouser legs and shook them loose, then opened the door to his home.

Faith was sitting back on the mattress on the floor, holding something out to him. He held the little, sheet-wrapped bundle in his arms in disbelief and looked over the head of his firstborn to lose himself in the luminous, dark, smiling eyes of his wife.

"Bout time you got here and took a look at your new son,' said Pearl, face beaming, wiping her hands on the hem of her dress. 'And we got corned beef sammiches for tea.'

Albert looked at the bundle in his arms. Something tight had hold of his heart. He felt like his grandparents were somewhere in the room, smiling at him with the same tight feeling around their hearts.

'We're comin' up in the world,' he said to Faith, his voice wavering but not taking his eyes from the baby. 'I was born under a shack, in the dark and onto clay. Now my son has been born right inside the house. Yep, we comin' up, all right.'

He gently placed the baby on the bed near its mother. 'Same day as John Mitchell's son,' said Albert. 'Damned funny thing, that. Very same day.'

Pearl lay in the dark on the straw mattress Albert had set up for her to one side of the room. 'I'll just stay nights till the little-un sucks,' she had said. 'Just one or two nights.'

Pearl lay happily, listening to the steady breathing of the others in the room and the night sounds outside. The heavy rain had stimulated creatures of her own into a cacophonous chorus of thanks. 'Listen to them croakers,' Pearl chuckled to herself. 'They having some party out there.' Water still dripped steadily from the hole in the roof into half a kerosene can.

Funny how often, when she lay quiet after helping with a birth, she heard a woman crying. It was the sound of the crying that took her back, picked her up and flew with her on blue-black wings, back to another time, almost another life. As if the woman's tears had grown fingers that held her, guided her, and would not let go. She concentrated as she had done countless times before, trying to remember anything at all from that day – sounds, smells, anything. But try as she would, she could not recall her mother's face. She remembered the bare feet, the soft cotton of her mother's skirt where she hid her face, but most of all she remembered the crying. And she remembered the collective feeling as if it were something she could touch, the feeling of the older people, their anguish, their hopelessness and their silent, restrained anger. She remembered the sounds her mother made, sounds that stayed with her in the train, through the long, anguished days, mixed with her own tears in her sleep, to come echoing back now, catapulted upwards from the depths of her own heart.

And then afterwards, always it seemed when the birthing was over and she was alone, or nearly alone, there was always the silent crying, the reaching out to her as if she had been given the gift of the birthing hands to make up for a mother's tears.

Pearl wondered if her mother were still alive, or if she had any brothers and sisters. Sometimes the shadow of words she almost remembered visited her at night to whirl around in her head, almost-words she never heard any more. She had no idea how old her mother might be or where she lived, no idea even of what she looked like. But as long as she helped with the birthing and later heard the crying, she felt safe.

She leaned up on her elbow and looked across to where Albert and Faith slept with their new son. They were family to her. James Mitchell himself had gotten permission from the State and read the words over the two youngsters a year or two back and given them the old shearers' quarters to live in. Pearl let her eyes roam around the room. It was bare but clean, and there was a feeling in the place – couldn't put it in words really. Kind of peaceful feeling, like even though they was dirt poor, they had some hope and they had dignity.

Pearl turned on her side and did what she had done at night for as long as she could remember. She buried her face deeply in the remembered soft cotton skirt of the faceless woman whose crying she heard, and slept.

New Year, 1931

Near the end of the decade, the worst fears of Brian Wills and his colleagues were realised; business collapsed and almost the whole world entered into the period of The Great Depression. Stock markets crashed suddenly and investors on stock markets were ruined without warning.

James Mitchell was among them. He had been speculating heavily with Sydney stocks and shares until his phone suddenly stopped ringing and he discovered almost immediately that his huge number of holdings were worthless. Due to the real estate he owned, he was far from destitute, but income from rents virtually ceased and would stay that way until the world righted itself.

Thoroughly mortified and ashamed that he'd chosen to ignore his Wellsford banker's gentle advice in his constant quest for increased wealth, James turned even more to the relief of liquor. At least, he thought, I can still afford that.

Like many country communities, though, the people of Wellsford banded together, with a common need to survive the period the best way they could. Those who didn't already draw on their own vegetable gardens quickly put whatever soil they could cultivate to use, and a barter system for a wide variety of basic items was soon thriving in the township. Everybody was affected to some degree by the Depression, so it caused a bond which drew people together for necessity's sake. Invention and creativity increased, with unrealised abilities being discovered and applied to provide another form of minor income or barter service.

Life on Wellsford Station went ahead much as it had in better times as the property was self-sufficient and had been for two generations. Several intended projects were shelved for obvious reasons, but the homestead and its staff continued to live in much the same way as before although Elizabeth introduced a process of providing produce for several of the town's charity organisations by the tightening of their own belts.

Elizabeth and John still had both his parents on the property most of the time, with Hilda slowly but steadily needing more supervision and James, now very sorry for himself, taking little interest in anything, rising late and spending far too much time with black moods and a bottle.

Oblivious to it all of course, the single member of the new Mitchell generation, Jamie, was happily consuming whatever was put in front of him, smiling at everybody and growing at a quite alarming rate. He was a constant source of delight to his young parents and kept Elizabeth fully occupied during his waking hours as she herself tended to his needs rather than call on Pearl, who had single-handedly brought up her husband during his babyhood.

Just as well, too, because Faith had now given birth to another boy, whom she and Albert named Benjamin, and the ever-smiling Pearl had her hands full as Daniel, their first son, now a very mischievous two year old, was into everything. He showed no sign whatsoever of jealousy towards his new baby brother; in fact, just the opposite, continually running in to check that Benjamin was all right, often waking him from sleep just to make sure.

Pearl absolutely adored both of the boys, feeling as if she were actually their grandmother rather than their closest friend. How Mary would have loved this time, she thought. And how unreal it seemed that Daniel felt so happy and secure in the love of his parents while outside their close little area, most of the world was worried sick about its means of survival.

In spite of the world situation, preparations for the New Year's

Eve party were a community effort. As the whole year had been a struggle for the townspeople, they'd unanimously decided to band together, pool their meagre resources and have a gathering at the school of arts, and the project had grown like Topsy. Every available person in Wellsford seemed to be busy with some particular job – sweeping, cleaning, placing chairs and tables, hanging streamers of linked chains made from newspaper while balancing precariously from ladders.

As the decorating came near to its completion, little Jessie Sanders stood, looking pensive. 'Penny for them' Isobel Craig asked.

'It's really lovely,' Jessie mused, 'but what a shame nobody could afford balloons this year.'

'Oh, Lord, I forgot!' Isobel cried and turning, ran out of the hall. In a few minutes, she was back with a large cardboard box of balloons. 'If nobody can afford to buy them, we might as well put them to use,' she laughed, opening the box. 'Now, who have we got with strong lungs, to blow these up?'

'I'd imagine that Stanley would be the champion in that area,' said Liz Collins, laughing. 'How come he's not here?'

'He's over at the hospital,' said Isobel. 'Maggie went into labour this morning, so I don't think he'll be around today.'

'Ye're wrong,' came a thick brogue from the doorway. 'It seems the bairn doesnae like this year, so it'll probably be the morrow. The doctor kicked me oot, so what can I do to help?'

Isobel plonked the box on the table in front of him and Belle Wills stood behind him with scissors and a ball of string.

'Ye'd better get a stretcher as well,' Stanley said, looking at the heap of balloons. 'I'll need it after this lot.'

'Isn't this marvellous?' Elizabeth said enthusiastically to Liz several hours later. 'Just like the night of the ball. It seems everyone's here, and all having such a good time!'

'You're right, Elizabeth, it certainly is marvellous. Looking around this room, it's hard to believe there's a world depression on out there. Thank God we can forget it for a while.'

'No news from the Clarkes?'

'Not since Stanley left, but as he's not here, I'm guessing the contractions must have started again. Not much of a way to spend New Year's Eve, I'd imagine.'

'No,' Elizabeth said, thinking back. 'I hope she doesn't have too hard a time.'

Liz looked up at the clock and said, 'It seems Stanley was right; only twenty minutes to midnight, so their baby must have chosen next year. I'd better top up some glasses. It's getting close.'

As if on cue, from outside came the skirl of bagpipes as the main door burst open and Stanley Clarke marched into the hall. Not only was he for the first time wearing the kilt, but as he passed people on a circuit of the room, there were shrieks of delight all around. Pinned to the seat of the kilt was a handwritten notice: 'IT'S A GIRL'.

All the friends of the town formed a line behind the Scotsman, marching, shouting, crying, laughing until, on the tick of midnight, Stanley stopped abruptly, took a deep breath and launched into *Auld Lang Syne*.

With the piper in the hall's centre, the people of Wellsford joined hands in a big circle and loudly sang the much-loved melody of celebration.

'Ye'll have tae excuse me!' Stanley cried out, 'but there's a couple of people waitin' tae greet the new year wi' me,' and he pushed through the crowd and out the door.

Regrouping

'My goodness, Maggie, isn't she growing,' said Fred Craig, pausing from sweeping the shop's entrance steps to peer into the pram.

Maggie bent forward to tuck in a tail of shawl, savouring the smell of freshly laundered baby clothes mixed with the unmistakeably natural, grassy fragrance from the cane exterior of the pram.

'Aye, that she is, Fred. Looks as if she'll take after my mother. She was a big, strong woman, no like me – I'm the runt of the family,' she laughed. 'We named her after my mother, so I suppose it's only right.'

Robbo leaned over the pram and very gently touched the baby's cheek with one finger, at which she immediately smiled. A beautiful baby, he thought, but it was the mother he was concerned about with her clothes hanging loose on her and dark circles under her eyes.

Maggie pushed the pram to the school of arts. God, she was tired. Maybe she needed a tonic or something, she thought. Now that Sandie was sleeping six hours at a time, she expected her health to pick up, but it was taking its time. She stopped at the bottom step to the hall just as Robbo the policeman came out the main entrance.

'Ah, perfect timing,' he said. 'I'll just lift that in for you. I presume you're here to see Isobel?'

Maggie felt relieved. She had been contemplating taking the baby from the pram rather than try to lift it up the steps herself.

'You've a visitor, Isobel!' Robbo called. Then, smiling at Maggie, he clicked his heels together and saluted before moving off down the steps again.

'Ah, Maggie, how lovely!' Isobel exclaimed as she and the students came over to admire Sandie in the pram. 'The girls were just asking me when we could expect you back. How's things?'

'Nae too bad, thank you,' Maggie answered, looking around for a chair. 'She's growing sae quickly that I'm kept very busy and I dae still get very tired. But oh, Isobel, I dae miss the classes.'

'Well, they're not going to stop, Maggie,' Isobel said, moving one foot on the underside of the pram to roll it to and fro. 'Just yesterday, I had an inquiry about entering students in a regional competition for highland dancing, so the girls are very excited about it all and dying to have you back here.'

'I'm as keen as them, Isobel, but I just don't feel up to it yet, ye ken? Besides,' she smiled, 'at the moment I'd make an extremely guid cow, but because I'm sae small built, I'm finding I hae to wear a nappy around my chest near feed times.'

Isobel smiled. 'Of course,' she said, 'but just as soon as you're ready, we're here. The competition inquiry covered a lot of fields, sword dances and all. Does that sound like you?'

Maggie's eyes shone. 'Ma Goad, Isobel, I can hardly wait! Just gie me a wee while tae get my strength back, then look out!'

Elizabeth looked across the dinner table at her husband. 'A penny for them,' she said.

John's eyes snapped back into focus. 'Eh? Oh sorry, love. I was miles away.'

'I could see that, but where? You usually discuss everything with me, so what is it?'

Looking unusually serious, John said, 'Actually, I wasn't miles away; I was right here. I'm worried about Dad, have been for ages. There's nobody else will have a go at him, so I guess it's up to me. And I'm not looking forward to it. Not one bit.'

She reached across the table and covered his hand. 'I knew it was that,' she said quietly. 'But we have to do it, or you do. For his sake. He wouldn't accept my saying anything, but he knows you'd be speaking for both of us. If it means a row, it means a row. We have to try and stop this awful slide.'

John looked up into his wife's face. 'Have I told you today that I love you?' he asked.

She squeezed his hand and smiled. 'Don't put it off, John. Think what you have to say and do it.'

John slumped in his chair, looking into space again. Quite suddenly he said, 'You're right,' stood up and left the room.

He walked down the hall to his office for a few minutes, then turned and walked into the parlour where James was sprawled in one of the big chairs, a glass in his hand and a bottle on the table beside him.

'Ah, John,' he said, looking up, 'come in, lad, come in.' Although he looked rumpled and bleary-eyed, he was not helplessly drunk. 'You look very serious, my boy,' his father continued. 'What's on your mind?'

'Well, you are,' answered John, sitting down opposite James.

Pearl walked into the dining room to clear the table where Elizabeth sat staring thoughtfully at nothing. As Pearl took her plate, she looked up at the older woman, sighed and smiled.

'You might like to leave the cleaning up, Pearl. It could get a bit rowdy in a few minutes.'

'Don't you worry about that, Miss Elizabeth. It'll only take a moment, and anyway, I've heard quite a few raised voices in this house over the years.'

Elizabeth grimaced. 'Yes,' she said quietly, 'I suppose you have.'

But this time, Pearl felt it was to be different. The blazing rows of years ago had been insoluble, impossible, between husband and wife; now it was a different kind of struggle between father and son.

The voices through the heavy walls became louder, then quieter with a sarcastic tinge, then rising, one side pleading, the other arrogant, then quieter for a while, then rising to an out-of-control crescendo: '… hell's the matter with … won't be spoken to like … used to be a force, now a farce … who the hell do you think …', steadily increasing until John's voice clearly shouted. 'Bugger it! I'm not talking about Elizabeth and me! What about Jamie?! You think we want him to have two pisspots for grandparents?!'

Silence.

A crash as a piece of furniture went over, followed by heavy footsteps, a door opening then slamming shut and the same footsteps leaving the house.

Pearl's eyes squeezed shut to hold back the tears. She stood holding the edge of the sink bench, took a couple of deep breaths, hung up the tea towel she'd been crumpling in her hands, had a quick check around the kitchen, flicked out the light and went outside.

The dining room door opened and John came back into the room, pale but red around the eyes. He pulled back a chair and sat by Elizabeth who was still sitting at the table. His head drooped forward, his breathing difficult.

For a short time, neither of them moved until Elizabeth stood up and, stepping behind her husband, leant over the chair's backrest and put her arms around his shoulders.

'In twenty-six years, I've never spoken like that to him – never,' he said, tears now slipping down his face. 'I hate it, Elizabeth.'

'Of course you do,' she whispered, 'but we both know it had to happen eventually. Only someone who cares enough can get through to him.'

'God, I hope I got through. I couldn't stand to go through that time after time, like he and mother used to. I'm exhausted.'

'No bloody wonder,' said Elizabeth.

John's eyes opened wide at even this mildest form of swearing from his wife, and then he involuntarily laughed as she placed her cheek against his and hugged him. 'That's probably enough excitement for one day. Let's get to bed.' She smiled.

James, furious, stormed across the verandah and down the steps out into the yard, glaring from side to side like some caged animal. He was on the point of shrieking, 'Charlie, saddle up!' when realisation hit him that it was the middle of the night. Instead he lashed out and punched nothing in the smooth night air then stomped the ground like a nervous, unbroken horse.

What had he done earlier, after those violent arguments? At first it had been easy to seek solace with his staff members. Then it was the card games and drink, the council meetings and drink, Ray Corcoran and drink, finally his own parlour and drink ...

His shoulders slumped, the fury passed and his breathing eased back. Goddamnit, he had almost punched his own son in there!

Starting with the disaster of his marriage, he'd progressed through one monumental mistake after another, always resorting to the bottle until now, he hardly left the house except to replenish his supply. The one constant through it all had been the property, which he had taken for granted right from childhood. He'd even handed it over to John before the boy was really ready, because it wasn't big enough for him. Not big enough! What bullshit! And now the boy was doing a great job of running things while he, James, was consigning himself to the scrap heap.

The boy was right. He and his quietly capable wife had seen it all happening and taken it on themselves to step in. John was certainly a steady lad, but that girl, the daughter of the banker he'd refused to listen to before the crash, she'd had a lot to do with all this.

James looked up at the endless black of the Australian night sky with its myriad of stars and the soft glow of the waning moon, and sighed.

The boy was definitely right. He was still young enough to start again. And he would, tomorrow.

Tonight, he would try and sleep.

★ ★ ★

Ian Sanders looked up from the last he was working at when the light from the doorway of his working area in the smithy was blotted out by someone's shadow.

'Good morning, Ian,' said James Mitchell, 'how are things going? Picking up a bit?'

The bootmaker put down his hammer and removed some nails from between his lips. 'Morning, James. Well, yair, I feel that business is finally on the way up a little, perhaps,' he said. 'At least people are thinking about new footwear, after years of repair jobs. Some of those boots have been fixed so many times, the uppers are like sieves.' Both men laughed.

'Did you ever think any more about those boots without laces you described to me years ago?' James asked.

'To be honest, with things going the way they did, James; no, I didn't. I made up a set of templates, but that's all. I've had a struggle getting enough repair work to make ends meet, so any innovation has been out of the question.'

'You still have the templates, I hope?'

'Of course.' Sanders opened a drawer under his workbench, searched through some papers then pulled out a large envelope which he tossed on the bench.

James watched with increasing interest as the craftsman explained his idea in detail, then finally thanked him for his time, apologised for having taken up so much of it, encouraged him to make some samples up and left.

Sanders watched his retreating back, shook his head and, instead of replacing the envelope in the drawer, put it to one side.

Early summer was hot, hotter than in previous years, and enervating. Wellsford summers were traditionally dry, but with the continuing rains through the spring, the levels of all the creeks, streams and dams were much higher than usual, and the townsfolk were sweltering in the unaccustomed daily high humidity.

Maggie Clarke was really suffering from heat exhaustion. To her relief, Sandie seemed to have reached a plateau and slowed her growth once on to solid foods, but she was a very energetic child and a handful for her mother to cope with, particularly with the added burden of this heat every day.

With the slow but steady upsurge in the business world, Stanley now had enough orders to keep him fully occupied for months ahead with more coming in every week. He worked extremely long hours, only pausing for meal breaks, so Sandie was completely Maggie's responsibility. At least now the girl was walking everywhere, but today Maggie had not felt well enough to handle anything much and uncharacteristically dragged herself upstairs to lie on the big double bed, leaving Sandie playing happily on the floor with her rag doll.

Ted Hunn stood at the bar, enjoying an end-of-the-day beer. Years of working with metal at his anvil with the fire of blazing embers going winter and summer had made him a genial giant of a man. His fingers had swollen to such a size that they all but buried the glass in his hand, but he held on; he'd always looked forward to that first taste. Bazza stood waiting for the regular refill, and as Ted put the glass on the bar, James Mitchell walked in.

'Hello, stranger,' said Bazza with a broad smile. 'You just passing through, or looking for accommodation?'

All three men laughed, as did several bystanders.

'I'll have a shandy, please, barman,' James said.

Bazza's smile was replaced by a genuine look of shock. 'A shandy, you say? Well, why not,' and began to draw one for James.

'Yes, Bazza, it's well past time I cut down a bit. I actually tripped over something yesterday.'

'That's not so hot.' Laughing again. 'What did you trip over?'

'My son,' said James, raising the glass to his lips.

'Your son!' Ted Hunn howled and slapped his bulky thigh with a huge hand. 'That's a good one.'

Bazza's smile remained but faded a little as his eyes and those of James locked in a moment of understanding.

Wiping his lips with the back of his hand, Ted asked, 'Is … is John all right?'

'Oh, he's right, all right,' James replied over his glass, flicking another look at Bazza who gently nodded.

'Lucky it wasn't you who tripped over him, Ted!' one of the other men called, 'you'da' killed the boy!' and the raucous laughter continued.

The big blacksmith turned to James. 'Ian Sanders has been hoping you'd drop in, James,' he said, still smiling. 'He's made the weirdest-looking pair of boots. Says he wants you to see them.'

'Thanks, Ted, I'll call in tomorrow. Are you still quite happy to have him in the smithy? It's been quite a while now. Can you still spare the space?'

'Funny you should ask that,' the big man replied. 'We've been glad of the extra company over the past couple of years, but now things are on the move and it is getting a bit cramped. Why do you ask, James?'

'Just a neighbourly inquiry really. But I wouldn't be surprised if those boots you mentioned take Sanders out of there and into larger premises before too long.'

'That would be great if it happens. The boy and I really like Ian and his wife, and I'm not looking forward to asking for the space at all.'

James drained his glass and Bazza stood ready.

'Another?' he said.

James shook his head, and again the two men's eyes met briefly. Slapping the blacksmith's shoulder, he said, 'See you tomorrow, Ted,' then called, 'G'night, all!' and left the bar.

Didn't it rain

James remembered his father, Hugh, talking of a huge flood soon after he'd first established Wellsford Station in the late 1870s, and although the long-forgotten memories were vague, in his mind's eye he could clearly see his father's face as he'd talked of it. Of course, there had been no township then, but if what he could remember of those conversations were reliable, they were all in real trouble if this rain didn't stop.

Nobody else remembered having seen rain like this. Whatever the ferocity grading is after 'teeming', that's what had been happening. Incessantly. It was as if God had filled the Big Dipper with water and turned it over. You could literally not see clearly through the rain.

The main road looked like a tributary of the river, water hosed off the rooftops and the gardens which had served everybody so well through the past couple of years were all quagmires. Unless it was of necessity, nobody ventured out on foot and almost all commercial transactions had come to a halt. The joking about the situation had stopped; it was now deadly serious. Although the river formed a couple of wide-open S-bends out on the station property, there was only one gentle, long bend above the township and it ran straight through and past Wellsford, down both sides of Devil's Rock, down into the rapids and another wide turn further down, so in normal wet weather, nobody need be concerned.

But this was not normal.

It became obvious to everyone, even without contact, that should the river overflow its banks, the town would be engulfed in no time. They had to try to do something, even if the huge volume of gushing water seemed to make any effort insignificant. Saturated men ran from door to door to search out bags and manpower to fill them with river sand, and the backbreaking task of building a retaining wall of sandbags began in the pelting rain.

Stanley Clarke was in the thick of it, with his organisational ability and quick mind put to good use, but like many of them, he was now near exhaustion. And, naturally, he worried about his family. Maggie always smiled but was continually tired, having to take a rest often during the day. Sandie was thriving and luckily seemed to be developing her father's type of mind, getting engrossed in what she was doing rather than rushing about getting into mischief. Stanley had much earlier built her a playpen and she was happy to sit amusing herself, not drawing on Maggie's limited energy to supervise everything.

During the morning of the fourth day of endless heavy rain; Ted Hunn, whose strength and good nature was a godsend for the line of workers at the river bank, was working beside Stanley when the Scot slipped in the slush and fell. He had trouble standing again and the big blacksmith lifted him to his feet, only to see him slip and go down again.

'Stanley!' Ted shouted over the storm's noise, 'you've got to rest for a while! Get yourself home and dry out! You'll be no good to anyone if you push yourself any further!'

Again he helped the Scot to his feet then down off the bank to flatter ground, gave him an encouraging pat on the shoulder and pointed towards the township.

By the time he'd reached his home, Stanley really knew how tired he was. Drenched, he had to hold his gatepost for a moment before stumbling the last few yards to the door. His orderly mind snapped into action as he thought how lucky it was that before last winter, he'd built the covered entranceway outside the front door, with the coat hooks and boot rack. At least he wouldn't carry all that mess into the house. He reached for the towel which hung for just such an emergency and took the worst of the wet from his hair, then opened the door.

'Daddy, Daddy!' called his excited daughter, standing at the playpen's railing with her arms outstretched.

Three days ago, Faith had called to the rain and watched it fall, gently to begin with, delighting in its regenerative powers, but the rain gathered momentum and strength as if the entire earth herself wept, and who was to know whether it was in joy or grief. By the fourth day, the little community of Wellsford was becoming anxious. The Wellsford River had not risen this high in living memory, but it seemed the rain well understood perspicacity; it displayed no sign of easing.

From her sheltered back doorstep, Faith watched as the muddy river, its water almost to bank height, swirled desperately through the land, too close for comfort. She watched a huge eucalypt, earth-laden roots sticking out at all angles and carried fast by the water, tossed around like a matchstick and allowed herself a moment's break from worrying to marvel at the water's energy. All we need is a logjam downriver, she thought, then we'll be in trouble.

She closed the door and looked around the small room, wondering what she would grab for first, what would mean most to her if the rain continued and the river broke its banks.

With the carefully hemmed spotted muslin held back by one hand, Faith rubbed at the condensation spreading on the inside of the glass with slender brown fingers. She was a good-looking woman, no doubt about that. Dark hair curled around a face that pleased, no matter which angle it was viewed from, a face that smiled frequently to momentarily counter an underlying look of sadness radiating from behind dark brown eyes rimmed thickly with long, black lashes. She stood for a moment then bent forward, both hands on the pads of her hips, just below her waist, a stance adopted from Pearl.

But now she bit her bottom lip with small, even white teeth and peered out through the rain then dropped the curtain and rubbed the palm of her right hand along her left upper arm. This kind of weather didn't just arrive out of nowhere; it meant something. Inside she nursed the fond hope that the meaning indicated something positive, but anxiety made her teeth worry her bottom lip even more nervously, wishing that Albert and the boys were home and not out in the weather sandbagging. She knew Albert would be looking out for them, but they were so young.

Faith moved across the living area of her home, knowing that the outer iron walls might be worn grey and weathered with streaks of ginger rust, but the inside timber glowed with a warmth that seemed to be reflected off the family life it surrounded. Her family life. She moved to her only chair, kicked off her slippers and let her feet feel the roughness of the faded rag rug, hooked from scraps of material thrown out through the years at Wellsford Station. There was a time when Pearl could identify all the scraps of fabric and where they came from. Pieces of old bedspread, blanket ends ripped into strips, printed cotton from dresses and shirts once worn by owners, some of whom were now gone, leaving behind only ghostly fragments of their lives to soothe the underside of weary feet.

She stretched her toes and walked to again hold back the muslin from the kitchen window as the rain swept noisily across the tin roof in large, boisterous waves. This water lashing all around the old shack reminded her of how Pearl would teach the small children at the station not to be greedy or to take more than their share, by telling them the legend about the big, greedy green frog.

'He was one greedy bugger all right,' she told them. 'Drank up all the world's water. Just kept on drinking and drinking and wouldn't leave a drop for anyone else. Everything for miles around – plant, animal, bird and human – cried out for water, but the mean old frog just shook his head from side to side, making the water inside him slurp noisily, taking great care not to release a drop. Ah, but like all greedy people, he met his match, Pearl recalled, smiling to herself. Little bitty fieldmouse came along and put on a show for the frog. Danced, stood on his head, turned somersaults, did handstands and spun like a Catherine wheel – you name it, this mouse did it.

'Pretty soon the frog started to shake. His great green shoulders heaved and he covered his mouth with a froggy hand. But before long, he could not contain himself and he started to laugh. He laughed and laughed, and as he laughed, he started to dribble and spill water from the corners of his mouth. Soon great rivers were flowing from the sides of his mouth and he shook so much that he completely lost control of himself. With a great hacking splutter, he released all the world's water, all in one huge, world-soaking deluge. That frog was what caused the Great Flood, just like the one you read about in the Bible.'

Faith pulled back the curtain again and peered out. Be needing an ark myself if this keeps up, she thought, dropping the curtain and walking back to her chair.

She had watched the local menfolk, as many as could, go past her window on their way down to the river early in the day, carrying their shovels to fill the sandbags. Looked a bit spooky, she thought to herself, most of them wearing oilskins, water running off their hats. She wondered again just what she would grab for if the river broke its banks, grateful for once that she didn't have much in the way of material things that might need saving.

But now, something made her stand and listen. Hearing nothing but the pouring rain on the roof, that same something led her to her front door. She opened it and heard the noise before she could see anything. A man's anguished scream for help.

Faith ran across the drenched ground until she could see down the roadway, mindless of the soaking rain on her clothing. There it was again, a wail like nothing she had ever heard before. A cry that seemed to come from another world. Suddenly a figure appeared running towards her, a man with no coat or shoes, carrying something in his arms, something limp.

With a shock, Faith recognised Stanley Clarke, carrying his wife Maggie, both of them drenched to the skin. At his heels, like some little mud creature, scampered their daughter Sandie.

'Help me, lassie,' the Scot pleaded, his eyes wild. 'I can nae wake her up. Help me, for God's sake, help me.'

Faith put her hand on the bewildered man's arm and quickly but gently led him into the shack. Tossing a towel to the little girl, she led Stanley to the bedroom where he tenderly laid his wife on the bed. Great God, she thought, she weighs nothing.

Faith suddenly understood that the rain was no accident. The world herself wept right now and this time, it was not in joy.

Stanley looked at Maggie, then at Faith. 'Nae, nae, nae!' he screamed, and fell to his knees beside the bed, crying uncontrollably.

Faith gently laid a hand on his shuddering shoulder, fighting back her own tears, then she moved out to look after Sandie. She had wrapped the child in another towel and was drying her hair when there was a heavy knocking at the door. She opened it to Isobel Craig, holding a battered umbrella.

'Faith, I hope you don't mind, but I'm worried sick. I was working near the front of the shop when I thought I heard shouting. For a dreadful moment, I wondered if the river had run over, but then I saw someone through the wet front window and it looked like Stanley lurching through the rain and yelling. I got my coat and brolly and tried to follow him, but he's gone somewhere. I'm sorry to butt in, but I'm …'

Faith held a finger to her lips and motioned Isobel inside. Isobel slipped the coat off, dropped the umbrella and immediately saw Sandie wrapped in the towels. She sucked in her breath, closed her eyes for a moment then followed Faith back to the bedroom.

'Oh, Jesus Christ – no!' she breathed, and ran to the bedside.

Some short time later, Isobel came out of the bedroom and dropped into the chair.

'Mummy's gone tae sleep.' Sandie's voice cut through her thoughts.

God, she'd forgotten the child was there! The voice unleashed a sudden torrent of emotion, and tears coursed down Isobel's face.

Faith came back in and quickly resumed drying the little girl. She had no more towels so pulled a tattered blanket from the one cupboard and wound it around the girl and under her feet. 'She's not shivering, she'll be all right,' she said to nobody in particular. She sat Sandie on the floor mat and stood back.

Isobel realised with a start that she herself was sitting in the only chair and made as if to get up, but Faith motioned to her. 'Just sit there, Mrs Craig. I'll get a cup of tea,' she said.

Mrs Craig, thought Isobel. In the midst of all this incredible madness, she still feels she should call me Mrs Craig?

'Let me take the wee one back to the store with me, Faith. You'll more than have your hands full when Albert and the boys come in. Can I bring you back some more towels or something?'

'No, no need, thanks. These'll be dried by the time they come in, and Pearl will probably be in later, so we'll be all right.'

Isobel put the still soaking coat back on, went out the door and opened the umbrella then opened her arms as Faith passed her the little girl, still wrapped up. Lowering the umbrella to cover the two of them, Isobel hurried out to the street.

Much later that afternoon, Stanley still hadn't moved, his cup of tea cold on the floor alongside him. As Faith peered through the window for the umpteenth time, the rain eased. She listened to the sound of water running off the tin roof into the water tanks and the steady splash as it exited the tanks from the overflow pipes onto the already soggy ground. In spite of her drained feelings, Faith smiled as she heard birds twittering at the break in the rain.

Faith jumped as the back door burst open and she ran to hand towels to the three rain-soaked members of her family. Albert took a towel and rubbed the boys' hair, looking only briefly at his wife. He knew instinctively. Something was wrong.

She pulled off the boys' sodden boots, rubbed their cold, wet feet and stood them in front of the wood stove. They stomped up and down, breathing on their hands and rubbing them together. Still Albert said nothing.

'Don't go in our bedroom just yet,' she said to him, close to tears.

He put his arm around her shoulders. 'It's all right, love,' he whispered.

Later, the wet-eyed couple stood for a long time, holding on to each other. Then Albert broke his grip and walked to the kitchen sink to fill the kettle. He stood, holding the kettle in one hand, looking at his wife.

'I'd be the same if anything happened to you or them,' he told her, nodding towards the lean-to where the boys slept. 'I'd be exactly the same.'

★ ★ ★

The bitterness that had filled every fibre of Phyllis Corcoran's being, from the day her husband Ray had taken off to meet his Pommie girlfriend and they'd both disappeared, gradually manifested itself physically. Little by little she developed an arthritic condition that invaded every joint, every muscle, every nerve end, a condition caused by a jealousy so intense it drew nothing pleasant or joyful to itself and in its own nurturing shunned help from well-meaning neighbours and would-be friends. It also bound Amy to her completely.

As soon as the girl was old enough, she ran the house for her domineering mother. Only at night, when her time was her own, would she take the doll from the bottom of her wardrobe and gently rock it in her arms. She talked to the doll as if it were real. Told it the things she never had an opportunity to share with anyone else, and she alone, in her solitude, heard the doll's replies.

Just after Amy's tenth birthday, on a day much like any other, Phyllis gave her daughter a shopping list and a basket and sent her down to Craig's to buy provisions. The shy, browbeaten little girl liked getting out of the house on these trips to the shops. She dawdled outside Stanley Clarke's, watching the Scot work on his furniture until he noticed her and called her inside. 'Och, ye wee bairn,' Stanley said, 'set ye doon.'

The girl picked up handfuls of sweet-smelling wood shavings and held them against her hair, wondering why she had to be dark-haired and not blonde and beautiful like the friend she kept in the bottom of her wardrobe.

At Craig's, Amy waited shyly while the shopkeeper filled her order, slowly sucking on the triangular packet of sherbet with the licorice straw that Isobel insisted she take.

Afterwards, Amy slowly dawdled home, enjoying both the break from her mother's constant demands and her contact with the townsfolk. But as she reached home and walked in the back door, she cried out in horror, dropping the basket of groceries on the floor. 'What are you doing?!' she shrieked.

'You're too old for dolls now,' her mother said as she quickly fed Amy's only friend into the wood stove. Amy caught sight of the blonde curls melting in the heat as she raced to the stove, pushing her mother out of the way. Mindless of the danger, she thrust her hands inside to retrieve her doll. It was too late. The celluloid melted all over her hands, causing excruciating agony, but the child uttered not a sound.

Horrified, Phyllis hobbled to the kitchen sink, filled a pitcher with cold water and plunged her daughter's hands into it. Still the child made no sound. Even later when Dr Sinclair dressed her hands and gently asked how she felt, Amy only nodded but did not speak.

For months the child remained speechless. While her mother harangued anyone who would listen about her lot and the useless mongrel who'd caused it; Amy, traumatised by the loss of her doll, locked her thoughts inside her head. The townsfolk, aghast at first at the tragedy, gradually accepted the child's being mute and chattered away to her without expecting an answer, never looking at the hands the girl kept hidden in the folds of her skirt in much the same way they hid the pity that filled their hearts.

'It's a damned shame,' Isobel Craig said to her husband. 'That girl has a beautiful face when she smiles, but she's so sad.'

It was a sentiment expressed over and over again by the people of the small town.

One Saturday morning, Faith knocked on the back door of the Corcoran household, carrying a basket of vegetables from her garden and half a dozen eggs. She nodded brightly to Phyllis, ignoring her bad humour, and placed the vegetables on the kitchen bench. Then, as she turned to go, she asked Amy to walk to the gate with her. Once outside, she handed the girl a small, brown paper package. The girl looked questioningly at her but would not show her hands, so Faith put the package on the gatepost. 'Undo it,' she said. 'It's something I made for you.'

The girl stood back, shyly shaking her head.

'It's all right,' Faith said gently, but Amy's hands remained hidden. Faith pulled at the string on the package. 'Here, I'll undo it for you, shall I?' The girl nodded.

Faith unwrapped the brown paper to reveal a pair of finely knitted mittens. 'Do you think you'd like to wear them?' Faith ventured.

Amy still stood with her hands firmly hidden, staring now at the mittens on the brown paper. As Faith moved to walk outside the gate, she reached to touch the girl on the shoulder.

Amy hung back, watching Faith's back until she'd moved well down the street. She reached out and hurriedly pulled the mittens on over her scarred hands. She quickly spun around to look down the street, but Faith was out of sight. As the girl turned to walk inside, a large tear rolled down one cheek, but she skipped up the path. *Free. Free at last.* Now at last she could bring her hands out in the open.

★ ★ ★

'Well, I've got good news and bad news. Which do you want first?'

James had walked into the bootmaker's section of the smithy and was pleased to see Jessie, Ian's wife, in the workshop with him. She was very much a part of the operation, and James liked to talk things over with both of them together.

Ian waved his answer to his wife, and she smiled brightly and said, 'We'd better get the bad over with first.'

'It's not really so bad, actually, just I suppose that I've always disliked getting beaten to the punch. I've had a letter back from the patents office and unfortunately, there's a company in Tasmania been making boots with elastic sides since before the turn of the century, so any kind of patent for your boots is out, Ian. But of course, there's nothing to stop you going ahead with the plan as they don't look exactly the same. They're called Blundstones, and I didn't know they existed till now. That's the bad news.'

'Whee, that's not so bad,' said Jessie. 'So, what's the good news?'

'Well, do you remember those children's harnesses you and Stanley came up with a while ago? Reaction to them is almost ecstatic and we've not only got a hold over the pattern but have a big children's wear company interested in marketing them – as many as you can produce.'

'Wonderful, James, and thank you!' Sanders exclaimed. 'And what a lovely coincidence.'

'Why so?' asked Mitchell. 'Only this morning, Jessie was talking about the possibility of producing them in bulk. You see, she's been more enthusiastic than me about the reins. I only really saw them as a bit of fun for Stanley and Maggie, God bless her, but Jessie saw them from a woman's angle, saw the practical advantage.'

'Oh, yes,' Jessie took over, 'I think they're a wonderful idea, have since the day Stanley suggested the plan. And fancy dear little Maggie being the first to own one. It's quite lovely really.'

'It is, it is,' said James thoughtfully.

'That reminds me,' said Sanders after a pause, 'that bloody Scotsman never paid for that work.'

'Ian Sanders, you're disgusting,' squealed Jessie, and all three burst out laughing.

* * *

Daniel was just about to sink his teeth deep into the roast beef sandwich Pearl had handed him when his father shook his shoulder. 'Come on, sleepyhead, wake up.'

Daniel shook his head. 'I was having a dream about this great big sandwich,' he said sleepily, pulling the covers back up around his head.

'No dreaming here,' Albert laughed. 'You got a short memory, boy. We going ferreting, this morning, remember?'

That's right. Daniel had quite forgotten. Today was Sunday and he and his father were going out rabbiting with one of the ferrets his Uncle Freddie had given them.

'What's the time?' the boy asked, stretching.

'Never mind that. The rabbits will be up, and if you're not, we'll miss.'

Although it was January, the wind outside was brisk. Daniel shivered, wishing the sun would come up over the eastern hills and warm his freezing bones. The male ferret Albert held in one hand was still sound asleep, its body falling from each side of his hand like a limp rag. 'Look at this,' Albert teased. 'Just like you half an hour ago.'

'Gawd, they stink a bit for such cute little fellas,' the boy told his father, rubbing a finger down the animal's snout. 'Think you'd better carry him downwind.'

'Mind yourself,' Albert warned. 'They've got teeth like needles.'

The ferret stirred and Albert slipped it inside a sugar sack, tying the top with a piece of string. 'They've got such lovely faces,' Daniel pondered, falling into step alongside his father.

'Not so lovely if you're a rabbit down a burrow,' Albert replied. 'Anyway, they do what we want, chase them rabbits up above the ground in no time. Kept a lot of us in meat during the Depression with a couple of these little beggars.'

They walked down the south side of the Wellsford River to a large paddock covered with tufted grass clumps. Alongside the river, brambles bent heavy with blackberries, making Albert think he had better come out again later with a bucket. On a nearby dead eucalypt, half a dozen sulphur-crested cockatoos cawed and squawked.

Albert walked to the middle of the paddock and undid the string around the top of the sack. He studied the ground in front of him and, seeing a hole in a low bank, almost hidden from view with long grasses, he undid the sack and let the ferret go. Then he undid another sack and held it over another opening further along the ground. Within minutes, a terrified rabbit jumped out of the opening and into the sack and as Albert whipped the sack out of the way, the attacking rodent also emerged, mystified by the disappearance of its prey.

Albert tied up the sack with the rabbit inside and put it over his shoulder. 'Rabbit stew tonight, young Daniel,' he said. 'Best way to catch rabbits. Now all we got to do is skin and gut the little devil.' He picked up the sniffing ferret and tied it in the other sack.

'We not gonna get another one?' Daniel asked, screwing up his face towards the morning sun.

'What for? One's enough for our mob,' said his father. 'We can bring Freddie's ferret out again any time.'

'You reckon that rabbit's scared of the teeth or the ferret's pong?' Daniel grinned at his dad.

They sat for a while at the side of the river, looking out at Devil's Rock. 'You know,' mused Albert, 'there's something evil about that rock.' Daniel looked over at the great, grey protrusion. 'It doesn't want any human being near it, that's for sure. I suppose that's why it's placed itself where it has, right in the middle of a river with rapids on one side and deep water on the other. And there's a feeling about it too, like if you get too close, it'll push you away, like there's some kind of force around it. I reckon it's holding some secret, that rock, maybe some secret from way back, something most of us aren't supposed to know about.'

'It's funny with rocks,' Daniel mused. 'Sometimes they feel welcoming and sometimes they definitely don't.'

''Well, when they don't, you'd better respect the message they're giving you,' Albert said. 'There's always a reason, even if we can't understand it.'

Daniel knew Devil's Rock felt unfriendly and there was also something menacing about its strange shape. When he squinted up his eyes, it took on an almost human shape, like a huge person bending over, ready to pounce.

Albert sat watching the rock for a silent minute or two. 'Didn't get that name for nothing. Something must have happened here once,' he said. 'Long time ago, something nobody knows about. Something happened here with that rock. Maybe even before anyone came here, long time ago.'

He stood up and put an arm around his older son's shoulders. 'Tell you what, young Daniel,' he said. 'Want to come out with me this afternoon to gather blackberries?'

Daniel nodded. He liked these trips with his father. It was kind of a restoring thing for them both. Like they came from a long line of hunters and gatherers and in a way, by doing this together, they were keeping not only their respect for each other alive and well but also their respect for generations unknown who walked this way before them in the past.

Poles apart

The pencil ran up and down the row of figures written on the page spread before her like a mouse running the stem of a full-blown sunflower. Except that whereas the sunflower might offer a seed in reward, the total at the bottom of the page offered the woman sitting at the table only mounting alarm.

She stood up and walked around the room, tapping the end of the pencil on a front tooth nervously, before returning to the table to once again check the total at the bottom of the page. It was as plain as the nose on her face: she had to tighten her belt yet again, or end up in the poorhouse.

Celia sat down, opened a drawer and took out the piece of yellowed newspaper she had read and re-read a hundred times. The headlines still took her breath away. Headlines that shouted the name of the ship her parents had boarded seven years ago to sail to Europe. Headlines that told of the ship's sinking in a violent storm in the Atlantic crossing from New York.

Leila and Wilf had waited years for that trip, then didn't even make it to England. The shock of it all had been terrible, and the aftershock when she discovered her financial position a little later was nearly as bad. She had known nothing of any second mortgage to pay for the trip, except that it made it obviously impossible for her to keep the house, her home. To keep up appearances, as Mama and Papa would certainly have wanted her to do, she used her grief to cover the true facts; putting the family home on the market was because she couldn't live with the house's memories, definitely not that she had no way of affording to keep it.

Once the transaction was through and the enormity of her problem obvious, she had no option but to sell the furniture and chattels as well, leaving Parramatta and her now destroyed status behind. There seemed only one place that she knew of that might be appropriate and affordable – Wellsford.

She remembered Wellsford fondly from the times she and her parents visited to stay with the Mitchell family when she was a child. The whole idea was not totally unpleasant, particularly as the Mitchells, if nobody else, understood her position in society. It never occurred to her that newspapers were also read in the country, so the Mitchells had guessed about her predicament.

With their help, she had found a little cottage for the right price, which meant that by investing her capital wisely away from the town, she could eke out an existence without anybody knowing of her fall from grace. There was nothing wrong with being a big fish in a small pool and she was, after all, well versed in the social mores and had known John Mitchell and his parents from childhood.

It had come as a shock to her how Hilda Mitchell had physically deteriorated. The woman had been one of her mother's best friends but was now quite dotty. Clearly inebriated when Celia met her last, she had been steadily getting worse over the intervening years and had now become an obvious cross for her family to bear.

John Mitchell had grown into a young man of class, and Celia found his wife Elizabeth to be delightful company. Her removal to this little country town had certainly provided some benefits.

Through her whole early life in Parramatta, Celia had never had any contact whatsoever with Aboriginal people and was surprised to witness the easy coexistence at the homestead with what she remembered her parents referring to as 'those people'. She couldn't conceive of their being in any way equals but had learned to accept that they did have their uses. Several times since she'd bought the cottage, she'd tried to no avail to repair or replace faulty things around the home, only to find that in no time, the leading hand from the homestead, Albert, arrived from nowhere and quietly made the necessary alterations for her. Generally without a word, sometimes a shy smile but with no expectation of payment.

And then there was Albert's wife, Faith. Quite lovely in a dark sort of way, and it was neighbourly of her to drop in some vegetables and eggs now and then, obviously excess to their needs at the homestead. Luckily they were left in the wood box by Celia's back door, so she didn't see any need to actually converse with the woman. After all, what could she say to someone like that?

★ ★ ★

Faith now sighed softly and picked up the empty basket that had carried fresh vegetables and half a dozen eggs from the chickens roaming freely around her kitchen door. 'I'll pop around next week with some vegies and things,' she said, expecting no thanks and receiving none.

Through conditioning from birth, Celia Branxton was rather given to excessive airs and graces, a legacy from her parents and particularly her late maiden aunts. Her thick, dark hair framed a pleasant enough face; that is, until she turned her nose up as if there was something offensive loitering directly underneath it. A slight shadow over her top lip suggested luxuriant growth in other areas, a suggestion enhanced by the dark, longish hairs on her lower arms. Shortish in stature with a generous bosom, she had been engaged to be married once, something she now chose not to discuss at all although she often announced to anyone who might listen that all men were tarred with the same brush and not worth the time of day.

Being a lady of high degree, even if only in her own mind, Celia never ever mentioned the three-letter word beginning with 's' and ending with 'x', nor did she acknowledge the ultimate outcome of the sexual act, and if in conversation she ever had to acknowledge that one of the town's daughters might be pregnant, she referred to the situation in a most refined way by calling it 'so so'. 'Yes, I believe Freddie Miller's daughter is "so-so",' as if it were some kind of contagious disease that should be spoken about in hushed tones.

Celia tried hard to hide her impecunious situation by saying to anyone within earshot, 'Oh, yes, I have a generous stipend left to me from Daddy's estate.' What the townspeople understood from the silver-blue shine on the seat of the skirt of her best navy suit was that Celia was close to skint. But she was now one of the locals and they tolerated her shenanigans with good-natured grace and tried to help without appearing to do so.

Like Johnno the butcher, who parcelled up her order knowing full well that Celia didn't have a cat. 'I simply can't understand what all the fuss is about,' Celia remarked haughtily, turning to cut up the cat's meat for the stew and sniffing distastefully at the dark, wrinkled kidney. She pulled a piece of greenish tissue from the kidney, held it for a moment then, thinking better of it, dropped it in the pot with the rest of the cut up meat. 'As far as I'm concerned, it all reveals itself in the breeding.'

'She'd skin a louse for its fat,' Albert once said to Faith when the subject of Celia arose. 'Tight as a duck's bum.' But underneath the sarcasm, both Faith and Albert knew Celia was not only living on a shoestring, but the airs and graces she affected were now a camouflage for the undeniable fact that she was lonely.

There was, however, one thing Celia loved and it was this attraction that finally stepped into her life to bring about a change. Bush orchids. She loved the bush orchids. Early summer, the hills surrounding Wellsford, and particularly the huge outcrop of basalt a short distance from the township, known as Minnie's Rock, were covered with the most exquisite display of these exotic blooms. Each October, Celia found her excitement mounting as she neared her November excursion.

Celia would leave early on the planned morning – wearing her straw hat and sensible shoes – take a flask and sandwiches and spend the whole day searching out her favourite flowers. There was another treat at Minnie's Rock as well: the wedge-tailed eagles flew with their young in November. And so did the falcons. She would take her binoculars (one of the few pieces she still owned from the Parramatta homestead) and spend the whole day enjoying what the area had to offer.

This year was no different.

At 7 am on a cloudless November morning, Celia set off, her stout shoes stepping purposefully. She had a good walk, two hours or more, to reach the rock and the sun was already hot. She slung her haversack containing the cut sandwiches, two apples and her water bottles onto her back, pulled her hat down to shield her eyes, adjusted the binoculars to a comfortable position over her ample chest and strode out, not stopping when she noticed Albert repairing a leaking water tank in the yard of his home, her nodding head indicating greeting.

Albert watched her retreating and chuckled to himself. He walked inside his back door and washed his hands in the sink. 'The Dopey Duchess just went by,' he said to Faith, wiping his hands on the towel hanging behind the kitchen door.

Faith rolled her eyes. 'Don't be cruel, Albert. She'd be all right if she could loosen up a bit,' she said. 'Nothing wrong with her, really, just a bit full of herself. She's scared that if someone gets too near to her, she might lose a bit of her self-made class.'

The Dopey Duchess meanwhile was feeling the heat – much earlier this year, she thought. *Probably in for an awful summer.* She stopped, removed her hat and mopped her face with a man-sized hanky. At the end of the dirt road leading past Faith and Albert's house, she started walking along the bush track leading to Minnie's Rock. 'Damned flies,' she said to herself, swiping her hands in front of her face as the beastly creatures searched the corners of her eyes for moisture.

Soon, in the distance, she could see the rock and high above it, floating on the air current, two eagles circling as if in slow motion. She stopped for a moment, looking through the binoculars for the lightning marks on the underside of the birds' wings and then, refreshed by their appearance, strode on.

Celia had to admit that Minnie's Rock mesmerised her. She was drawn here as if by some kind of destiny although she had no idea what could possibly be life-changing about wanting to look at orchids. But today the sun was hotter than she remembered. She had almost emptied one water bottle already, long before ten o'clock.

She trudged up the side of Minnie's Rock, heaving herself up a slope that this year seemed unfamiliar and difficult. Then there they were, directly in front of her, sprays and sprays of wonderfully delicate mauve and white orchids. The heat and her thirst momentarily forgotten, she sat on the ground, slipped off her haversack and drank in the magnificent display. Above her, ahead of her and particularly below her, the gorgeous blooms were everywhere. This year they seemed better than ever before.

Completely hypnotised by the orchids, Celia was soon crawling among them, lost in the sensation of being surrounded by the sprays, being careful not to damage any of them and feeling totally at one with nature as if she and she alone knew of the existence of this area and its beauty. Now, lying full length on her stomach, she inched forward under a bush to look more closely at an especially beautiful spray which swooped down ahead of her, gently bouncing in the morning breeze. Another few inches and she would be able to touch the gorgeous branch.

Suddenly she realised that it was not only her but the ground that was moving, then there was a terrible splitting, crashing sound like a tree being felled and in a split second, she and some of the ground around her were hurtling down the sloping side of the rock then out into space off a ledge and down towards the ironbarks far below.

She tried to open her eyes but couldn't. Her head buzzed agonisingly and there was a ringing sound in her ears. With an effort, she forced her eyelids to lift slightly and immediately wished she hadn't. Weird, out-of-focus shapes weaved and spun through her vision. She felt as if she was on fire, the buzzing sensation became worse, then everything went black.

Once again, Celia heard the sound, like a high-pitched vibration, but now the fire in her head had lessened and after a few moments, the sound decreased to a steady hum. She didn't want to try opening her eyes yet, but as she slowly regained consciousness, she experienced a curious sensation of being cooled with a covering of dew. Then again. As if someone was gently bathing ... She was alive! Someone was cooling her forehead with a damp cloth!

She snapped her eyes open – still no focus – and made an attempt to sit up. Absolutely out of the question. Everything ached; she could hardly move. To her astonishment, through the painful haze, she heard a voice, a male voice.

'Please, Miss Celia, don't try to move, just lay still.'

She was very pleased to do just that. The humming was slowly subsiding, but she again felt as hot as fury although the cooling cloth helped.

'Just you rest, Miss Celia, just lay quiet. Everything's going to be fine.' A soft, reassuring voice, one she vaguely recognised. But not only could she not see, she couldn't think either. All she knew was that she was alive, and someone was looking after her. Again everything went black.

This time Celia felt much better. The humming was still there, but softer, and the fire had subsided to an enveloping warmth. Her eyes opened quite easily and to her enormous relief started to focus almost straight away. She was looking at the inside of a rustic roof with roughly-sawn rafters – some kind of hut, she guessed. It was daylight; sun was streaming into the room. She tried to lift herself but with a groan realised that movement of almost any kind was impossible. Even moving her head was extremely uncomfortable, but soon she was able to see around her enough to ascertain that she was on some kind of lean-to bed in a corrugated iron hut with a coal sack over its only door and an open fireplace with its chimney forming a part of its outside wall. The floor was packed earth and there was no other furniture, or in fact anything useful that she could see.

She became conscious of sounds, someone moving things around outside the hut. Then she remembered the voice; the soft, encouraging voice. A man's voice. Panic gripped her and her head started to spin again. Who was this? What was she doing lying in this shed? What could have … wait! Images came flooding back, images of orchids, beautiful orchids, hundreds of them, and one unbelievable spray just out of her reach. Then … chaos, total chaos, a totally unreal feeling of falling, and nothing more.

She closed her eyes to try and concentrate on making some order of the jumbled thoughts in her head then snapped back to the present as she heard the voice again – very close.

'You looking better, Miss Celia, gonna be all right.'

This was no European voice; it was Aboriginal! Great heavens, she was helpless in a hut somewhere with an Aboriginal!

Suddenly terrified, she opened her eyes and looked right into the face of the man she only knew as Albert's cousin who occasionally turned up at Wellsford. She had never spoken to him, never even been close enough, but she thought his name was Freddie.

The face grinned and the soft voice continued. 'Oh, yes, you surely looking better. Now, just relax and rest.'

Instinctively, Celia's panic forced her into another fruitless attempt at getting up. Pains seemed to shoot through her whole body, and she cried out.

Strong but gentle hands rested on her shoulders. 'Please, Miss Celia, don't do that. You lucky to be alive after a fall like that, let alone only bruised. Just you rest now.'

Only bruised, she thought. *Thanks very much!* With a start, she realised she was thinking clearly again, so probably he was right. Surely if anything was broken, she would know? But when she'd tried to move, every fibre in her seemed to ache, so she obviously had no option but to do as the man said – relax and rest.

To her astonishment, Celia found that she could. There was a feeling of confidence and safety about this gentle man, and she felt her panic and anxiety fading.

'I'll just go outside and make us a drink,' he said.

Make us a drink. Us! She had never even spoken to the man – still hadn't, yet – but he seemed to have assumed the responsibility for her wellbeing. Nobody had done that since she was a child and even then, she had often felt uncomfortable and somehow responsible as her parents had so seldom showed much affection for each other.

Puberty had been a lonely time and the memories of her own brief courtship now appalled her. On her part, there had been a desperation for a personal friendship of her own, not one selected and domineered by her mother, but the man had been unfeeling, rather uncouth and totally unconscious of Celia's need for help in changing her life's direction. Soon after this mismatch and her withdrawal into her safe little shell, there was the separation with her parents and all the accompanying trauma, then Wellsford and her retreat from almost all social contact.

And now where was she? Leila would certainly have died of embarrassment with her daughter's predicament, but Celia was now realising how lucky she was. This man, Freddie (heavens, she'd lived some years quite close to these people and didn't know if they had surnames!), had almost certainly saved her life, but how?

It was all too much, too many loose ends. One thing was sure enough: Freddie was right. She could do nothing else but rest.

A few moments later, Freddie appeared again beside her, holding a rough mug of steaming liquid which he put on a box on the ground.

'You got to have something to drink, Miss Celia. I'll give you a hand to sit up a little.'

Inside, Celia cringed slightly. Great God, here she was, totally reliant on this man. If Freddie noticed her reaction, he didn't show it but slid his arm gently behind her head and across her upper back. To her surprise, he lifted her quite easily then supported her while a dizzy spell came and went. Then he picked up the mug with his free hand, after testing it for heat, and held it carefully to Celia's lips. She didn't recognise the smell of the steam and looked inquiringly at him.

'Don't worry,' he said, grinning, 'it's not your tea, it's ours. It'll help fix you up.'

Very tentatively, Celia sipped the liquid and as it passed into her system, she felt a wave of relief which registered with her still-grinning companion.

'All right?' Offering the mug again.

'Yes,' she replied, gratefully accepting more of the steaming drink, and as her body reacted to the calming fluid, she realised that the first word she had uttered to her benefactor was a definite 'yes'. How strange.

To add to her confusion, Freddie casually put the mug to his own lips and took a strong sip then looked at her as if reading her mind, grinned and said, 'Sorry, Miss Celia, only one mug,' before offering it to her again.

Internally, her immediate reaction, built on a lifetime of instruction in formal behaviour, was 'I couldn't possibly', but in this situation, with her aching body crying out for sustenance, she gratefully accepted the mug, this time a longer draught, then another. With each swallow, she felt better, a little more relaxed. Then unexpectedly she felt tired again, sore and tired, and her body sagged a little.

Freddie put the mug back on the box and again supported her as she lay back on the pillow. *Pillow? Where did a pillow come from?* Never mind; she was glad it was there and gratefully settled back.

Suddenly she was conscious of something painful on the inside of her right thigh and with an effort, cautiously moved her hand to the area, immediately withdrawing it as pain shot through her leg. Lifting her hand slightly, she noticed a trail of blood on her fingers.

'It's all right,' Freddie said gently. 'You gashed your leg in the fall, but I've bathed it and the wound is clean. Nothing to bandage it with yet.'

Celia felt dizzy. Great God, she thought, for a dreadful moment, I wondered …

Freddie stood beside her, the now empty mug in his hand. 'You feel better?'

'Yes.' There it was again. 'Thank you,' she added.

'Right. Now you just try to sleep, and don't be frightened. I'll go and get Albert and we'll see about getting you back to town.'

Celia nodded slowly at him, and in a flash he was gone.

She dozed fitfully for some time, in between times still trying to piece it all together. She remembered the climb, the orchids and the terrible falling sensation, but how did Freddie fit into it all? How did she survive without any breakages? And how did Freddie know that … She felt her face redden with the realisation that he must have physically checked her over! Where had he come from? How did he know she'd fallen, and she didn't fall into this shed, so how did she get there? And another thing: from the light and heat in the shed, it was quite early, so this must be another day!

With her head full of unanswerables, she drifted off to sleep once more.

Almost immediately, it seemed to Celia, she awakened to the sound of horses' hooves outside the shed, then was greatly relieved to hear Freddie's voice calling.

'Don't panic, Miss Celia, it's only me and Albert!'

The coal sack was flicked back and the two men came through the doorway. Albert looked at her, smiling.

'Freddie tells me you decided to try to fly, Miss Celia.'

Although she was in no mood for jokes, Celia was delighted to have these men here, casually but confidently taking over.

'We got lucky, Miss Celia,' said Freddie. 'Albert was coming to look for you and we met just down the track, so we'll have you home soon.'

Once again Celia could only croak 'thanks' as four capable, caring hands picked her up effortlessly, mattress and all, and carried their load to a stretcher they'd rigged between two horses. They made everything fast and set out slowly for Wellsford.

* * *

Celia sat in her only armchair, enjoying the sunlight spreading over her from the window. Several weeks had now passed since the ordeal and she was reasonably mobile again. Still bruised, but thankfully not broken.

She'd had plenty of time to ponder on the recent events and had found herself questioning many of the attitudes she had harboured through her life to date. This feeling of superiority that had been taught and ingrained into her since childhood; what was that all about? Her very life had almost certainly been saved by a man who her parents would never under any circumstances have considered having any contact with, a man to whom she owed an enormous debt of gratitude.

And the importance of possessions that she had always been party to. Heavens, it had been that impulse that had made her reach out for the orchid spray, the action that had set off this whole chain of events. Anyway, since her move from the city, she had discovered how much easier it was to live with fewer possessions although she knew that her mother would say, 'One has to keep up appearances, come what may.' What a load of tosh, Celia thought. Her parents had spent their lives overindulging themselves, with the result that Celia was now in the position she was, with little or no experience of 'the world of the common people', again one of her mother's favourite phrases.

The 'common people' of this town had been kind to her since her arrival; probably, she thought, more so than she deserved. Elizabeth Mitchell, for all her position, had not reacted at all unfavourably to Celia's sparsely-furnished home when she had dropped in to check that things were all right. In fact, she didn't appear to notice the situation at all.

And as for Faith and Albert who, she'd discovered, did have surnames – Franklin – she couldn't believe how considerate they had been. From the day the men had returned her to the house, Faith had quietly taken over her recuperation, coming and going with food and drinks through each day, gently encouraging her on each visit.

On the day after her return, Faith had brought the older woman from Wellsford, Pearl, with her, and after they'd given her something to eat and drink, Pearl had suggested questioningly that perhaps Celia would like a wash? She'd nodded, which was about all she could manage as everything ached so much. Pearl had put the kettle on to heat some water, then to Celia's momentary astonishment had removed her blanket and sheet, then her clothes!

'My goodness, girl, you certainly did land hard,' was all Pearl had said, and as she'd gently sponged Celia's body with the warm cloth and towelled her down, Celia had lifted her head with an effort and looked down at herself. There were bruises and scratches everywhere, it seemed, certainly in the parts she could see.

Once again, Pearl's voice had cut into her thoughts. 'Sorry, girl, this may hurt a bit, but I've got to turn you over,' and she had casually done just that.

Celia couldn't believe how quickly and easily she'd done it, and although it had hurt for a few moments, the feeling of the strong hands and the warm washcloth on her shoulders and back had been absolutely wonderful.

Once finished with the towelling, and without another word, Pearl had flipped her over again, then fluffed up the pillow.

'You're a good-built woman, Celia, a good-built woman,' she'd said, then covered her still naked body with the bedclothes.

Celia had blushed crimson. In her whole life, nobody except her mother in the early days had seen her naked, and now this quiet and capable woman had not only washed her, she'd paid her a lovely compliment.

'You just rest, Miss Celia, and don't worry about your clothes. We'll wash them and bring them back this afternoon.'

With that the two women had left.

Celia had gaped, wide-eyed, at her ceiling. Not only was she helpless in her bed, she was naked as well. And these two neighbours had shown no embarrassment whatsoever, just gone about the business of helping her in all ways they could, giving everything, expecting nothing.

Soon she'd begun to relax, realising full well that she had absolutely no option. She'd closed her eyes and thought about this amazing turn of events. It had all happened so quickly that it frightened her. But as she'd lain still, the fear and embarrassment subsided to be replaced by a very different feeling of contentment. Not the contentment she'd experienced in her family environment with the acquisition of more worldly goods, but one of a different kind, a relaxed feeling of safety in the company of people who, like her, had little or nothing to call their own but were still ready to share what they had, their food, their abilities, even their personalities. It was quite a delightful change, even a luscious feeling.

The woman, Pearl, while capably tending to her needs, had complimented her on her body. Nobody had ever said anything like that to her. She'd been brought up to regard everything in the physical area as being outside comment or conversation. Faces, yes, but bodies? No, no, no!

But for heaven's sake, why not? Pearl's statement had been purely one of fact, and Faith had not reacted in any way to it, so why had she, Celia, felt shame? Perhaps she did have a good body, but how was she to know?

One thing was clear; that she was at that moment completely unable to alter her current situation in the slightest.

As Celia had settled down, another disquieting thought had entered her awakening mind. The warmth of the mattress and sheets had felt quite wonderful against her skin. Nakedness wasn't disgusting; it was marvellous.

* * *

A gentle knock at the door had awakened Celia again and she was conscious of feeling a little better. The door had opened and Pearl's face appeared around it, smiling. Celia had noticed Pearl was carrying her clothes, clean and folded, some sheets and a small container. As Pearl had crossed the room, Celia had said, 'I'd like to thank you, Pearl, for your kindness.'

Pearl put Celia's clothes and the sheets on her armchair and approached the bed with the container.

Quite a strong smell of eucalyptus had reached Celia's nose and she'd stretched her head forward to look for its source.

'Don't you worry yourself, now,' said Pearl. 'I've mixed up some poultices that should do the trick for you.'

Folding back the bedclothes, Pearl had dipped her fingertips into the container and, starting from Celia's neckline, gently dabbed and spread the poultices over the parts of her body that showed signs of her ordeal. Rather than recoiling in pain as she had expected to do,

Celia had found the process soothing, another lovely experience. And when Pearl had attended to the trouble spots and gone over those areas again, gently massaging the poultices into her skin, Celia had all but forgotten the discomfort in this new feeling of arousal in her nerve ends.

'Sorry, girl, but I'm going to have to turn you again,' said Pearl, and once again Celia had been surprised at the ease with which the woman did this. In a flash she was lying on her stomach and the worst discomfort had been moving her head up from the pillow to breathe.

Pearl had repeated the applications and the delightful massage to her back and Celia had been amazed at how soothed she'd felt in such a short time. Then Pearl picked up a sheet from a chair, flicked it open and draped it over Celia's body.

'All right, girl, here we go again,' Pearl had said, and a moment later, Celia was face up with a clean sheet under her. Pearl had then removed the underside sheet, slid the clean one under the pillow and tucked it in all around. Then she'd taken the top sheet off and put it with another on the floor, collected another from the chair, thrown it over the by now flabbergasted Celia, covered it with the blankets and gone to put the kettle on, presumably for a cup of tea.

'How on earth did you do all that so easily?' she'd said later to Pearl.

She'd looked at Celia over a steaming cup, smiling broadly, and said, 'Nice to know you're getting better, Celia. Till right now, it seemed you could hardly talk! In my time, girl, I've tended to and lifted a whole lot of women, most of them pregnant, so you're easy. You're not only not very big, you're not pregnant.'

'It's silly to put clean clothes on over those smelly poultices,' Pearl had said, 'but maybe I should have asked if you'd like a nightie?'

'No thanks, Pearl, I'll be fine,' Celia had said, snuggling into the warmth of the bedding against her skin.

Pearl had given her a knowing look, then said, 'You're going to be all right, Celia, just fine. I'll come by and see you tomorrow. You rest now.' She'd picked up the sheets and her container and walked to the door.

'Pearl!' Celia had called.

The older woman had turned. 'What is it, girl?'

'Thanks so much.'

'Aw, come on,' Pearl had said and, grinning, left the room.

Yes, it had been quite a learning period for Celia. More, by far, at a personal level than all her years at school. Now she was really starting to understand people and the importance of close co-existence. The Mitchells, and in fact almost all the townspeople, had been kind and thoughtful and had supervised her recuperation just as if she were family.

Celia felt that she had only just been introduced to her own body. How wonderful it was not to be restricted by the absurd clothing she'd worn all her life, and the constant reminders: 'Modesty at all times, m'dear, everything must be kept covered', and the other one: 'Stays, Celia, a well-bred woman always wear stays. Without stays, you'll spread'. In this country, where the temperatures could sometimes soar to twice the English average, where was the sense in that?

And since the first time she had felt the delight of sheets against her bare body, she had become much more conscious of herself, both inside and out. Right now, for example, she was enjoying the sunshine, sipping a cup of tea and feeling the healing warmth through her unbuttoned light blouse, letting her mind drift into areas that would have been unthinkable some few days ago.

Her thoughts were interrupted by a knock at the door. Still holding her tea, she opened the door to see Freddie standing there, looking uncomfortable.

'Freddie,' she blushed, 'how nice to see you. I've just made tea, come in, come in.'

He shuffled his feet on the doormat. 'You sure that's all right, Miss Celia? I dunno ...'

'Of course it's all right, come in! I'll pour another cup. I do have two, you know.'

Freddie grinned at the memory of the mug incident, then stepped into the room.

'Sit down, sit down,' she said, pulling the chair from her table for him. 'Two cups, but only one chair.'

Both of them laughed and Freddie felt a little less uncomfortable being inside the home of this woman he felt he hardly knew.

'I'm sure you know how grateful I am for your help, Freddie, but what still mystifies me is how it happened. How did you know I was there?'

'I didn't, Miss Celia, at least not at first.'

'Before we go on, Freddie, will you drop the "Miss", please? After all, I almost certainly do owe you my life.'

'You don't owe me anything, Miss Celia. These things happen in the bush sometimes and you just do what you can to help. I just happened to be up there and I heard you scream – and the crashing. I followed the sounds and found you under the tree. It was obvious from looking at it what had happened. You'd snapped off a couple of branches on the way through! A couple of feet either way and you wouldn't have been so lucky. I knew where there was an old shearer's shed not far away, so I took you there.'

'But how?'

'I carried you, Miss Celia.'

'You carried me. Heavens above!'

'Sorry, Miss Celia, but I couldn't leave you where you were.'

'Oh, Freddie, I didn't mean it to sound like that! I'm truly so grateful to you – you carried me! But how did you know about the shed; you're not from around Wellsford?'

'No, Miss Celia ...'

'Please, do you want me to call you Mr Freddie?'

'Well, it's just not that easy. The few people I've had anything to do with have always expected that.'

'All right, Mr Freddie,' Celia said pointedly, smiling. 'Now, let's get back to the shed.'

'Yair. Well, there've been lots of times over the years when things got too hard to take where I've always lived and worked, and I often took off and headed for Albert, my cousin. He told me about the old shed, and sometimes I'd hole up there. That's how I knew there was blankets and things there; we'd put them there.'

Celia listened to him talking, hardly able to believe that this chain of events involved her. 'But how did you happen to be up there at that time?'

'Well, this might sound strange,' Freddie said, moving uncomfortably, 'but years ago when I was hiding in the hut and in the bush around it, I started to notice the eagles and their young around the area, and I went to find their nesting places. Climbing up Minnie's Rock one November, I discovered all those bush orchids – beautiful, they were. So, nearly every year, I come back in November to see it all again. And that's what I was doing when I heard you yell.'

Feeling a little faint, Celia just looked at him.

* * *

From the purposeful way her feet hit the ground as she walked across the yard, Albert knew his wife had something to say. He was in the tin shed working at patiently shaping a new half-sole for his well-worn boots.

Faith stood outside the door of the shed, one arm half around the doorjamb, enjoying the sun's warmth on her back. She watched the slivers of leather fall to the ground under the knife, from along the side of the boot, held tightly in the vice. She breathed deeply, savouring the smell of new leather.

'I've been thinking,' she said.

'I know,' her husband replied. 'Could tell from the way you walked over here.'

Faith smiled. 'I went to Celia's today. You know she's really changed since the accident. Asked me into the house and made me a cup of tea and then, you won't believe this, pulled damned near everything from her garden, insisting I bring it home.'

Albert continued his shaping, pulling in the corners of his mouth in concentration.

'I can't believe the change,' Faith continued. 'When you think of how up herself she was before.'

'Yair, well, you got Freddie to thank for that,' her husband said, concentrating on the job at hand. 'Been slipping her a length.'

Faith gasped, then laughed. 'Albert Franklin,' she said, 'there's no need to be crude.'

Albert placed the knife on the bench alongside the vice and grinned at his wife. 'Not being crude, love,' he said. 'It's a fact.'

Little sparks of cognition ignited for a moment in the deep brown of Faith's eyes. 'You're kidding!' she exclaimed, one hand half covering her mouth as if to prevent herself uttering any unkind words.

'No,' Albert continued, 'been going on for a while, apparently. Seems she asked him around to tell her what happened and she must've been in some kind of shock, I reckon. Didn't want him to leave. One thing just led to another.'

Faith walked into the shed and sat down on the upturned apple crate Albert kept in the corner.

'But Freddie?' she queried. 'Freddie is the one who said they're all arseholes.'

Albert wiped his hands on the sides of his trousers. 'Hasn't said that for months.' He grinned. 'You see. what we think is shaped pretty much by our experiences. Freddie only thought that way because he was surrounded by people who deserved to be called that.'

Faith shook her head. 'But Celia, she was such a snob. Always held the Wellsford staff at arm's length, even as a child.'

'Same thing though, isn't it?' Albert questioned. 'That's the way she was taught and that's the way she thought until life stepped in and showed her the penny has two sides.'

Faith walked to the door of the tin shed, shaking her head. 'But Freddie?' she said as the idea tried to sink in.

As the sun warmed and comforted, Faith stood watching her husband, thinking about what he'd just said. She wondered if understanding was the answer to all problems, or if good and evil were like a pair of inseparable Siamese twins. You couldn't have one without the other. Certainly no one had any say in the time and place of their birth, nor did they choose their parents. Or did they? It was as if you were placed in a certain area at a certain time and from then on, it was up to you. So, if you decided, as she and Albert had done, to make the best of it, did that add to things?

Sometimes Faith felt that there could be a great cloud of negativity surrounding the earth with such a strong magnetic force, it could almost pull you under. Albert had experienced that as a child when his grandmother had died, almost given in to it, and so had she in moments of despair. But then they had striven to fight back, and help had arrived from somewhere. Somewhere beyond that cloud of negativity. And then people surprised you – Freddie and Celia, for example. A few weeks ago, neither of them would have thought in their wildest dreams that they could form some kind of affection for each other. But then the fates arranged Celia's accident and in so doing adjusted both her and Freddie's vision, allowing them to see with new eyes.

Faith sighed. 'It's kind of nice, isn't it?'

Albert smiled fondly. 'Nothing wrong with people caring for each other,' he said, 'nothing at all.'

Yule tidings

Elizabeth stood on the verandah of the homestead, waving to Jamie to come inside. He ran across the yard, smiling at his mother and thinking, as he usually did, how pretty she was.

'What's on?' he queried.

She put her arm around his shoulder. He was growing, all right, her boy.

'We're going to have a house guest for a few weeks,' she said. 'Phyllis Corcoran has to go into hospital in Sydney for some prolonged treatment and we will have her daughter Amy staying here.

Jamie nodded. 'She doesn't talk, does she?'

'No,' Elizabeth answered. 'She's been mute ever since she had an accident a while back. It's caused by shock, and I want you to be kind to her, to try and understand that she needs encouragement and befriending.'

The boy nodded. 'Okay by me,' he answered. 'Now, can I go outside again?'

His mother smiled. 'In a minute,' she said. 'There's just one other thing. Do try not to talk about her hands. They're badly scarred and she hides them all the time. Please remember to try not to mention them.'

'That's no trouble,' the boy answered as he moved towards the door.

Three weeks before Christmas, Amy Corcoran arrived at the station. Elizabeth really liked the young girl with the sad face who hid her hands in the folds of her skirt, but though the child seemed quite comfortable, nothing would induce her to talk.

'What happened to your hands?' was almost the first thing Jamie asked. Elizabeth closed her eyes and sighed, fearing for the worst, but the girl just shrugged her shoulders and smiled; didn't seem to be offended at all by the boy's question.

'They're lovely mittens you're wearing, Amy. Did Faith knit you another pair?' Elizabeth asked.

The child dug her hands further away but nodded her head.

During the week prior to Christmas, Elizabeth had John cut a small tree from the pine plantation, which they put in a large pot alongside the fireplace in the old parlour, ready to dress up for Christmas morning.

'We're going to decorate the tree today,' Elizabeth said to Amy. 'Would you like to help?'

The girl nodded, smiling shyly.

Elizabeth laid out the tree's decorations on the table – tinsel, silver and gold balls; tiny carved, handpainted wooden figures and for the top, the silver fairy with blonde curls and tinsel wings. And, of course, the bag of cotton wool, part of the Mitchell household tradition, placed on the branches every year since its introduction in Grandfather Hugh's time, a vain attempt to return him momentarily to England for the Christmas season. Every year, John wanted to discard the now grubby cotton wool but could not bring himself to do it. This year was no different, and it had over the years become his job to lay the fake snow out.

Over her shoulder, Elizabeth noticed Amy's hand reach out and touch the fairy's hair briefly, disappearing into the folds of her skirt again when the woman approached. The child's sadness cut Elizabeth deeply. Apart from her scarred hands, her silence bore witness to a hurt so personal that the girl had retreated into a world she chose not to share with others by giving voice to her thoughts.

The incident had occurred over two years earlier, one sixth of her life, and during that time, nobody had heard the girl utter a sound. But

Elizabeth had seen the pencil drawings Amy had brought with her in a folder and it was clear from those images that there was something behind those haunted eyes that sought self-expression. Every day, Elizabeth made sure a supply of paper and pencils were left where the girl had access to them.

Elizabeth had watched her drawing, from a distance, and was fascinated by the way Amy concentrated her entire attention on what she was doing. All else became secondary as the pencil, held firmly but delicately in Amy's mittened hand, moved effortlessly and confidently across the sheet of paper, but as soon as the girl realised someone might be near, the pencil was dropped, the work covered and the hands immediately hidden again. Under the table, anywhere out of sight.

'This is a magic fairy,' Elizabeth said to the girl, holding out the Christmas tree decoration. 'If you wish hard for something you really want, she'll do her absolute best to grant your wish.' She looked sideways at the child. Amy was staring intently at the decoration. 'Don't tell anybody your wish, though, or it may not come true.'

Jamie passed the various pieces to his mother and tried to encourage Amy to do the same, but the girl, while watching it all with glowing eyes, would not show her hands. The fairy was put on the very top of the tree, wings adjusted, blonde hair shining. Lastly the coloured lights were added and John plugged their lead into the power point.

Amy sat cross-legged, staring at the now brightly-lit tree in wonder. It suddenly occurred to Elizabeth that the girl had in all probability never before had a Christmas tree of her own.

'What do you want Father Christmas to bring you, Jamie?' she asked, winking at her husband.

'A bike,' Jamie said. 'I'd really like a new bike.'

'Wonder what Amy would like,' John said to no one in particular.

'Paints.'

The word hung on the air for a second, just long enough for everyone to wonder whether or not they'd heard right.

Still Amy stared at the tree.

'Sorry,' said John, moving to put his arm around his wife's shoulder. 'What was that you said?'

'Paints and crayons,' the child said. 'I'd really like him to bring me some paints and crayons.'

'Well,' said John, tightly holding his wife's hand and motioning to her to not say a word. 'I'll have to see what we can do about that.'

★ ★ ★

In the old shearer's quarters, ten year old Daniel scuttled around the kitchen floor area like a Cossack dancer, busying himself spreading the folded newspapers lengthwise on the floor then sitting back on his haunches, surveying the piece thoughtfully before reaching for the scissors and carefully cutting a uniform design from one end. Faith had watched her elder son tenderly. He was different, this boy, a mother knew that intuitively. His nature was a mixture of extremes; sadness sometimes then boundless joy and unlimited patience like he displayed now, cutting that newspaper, but that patience could be instantly replaced by a deep intolerance. Still, he was special. Not that she loved Bennie less, not one bit, but Daniel had always been close to her and eager to share with her. She worried about him of course, worried about the time she might not be there to direct his energies or have the right to interfere in his life. He had to be his own person; she knew and accepted that. She had the time now to love him, that was all.

The boy on the floor had flashed her a smile. 'Nearly finished, Ma, just wait till you see.'

He stood up and unrolled the piece of cut out newsprint to reveal a string of little people standing in a line, holding hands. He dragged a packing case to one side of the room, climbed up and tacked one end of the line to the wall, high up, then climbed down, gently pulling the other end to stretch out to reach to the other side of the room where he also tacked that in place the same way.

'What do you think?' Expectant, wanting her approval.

Faith stood with both hands on the pads of her hips and walked up and down, looking at the row of cut out characters. 'Beautiful,' she said to him. 'Just beautiful. Beats that silver stuff. But who are they? Any idea?'

'Ma,' said Daniel, unable to hide his disappointment. 'Just think about it.'

Faith smiled at her son then stood behind him, folding him in her arms while together they looked at the newspaper people.

'Well,' she said, 'you've got me. Tell me who they are.'

Daniel turned to face her; his large, sombre brown eyes thoughtful. 'It's Christmas, right?'

Faith nodded.

'And every Christmas, it's just you and Pa and Bennie and me and Pearl, of course.'

'Of course,' Faith replied. 'We're family, aren't we?'

'Ma, that's just it.' Danny kissed her on the cheek and pointed to the line of people hanging across the ceiling. 'Now they're all here. Just in paper of course, but they're all here. The grandparents and parents and uncles and aunties and cousins we never knew. The mother and father you and Pa never knew. We had them, didn't we? We had them, and they had us, and they never knew us either.'

Faith felt her eyes sting. She hugged her son tightly.

'Well, they're here now, boy.' She choked back her tears. 'Every Christmas, we'll put them up and know that they're here with us.'

The crash of the back door opening startled them both. Benjamin entered hurriedly, stripped to the waist, throwing something heavy on the table, something wrapped in his shirt. Then he opened the door a crack, peered out and closed it again, leaning with his back against it, breathing hard but smiling. He grinned broadly at his mother and

walked to the table to bend and, with a flourish, pull his shirt away
to reveal what lay beneath.

'Courtesy of Lord and Lady Muck from Turd Island, have a Merry
Christmas.'

Faith stared at the leg of lamb on the kitchen table. 'Bennie, you
didn't, you couldn't.'

'Sure I could.' Benjamin felt cocky now, the deed done. 'And why
not? Why should we have a blimmin' chook or a skin-and-bones rabbit
while Lord and Lady Shit-for-brains stuff their faces and throw away
more than we eat?'

'But Bennie, that's stealing!'

'Think of it as sharing, Ma.' Still grinning. 'Anyway, I'm not takin'
it back.'

Faith gingerly rubbed her forehead in the hope that a solution of
some sort might present itself and as if on cue, Albert walked through
the back door, one glance taking in his wife's face, his two sons and
the purloined joint on the kitchen table.

'What can we do, Albert? Tell us what to do,' Faith pleaded with
her husband.

Albert looked slowly from Faith to Daniel to Benjamin and then
back again. He sighed and walked to the table, looking at the stolen
lamb. He turned and stood for a moment, stern, unsmiling. Bennie's
grin quickly faded.

'All right,' he answered. 'You asked me, so I'll tell you what we're
going to do.'

Three solemn faces anxiously studied his, intent, waiting. Suddenly
Albert's face broadened into a wide grin. 'Tomorrow we dig some
spuds and pick a bit of mint, light the wood stove, and cook it. This
year, Albert Franklin and his family are having a real Australian
Christmas.'

A knock at the door cut short the laughter. Albert opened it, just
a crack.

'It's only me,' said Pearl. 'Who'd you expect? Police? Got half a Christmas puddin' for us from Elizabeth Mitchell. If you're lucky, you might still find a threepenny bit.'

Pearl moved towards the table, her eyes as wide as her smile. 'Oh, Gawd,' she said, laughing, 'that where it went? Ah well, it's true. Blessings fall from the sky at Christmas, don't they?'

'Or off the back of a truck,' Albert grinned.

Everything was tidied up, the leftover lamb wrapped in muslin in the safe, both boys and even Pearl sleeping soundly, and still Albert couldn't get the grin off his face. Lying on his bed with his wife's head on his shoulder and his arm around her, he felt totally contented. He gently squeezed her elbow and whispered, 'Are you asleep?'

'Of course not,' Faith answered. 'Don't you know me yet?'

Albert snuffled quietly. 'You know I can't believe how good that stolen lamb tasted,' he said.

Faith stiffened slightly. 'Oh, God,' she said, 'don't remind me! How could Bennie do that?'

'Maybe he knows people better than we do, Faith. Pearl just told them today that a fly got to the joint so she couldn't cook it, and they didn't even notice it was missing from the coolroom. The boy was right.'

'Some fly. A great big, two-legged one,' she said.

The two of them shook gently as they laughed.

'Things are changing, though, aren't they?' she continued. 'We've always accepted our lot and been happy to have a roof over our heads and fair people to work for because that's all we've known, but today's lot, even our own boys, question things much more.'

'Guess we were just lucky, Faith. We got through before things started to fall apart. Even Mr James changed with all that council stuff, so the boys couldn't know how things were years ago. They only know about now, and I reckon that's why Bennie uses all those names for the Mitchells. Where do you think he got them from? He's only a kid, remember.'

'Where did he get them from, then?'

'From other kids he spends time with, that's where. When we were kids, the homestead and farm were our life, but that's not enough for today's kids, so they're going to get up to mischief. If they think things aren't fair, they'll kick up now, where we never did. You think of Freddie; he's as close as any of our lot ever got to fighting back, and where did it get him, then?'

'Never mind where it got him then, how about now?' Faith asked, and again they laughed softly.

'Albert?'

'Yes?'

'Make love to me?'

'Oh boy, what a Christmas,' Albert breathed.

★ ★ ★

Getting the chair onto the metal basket on the front of the delivery bike had been difficult enough. Stanley had padded the metal surroundings of the basket with hessian, then put the two arms of the chair over the handlebars which had also been rolled in lagging, resting the bulk of the chair on the basket itself. The tyre on the small front wheel of the bike flattened threateningly with the chair's weight. I cannae do it, Stanley thought to himself. It was obvious he would not be able to ride the bike, but nevertheless, he put his bike clips securely around his trouser legs, pulled his old tartan tam o'shanter with its pompom holding on by a mere thread down to one side of his head and started to gingerly walk his load through the main street of Wellsford. It wasn't so bad on the sealed road, after he got the balance right, but the bike developed a mind of its own, lurching every which way once he reached the end of the bitumen.

Stanley guided his load up the crushed-shell path to Faith and Albert's front door. He had wanted to do this for a long, long time, but first he had to wait until his heart had gathered strength enough to once more guide his hands. For a long time after Maggie died, he seemed to just lose interest in furniture making. Then he got the idea to make a chair for Faith as a way of saying thank you. Besides, he couldn't help but notice that she had hardly a stick of furniture in her little home. Clean as a whistle it was, he had noticed that, and with all the love she had put into it, it felt nothing like a shearers' shack. She could put an old baked bean tin full of wild flowers on the table and give it a feel of home.

Stanley held the bike carefully with one hand and knocked lightly on the door. Faith looked startled for a moment when she opened the door, taking in the overloaded bike overflowing with the armchair, her surprised eyes questioning Stanley's face.

'I made it for you,' Stanley said, almost apologetically. 'I wanted you to have something I had made, lassie. I want to say thank you.'

Faith put her hand to her throat. She stared at the chair in the front of the bike.

'Here,' the Scotsman said gruffly. 'Hold these handlebars while I get it off, then.'

Faith held the bike steady while Stanley lifted the chair off and into the front room of the house. 'It's covered with moquette,' he told her. 'Green, uncut moquette. I thought green would go with anything.' Not that there's a thing here for it to clash with, he thought.

Faith was speechless. Her hands caressed first the fabric of the chair and then the carved arms. She had never had a new piece of furniture and thought she would never, if she lived to be a hundred, see a piece quite so beautiful.

'It's Jacobean,' Stanley told her. 'It's a style my Maggie particularly liked. She would have wanted me to say thank you.'

'But there's no need.' Faith was trying to find words to express her feelings. 'You don't have to thank me for being a human being. I only did what anyone would do in similar circumstances.'

Stanley touched her arm gently. 'No, lassie,' he said, 'that's not so. Human beings very often close their eyes to another's pain, rather than become involved. You didnae do that. You opened your heart.'

Stanley pulled his tam o'shanter out of his pocket and put it on his head. He tipped the edge of it as he walked through the front door of Faith's house and then he turned. 'Thank you, lassie,' he said again. 'Thank you.'

He walked to where he had placed the delivery bike and stood for a moment, scratching his head. He turned when he heard Faith laughing, one hand over her mouth, the other pointing to the end of the street. There was his bike wobbling back towards them like it had had one too many, with Daniel pedalling and Benjamin sitting in the wire delivery basket. As soon as Daniel caught sight of Stanley, he stopped pedalling, whether from guilt, embarrassment or both, the bike and both boys dropping into a squealing heap on the road.

'Serves you right,' said Faith later, bathing Daniel's grazed knees and palms with vinegar. 'You don't help yourself to things that don't belong to you.'

'Well, Bennie did at Christmas time, didn't he?'

'That's enough of your cheek,' she said. 'That was different.'

They both smiled at the recollection, Daniel proud of his brother's daring, Faith embarrassed still.

Benjamin walked away to where the chair stood, throne-like, in the corner of the living room. He bent to smell the freshly lacquered timber, rubbing his fingers over the barley sugar twists on the arms. He couldn't quite comprehend how anyone could make a piece of timber look quite so magnificent. 'Jack of Bean,' he whispered under his breath. 'When I grow up, that's what I'm going to do. I'm going to work with timber, make chairs of Jack of Bean.' He lay flat on the floor, arms folded under his head so that he could get an uninterrupted view of the chair, drinking in the glow of the timber, the green of the moquette, more happy at that moment than he could remember.

Later in moments of retrospection, Faith often remembered how happy she had been that day with her family around her. She remembered the rich aroma of lamb sizzling on the stove. She had had her Jack-of-Bean chair to sit in and, holding hands across her ceiling as if reaching down through the years to include her, she had the essence, at least, of belonging. Not just to the people in the room but way, way further back. Way back further than anyone could imagine. Way back to when her country was young. That night, for a moment at least, she had held to her heart the essence of her heritage.

'Penny for them.' Pearl leaned across to tap the table as Faith realised she might have been speaking to her for a while.

'Oh, I was just thinking about last Christmas,' Faith answered, 'about us all being together and Daniel making those little people out of newspaper. About how good it all felt.'

Pearl nodded and stuck the darning needle through the sock in her hands. 'Funny, isn't it?' she said, not waiting for a reply. 'Here we are without any family and yet that Christmas was the most family feeling Christmas I bet anyone ever had.' She picked up the needle and continued with her mending, humming to herself some song she remembered from somewhere long ago. Some almost familiar tune that just seemed to come to her from way, way back.

Losing and finding

'Hail Mary, full of grace, the Lord is with thee.' Words uttered in a monotone accompanied by a relentless pacing backwards and forwards along the length of the timber verandah. Feet turned the corners with almost military precision before gathering the urgency to turn again, following back on their own unvarying tracks.

Madness walks its own path, Pearl thought. She was scratching at nothing in particular on her upper arm, cocking her head to one side to listen sadly to the message of increasing dementia being tapped out by Hilda Mitchell's tireless feet. She sighed softly as she heard the bang of the screen door followed by Elizabeth Mitchell's voice gently urging her mother-in-law to come inside.

Hilda appeared not to recognise her daughter-in-law. She ignored her offered outstretched hand and continued the relentless walking. 'Hail Mary, full of grace …' She stopped and looked over her shoulder. 'He'll be here soon.'

For a moment, Hilda had ceased her pacing to look briefly down the driveway leading from the house. Then, seeing nothing, either in reality or in the recesses of her own mind, continued, 'Hail Mary, full of grace …'

'No, Mother, he's not coming today, not any day. Now please, come inside.'

Hilda pouted and folded her arms over her frail body as if to prevent the escape of the demons inside her. 'He's coming, he's coming soon. Daddy fell asleep and they couldn't wake him up, but he's coming soon. He'll come and get me soon and we'll go back to Parramatta.'

She stopped walking momentarily to rummage in the string bag thrown limply over her arm. Her right hand emerged triumphantly clutching an old red and blue tea-cosy purloined at some stage in the past when Pearl must have pretended not to notice. With a gesture of defiance more suited to an operatic dowager, she placed the cosy on her head, a manic replica of some royal toque, tossed a disgusted look in the direction of her daughter-in-law and continued to relentlessly pace and pray.

Pearl bent over the blackberries she was hulling, flicking across their surface with one finger, looking for any overlooked piece of leaf or bug. 'Just put a gun to me head if I ever go that way.'

Faith nodded her agreement, flouring and folding over the pastry she was rolling to house the freshly cleaned blackberries.

'It's a wonder,' said Pearl, rubbing along the tops of both legs with her hands as if pushing her thoughts out through her knees, 'that she hasn't worn those beads down to the size of a tomato seed. She's hailed Mary so often you'd think the Holy Mother would go for a name change.'

Faith nodded, wondering what particular madness caused the demented woman on the verandah to finger her rosary with such determination. 'Don't you think the whole religious thing, according to their thinking, is a little strange?' she asked the older woman. She cast a quick glance over her shoulder as if fearing the topic of discussion just might invite divine intervention. 'I mean,' she continued without waiting for a reply, 'it's rather odd to take a man in the prime of his life, torture him, press a crown of thorns on his head, nail him to a cross and then expect generations that follow to worship that horror, don't you think?'

Pearl nodded. 'Bit strange, I suppose,' she conceded thoughtfully, popping a ripe, blue blackberry into her mouth.

'There must be more to it,' Faith continued, on a roll now, 'something we have to search for, something on the inside. She looks at everything from the outside. Take a tree, for example. When we look at it, we don't just see the trunk, the limbs, the leaves, its flowering cycle, all the outside things, do we? We see the inside working constantly away there, the roots pulling the sap up through the inner system, feeding and sustaining the tree. We see the rain nourishing and know the inside of the tree is working hard to turn that water into energy. I wonder if that's the main problem with their religion?'

Pearl stopped rubbing her knees and instead rubbed at her lower lip with her top teeth.

'Maybe,' continued Faith, 'they've got this whole religion thing arse-up along with their thoughts about the land. Maybe they're supposed to look at the nailing to the cross the same way they should look at the earth – from the inside, look for the inner meanings. You think about it. They look at us and what do they see? Nothing. We simply don't really exist. But if they looked at the inside then they might realise that we're all just the damned same. It's all in the way they've grown used to looking and they just look the wrong way, I reckon.'

A gentle swish, soft as a handful of corn kernels thrown to hungry chickens, sounded on the verandah outside, then the sound of a woman crying and another comforting, leading her away.

Pearl stood up and wiped her hands on her white apron. 'Better pick up those rosaries,' she sighed. 'She'll be pulling the place apart looking for them in a little while.'

She returned, putting the pestered beads on the table. 'Poor Elizabeth,' she said. 'She'll get her inside, get her into her nightdress and into bed, but before she walks the length of the hall, the crafty old girl will be back outside, walking up and down Madness Road again.'

Faith stood and straightened her back, one floury hand on her hip. 'How many pies does Elizabeth want made for the picnic on Sunday?' she asked.

'Beats me,' Pearl replied. 'There'll be no picnic on Sunday anyway. Take a look out the window at the ironbark trees. They're all sending green shoots out their tops. Rain's coming.'

Faith swished flour from the scrubbed kitchen table and smiled at the older woman. 'Who told you that one? You got some inbuilt weathercock?'

A smile flitted across Pearl's face to be instantly replaced by a look of thoughtfulness. The heaviness of the thought being weighed in her mind slowed down her ability to speak. Where had that knowledge come from? Maybe Faith stirred it up with all that talk about looking inside things. Certainly she and Mary both knew that when ironbark trees sent out tiny, umbrella-like green shoots from their tops, rain was imminent.

'Your mother knew that,' Pearl replied. 'We both knew it. It was just something that was there, inside both our heads.'

Hope, fluttering like sparrows' wings, made Faith clutch at her middle with one hand while steadying herself on the kitchen table with the other.

'But who told you?' she insisted. 'If you both knew, who told you?'

Pearl sat on the wooden bench at the opposite side of the table. She folded her arms across her knees and let her mind wander back. Way, way back. Before Wellsford Station, back to someone else, someone she couldn't quite see, but she could feel his presence. *His* presence. A man. Was it her father? Her grandfather? She would never know now.

'He told me,' she answered simply, 'but I dunno who he was. We must've been out in the bush and he told me, about how wise the trees are, how they always know when it's going to rain, specially the ironbark. That's why they send up their shoots. Because they know. All that religious chat you was doing before, probably loosened something inside this old head.'

Faith put her arms around the older woman, neither trying to disguise their brimming eyes.

'You had them,' Faith told her. 'You had folks of your own. It's just that you got robbed of the time it takes to make memories. But you know you had them and they know they had you. You have to hang on to that knowledge.'

If Pearl heard Faith's last comments, she showed no sign. She continued to sit with half-clasped hands in the folds of her apron, looking into space. 'He told me about the rocks as well,' she said slowly.

Faith's breathing quietened. She didn't dare move. She wanted nothing to interrupt the flow of the older woman's thoughts.

'There were these huge rock outcrops all around where we lived,' Pearl continued. 'He told me about how they had been there for centuries, probably since the Dreamtime. How they had witnessed all that had happened through generations of human lives. Sometimes they're spirits from the beginning who turned to stone, knowing the truth but not revealing, waiting for us to learn how to look. But you learn nothing, unless you learn to look behind the exterior. Just like you were saying.'

'Taken me forty-odd years to remember that,' Pearl smiled. 'Probably find I'm as gaga as the old girl, but I just don't see it in myself.' She giggled girlishly. 'Better lock up the tea-cosies just in case.'

She stood up and sprinkled the blackberries into the open pie crusts before her. Faith was right; she'd had family who cared and people around her once, who were her own. Now they were coming back to her. Now, at this time of her life when she was sixty years old. She brushed a piece of hair back from her face and retied the twine around the thick mane at the back of her neck.

'You can still put a gun to me head if I start raving,' she laughed, wondering why she felt so good. Even at sixty years old, I can run through the ironbarks, she thought. Run like the wind with her hand secure in the remembered warmth of the larger hand belonging to the person with the face she could still not quite see but who was nonetheless coming closer, ever closer.

'Better get these pies finished,' she said, bending over the kitchen table. 'Even though there's going to be no picnic because of the rain.'

The two women laughed softly together, enjoying the secret knowledge that had been somehow returned to them from a forgotten past. A past they were only now beginning to feel strong enough to believe in.

Adding to the line

Daniel stood in the shadowy gloom behind the Wellsford school toilet block, rubbing his bare hands up and down his shirt sleeves, shivering with the evening's chill. The nights were drawing in, all right, and Jamie was late. He stood, ears straining, waiting for the familiar whistle that asked for his call of return, a signal that all was clear for their meeting.

He sucked the inside of his soft-skinned cheek. There'd be hell to pay if the Mitchells realised that the son of their farm help and their own son were indulging in a bit of hanky-panky after school. Oh, he knew that to Jamie, it was all a bit of a game, nothing lasting in it. A bit of sexual experimentation to relieve the monotony of a town that boasted only one picture show in the school of arts hall and damn all else. For Jamie, it was just something to fill out the boredom of the school holidays before he was returned to the city to boarding school.

But Daniel remembered how his heart had leaped when he had first asked to meet him behind the toilet block. 'We'll have to have a signal,' Jamie had said. So, they'd invented the whistle and the long whistle call of return and now Daniel couldn't hear any whistle without remembering that first time. The time he'd stood in the cool darkness with his eyes closed, head leaning back against the cooler brick wall, his hands in the blonde softness of Jamie Mitchell's hair. Now the long, dragging week had somehow to be lived through while his heart waited for the ten or fifteen stolen minutes on Saturday, realising even so that fate was usually less than generous with those of her children who were different. Sometimes a side of her seemed to save the worst for them.

It was then he heard it – from outside, interrupting his thoughts. Their signalling whistle. He put his hands to his mouth to give the familiar return.

'Not what you expected, is it, matey?'

Daniel felt himself pushed back against the brick wall, his shocked face not quite comprehending. The two heavy set men who stood in front of him were not from Wellsford, he was sure of that. He'd never seen them before.

'Heard your little poofter whistle,' said the larger of the two. 'Expecting someone?'

'No, no,' said Daniel cautiously. 'Just come around for a leak. I'll be off now.'

'Oh no, matey, not for a minute or two yet. We saw you and your boyfriend here last week from our parked truck – nice-looking fella. Matter of fact, we heard your pretty little bird whistle. Thought you were whistlin' us at first, then your mate arrived. We guessed it might be a regular. Looks like we guessed right.'

The second man – piggish, aggressive; fat, rough hands; short, thick fingers sprouting little tufts of hair on their backs like spinifex grass; a wedding ring on the left hand.

'Yer know,' said the first, the more brutish of the two, 'can't stand bloody poofters. Reckon a boong poofter's right from the bottom of the barrel. From right down among the crap, because that's where they like it.' He laughed, revealing a line of small, brown, broken teeth.

Daniel's throat constricted. He knew he didn't have much hope of defending himself against the two men, but he was more worried about what had delayed Jamie. He was sure the two were off-duty policemen, piggish brutes, but what were they doing in Wellsford and how did they know about these meetings?

'You look like a church-going man,' said Danny, head clearing now, trying to stall.

'Damned right,' said the larger of the two, lashing out with his fist, hitting Daniel on the shoulder. 'That's why I can't stand little poofters like you.'

'Go to church every Sunday, do you, with your family?'

'Yep,' came the reply, accompanied by another practice punch, hitting at the air.

'So, you only do this on days other than Sunday?' Daniel asked.

The words were hardly out before the clenched fist hit him right above the eye, the force sending him staggering backwards into the brick wall, the momentary numbing of his senses conversely kindling his defiance.

'Pity your wife can't see the hard-on beating me up gives you. Bet she's never enjoyed one like it.' Insolence used as a coin to buy time allowed Daniel the fleeting pleasure of noticing the dark look covering the stranger's face, replaced almost instantly by red, roaring anger.

'Poor little poof can't even defend yourself, I bet, poor little baby ...'

Daniel made no attempt to defend himself; his mind was working overtime trying to figure out how the two men knew about the arrangement. He and Jamie had been so cautious, so alone in making their plans, discussing the situation with anyone else was unthinkable, even though Jamie had hinted at similar activity occurring at boarding school in Sydney.

Something warm trickled into Daniel's eye and down his face as the two men, now thoroughly enjoying the imagined growth in their stature gained from the power in their fists, punched in turn. Daniel shook his head, still unable to quite work out just what was going on. Where was Jamie? A bell was ringing somewhere outside, or was it inside his head? He hurt, he hurt so much. Jamie, he must warn Jamie.

The two men punching in sadistic rhythm now, hitting harder, enjoying the short-lived feeling of a warped superiority which bypassed intelligence to survive, if only briefly, in clenched fists. A blinding force caught Daniel in the middle, doubling him over, making his knees sag, sending the concrete floor spiralling up to meet him.

'Ma ...' Somehow, somewhere in the back of his mind, Daniel thought he was ten years old and had just finished cutting out a string of newspaper people; his long, long line of generations past. He had handed one end to Faith who smiled lovingly at him. He was standing waiting for her to move back from him, pulling the paper out, right out to its full length, stretching it across in front of them so they could see them. All of them, all in a line. Their ancestors.

As if in slow motion, Faith moved smilingly back from him. At that precise moment, the steel-capped toe of the black leather boot connected brutally with Daniel's skull, adding in its senseless ferocity one more figure to the line of paper people waiting. Waiting in some other place. A paper thin string of people already holding hands in resigned anticipation of the young one about to join them.

Faith was in her kitchen, humming to herself and setting the kitchen table when she saw it, standing on the window ledge. It simply landed and stood, moving its tail backwards and forwards. One hand flew to her throat as she stood watching the bright blue undertail of the Willie wagtail. She felt faint, the blue of the undertail filling her thoughts, then gradually her head, until her vision seemed to encompass nothing but the bright warning wagtail streak of blue. She groped her way to the drawer in the old dresser and rummaged about until she found the string of paper people made by Daniel to be brought out each Christmas. Without putting on a light, she moved to the Jacobean chair and sat trance-like, holding the folded newspaper cut-outs against her.

She knew what it meant. From somewhere way back, she knew what it meant. The wagtail had come to warn her. She wished Daniel were here, home with her. God, why did she know it was Daniel she was being warned about? He had always been different, her firstborn; sensitive, artistic and caring, and sometimes stubborn and unyielding as well. Injustice didn't sit easily on him. It had always seemed to her that he was someone special on loan, someone who came into this world to brighten and add to people's lives, and always in her heart, she had worried that it might be at the expense of his own.

Somewhere outside, someone was beating on a kerosene can. *Thump, thump, thump.* The noise made Faith cover her ears with her hands, but that didn't stop it – nothing stopped it. Everything about the moment seemed totally unreal. As if it were frozen along with her ability to feel. *Thump, thump, thump.* Not outside at all. Inside. Inside under her own ribs.

Faith sat motionless until way past dark. She was still sitting there immobile in the dark, the newspaper people on her lap, several hours later when a grey-faced Robbo knocked on the door.

★ ★ ★

The small bell connected to the hinge tinkled as James Mitchell pushed open the door to Stanley's workshop. Stanley moved the wood plane up and down the piece of timber then rubbed it tentatively with sand-paper-sounding hands before turning to acknowledge the visitor.

'I've come to pay for Faith's boy's coffin.' James held a roll of notes in his hand.

Two bright pink hot spots of colour appeared on Stanley's cheeks, but his voice was controlled and cool.

'There's no bill to be paid for that,' he said matter-of-factly, picking a curl of wood shaving from the blade of the plane and then blowing on it to remove any trace of sawdust.

'Oh, but I insist. Faith works for me, you know.'

Something very blue in the centre of Stanley's eyes focused a steel-like grip on the rheumy eyes of the older man. 'You dinna hear too well.' Stanley's voice was steady, but the colour in his cheeks was rising. 'I said there's no bill to be paid for that.'

He put down the plane and leaned both his hands on the bench separating the two men. His palms were flat, the fingers pointing towards each other. 'I don't expect for a moment,' he continued quietly, 'that you might understand, but that coffin was made specially.'

He leaned further across the counter, not raising his voice. 'I made that coffin utilising every smidgen of skill I've ever learned. It was made from my heart, cried over, caressed and loved. You see, that way Faith at least would know that someone, someone in this godforsaken world understood and cared enough to try and ensure that Danny was laid to rest surrounded by something that came from the heart.'

Stanley moved back from the counter but never took his eyes from James's face. He shook his head, his voice uneven now. 'God knows it's no compensation for her. No compensation at all.'

James Mitchell, with difficulty, averted his eyes from the magnets in the Scotsman's face and walked to the door. He turned, thought about saying something but changed his mind and silently, except for the bell's tinkling farewell, closed the door behind him.

'Keep your fookin' filthy money.' The unfamiliar oath fell forcefully from between Stanley's lips. He looked at the plane on the workbench and for a moment fought an overwhelming urge to smash it through the plate glass window of his shop, but years of logic nurtured in a land of heather placed a restraining hand on his shoulder and guided his energies back to where he had always placed them: in his work.

As the plane swished backwards and forwards, backwards and forwards, Stanley found himself thinking of another time, another funeral. It was such a strange thing. After his deranged run through the streets of Wellsford carrying his dead wife in his arms, he had not expected a soul to attend her funeral. But he was wrong, so wrong. Shuffling and sheepish, wet-eyed and embarrassed, half the town filled the church, and later his small kitchen, to overflowing. Plates of food, flowers and people materialised miraculously as the townsfolk gathered to pay their respects.

Gradually, through the months of healing that followed his wife's death, Stanley realised that the residents of his new country were not heartless; they simply didn't want to be the first at anything. Once one person made a gesture, that gesture expanded into a unanimous one of mateship, with whoever made the initial gambit becoming safely faceless in the crowd.

Backwards and forwards, backwards and forwards, gently, feel the timber, gently … 'Aye', he had been pleased with Danny's coffin; it had turned out to be one of his best yet. It had been a surprise to him how emotional he had become over this whole horrible incident and what people were saying about it. He could have smashed James Mitchell fair in the centre of his face for a moment there, but what good would that have done? It wouldn't bring the lad back – violence begets violence. Besides, the poor bugger was probably finally understanding that certain valuables in life do not have a price ticket.

'You canna buy love, Stanley.' His Scottish father had told him that. 'You canna buy anything of true value, laddie, yet it takes some people a lifetime to understand that.'

Stanley enjoyed these remembered conversations with his father. They made him wonder if the difference between life and death might, after all, only be a point of perspective. Was there a chance that in some other unknown place, his father occasionally remembered past conversations as well?

'We don't know very much about anything,' Stanley said. 'Not very much at all.'

Sands of time

The currawong's territorial call at sundown had always pleased Faith and now she stood in her doorway smiling to herself as the large black bird in the nearby eucalypt filled the air with its loony warbling. From a perch in a distant tree, another bird opened its throat with the trill of reply. Something about the currawong's call gave Faith a sense of belonging, a feeling of connectedness with the country of her birth, a country watching sadly as the cream of its male youth, dressed in khaki, was leaving its shores in great, grey troop ships, determined to defend her, even if from half a world away.

Now Faith could no longer look at her Benjamin without the hurt of Daniel's death overwhelming her thinking, her heart aching for other women with children a few years older than hers. Women whose fear-filled eyes watched the telegram boy's bike as he pedalled down their streets, praying to God that it was not their gatepost he propped his bike against while he delivered the news all wives, mothers, sisters and loved ones feared most.

Her life at Wellsford Station was different as well now with most of the men away. With James Mitchell no longer able to undertake some of the heavy tasks and John called up for service, Elizabeth Mitchell had emerged from her formerly shy chrysalis-like state, trying her best to hold the station together, calling on all hands to do their bit for the war effort. Jumpers, worn through at the elbows, were now unpicked, the wool rolled into fat balls to be knitted up on four needles into socks for servicemen, or squares for blankets. Large, sweet-smelling and long-keeping fruitcakes were baked and placed in old biscuit tins, the entire package rolled in scrim which Pearl and Faith sewed together, making sure the joins were secure enough to withstand the long sea journey to some faraway army camp.

Black paper coverings were cut out and fitted over windows to prevent light escaping at night in the unlikely event of some enemy bomber pilot finding his way to Wellsford, and backyards were dug up and turned into bomb shelters where hard biscuits, water bottles and grey blankets were stored in case of invasion.

If Faith felt secure in the knowledge that Albert, according to the census, did not exist and therefore could not be called up for duty, that security swiftly left her the night her husband appeared in their doorway clad in the all too familiar khaki uniform.

'I went and enlisted.' The words hesitant, apologetic. Albert rested his hand on his wife's shoulder. 'I had to, luv,' he continued, 'if there's an answer to our problem, it lies within the problem itself. Can't you see that? Besides,' he continued, 'it might help me forget ...' The words trailed off, too hard to say.

In spite of the ache surrounding her heart and invading her whole being, Faith knew he was right. Albert looked fondly at his wife. 'For our dead son and our living son and us, I got to go.'

Faith nodded, indicating her understanding, not speaking lest words in their inadequacy broke the banks to her already brimfull eyes. Elizabeth Mitchell had watched her husband and some others leave Wellsford Station to answer the call and had managed to reach deep inside herself to find a strength she probably never even suspected. Faith felt she would have to manage in much the same way. She would just continue in the station kitchen with Pearl, she would care for Benny and she would wait and pray for Albert's safe return.

'You look good,' she managed to say at last. 'Handsome in that uniform. Just wait till Benny sees how good his Pa looks.'

She walked to remove her apron from the wooden peg behind the kitchen door, silently tying the strings at her waist and busying herself with the flour and lard, making a pie crust. Life would be difficult without Albert, no matter how she tried to avoid thinking about it. He had just always been there, way back, as long as she could remember. He had come to Wellsford Station not long after her mother had drowned although when she thought of her mother, it seemed her face somehow merged with that of Pearl's.

From the time James Mitchell had brought Albert in to work at the station, it just seemed the most natural thing in the world that she and Albert would be together. Mitchell had approved and gone out of his way, giving them the shack to live in and saying the words over them to please Hilda who was already well on the road to gaga. That was another reason she admired Elizabeth Mitchell; she had taken on the responsibility of her mother-in-law which was no easy task. The old girl's mental faculties had deteriorated to the stage where she eventually had had to be locked in her room at nights for her own safety, her nocturnal wanderings ultimately leading to her downfall.

'There's something in her world the old girl can't handle,' Pearl had once said to Faith. 'That's why she went nuttier than these cakes we send the soldiers. It's no wonder Mister James used to drink his whisky and sleep to oblivion in the barn or shearing shed.'

Faith busied herself setting the table. 'When do you go?' she asked Albert, surprised that her voice sounded so calm.

Albert put both arms around her from behind, leaning his head on her shoulder. 'I go to camp tomorrow, luv,' he said. 'They tell us it's just about over, so I suppose we have to get there soon. Anyway, I leave tomorrow.'

For a long time the couple stood, not wanting to break the moment, stretching it as far as possible, gathering together within it all the other moments taken for granted, willing them to stay and expand, to prevent tomorrow's inevitable arrival. Then reluctantly Faith pulled away.

'I'm proud of you, Albert,' she said, not looking at him. 'I'm proud of you and so will our son be. You'll see.'

Even though her pride was shaken by the feeling that life might never be the same again, Faith did not show it. She cleared her throat and set the dinner table. 'Well, come on,' she said to her husband. 'Last dinner cooked by me for a while. Don't stand there and let it get cold.'

Albert picked up his knife and fork and looked lovingly at his wife. 'I am coming back, Faith,' he said to her gently. 'No way in the world I'm not coming back.'

★ ★ ★

Thank God for the army short back and sides, Albert thought as he ran his hand around behind his head and through the dampness seeping into his shirt collar. God, it was hot, hotter than he had expected. Somehow he thought his last day in Egypt would be more comfortable, as if the end of the war in Europe would bring with it such a wave of relief it might also mellow the Eastern climate. He didn't particularly want this last day's leave. It would be better to get on the darned ship and just go, he thought, wanting to be home and over the horror of a crowded troop ship as soon as possible.

He looked at the other soldiers sitting alongside, most of them anxious to be off the truck and into the bars and whorehouses. No thanks, thought Albert, mouth watering momentarily at the thought of a cool ale but finding the idea of a possible dose of clap from an Egyptian brothel a decided turn-off. Anyhow, he wanted to see the sights, the Sphinx, pyramids, even if he had to go there alone. There was a history here that drew him, an ancient knowledge that seemed to almost parallel things he remembered his grandfather had taught him. Not that he could remember much; his grandfather died before Albert reached much of an age. Still, he had a feel for the history and sanctity of things, and he felt close to it here, in the heat.

The truck lurched to a halt with a smell of burning rubber and the men jumped out. Maybe just one ale, Albert thought, the dry desert dust invading his nose.

He made his way over the street to a nearby bar, ordered the drink and let the cooling liquid flow pleasingly down his throat.

'Lucky Strike?' inquired a voice next to him.

Albert turned to find a young US marine standing alongside at the bar, offering a packet of cigarettes.

'No, thanks,' Albert replied, 'don't smoke. Just having a beer before I go for a walk around the sights.'

The young man extended his hand. Something about him registered although Albert was sure they had not met before. Strong face, too, he thought, the kind of face that sees all but reveals nothing.

'You're an Ossie, aren't you?'

Albert nodded. Funny how the Yanks mispronounced names, just like they said 'Ay-rabs'.

Albert drained his glass. 'I'm heading down towards the Sphinx,' he said, 'taking in some history.'

The American laughed. 'Me too,' he said. 'How about that? Want some company?'

Company was the precise thing that Albert didn't want, but for some reason he never got around to saying so. Instead, he and the long marine walked out of the bar and down the street past the stalls laden with brass pots and hookahs and draped like some Aladdin's cave with richly woven tapestries and rugs to where a shifty-looking camel driver haggled over the price of a fare. Once agreement had been reached, each soldier climbed onto a camel's back which the owner then poked with a pole till it lurched upright, almost dumping the rider in the dust before they had taken a step.

'No wonder they call 'em the ship of the desert,' Albert laughed. 'A bloke'll be queasy as hell after half an hour of this. Bad as the bloody troop ship.'

At the end of the uncomfortable trip, the bad-tempered animal and the heat were all immediately forgotten as Albert and his new acquaintance took in the sight before them. A sight so stunning, Albert wondered what on earth he might have been expecting. Certainly not the surge of emotion that overflowed through his eyes that moment, making his pulse race and filling him with an intense awareness of his own insignificance. The flies, dust and the dark half-moons spreading under his arms from the oppressive heat failed to register as he drank in the majesty of the great pyramid rising timelessly through the haze as it had done for centuries. He wondered when he later looked at the Sphinx if he might have had a touch of the sun, so sure was he that the great, impassive face recognised and returned his gaze. How many other thousands of people had stood in this very spot, centuries of footprints within footprints, he wondered.

'Kinda takes your breath away, don't it?'

Albert had forgotten for a moment that he wasn't alone.

'Name's Larry Zephier, US Marine Corps. 'Bout time we introduced ourselves, I guess.'

Albert shook the offered hand again. 'Albert Franklin,' he answered, noticing the strength of the handshake.

'I'm a Sioux Indian,' Larry explained. 'Straight out of South Dakota and into the army. Kinda funny that my surname starts with the last letter in the alphabet,' the American laughed, 'because that's where we Indians usually end up. Right at the end of everything.'

'Yeah,' agreed Albert, 'that does have a familiar ring to it.'

The two men walked along the west side of the pyramid now dwarfing all in its proximity. They stopped and sat, saying nothing, drinking in the visible history in front of them.

'I'm not sure,' continued the American slowly, 'where my surname comes from, come to think of it. It's certainly not a tribal name. But I think you and I probably have a lot in common in our outlook and attitude to life,' he continued. He reached into his breast pocket and pulled out the packet of cigarettes, lit one and breathed deeply.

'Probably why you and I, the oddballs, are here looking at history while the good ole guys with all the intelligence are in town chasing booze and broads.'

Albert smiled. The day after tomorrow, he would sail for home, a vastly changed person from the Albert who left the sunburned country twelve months earlier. He had fought alongside people born in the same land as he, made friends, been accepted as one of them. But how long would that last, he wondered, once he returned to Australia?

'Funny thing about the US,' Larry continued, as if reading his thoughts. 'They didn't even want to allow that such an animal as the American Indian existed, let alone notice the possibility that he might have a useable talent. Not, that is, until they needed some way to confuse the enemy in the war area. That's when they discovered that not only could Navajos actually speak English intelligently, but they spoke another language, their own language, that very few people would ever hear or understand. So, suddenly, US Intelligence formed the Navajo Code Talking Corps for radio contact. They figured it was a great way to keep information from the enemy, although most of us Indians wonder if the real enemy will ever get the message.' He laughed.

'We couldn't keep our language,' Albert said. 'My grandmother spoke the lingo, but she wasn't allowed to use it, so I never learned.' He leaned back, supporting his upper body with his forearms. 'Going home in a couple of days,' he offered. 'Battalion's moving out.'

'Oh yeah? Me too,' said Larry, tentatively toying with a scar on the back of his hand. 'Back to no work, no status, a no-win situation.'

Albert understood precisely what the other man was saying. He harboured no illusions at all that any slight status he had gained through the war would be removed and hung on a peg to gather dust along with his khaki uniform. He ached for his simple cottage, for Faith and Benjamin and for the relative simplicity of his prewar life.

'You know,' continued his companion, 'my home is a two-roomed shack – no running water, no plumbing. It's the most beautiful place in the world. I grow corn this high,' he laughed. 'I grow corn and I make silver and turquoise jewellery to sell to white traders for whatever they'll pay me, then they take it to the cities and clean up.' He laughed again. 'But, you know, we are richer by far, by far. They never seem to learn that although you can't eat money, it can eat you. At least we know that, if we know nothing else.'

Albert nodded. He thought of the little shearers' house by the Wellsford River, of the garden where he and Faith grew their vegetables, where their chickens ran unhindered.

'You got any children?' Albert asked.

The Indian nodded and grinned. 'Just one, a daughter, born after I left. I'm looking forward to meeting her. How about you?'

'I had two boys,' Albert tried to say, but only the last two words sounded. 'Different as chalk and cheese.' He looked at the impassive face of the Indian, a face housing the most compassionate eyes Albert had ever seen.

The two men sat without speaking for a long time.

'You're sure lucky you got those two boys.'

Albert couldn't answer although he felt safe with this man. He'd already revealed a lot of himself to someone he had only met an hour or so ago.

'Lost one of my boys.' There, he'd said it. Now the words tumbled over each other, out of control in their eagerness to reach the air and so attain life in the hope that that life might dull some of the hurt.

The Indian said nothing as if he knew there was nothing he could say; that for the moment at least, he was to play the role of listener.

'One that died didn't ever seem interested in girls,' Albert said. 'He was a beautiful boy, but he didn't seem to like girls. He was killed because of that. Just that. Can you believe someone beating someone to death because ...' The words trailed off as if the steam propelling their exit from Albert's consciousness had run out. He sat quietly.

'We consider that difference to be very fortunate,' the Indian said gently after a long silence.

Albert was puzzled. What was fortunate? Danny had been killed because he was different. What the hell could be called fortunate about it? But he said nothing and sat, waiting.

'Many Indian tribes consider it very fortunate to have a person in their midst who is of a different sexual persuasion,' the Indian continued. 'The old ones tell us that before birth, such people choose to live a different life, therefore willingly taking the chances that their chosen life presents to them. This life can be very lonely although sometimes they find a life partner. The Sioux call them 'Wincti' and when Indian children are very young, their parents call a Wincti to their house and ask him to give the child a secret name. This name is very special and we never reveal it to anyone, ever. To do so would mean diminution of the sacredness surrounding the name and the giver of the name. These people enter the world to sometimes leave it earlier than others. But we believe they come with a mission. There is always a reason when they leave us. Maybe it is to open our eyes. Maybe it is to open our hearts.'

Albert felt something overwhelming and special for the person sitting next to him, a person he hadn't even known when he woke up this morning.

'You know,' Larry continued, 'there are no accidents. We were meant to meet today. We may never meet again, but each of us will remember today as the beginning of our friendship and the end of the war.'

Albert stood up and stretched. 'Gotta be getting back,' he said. 'Not much of a writer, so no point in getting your address.'

Larry stood up, smiling. 'Don't worry about it,' he said. 'If I want to get a message to you, I'll find a way.'

Albert extended his hand. 'See yas, mate,' he said, reverting to Australian habits to avoid the goodbye. He walked over to the camel and climbed aboard. He turned to wave to the American and suddenly cupped both his hands to his mouth. 'If you get Down Under, I live in Wellsford, in New South Wales!' he hollered. 'You can't miss it, belongs to the Mitchell family, Wellsford Station!'

'Gotcha!' the other man called. 'I might just do that one day! Show you how to grow corn!'

The two men laughed.

From the back of the lurching camel, Albert looked back until it was pointless to look any more. The Indian was just as another grain of sand, a speck in the distance dwarfed by the breathtaking structures behind him.

Something new and free was circulating within Albert. He had spoken of his family, spoken of his sons, laid his innermost feelings bare, and at last he had a male friend. A true friend, he was sure of that.

Constant loneliness companioned by ever-present uncertainty served a dual role, drawing the womenfolk of Wellsford closely together as WWII ran its course. A large hoarding at the west entrance to the main street of the town had lost, for the duration, its familiar advertisement showing billowing, white sheets pegged to a propped clothes line against a royal blue sky with the promise that 'Out of the Blue comes the whitest wash' and replaced it with the stern command to 'Buy War Bonds'.

Added responsibility rummaged deep down inside Elizabeth Mitchell's psyche, uncovering hidden strengths as she valiantly managed ration books for clothing, food and petrol, made regular trips to share produce grown in the station's kitchen garden with less fortunate townsfolk and developed her ability to provide herbal cures from that garden for whatever ailed them.

'You know, it's a funny thing,' said Pearl one day as she and Faith pounded rich orange petals of calendula for one of Elizabeth's cure-alls. 'Reckon if she gave one of them old geezers plain green grass and told them it would heal them, it damned well would.'

Faith nodded. 'Wait a minute, isn't that what you've been doing for years?' The two women laughed. 'Just that someone cares, that's what does it. The minute someone cares, they feel better.'

Pearl sat at the large farm table, drawing the needle over and under, over and under, mending what was left of an old sock. 'Don't feel like Christmas this year, does it?'

Faith shook her head, her hands folding the large, white pillowcases in half, sprinkling the water over them from the bottle in her hand before folding them again and putting them in a stack to be ironed.

For years now, their nights had been spent extending the life of worn through station socks by stretching them over wooden mushrooms and darning with neat tapestry stitches in an effort to save clothing coupons which could pass on to someone with greater need. Luscious, heavy fruitcakes whose aroma had filled the house in July with early Christmas promise, and Christmas puddings filled with threepences that could never be spent in the country of their destination were packed in tins to be shipped to faceless men in khaki. Hilda's old school building was now a storeroom for every kind of dried and bottled fruit and vegetable, labelled and stacked for future use either at the station or by needy townspeople.

Then suddenly, it seemed, it was over. The men were returning home. Some being carried, some wheeled and the luckier walking, all of them knowing that life would never be quite the same again, their stolen innocence never to be returned.

A huge banner hung across Wellsford's main street, welcoming home her menfolk. At the station, Jamie teetered on the edge of a ladder attaching streamers to welcome men back to the farm. Pots on the stove bubbled as Pearl and Faith cooked the entire ration book's allowance and more in celebration. Nothing would be too good for them. Their men were coming home. True to his word, Albert was coming back.

Dementia

During the war, Hilda Mitchell's mental faculties had deteriorated to such an extent that locking her in her room 'for her own good' was now the norm. Her daytime antics observed by her staff saddened more than they amused.

Pearl heard the scurrying just moments before Elizabeth Mitchell burst into the kitchen, wild-eyed, breathless, clutching her nightdress. 'Quick, Pearl, quick!' Agitated, unusually commanding. 'Come and help me.'

Pearl followed her back down the hallway to Hilda's room. The door was wide open and the bed hollowed but not folded down. No one had slept in it.

'She's gone,' gasped Elizabeth. 'The French doors are open and she's gone.'

Hilda's jumbled mind had had no regard for time or date. Tonight her short-term memory had been almost nonexistent, her long-term memory agonisingly sharp in its clarity. She had awakened lying on the top of the bed, thinking it was another time, a long-ago time she had pushed firmly back into the dimmest recesses of her mind. A time that now tantalisingly placed itself first and foremost in her thoughts to befuddle and confuse. A time when she stretched herself out on the bed, enjoying the jarring, creaking and groaning of the house timber cooling. She heard Pearl and Mary cleaning up the kitchen, then the familiar click as they pulled the long cord on the light switch and the thud indicating the closing latch of the kitchen door, signifying their retirement for the night. The memories flooded back.

Outside in the Moreton Bay fig, gluttonous bats screeched as they blindly swarmed to eat more than their fill. The night was warm, humid. Hilda ran her left hand over the rise of her breasts, her hard nipples and flat stomach, finally letting it rest in the soft down. Half an hour, half an hour she had to wait before she could make her move. Zephyr breezes gently moved the muslin covering the slightly open French doors leading to the balcony. The cicadas were deafening tonight in the heat, just the kind of cover she needed, although the moon shone like a beacon. She would have to be cautious.

Slowly, luxuriously, without a sound but enjoying the moonlight, Hilda dressed herself. Then she fluffed up her bedclothes, placed two pillows down the centre of the bed and covered them over with the quilt. If anyone looked in from the door, they would think she was lying on her side, fast asleep.

Silently she tiptoed to the French doors, gently, gently opening them further before pulling them quietly behind her and stepping out onto the verandah. She moved like a cat, making her body thin to avoid the moon's telling glow, padding on feline feet. She knew exactly where to go; she had traversed this path before many times, sometimes in person, sometimes through the darker, devious, more circuitous pathway of her mind. Soundlessly she stepped down from the balcony, stopping for a moment to check for any sound from the house then, hearing nothing, glided towards the path that led down to the river.

Now she ran, half crouched, past the old barn where the station hands slept, shuttered in the darkness. Down along the river bank, past the pepper trees housing the deafening cicadas, over the wooden fence. Along the walking trail she ran, then into the bush, around behind her favourite jacaranda tree, its heavy blue blooms almost purple in the moonlight. Through the stringy grass, gently now, down on all fours.

Then she heard it; the expected sound that nevertheless made her stop, stock still. The sound of laughter and water splashing. James's laughter. With animal cunning, Hilda hid herself behind the blue rock outcrop and eased herself into a position enabling her to see what James was doing.

He was having a good time, all right, laughing and splashing. Now running out of the river, stark bollocky – not alone, though. Oh no, not alone at all. Not laughing now; his mouth was too busy for laughter now. Running itself all over the welcoming thighs of the person he was with. Hilda had never seen her husband quite like this. She stepped forward a little, breaking a twig underfoot, the surrounding bush exaggerating its sound in the night.

'What the hell was that?' The woman, breathless, anxious.

'Nothing. Nothing, Girlie. A kangaroo perhaps.'

The woman groaning now, on her knees, bending down in front of James. And James, James with his head tilted back, matching the faceless woman's groans. Matching them with his own increasing delight, the two of them oblivious now to anything but each other.

And then after, the caressing, the touching; the tender, lingering hands and eyes. Both of them standing, prolonging the agony of parting as James kissed the unknown face, her eyelids, her hands, fingertips, and the two of them stood unable to let go until the fingers themselves reluctantly broke the grasp and James hesitatingly collected his clothes and walked off towards the barns.

The woman lay on her back with her hands behind her head, softly singing into the night. Something red erupted in Hilda's head, blocking out all but the insane jealousy that suddenly controlled her very being. She bent down to pick up a sharp bush rock and then sprang like a night animal to the side of the startled woman lying on the ground. Like someone possessed with superhuman strength, she hit and hit and hit again. Then, placing her arms under the armpits of her husband's unconscious lover, she dragged her to the water's edge. Puffing, heaving, panting, sweating, Hilda dragged the dead weight load along the river bank past the safe swimming area, along the bank towards Devil's Rock. More demon than human now, with a strength temporarily borrowed from evil forces, she pushed and heaved and rolled the heavy load over the bank and into the river, then feeling all around until she found the blood-stained rock and hurled that also into the enveloping water.

She half walked, half ran back to the jacaranda tree and the safe swimming area where she dropped her clothes and walked into the cooling water. She lay floating on her back for a few moments then climbed out onto the bank, shook off the excess water and dressed. She felt an exhilaration she had never experienced before, a kind of rush known only to those who momentarily and willingly step outside the bounds of sanity to place themselves in league with the Devil.

James, she knew from experience, would not go straight to the homestead. He would wake up one of the hands to drink whisky and play cards long into the night.

Humming gently to herself, Hilda retraced her way cautiously back to the house. Once back in her bedroom, she undressed, placed her stained clothing in a paper bag to be burned in the rusting 44-gallon drum used as the kitchen incinerator and climbed into bed.

She lay back under the sheet, once more running her hands over her body, only this time the feeling had a different intensity, a different dimension. As if some evil force, pleased with her efforts, guided her hands in reward.

But now Pearl took one look at the unruffled bed and called for Albert who saddled up and rode to the eastern paddock to try and find John. Elizabeth didn't relish this confrontation with her husband. She knew it had been her job to lock her mother-in-law in her room at night to prevent her wandering and last night, she had simply forgotten.

She glanced in James's room then raced to the shearing shed where she thought he would probably be asleep after playing cards half the night with Charlie. All hands, including Jamie, banded together, assigned various areas to search. 'She's wilful,' Elizabeth said. 'Even though she's not in control of herself, she could easily be just hiding.' There was a touch of something bordering on hope in her voice.

By the time John arrived at the house, all outlying buildings had been searched to no avail. While Jamie held a torch, Albert climbed the ladder down to water level in the well but was sure she had not ventured down there as the pail on top of the well was always held in place in a certain position and had not been moved. If Hilda had decided to go down the well, she could hardly have replaced the pail so carefully.

John wiped the wetness from his forehead with his shirt sleeve. 'We'll have to go to the river,' he said. 'It's the river that attracts her sometimes.'

The party divided, one part going east and the other west at the river. Pearl expected to find the old lady sitting where she usually sat on the river bank under the large jacaranda that was her favourite tree, now heavy with blooms. Pearl let her eyes rest on the purple haze of its blossoms then drop to the base of its trunk, but there was no sign of her.

Reluctantly the group moved towards Devil's Rock. 'She wouldn't come this way,' James insisted. 'She didn't like this area. There was a feeling that made her even more disturbed around here.'

Pearl sighed gently. She didn't like this area either and hadn't been here since the day they pulled Mary out of the river, bruised all over with a great, bloody gash on her forehead, and Black Mary was a strong swimmer. The water was treacherous around this part; one side of the rock was safe but the other side pulled in a strong undertow over the rapids towards the waterfall.

Down behind the pumpkin patch, the river turned sharply, deepening, gathering speed, preparing herself for the dive over the Wellsford Falls half a mile downriver. Spring wild flower-covered banks combed by anxious, squinting eyes remained conspiratorial, revealing nothing.

It was Albert who saw her first. 'There she is, out there! Out on Devil's Rock!'

Eyes moved in slow-motion and disbelief. No one spoke. Out in the middle of the river, Hilda Mitchell sat stark naked on Devil's Rock, blissfully unaware of the panicking group on the stop-bank. She was cradling something in her arms, staring at the water and singing softly to herself. As they watched, she stood up; her thin, white body bent with the weight of the object in her arms.

John had dark, damp patches creeping from his underarms down the sides of his shirt. He wiped the perspiration from his face and gently touched the sleeve of his now speechless father. 'How the hell did she get out there?' he asked, not expecting a reply. 'She used to be a strong swimmer years ago, but how the hell did she get out there?'

Around his mother's neck, a thick rope led down to the object she cradled in her arms. She turned around slowly, still not seeming to see the group on the nearby river bank but revealing in her movements a large rock in her arms. Silently she took a step forward to the edge of Devil's Rock, her body bent forward, staggering with the weight.

'Jesus Christ,' said Albert, dropping his shirt and running to the water's edge.

It was too late. Softly Hilda Mitchell jumped, still humming to herself and fondly cradling in her arms the surety for completion of her plan.

'Albert, stop!' It was James's voice; a tired, old voice. 'No, Albert, it's no use. We will have to go down to the bottom of the falls.'

Pearl walked away from the group and sat down under the jacaranda tree that was Hilda's favourite. Faith followed and sat down silently beside her.

'You okay?' she asked the older woman.

Pearl nodded and reached out and patted her hand.

'Yeah, Girlie, I'm all right.' She looked briefly in the direction of Devil's Rock and then rose slowly to her feet, standing for a moment with her hands on the pads of her hips. 'I'm all right,' she repeated. Then she silently walked ahead of Faith back to the house, lost in the chaos her unfolding thoughts were creating.

The bombshell

A grandad body with a tongue of brilliant blue kept Benny spellbound. He lay on the dry grass hardly daring to breathe while the blue-tongue lizard leisurely rolled out its magnificent tongue to catch whatever unfortunate, airborne insect chose that particular moment to pass his way. There were three lizards – two adult and one smaller. Benjamin believed they knew full well he was there and had accepted him.

Pearl had told him years ago about watching wildlife, about how quiet and still you had to be so as not to frighten or intrude. The boy-man and the lizards all lay sharing the same sun, and when the family of three had had enough and had lumbered off to disappear in the hollow trunk of a long-dead tree, Benjamin rolled over onto his back, squinting up his eyes, letting his imagination make shapes in the overhead clouds.

For two years now, he had been apprenticed to Stanley Clarke at the furniture shop, a stroke of luck he still hadn't quite recovered from. He had wanted to make furniture ever since the Scot had brought the handmade Jacobean chair for his mother. Benjamin remembered touching the barley-sugar twist legs, the way the timber looked to be alive so that if you touched it, you almost expected it to be blood warm. He had decided then and there that he'd love to work with timber, but never in his wildest dreams had he thought he would be given the chance.

Everything had gone haywire, all at once. His father had joined the army and gone overseas for a year after Danny, dear Danny … he stopped. He still couldn't bear to think about what had happened to his brother. But he had to think about it; he couldn't put his head in the sand any longer. Danny had died, his death had to be dealt with; otherwise there was no point to his life. Oh, he knew what everyone suspected about Danny's death, but it was all conjecture; no one actually knew who did it. And probably no one ever would. But now he had to try and help his father. Danny and the war had really messed him up.

Benjamin sat up and stared down at the river. 'Bloody funny thing, life,' he said to himself. Funny, all right. Look at him and Sandie; couldn't keep their eyes off each other, but he'd watch his hands. Even if he had to sit on them, tie them together behind his back, he'd manage his hands until the time was right. Too much had gone wrong, too much had hurt Faith and Albert and he had no intention of adding Sandie and her dad to that list. No, if there was a life ahead for Sandie and him, they would start the way they intended to go, the way Albert and Faith had always taught him. With respect.

★ ★ ★

Only in retrospect did it occur to Albert that he had once again had no awareness of the space between wakefulness and sleep. This was happening to him constantly lately – the consumption of too much alcohol nicked from the station storeroom before he fell, almost from habit, into bed and straight to sleep robbed him of the delicious, slow slide that heralds the onset of the night's rest.

Later he recalled his first sighting of the willy-willy with startling clarity. He had watched its approaching, dark, tornado-like shape as if from way in the distance, spinning like the toy top Stanley Clarke had made for Daniel years ago, gathering dust and increasing dimension in its movements, looming larger and larger as it had advanced almost menacingly towards him, gathering up pieces of spinifex grass, stones and leaves in the long-fingered darkness of its spiral dance. He had watched as if paralysed, helplessly mortal, as the cone-shaped cloud grew to something hugely powerful, advancing steadily towards him, bringing with it a razor-sharp clarity of his own insignificance.

Albert felt the wetness on his forehead increasing and sweat running down the back of his neck, the shuddering fear overwhelming him as the black, dust-filled cloud taunted, making its way directly towards him one moment then darting around and behind him the next.

With an almost superhuman effort, he managed to raise one arm in an attempt to cover his face just as the cloud completely changed its shape, turning from a spiralling cloud of dust into a very old man, his face and hair painted with clay and feathers, a pair of song-sticks in his hands beating, steady, haunting, primitive in their repeating sound.

Slowly the man advanced towards Albert to stand silently looking at him; his large, dark eyes filled with sadness. Albert lay mesmerised as the figure began to very slowly dance around him, song-sticks beating together, chanting in a language foreign to his ears. Slowly, as if following some unwritten ritual, the stranger circled Albert, the sticks hypnotising, his chanting voice reaching far deeper than Albert's hearing, penetrating way down inside him to touch and disturb.

Suddenly Albert jerked wide awake to find himself bathed in a heavy sweat but still in bed alongside his sleeping wife. He listened for a moment to her regular breathing and the sound of the night breeze gently rustling the stringy-bark outside then quietly slid out of bed and walked to the jug and washbowl in the kitchen and bathed his face with the cool water. He let the water trickle down his neck and bathed his arms and upper chest. Then he sat quietly in the dark in Faith's favourite chair.

He stilled his unsteady hands on the chair's arms, knowing his dream, if that was what it was, had just touched on something sacred. He sat recalling the face of the willy-willy turned human and felt a flood of shame at the sadness he had seen in the large, brown eyes,

eyes that were not unlike his own. Through the rest of the night, Albert sat unmoving, watching the light changing outside with the approaching dawn.

'Who were you?' he asked of the fading darkness. The only answer came to him from a lone currawong, heralding the beginning day with its warbling call.

Albert turned the postcard with the Statue of Liberty on the front over and over in his hands and shook his head. He simply could not get the grin off his face. Of course he had never doubted that his friend would remember him, but he felt like jumping in the air with joy. He held the card out to show Faith, her brown eyes shooting sparks of pleasure.

'Read it again, Albert,' she said. 'Read it again.'

Albert needed no prompting to read the only personal communications he had ever received in the mail. He cleared his throat, held the card at arm's length and, trying to suppress the smile that constantly pulled at the corners of his mouth, began.

'Hi Albert, just so you know an Indian never forgets! Our time shared together has never left my heart and how well I remember our conversation, as if it were yesterday. I have something here for you that will be delivered when I find a way. In the meantime, hang in there, my friend. Signed,' Albert read, 'Larry Zephier.'

Faith touched her husband's shoulder. 'You got a real friend there,' she said softly. 'A real friend.'

Realisation

The united forces of boredom and sadness propelled the leg that kicked the stone into the calm of the river, its splash sending the water into ever-expanding rings. The stone kicker picked up a piece of grass and, driven by the same boredom, placed it across his lips and blew the blade into the wind. He wondered about his future. It was all too secure, too organised. Almost as if his father had mapped his life out for him so that decisions about what was ahead had been taken out of his hands as if he were incapable of deciding for himself in a way, though he knew his parents wished the best for him.

He supposed rebelling against that expectation was the reason why he had allowed himself years ago to create the diversion with Daniel. Certainly there was nothing serious in it for him; it was just a bit of an experimental change – boys together. But soon after it started, he knew it was very different for Daniel. Poor Daniel.

Jamie lay back as the dried out grass made his nose twitch. Oh, he would go ahead and marry. His father had a thing about heirs. If he didn't feel future grandchildren were certain to arrive, he would be terrified that somehow the Wellsford land might not continue to belong ad infinitum to the Mitchell family. But for someone to kill Daniel the way they had, beaten him and kicked him to death, simply because he was 'different', the thought left him empty and sick to his stomach. And who could possibly have known they were meeting?

Jamie had gone over and over this in his head during ensuing months. It was harmless, dammit, just a bit of hands-on stuff, no questions asked and not going anywhere. It seemed that everything you did and thought was perceived by others, particularly your elders, as some kind of sexual perversion to be stamped out.

Was that a throwback to their own inadequacies in that area? he wondered although he immediately countered that that couldn't be so. His grandfather, he knew, had visited that establishment in town regularly. It had even been suggested that he once owned the old brothel. So why was that acceptable and his experience with Daniel forbidden? Not that he blamed his grandfather, what with his grandmother going completely round the bend, holding conversations with the furniture and parlour palms and ignoring human beings. Then that awful day when she'd lost it completely at Devil's Rock.

Jamie found himself wondering if there was some kind of a hoodoo on Wellsford Station. He had heard about Faith's mother, Mary, who drowned mysteriously years back. Way back in the beginning, his great-grandmother had walked out on his great-grandfather who built the place. Then the old man himself skipped out, back to the old country because he couldn't stand the ferocity of this new land. Jamie found that a bit hard to understand. Although he didn't like being told how to spend his life, he loved Wellsford Station as well as the civic life he was just entering. He had recently tasted status and wanted it on his life's menu.

He leaned back and looked at the cloudless, blue sky, the ironbark trees; and melaleuca with their tiny, white, bottlebrush blossoms; the blossoming eucalypts attracting the honey-making bees; and the cleared, rolling fields where the contented Herefords grazed, and wondered why anyone would want to go back to a country renowned for being foggy, damp and cold. He stood and brushed the grass from his clothes.

There was something else worrying him and he just couldn't put his finger on it. Something that just didn't sit right. Something to do with his grandmother's dementia. He thought about Faith and Albert,

Daniel's parents. Faith with her beautiful, calm, sad face, and Albert. You never quite knew what Albert was thinking, or what he had seen in his life.

Anyway, he had made up his mind. He was going to go to Canberra. Politics attracted him and it would not sit easy with his father – he knew that. Better make the announcement and get it over with, though, and if skin and hair flew; well, so be it. He had made up his mind.

* * *

There was no escaping the merciless heat. Death comes on the west wind, Pearl thought as she slapped out with the tea towel. 'Damn flies drive you mad,' she mumbled. 'Pick up the butter; it's runny, and there's a little black fly-leg in it.' She ran a muslin cloth through a bowl of now lukewarm water on the bench and held it to her forehead, letting the water run down her face and neck. The hot, breathless air, besides being enervating was vexing. She didn't like the feel of things at all.

From the back kitchen porch, Faith shielded her eyes against the sun with her hands as she looked anxiously in the originating direction of the hot, gusty wind. There was a huge, reddish cloud in the sky, making the sun seem hazy and dull and giving an eerie glow to the landscape but in no way diminishing the heat. The stabled horses were uneasy, whinnying and restless. Cattle had been rounded up and penned, as had sheep, although God knew how many might have perished in the outer paddocks.

Faith found herself praying for a wind change to alter conditions. The kitchen garden looked like she felt; spinach, tomato and lettuce plants all wilted, hanging, devoid of moisture, half dead. She walked back inside to where Pearl stood mopping her face.

'All we need now is rain,' Faith scoffed. 'The way they've got the house all bagged up, the next thing we'll have to contend with is cleaning up the flooding inside because the water can't get away.'

Pearl nodded. 'At least we could stand out in it and take a deep breath.' She walked to the pantry and pulled out the remains of a leg of ham. 'Better make this into sandwiches for the men before it goes off. Won't last in this heat.'

The two women, their movements slowed by the breath-grabbing heat, avoided each other's eyes as if in their meeting, each might recognise and give life to the fear neither wanted to express.

The day before yesterday, James Mitchell and Charlie had ridden to the outskirts of the land to inspect stock and visit the Campbells, a newly-arrived Scottish couple who had taken over the McManaway property adjoining his, worried that they may not know how to protect their place against fire. Pearl hoped they were all all right. She knew how quickly the bush burned. She had seen the eucalypts just erupt into flames with the heat, knew how quickly those flames moved through an area; their hungry, red tongues devouring everything in their path. It could be all over in a matter of minutes, leaving nothing but black smouldering ruins behind. She also knew about the trees that needed the fire to regenerate their growth, recalling vaguely how her people used to burn off.

She stopped mopping her face, realising that it had happened again. From way back somewhere, memories were returning to her, things she had forgotten completely creeping back into her awareness. She poured a glass of water and took a long, cool drink. How much more was there tucked away? How much more would reveal itself to her through her slowly returning memory?

Her thoughts were scattered by the sound of a commotion in the yard, raised voices and two horses pacing, breathless and agitated. She closed her eyes briefly then walked outside the door of the kitchen to confront the fear that had come to her on the hot wind. Across the back of his favourite horse was the body of James Mitchell, his unclosed eyes staring fixedly straight ahead. His white hair was blackened and singed and a large, bloody gash oozed on one temple. Albert held the reins of the distressed horse as John tried to free his father's left foot from the stirrup so as to ease him to the ground.

'What the hell happened, Charlie, for Christ's sake, man, what happened?' John spat out the words to the old man who'd been like a shadow to his father all these years.

Charlie sat in the red dust of the yard with his head in his hands. 'Bloody awful, boss, that's what. We got to Campbells' place and it's gone. Burned. Nothing there but black sticks and the remains of their brick fireplace. We start to look for them, they nowhere. Boss looks all around and then calls out, "I found 'em, Charlie!" Found 'em, all right. What they done is get in their water tank. S'pose they thought it the best thing to do when the fire come close. Just boiled 'em to death. Then Boss so upset he get on his horse and pull her around to gallop. Don't notice branch right in front of his nose. Hit him wham on the side of the head and the horse take off, got one foot in stirrup, but he's gone. I know from that hit on the head, he's gone, all right.'

Later as the first large drop of rain fell on the tin roof of Wellsford Station, heralding the onset of the life-saving change of weather, Pearl filled the huge, black kettles on the stove with water. She'd be needing that now because she and Faith would have the job. The job of laying out the person they had spent their lives working for; preparing him, getting him ready. She felt a sadness for the man, not because he had treated her as anyone special or made her life any different but because she had known him as a man, older than herself, through all of her life with the family. Through all his problems, she had watched James Mitchell and known him, possibly known him as well, if not better than any other.

She sighed to herself at the thought of the preparation ahead of her for the coming funeral. James Mitchell had been well known, admired by some, envied by others. There would be a large funeral – she was sure of that. A very large funeral with all coming to pay their respects. She thought of Hilda Mitchell and shuddered. Would there be some trace of her at her husband's funeral? Some ghost-like creature dancing through the congregation in a state of disarray, her poor mind not even comprehending just what it was she had to dance about?

★ ★ ★

'Albert got another one of them postcards in the mail yesterday,' Faith said, smiling. 'They really give him a buzz. Funny that he only met that Yank the day before he left, but they really liked each other. That makes three he has now, all pinned up on the wall at home.'

'You know, in all my life, I never met a real live Indian,' said Pearl. She leaned forward on the big farm table, cupping her jaw in her palms. She exhaled a long, tired sigh. 'Gawd, I'm tired lately,' she said, 'tired when I go to bed and just as tired when I wake up in the morning. Must be gettin' old.'

Faith looked at her. 'I know you and that tired stuff. There's a lousy job coming up and I'm going to get it, aren't I?'

Pearl grinned at her. 'Tell you what, girl, you're right. You take the polishin' wax there and go rub up that desk of old Mitchell's. Elizabeth has taken off for town and she doesn't want that hideous old thing here any longer, and it has to look good as new before it goes to auction. Go on, girl. Meanwhile I'll shell these peas here.'

Faith sighed, knowing full well that sighing made not the slightest difference. She picked up the wax and cloth and moved down the hall past the framed photographs of earlier Mitchells. *All got a look like someone stuck a toffee apple up their bum.* She giggled to herself at the thought, stepping into what used to be James Mitchell's study.

Although the room had generous proportions, it had hardly been used for years. James had stopped using most of the house once he'd decided that life with the hired hands was preferable to sleeping with

Hilda. Elizabeth had always considered the room gloomy, as if the years spent there by her father-in-law left some physical trace of him in the accumulated dust. Now she had decided she needed the space rather than the memories induced by the presence of the desk.

Faith stood holding the wax in one hand, her other hand resting lightly on her hip, and looked at the mahogany monstrosity. Pretty damned ugly, all right, she thought to herself as she knelt down and started waxing one side of it. Ugly though it was, the combination of wax and effort slowly brought the mahogany to a rich, reddish sheen.

Faith straightened up then moved back to check her handiwork, involuntarily touching the tin of wax with her toe, sending it skidding underneath and behind the desk. She pulled her lips downwards in a gesture of annoyance and lightly leaned down on her hands and knees, reaching one arm back and under the writing ledge; then, holding on to the front shelf with the other hand, stretched back for the polish.

A click, gentle but definite. She heard the sound almost without it registering. It was only when she stood up that she saw a drawer she had never seen before extending open, out past the front ledge of the desk. Nothing much in it, just a folded piece of paper.

She looked briefly over her shoulder as if expecting someone to materialise in the doorway – why, she didn't know. I must have dusted that desk at least a hundred times, she thought, so why should fate choose today to have me find this drawer?

She took the paper out, opened and read the contents. Once done, she folded the paper gently and replaced it in the drawer which she pushed to close. Again she heard the click as the secret drawer fastened.

For a minute, or was it an hour, Faith sat on the floor of the Mitchells' den, gently rocking backwards and forwards on her haunches. Then she stood up, picked up the wax and cloth and strode purposefully back down the hall and into the kitchen.

'Peas goin' on forever,' Pearl said, not looking up, shelling the peas into a basin and dropping the pods into a laid out sheet of *The Wellsford Herald*. 'Chooks'll enjoy these pods, though.'

Faith said nothing. She walked over to the dresser and picked up the water jug which she hurled like a woman possessed against the opposite wall, sending shattering glass in all directions. With manic force she wiped her arms across the table, sending everything in front of her crashing to the floor. Pearl pulled the peas and paper towards her, wide-eyed, but said nothing.

The girl picked up a kitchen chair and hurled it at the kitchen window. Either the sound of splintering, crashing glass or the energy required to cause it seemed to release something inside her. She stood in front of Pearl with both hands on her hips, defiant, wild-eyed, perspiration standing out on her forehead, wide nostrils breathing like an overrun horse.

Pearl still sat podding her peas; otherwise not moving. 'Something upset you, Girlie? What is it, then?' she asked gently, soothingly.

'That rotten, mongrel bastard!' Faith yelled. 'That rotten, mongrel, dirty Mitchell bastard … that bastard … that bastard …' She was crying now, wet-faced, throwing her arms around above her head in disbelief. 'Did you know?' She stood in front of Pearl, pulling the pod-laden newspaper onto the floor, sending the basin of shelled peas racing after them. 'Did you know?' She grabbed Pearl by the shoulders, shaking her, incoherent now, words jumbled in with her sobs.

Pearl sat motionless, not answering. Faith slumped to the floor, eyes suddenly swollen, exhausted now. She looked at Pearl. 'Did you know,' she asked quietly, 'that that bastard was my father?'

Faith rolled to her knees like a rag doll and looked to Pearl expectantly, wishing, willing her to deny her statement.

Pearl bent half-heartedly to pick up some spent peas. Dear God, she was tired. 'Yes,' she said quietly, 'I knew.'

Faith looked like a whipped dog. She tried to speak, but her mouth would not form the words. She reached out and pulled Pearl around to face her. 'What?' she questioned uncomprehendingly. 'All my life, you have been my closest friend. I've trusted you ... Pearl, for Christ's sake ...'

Pearl's eyes filled with tears. 'I said I knew, but I didn't know – not for years. I felt that something didn't quite add up, but I left well enough alone. But I knew for sure that day Hilda Mitchell stood on the rock with the door in her face wide open. That's when I knew.'

Faith sat on the floor. How much more was there? What else was there for her to hear? Was her life so controlled by outside circumstances that she was helpless, and totally without hope?

'Was he so ashamed of me that he could never find the courage to tell me?' Faith asked, her voice lifeless.

Pearl got up from the table and lifted Faith up, holding her, moving her slowly towards a chair. She held the younger woman's hand gently, as gently as she spoke.

'I had the feeling years ago that James Mitchell cared for Mary. Oh, he was careful, so careful. When you was born, they blamed you on that itinerant station hand who had been here for about six months. I never really believed that, but your mother said nothing, kept it to herself. But then I noticed Hilda change. She had always been a strange one, but after you was born, she became unravelled. James was the one who wanted you and Albert to have that old cottage to live in. He always had a leaning towards you and although he was not man enough to ever be able to admit it, he cared, Faith, he did care.

'When they pulled your mother from the river, the whole station knew something strange had happened. To start with your mum, she was a great swimmer, loved the water. Second, she didn't like that area near Devil's Rock – never went there. She must've gone there thinking no one would know she was going to meet him.'

Faith said nothing, feeling totally exhausted.

'No, she didn't drown by accident,' Pearl continued. 'I only really saw that for sure the day Hilda's face door opened. That's what sent her bonkers, I reckon. She was so eaten up by jealousy because she knew that your father cared for your mother, that she must've followed them, waited for her chance, then killed her. Must've hit her on the head with something. That's where the cuts must've come from. My guess is that she expected the body to go over the falls and down the river, not be caught in the reeds.'

'When they pulled your mother from the water, James went crazy. Just saddled up his horse and didn't come back near the station for ages.'

Faith pulled herself to her feet. She blew her nose loudly and straightened her dress.

'You all right now, girl, can I get you anything?' Pearl moved towards the teapot.

'Yeah, yeah,' replied Faith, the fight gone out of her now. 'You can. You can get to buggery.' She looked at Pearl and laughed, then sniffed loudly. 'Christ, look at this mess,' she said. Slowly Faith started to pick up the broken pieces off the floor. 'Better get on with it,' she said, pulling her hair back into place. 'What's done is done.'

Behind the kitchen just through the wall, in the wine racks between the flour and sugar sacks, the bottle of wine on its way to Albert's pocket suddenly lost its appeal.

Journey home

Pearl watched with a kind of detached interest as the thin, red trickle of blood ran sluggishly from the rose thorn puncture down the full length of her finger before she shook off the surplus then sucked away all sign of it. Slowly she cut another half dozen or so of the pale pink Rome Beauties that were once a young Hilda Mitchell's favourites, struck from a cutting brought from the old Parramatta homestead.

She walked back into the station kitchen to crush the base of their stems with a rolling pin, reaching into the long pine cupboard for the crystal rose-bowl and then stopped still, steadying herself with one hand on the benchtop, breathing irregularly.

'Gawd,' she muttered, 'I feel a bit strange. Must've ate something off.'

Beads of perspiration glistened on her forehead like early morning dewdrops on paspalum, to be dissipated almost instantly as her body convulsed with intense shivering. She folded her arms over her torso to keep in its warmth, rubbing the tops of her arms with her hands. The room was playing tricks with her, changing its shape, moving away from her one minute and the next folding itself menacingly in towards her.

The pale pink blooms lay forgotten on the kitchen table as Pearl felt the sudden surge of fever grip her body. Something itched and burned like an army of ants wearing hobnail boots, a regiment marching just under her skin. Something had hold of her, all right, something demonic, something that pushed its hot breath right in her face then almost immediately changed itself into icy needles to chill her bones and chatter her teeth.

She watched dispassionately as the kitchen floor raised itself towards her, slowly at first then gathering momentum, shook loose from its moorings to rush towards her, bringing in its upsweep a merciful, all-enveloping blackness to claim her consciousness.

Clicketty-clack, clicketty-clack, the cold glass of the train window pressed against Pearl's lips as she pushed her tear-stained face as far away as possible from the hands of the woman sitting opposite her. *Clicketty-clack, clicketty-clack.* Why were they taking her away? Every minute, the great iron monster took her further and further away from the soft folds of her mother's skirts, from her warm hands and the anguish of her crying. *Clicketty-clack, clicketty-clack.* She tried to move her lips from the cold glass of the window, but they were stuck now, stuck on the watery glass. Nothing she could do now; something had taken her energy. Nothing would remove the cold glass window from her lips.

'Come on, Pearl, try and drink a little bit, you're burning up there.' Faith's wavering voice, brimming over with concern, Faith cradling Pearl's head and holding a glass of water to her lips, trying to urge her to drink. She was burning up, all right. The room was alternately freezing then on fire. She could see the flames, feel the heat from their reddish-orange glow as they crept and leapt up the sides of and along the bed, inching closer, closer, ever tormenting the body she was incapable of moving.

The cold water trickled across Pearl's lips, down under her chin and along her neck. Words fought each other for existence; then, stumbling over themselves inside the ill woman's furnace-filled head were destroyed in its fire before she could utter a sound. She wanted to tell Faith not to worry and fuss so. The girl looked drawn, sitting alongside the bed, pressing the ice cold washcloth onto the forehead of the only mother she had known, bathing her neck and hands, trying to trickle water into her hot, parched mouth, stopping to gently rub Vaseline into the parched lips.

As Pearl again lapsed from consciousness, Faith stood up and walked to the window, watching the muslin on either side of it fly gently in the evening breeze. She felt sadder than she could ever remember, looking at her oldest friend and feeling totally useless and inadequate. She wished Albert would hurry up; it wasn't so bad with someone else there. It was when she was alone that the burden seemed unbearable.

Panic rose inside her like some vile bile. What would she do if something happened to Pearl? It was Pearl who'd looked after her when the mother she could hardly recall died, it was Pearl who'd delivered her children, who'd comforted when Daniel was murdered and it was Pearl who was always there after Albert had enlisted.

Faith dropped into the wicker chair by the window, telling herself that she was overwrought and overtired. 'It might all look different tomorrow,' she told herself. 'She might be well again tomorrow.' All time seemed welded to the woman in the bed who consistently lapsed in and out of consciousness.

Around the fourth morning, Pearl felt a change in her condition. She opened her eyes to see both Faith and Albert standing alongside her bed. Albert stood with his arm around his wife, trying to comfort her. Pearl tried desperately to talk, to tell them everything was as it should be. If only she could open her mouth to tell them to look around and see what was happening in the room. The two poor dears were so involved in their grief, they failed to see just what was going on.

Don't cry, loves, don't cry. Pearl thought the words, wishing her thoughts to enter the minds of the two people she loved most in the world. She wanted to somehow tell them she was happy now. For the first time since she had arrived at Wellsford Station, she was going somewhere. If she could just tell them to turn around, they could see for themselves the people coming for her, coming in through the door. It was funny how familiar all those people looked to her. She didn't know their names, but it was obvious that they were her kin. *Just look at that woman walking through the door now, look at her with her gentle face.* Pearl looked at the woman standing in front of her, the woman wearing a faded print dress reaching out her hands to her, and inside, her whole being smiled.

Gently sobbing, Faith bent to delicately close the eyes of her almost mother. Albert stood with hunched shoulders, his face buried in his hands. Faith touched her husband on the shoulder. 'Don't cry, love,' she urged. 'Be happy for her, be happy for our Pearl. She's gone home at last, just like she always wanted.'

Faith rested her head on her husband's shoulder. There was a strength coming to her from somewhere. She felt exhausted but strong. She looked at Pearl in the bed and understood. The strength was coming from behind the smile that still filled the room, a gentle smile radiating off a dead woman's face.

Forward steps

*L*ife changed enormously at Wellsford Station following Pearl's death as it was to change everywhere. Faith and Albert settled back into something of a routine, except that now their life felt different.

Jamie left Wellsford Station to work in Canberra, his father agreeing grudgingly after his mother shrewdly pointed out for the umpteenth time how beneficial his gaining a degree in economics had been for Wellsford and the bush and that from Canberra he could also help Wellsford. If Elizabeth had any knowledge of the associations Jamie had made at university, she'd kept it to herself. She knew her husband had been depressed since the death of his father, and Pearl's passing had only added to this depression. Although her son Jamie needed to get away, underneath she worried about his not continuing the tradition with the land.

Restoring

Sitting on the train was pleasant enough. It was only when she opened the window to relieve the stifling heat and a tiny piece of soot landed in her eye, causing it to redden and water continuously, that the sheen she had placed on the trip to Sydney dulled a little. The situation worsened when the face of the woman sitting across the aisle set in a mask of smug, self-assured knowingness; she had taken a good, long, lingering look at the hand rubbing the offending eye and noted the home-knitted mitten, worn in the heat of summer.

Amy gave up trying to remove the tiny piece of soot and merely blinked constantly, only adding to the smugness on the face of her fellow traveller. She hid her mittened hands in the folds of her skirt and wondered if she might really be as mad as everyone around her, all through her life, had seemed to think. She stared out the window and thought about eating the sandwiches she had cut this morning. She looked at the tomato fillings now bleeding through the bread inside the greaseproof paper wrapping and thought better of it. Anyway, she wasn't a bit hungry – too nervous to eat, really. She could feel her hands perspiring under their woollen covering and for once was grateful for the concealing homemade mittens.

Well, she had nothing to lose if this trip led nowhere, did she? She would get off the train in Sydney, take a cab to Paddington and if Rudi what's-his-name told her he didn't like her work, she could just turn around and forget all about it. It was all Jamie Mitchell's idea, anyway; he made the appointment and set the whole thing up. He and particularly his mother Elizabeth had encouraged her through the years, ever since she'd stayed with them that time when her mother had had to go to hospital in the city.

She observed the passing landscape lazily as the scene gradually changed from paddocks and trees to red brick and tiles. They must live on silverbeet and carrots, she thought, taking in the regimented vegetable gardens. She strained her neck for the sight of the famous coathanger – the Sydney Harbour Bridge – and felt a slight tingle as she caught a glimpse of its Meccano-like structure in the distance.

Her eye had stopped watering. Somehow the piece of grit had dislodged itself and she snapped open a powder compact expecting a dark, sooty piece sitting on her lower eyelid. Slowly, Amy took in a deep, long breath. The city smelled differently from the country. The air was thicker somehow, warmer in a way, as if you were breathing in the accumulated outbreath of the population.

As the train slowed to a belching, steaming halt, she gathered her belongings together, cursing softly under her breath at the awkwardness of her portfolio, and made her way to the taxi stand at the front of Central Station.

'Yis just in town for the day, luv?'

She wondered if the eyes in the rear-vision mirror had themselves spoken to her and wished they would pay more attention to the road ahead. 'Overnight,' she replied hesitatingly.

The eyes in the front mirror crinkled at the corners. 'Where yis from?'

'Wellsford,' she answered quickly, wishing he would just drive and forget the conversation. 'Wellsford, north-west NSW.'

The head in front shook and the eyes left the mirror, but the mouth pursed itself and started to whistle 'I've got a gal, in Kalamazoo ...'

Amy concentrated on the rows of Paddington terraces when the cab suddenly slowed to a halt. 'Here yis are, luv, safe and sound.'

She paid her fare and studied the building in front of her. Not too terrifying, an old English styled, terraced house, painted white, shuttered blinds, iron lace balcony. She opened the iron gate, walked over the terrazzo path and tentatively lifted the brass doorknocker.

Inside, Rudi van Geldorn laid out Amy's folio on the desk in front of him, sat back in his chair with the palms of his hands together and rested his index fingers on his chin. He took a long look at the young woman sitting on the other side of the desk, noting the slender figure; the dark, haunted eyes in a finely boned face framed with a shock of curling, brown hair, and the hands hidden in the little woollen mittens. Yes, the mittens; Jamie Mitchell had warned him about those.

Rudi stood up and walked to a side table, picked up a silver coffee pot and poured two cups. He noticed her hands trembled slightly when she took the coffee and that the visible parts of her fingers were long and slim, the nails unpolished and well shaped.

He stirred and stirred his coffee beyond aggravation point. She wanted to bend over and ask him to stop but controlled the urge. Finally he put the coffee to one side and leafed through the folio.

She watched his face for a suggestion of response, but he just looked very slowly through the contents and, once he had come to the last one, looked through again. He said not a word, but she noticed that a small pulse to the left side of his forehead beat a slow tandem.

Inside he was breathless. Christ Almighty, he thought. *Where the hell has this girl been?*

He leafed through the folio again, his excitement steadily mounting, unable to believe what he was seeing. The pieces were so emotionally loaded that the initial impact was overwhelming. The first piece was the back view of a man walking down a long passageway to a door, obviously a front door. It was the jacket that said it all. The way the jacket hung on the man's shoulders, cloaking his obvious feeling of despair. And the child. The child in the doorway with her head down and hanging from one hand the limp, devoid-of-life doll. A doll staring into nothingness, trapped in the circumstances surrounding it.

'You have a lot of talent, young woman.' She smiled, almost looked relieved. A lot of talent, Christ, how condescending, he thought. *The woman is unbelievable.*

He slowly leafed through the drawings again. Noticed she'd included a doll in just about every piece. Not a curly-headed, Mama doll, but a limp, lifeless, helpless doll. And the light, the way the woman captured the light. He hadn't seen that kind of work since he left Europe.

'This is an interesting piece,' he questioned, pointing to a painting of a woman sitting in a rocking chair by the fire. You could not see the woman's face; just the top of her hair showed, hanging over the back of the chair, viewed from behind. On the other side of the room a younger, slender woman poured tea into a cup from a silver teapot, the sun from the sole window in the room reflecting right on the teapot. And there, there on the floor in the shadow, huddled against the leg of the table, almost hiding itself, was the doll.

She nodded. 'The light worked well for me that day,' she said. 'I had to work fast to catch that light.'

He smiled. 'I notice that you often include a doll in your pictures. Does that have any special meaning?'

She didn't answer immediately, looking slightly startled as if the knowledge was new to her. 'No, no, I don't think so. No significance at all. Must just be coincidence.'

He tapped the folio with his right hand. 'I think we can mount something special with these,' he said. 'I would like to arrange to show you in Sydney, in the not too distant future.'

She gasped, then for the first time, she smiled. 'Are you serious?' she asked. 'Do you think the pieces are good enough for a showing?'

He nodded. God, the woman was beautiful when she smiled. 'Quite serious,' he said. 'Very much so.'

Embarrassed but delighted, she stood and purposefully smoothed the folds of her skirt. 'Will you phone and let me know what is to happen?' she asked.

He took her by the elbow and led her to the door. 'As soon as I have something arranged, I will let you know the details and we can discuss whether or not they suit you. In the meantime, you must keep on with your work. Keep at it, my dear. Please.'

He closed the door behind the slender figure and hurried back to his desk. There was something about this work that was compelling. It was the overwhelming sadness that reached out to you from the images. Reached out and took a firm, not totally pleasant grip on your heart.

Rudi reached out for his telephone and dialled Canberra, leaving a message for Jamie Mitchell to phone him back. He was feeling a sense of exhilaration, the very reason he got into the art business in the first place, come to think of it; however, too much of the work that passed over his desk left him feeling more despondent than confident. But this woman … He had to find out more about her, this country-born, self-contained woman with the desperate eyes who had no idea at all of her genius.

In spite of the fact that she'd hardly slept at all the night before, the long daytrip home on the train seemed to Amy to pass almost without her awareness. She suddenly found herself on the outskirts of Wellsford without having noticed any of the preceding rail stations. She was experiencing a kind of nervous feeling in her abdomen and wondered if, now that someone had indicated a professional interest in her work, she might suffer some kind of artistic paralysis and not be able to find the inspiration to continue. She then immediately dismissed the feeling as one of nerves and concentrated on watching the changing light on the passing landscape.

Wasn't it Monet who said that he'd once tried on four different occasions to catch the correct light for one of his canvasses? She understood completely how fast you had to work to capture an elusive moment of light that made something special, turned it into something you wanted to share with others, but it was overwhelming to her that someone else had immediately seen it in her work.

As the train thundered into Wellsford, Amy mentally rearranged her future life. She would simply tell her mother that from now on, the painting came first. Living frugally was not a problem as she had done that most of her life and she could continue that way quite happily, so long as she could paint. Nothing in the world was as important, and for that very reason, without her comprehending the fact, that very moment heralded the beginning of Amy Corcoran's healing.

Honesty time

Jamie Mitchell straightened the papers on his desk, ripped the day's calendar from the pad in front of him, pushed back his chair and checked his watch. The stresses and strains of the last few months were showing in his face. Fine lines now fanned out from the grey-green eyes and already he noticed one or two silver threads among the gold. Good line for a song, he thought

He clicked off the light and closed his office door to walk down the long hall, through the front doors of the building to the car park. 'God, it's cold,' he muttered, pulling his coat collar up as the unfriendly wind blew across the lake to throw a sampling of her winter promise full in his face.

It was a strange feeling this time, going back to Wellsford. His father, who had been ailing for some time, could never write a letter without urging his son to come back to the land 'where he belonged'. Must be damned hard for them to understand, he thought, putting the car into gear and gliding out, heading towards the main road north. I'm sure she understands, he thought, seeing his mother's face in his mind's eye. She knows what it's all been about, surely.

What they didn't know was what they said about him in Canberra. 'Rich landowner, fatted calves', all that stuff. Especially the press when they wanted to make a point. They could take a piece of two-be-four and build it into an estate if it suited their purpose. And now all this shit with Vietnam, moratoriums, the lot. He'd never believed that South Vietnam called on Canberra to join the war; he was sure the head man suggested sending their boys to further his own ends. Christ, it was all so depressing, and going to get worse, and the insidious thing was that the public, other than for a few, believed the crap the newspapers and television fed them. That was all part of the whole continuing ploy.

He checked the petrol gauge and moved his body backwards and forwards in the seat. It was a funny feeling this time, going back. It was not a decision taken lightly. He wasn't at all sure what the reaction would be when he told them. He remembered he used to feel like this coming home from boarding school in Sydney. Always wondering if he was going to please or displease. And as of now, he was no closer to marriage. That wouldn't please his father.

He smiled wryly to himself, recalling the pot-smoking abandon he had thought so free when he first arrived in the ACT. Now it bored, like everything else in the city. Once a thing became routine, it simply bored as much as any other routine.

He was dog tired when the car reached the old road just outside Wellsford. The town looked exactly the same. You could shoot a cannon down the street and not hit anyone this time of night.

He hit the cattle grid at the entrance to his parent's land and slowed the car. Don't want to hit a kangaroo, he thought, knowing there would be plenty around with the dry. The light was on in the old shearing shed Albert and Faith called home and for a moment, he was tempted to call in. No, better wait. All in good time.

The house looked smaller in the headlights, but it still gave him a lump in his throat. Three generations. He supposed it had to touch you somewhere, even after the cynicism of the last few years. The light was still on in the parlour. He knew they would be waiting with the cup of tea, the time-honoured remedy to cure all ills.

He hugged his mother and shook his father's hand. Christ, he still had a grip. No monkey business with that one. Then family talk, reminiscences until too tired to talk any more, and the three retired for the night.

His father hadn't asked. This time, Elizabeth must have been in his ear because he made no mention of his 'staying on the land, where he belonged'.

Next morning, he and his parents were sitting in the kitchen at the scrubbed pine table. 'You'll be wondering why I've chosen now to visit?' said Jamie.

His father rolled his head, a resigned kind of a nod which could mean anything.

'It's just that I've got a few things to say to a few people and Canberra in May gives you the horrors,' Jamie added.

His father got up from the table to put his cup and saucer on the bench, disappointment buried deeply under the cover of a loud cough.

'And there's something else,' he continued.

His father didn't turn around but stood, rinsing and re-rinsing the teacup and saucer.

'I'd like to come back here to live if its all right. I want to spend the rest of my life working the land.'

Silence. The silence of disbelief. Then a flood of tears from his mother, and his father's hand pumping his. Jamie was surprised at how emotional he felt. He was home, all right, home at Wellsford.

Later in the day, Jamie checked the newspaper billboards. It was all there, all right. The news had broken; he really had resigned.

He drove out through gentle rain to Faith and Albert's. They had aged, it shocked him momentarily. But then after talking for a while, he found he wasn't aware of it any more; they were exactly the same people.

'I'm coming back to live,' he told them. 'Just wanted to call in and tell you both.'

'Listen to that rain,' said Faith, carrying teacups from the kitchen. 'It's raining like the heavens have parted. Do you have to drive back?'

'Only to the homestead, not to Canberra, thank God.'

He refused the umbrella Faith offered and ran to his car. It certainly was pelting down now.

He leaned forward in the car, wiping the inside of the windscreen with his sleeve. He hated driving in this kind of weather, unable to see more than a few feet ahead, with the car windows fogging constantly. *At least it seems to be easing,* he thought hopefully, wondering if it was merely his wishful thinking.

He braked suddenly, noticing the yellow Volkswagen that had pulled up on the side of the road, easing in front of it and peering through its steamy windows. He rummaged in the back seat and found an old umbrella with a broken spoke, remembering the unwritten country rule of checking on fellow travellers in treacherous weather conditions.

'You okay?' he said, tapping on the driver's window of the parked car. The door opened.

'Oh yeah, I think so. Thank you.' An American voice from somewhere inside a sou'wester and oilskin. 'Can't get the car to start, though.'

'Let's have a look,' Jamie said. 'Hop out a minute.'

The sou'wester lifted and Jamie found himself looking into the brownest eyes he had ever seen. *Christ,* he thought to himself. *Baby, ain't your brown eyes blue.* He tried the ignition and then moved round to the back of the car, raised the engine cover and fiddled. 'Dead as a dodo, I'm afraid,' he told the brown eyes. 'You'll have to leave it here. Better hop in my car and come on down to the station. You can't spend the night out here.'

The brown eyes widened. 'Is that all right?' she questioned. 'I don't want to inconvenience anyone.'

'No, no, it's fine,' Jamie answered. 'They don't get too many visitors at the station and my parents will be happy to have you.' He reached in to the back seat and lifted out the suitcase.

A long-fingered hand reached up and removed the sou'wester. Jamie noticed the dark, shining plait of hair that fell from under it, with the thought that it could tie up a steamship to a wharf. The hand extended itself towards him. 'Hi, I'm Sunnie Quick-to-see Cobiness.'

'Jamie Mitchell,' he answered, gripping the fine-boned hand and smiling. 'What kind of a name is Kwiktisse?'

'Oh, it's a name that was given to me. Because I'm quick to see,' she laughed.

'Oh, quick to see – ask a dumb question. I kind of missed that part.'

'How far is your place?' she questioned, rubbing the condensation on the inside of the window and peering through as they passed Devil's Rock.

'Not too far, only a few minutes. You'll be just in time for dinner. Roast lamb, Australian style.'

She laughed and pushed a wisp of hair away. With a slight pang, he noticed the gold band on her left hand.

'You travelling alone?' he asked. 'Wellsford is not exactly a tourist mecca.'

'Mmm-hmm,' she replied, smiling. 'I came here to make a delivery for someone.'

He pulled up in front of the homestead. 'This is it,' he said smilingly. 'Home sweet home.'

Elizabeth chopped the mint for the sauce, humming to herself. She loved having visitors, especially unexpected ones.

'How long are you here?' she asked the young woman later when they sat around the fire with Jamie and John, enjoying an after-dinner port.

The brown eyes looked thoughtful. 'I suppose that all depends on how long it takes me to find the person I came to see,' Sunnie replied.

'Well, you're more than welcome to stay here,' Elizabeth offered. 'In fact, we would really love to have you.' She was taken with the girl. There was something about her.

Sunnie looked around the room. 'It feels real nice here,' she said. 'Feels like a real home.' She leaned across to place her coffee cup on the table. 'I wonder,' she asked, looking from face to face, 'if any of you know the person I have come to see. His name is Albert Franklin?'

Jamie looked shocked. 'I don't believe this,' he said. 'I'd just been to Albert and Faith's place when I almost ran into your car last night.'

Sunnie laughed. 'Oh, so you can tell me how to find him, then. I have something for him.'

John stood in front of the fire, pushing the tobacco down in his pipe. 'Albert Franklin has lived all his life on this station. I didn't think he knew anyone much, apart from the people he's met here.'

The woman laughed and rubbed at something invisible on her skirt with her left hand. Once again, Jamie caught sight of the gold band. 'Did you bring your husband with you?' he asked, immediately wishing he had bitten his tongue instead.

The brown eyes widened for a moment. She shook her head. 'Tsonokwa woman took my husband,' she said softly, her voice breaking.

'Oh,' Jamie replied, noticing the look that passed between his parents and wondering who the hell Sunokwer woman might be.

'In the morning I'll drive you over to Albert's if you like,' he offered, eager to make amends.

She flashed a smile. 'That would be wonderful,' she said. 'Quite wonderful. As long as it's no trouble.'

'None whatsoever,' he assured her.

She stood, throwing the heavy plait of black hair back over her shoulder. 'If you don't mind, then, I might turn in,' she queried. 'Tomorrow could be a big day.'

The gift

J amie had left well before breakfast to arrange for Sunnie's car to be towed into Wellsford for repair. It was now five to ten, five minutes before he was to meet her. He was surprised at how anxious he felt. 'Not to worry,' he reassured himself. 'Sunnie by name, sunny by nature.'

He walked into the hallway of the homestead just as Elizabeth knocked on her visitor's door. 'Ten o'clock,' she called gently, 'time to go.'

Neither Elizabeth nor Jamie were prepared for what they witnessed when the door opened. Sunnie stood in front of them dressed in a pale cream buckskin dress. Long fringes swayed around her calves and forearms. Around her head she wore a beaded headband with two thick braids of hair neatly tied. Beaded moccasins encased her small feet.

'Oh, Sunnie, you look beautiful,' Elizabeth whispered.

'Yes. Beautiful,' her son echoed.

Sunnie smiled. 'Today is a very special day. It is the reason I am here. I am a Sioux Indian and it felt right for me to dress for today in ceremonial clothing.'

Jamie held open the car door as Sunnie arranged her clothing. He noticed a small package on her lap, but she refused his offer to place it on the back seat.

'I hope you don't mind,' she said as they drove to one side of the road, trying to avoid the mud left by the previous evening's storm, 'but I would prefer not to talk until we get to the Franklins'.'

Jamie looked at her, puzzled.

She smiled at him. 'The Sioux have a belief that words weaken an occasion if used too freely, and for this special occasion, I would prefer to strengthen my feelings.'

Jamie nodded. 'Okay with me,' he said.

As if by some predestined arrangement, when Sunnie knocked at the Franklins' door, Albert opened it. He stood looking, puzzled initially, then after a very long moment and without question motioned to the young woman to come inside.

Faith held her husband's hand as the young Sioux woman pointed to the chair, indicating Albert should sit down. Still holding his hand, Faith stood just behind his chair.

'My name is Sunnie Cobiness,' she said gently, 'but I was born Sunnie Quick-to-see Zephier.'

A large tear rolled out of Albert's eye and down his cheek. He went to speak, but the young woman put up her hand.

'I am here on behalf of my father who has moved on to be with the old ones. He asked me to bring some things to you that he wanted to bring himself.'

Sunnie knelt down and partially unwrapped the cloth package she held. From it she took a smaller package which she unwrapped. She leaned across to Albert and gave him two rings; a large one, and one smaller.

'The circle,' Sunnie said, 'has no beginning and no end. This is the way of true friendship. There is no division, no separation. These rings were made for you by my father. One for you and one for your wife.'

Albert took the smaller turquoise and silver ring and placed it on his wife's finger. The larger one he placed on the third finger of his left hand. He registered no surprise that both rings fitted.

'I have something else,' Sunnie said.

She unwrapped the cloth in front of her and took out a long, black and white feather, its quill wrapped in beaded, red cloth, and handed it to Albert.

'This feather is one of three from my father's pipe. He often smoked it and thought of you. Of the other two feathers, one is mine as daughter and the other remains on the pipe which will one day be given to my son.'

Albert felt the gentle softness of the feather against his cheek.

'The feather symbolises good health, truth and friendship,' Sunnie told him. 'We would ask that you hang the feather on your wall. Indian people believe that when the feather moves, it is because the spirit of one who has left us is visiting.'

Faith wanted to run to the young woman and embrace her, but she stayed still, alongside her husband. Her heart was thumping so loudly she felt the whole of Wellsford might hear it.

Sunnie stood in front of Albert and his wife and placed her right hand over her heart. She extended her left hand toward them both. 'Oihan Kesruya Cantocignakinte,' she said.

Albert leapt from his chair and embraced the young woman, his eyes wet and shining. Faith put her hand out and got caught up with Jamie's on its way to shake Albert's hand. In the middle of it all, somehow, rested the Sioux woman's small, brown hand.

'I never forgot him,' Albert said shakily. 'We only had a very short time together, but I never forgot him.'

Sunnie smiled. 'Friendship is not measured by the length of time spent together,' she said, 'but by the intensity of the sharing and the understanding it carries. Now that I have delivered these things to you, my father can rest in peace.'

'Now you're quiet,' Sunnie said to Jamie on the way home in the car. 'What's on your mind?'

'I was just thinking that it would be nice, now that you've carried out your mission, if you could stay a while and get to know some of the other people at Wellsford. Have a look around the place ...'

She put her hand out towards the steering wheel and brushed his. 'I'd like that,' she said. 'I'd like that very much. And what I'd like first of all is to visit that rock I saw through the rain on the first night.'

'A deal,' Jamie answered, wondering why he felt almost drunk. 'I'll take you there.'

In the shearing shed-cum-home, on the banks of the Wellsford River, Albert fingered the turquoise stone in his new silver ring. Then he rummaged in the kitchen drawer and found a nail and hammered it into the wall. To it he tied the black and white feather, then he turned to embrace his wife. He turned quickly, too quickly. Too quickly to notice the feather gently moving behind them.

* * *

Walking along the river bank past the huge jacaranda and down the well-worn track to Devil's Rock felt good today, Jamie thought. He noticed a slight hesitation darken Sunnie's eyes as she glanced at the rock. Well, it was an ugly old thing. He didn't much like looking at it himself. But today the sun was warm on their backs and a gentle zephyr breeze caressed the grasses to either side of the path, the perfect day for a picnic and he knew just the spot a little further on near the waterfall.

Sunnie shook out the tartan picnic rug she was carrying and placed it over her shoulders. 'Look like a real Indian now,' she laughed.

Jamie felt a tug at his throat looking at the slim body, the plaited rope of hair. 'You make me realise,' he said, 'why that Scotsman raced off into the night with – what was her name?'

'Pocahontas?' Sunnie queried. 'Is that who you mean?'

Jamie shrugged, taking the rug off her shoulders and spreading it out on the ground, enjoying the sound of water falling over the Wellsford Falls.

Sunnie sat down and leaned back, stretching herself out cat-like towards the sun.

Jamie placed the picnic basket to one side of the blanket and lay down on his stomach, the better to observe the young woman at his side. 'When did your husband die?'

She looked shocked. 'I didn't say he died,' she replied.

'No, but he did, didn't he?'

She rolled onto her stomach and twirled the gold band on her left hand. 'We were just kids,' she said. 'Met at university. You know, young love, all that stuff.'

Jamie reached into the basket and brought out a thermos and poured two cups of tea. 'Still hurts you, doesn't it?'

She nodded. 'It hurts, but it hurts less than it did. In a way, I always knew Tsonokwa would get him.' She lifted the plait of hair from her shoulder and threw it down her back.

'You see, Kevin was Indian as well. He came from up above Vancouver and part of his tribal mythology, if you want to call it that, was about the legendary Tsonokwa woman. She was fearful, this woman. She controlled the magic water of life and I honestly believe she controlled him.'

Jamie nodded, saying nothing, understanding less but handing her the hot cup of tea.

'Sometimes when we stayed with his parents, we would go out on the lake in the canoe. Long, green weed floating in the water looked to him like Tsonokwa woman's hair. If the weather changed, he would say that Tsonokwa was angry. At night, we would hear a loon warble and he would tell me it was Tsonokwa laughing.'

She held the teacup with both hands and sipped gently. 'Don't get me wrong,' she said. 'Kevin wasn't a nut case; he was Indian, an artistic, intelligent Indian. But one night, he went out to catch salmon and never came back. Somehow the canoe capsized and he drowned.'

He heard the catch in her voice and fought the urge to hold her. Space, he must give her space.

'I guess you could say that Tsonokwa won out in the end,' she said.

'Anyway, I suppose I went a little crazy for a while there. Then one day, my father told me that Manitou had something else in mind for me and that I should come to Australia to deliver his gift to his friend Albert.'

He ran his finger along her arm. 'I'm glad you did,' he said.

She smiled. 'I like your parents,' she said. 'They're almost Indian.'

He smiled, reaching out to remove a piece of dried grass from her hair. 'People are people,' he said. 'They're all the same, basically.'

'I don't think so,' she countered. 'Take the night you first took me to your parents' house. Your mother never hesitated to invite me in. She made dinner and asked me to stay.'

'That's how it is in the country,' he laughed. 'People are more hospitable. It breaks the monotony.'

'I could get to like it here,' she said, 'really get to like it.'

Charlie Saddleup

'No, I don't mind talking to you at all,' Charlie wheezed. 'Funny to think I been living here longer than anybody now. Heard you were staying on a bit.' He gave a throaty chuckle. 'In my day, they'd say you and young Jamie got struck by the thunderbolt.'

Sunnie smiled at the old man. She liked him; he was like the old Indian people at home. He made her feel more sure than ever that underneath, all people are the same. 'All blood is red', her father used to say to her.

Charlie lay back in his chair and closed his eyes. For a moment, Sunnie thought he had fallen asleep, but he opened his eyes, unaware of the time lapse.

'He was all right, you know, old James Mitchell. I knew him better than anyone. He never meant anyone no harm. He was kind of like we all are, conditioned by the times. You can't escape the harness fate slips around your neck. And he loved the land. Oh yes, it was the land that was his mistress, all right.'

Sunnie bent over and kissed the old man on the forehead. 'I'd really like to listen to you talk again some time,' she said. 'This next week, I'm visiting Sydney with Jamie and his parents, but we'll be back in a few days.'

'Oh, Gawd,' Charlie mumbled, 'you can have that. I hate the city.'

Sunnie smiled. 'Do you happen to remember Amy Corcoran? Jamie tells me she came here to stay when they were both young.'

Charlie rubbed his watering eyes. 'Is she the one didn't have any hands? Well, she hid them all the time and it looked like she didn't have them.'

'That's her,' Sunnie replied. 'She's got them, all right. In fact, they're like magic wands at the ends of her arms now. She's having her first art show and we're all going down to the opening. Everyone is very excited. Amy is considered to be a major talent.'

The old man smiled. 'That's nice, real nice. She was such a serious looking kid. Had a hard time for a while there.'

Sunnie toyed with the end of her plait. From where she sat alongside the old barn, she had a full view of the homestead with its green roof and white painted walls, so typical of so many Australian scenes she'd seen on calendars that had seemed so exotic and remote to her in Midwest America. In the kitchen garden alongside the house, Faith bent double picking tomatoes, and behind her in the stables, the soft snuffling of horses warmed her heart, dampening her eyes.

Sunnie took in the far-reaching sky. Looking up, she remembered someone back home saying to her, 'You'll love the Australian sky. It just goes forever,' and they were right. Not a cloud in sight, for what looked like a million miles.

'I'm going to love being here, and being able to talk with you, Charlie. You give me a real feel for Wellsford.'

'It's not me, Girlie,' the old man replied. 'You can get that feeling without even speaking to anyone. That's what got old man Mitchell in the first place. It's this land. The feel of the land.'

Sunnie stood up and picked up her camera. She knew he was right. She felt a flood of affection for the old man half asleep in front of her. This land had got to her as well. He had read her, all right, and made her feel right at home. Read her just like an Indian.

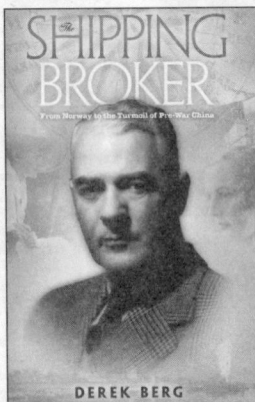

Best-selling titles by Kerry B. Collison

MERDEKA SQUARE
KERRY B. COLLISON

THE TIMOR MAN
KERRY B. COLLISON

JAKARTA
KERRY B. COLLISON

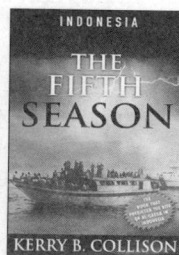

INDONESIA
THE FIFTH SEASON
KERRY B. COLLISON

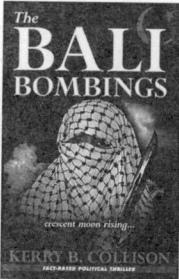

The BALI BOMBINGS
crescent moon rising...
KERRY B. COLLISON
FACT-BASED POLITICAL THRILLER

THE HAPPY WARRIOR

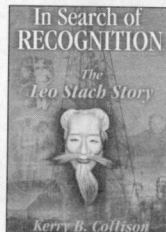

In Search of RECOGNITION
The Leo Slach Story
Kerry B. Collison

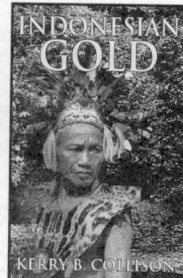

INDONESIAN GOLD
KERRY B. COLLISON

SID HARTA PUBLISHERS

Readers are invited to visit our publishing websites at:
http://sidharta.com.au
http://publisher-guidelines.com/

Kerry B. Collison's home pages:
http://www.authorsden.com/visit/author.asp?AuthorID=2239
http://www.expat.or.id/sponsors/collison.html
http://clubs.yahoo.com/clubs/asianintelligencesresources
email: author@sidharta.com.au

Purchase Sid Harta titles online at:
http://sidharta.com.au